ISOLATION

DARK NEBULA
BOOK 1

SEAN WILLSON

WELCOME TO DARK NEBULA

Thank you for buying this book!

If you're interested in a free novella entitled **Dark Nebula: Contact**, hearing more about the series, seeing new cover art as it's released, or getting exclusive access to sales as they happen, then you can subscribe to my newsletter online at:

seanwillson.com/subscribe

You can also drop me an email at:

author@seanwillson.com

I always love hearing from my readers.

DARK NEBULA SERIES
Novella: Contact (FREE)
Book 1: Isolation (This book)
Book 2: Discovery
Book 3: Generations
Book 4: Beacon
Book 5: Graveyard
Book 6: Nursery

PORTAL SERIES
Book 1: Drowning Earth
Books 2-4: Coming Soon…

CONTENTS

Abigail Olivaw — 1
Data Sheet — 5
1. Abigail Olivaw — 7
2. Zachary Olivaw — 22
Data Sheet — 31
3. Joyce Green — 33
4. Lync Michaels — 45
5. Steve Ericsson — 48
6. In Orbit — 51
7. Abigail Olivaw — 53
8. Zachary Olivaw — 65
9. Steve Ericsson — 77
10. Joyce Green — 85
11. Lync Michaels — 89
12. Abigail Olivaw — 98
13. Zachary Olivaw — 105
14. Steve Ericsson — 113
15. Joyce Green — 115
16. Lync Michaels — 119
17. Abigail Olivaw — 133
18. Zachary Olivaw — 151
19. Steve Ericsson — 157
20. Joyce Green — 170
21. Lync Michaels — 178
22. Abigail Olivaw — 184
23. Steve Ericsson — 202
24. Lync Michaels — 209
25. Abigail Olivaw — 220
26. Lync Michaels — 224
27. Joyce Green — 242
28. A Spy Satellite — 260
29. Harold — 262
30. Joyce Green — 268
31. Lync Michaels — 275
32. Harold — 284
33. Nguyễn Due — 291

34. The Medic 297
35. Joyce Green 304
36. Lync Michaels 311
37. Abigail Olivaw 328
38. Harold 331
39. Nguyễn Due 339
40. Minula Clarke 353
41. Joyce Green 358
42. Lync Michaels 373
43. Nguyễn Due 393
44. Joyce Green 402
45. Lync Michaels 413
46. Nguyễn Due 420
47. Joyce Green 432
48. Lync Michaels 447
49. Abigail Olivaw 458

Thank you for reading! 463
Also by Sean Willson 464
About the Author 465
Acknowledgements 466
Glossary 468
Four Laws of A.I. 473

"You failed them. You failed all of them," whispered a voice that sounded remarkably like her father.

"Who're you kidding!" a fourth voice screamed. "You'll crash and burn at this, too."

She hated the voices, and if she could, she'd mute them all and focus on the climb. They were nothing more than an echo of her self-doubt. It's the truth they represented that hurt the most.

Her retinal comm chimed and a priority alert flashed in the corner of her vision. Having a computer screen embedded in her eyes was humanity's greatest blunder, and that alert was yet another reminder of how she'd failed. That same alert had appeared for so many days that she'd lost count. It was like living in a bad dream with aliens, but on infinite repeat.

When her grip released, gravity stood still for a moment until she slid down the cliff face of the mountain. She rolled onto her side and did her best to dodge the sharper outcroppings she'd been working past for the last hour. As the rocky surface ripped at her skin, her hip exploded in pain.

Each and every one of her preceding failures flashed before her eyes as the ledge approached. Sticking the fall was her only option. Either that, or she'd careen off the edge into the…

"No!" she screamed and shook her head. She couldn't think about that again.

Time seemed to slow, like the seconds after that mottled green alien bastard touched her shoulder. She'd regret letting him walk behind her for an eternity. She knew better, but she'd gotten smug.

Her retinal comm flashed brighter, and the chime echoed eerily. The priority alert wanted her attention, but she had more important matters to deal with right now, like not plummeting to her death.

The only route she could see involved catching the edge

ABIGAIL OLIVAW

UNKNOWN

S elf-doubt was a real bitch. No matter how hard she worked, she couldn't shake feeling as if nothing she did was good enough. Like she wasn't a leader capable of protecting her people. Add to that, her family being broken apart, her living to work, and when she wasn't in front of a camera, she was effectively alone with only her inner thoughts and an A.I. to keep her company. And worst of all, no amount of blood, sweat, or tears helped to change her destiny.

Her arms trembled and her grip was failing. She swayed back and forth on the edge of the rock-face, and adjusted her hands to wipe the sweat onto her dirt stained shirt. With her handhold firm, she stabilized her core to stop the movement and pulled down with everything she had. As she inched upward, she pushed her chin toward the next ledge, but at the halfway point, her torso started swaying again. The burning in her arms was unbearable, and then the voices began screaming in her head.

"You're the President, you've got this," the first voice said.

Another voice chuckled. "Not this time. She's a coward."

below and trying to roll laterally. Whatever she did, she needed to break her fall and not slide forward.

When the ledge hit, the crushing blow of the collision contorted her legs in unnatural ways until she felt a pop. A second later, excruciating pain coursed upward and the oxygen burst from her lungs as she struggled to gain control and roll sideways.

Slowing the continued descent was her only option. She reached out to her side, looking for a handhold to grasp. Everything was happening too fast, and her legs weren't cooperating and tucking in tight like she wanted. She must've broken something.

The edge was only centimeters away, and her momentum was still too high.

It was then that she noticed a rock that should be big enough to slow her. The jet-black stone was just out of reach, so she stretched forward as far as her already battered muscles would allow and rolled toward it. Her hand barely caught the coarse surface, and she squeezed with everything she had.

Suddenly, the faces of her brothers flashed before her eyes as the pain surged higher and momentum yanked at her arms. They were screaming at her, pleading with her not to let go.

She wasn't a quitter, and didn't plan to start now.

When she squeezed harder, the world froze and everything went quiet. Looking skyward, she could see hundreds of black teardrop shaped pebbles floating just out of reach above her head. Her breathing had stopped too, but strangely, the incoming message was still flashing in the corner of her retinal comm.

She must've survived, because pain was coursing through her. Each wave more intense than the last.

After nearly a dozen attempts to summit this blasted cliff, this one hurt the most.

Finally, she gave into the pain. Another climb wasn't in the cards. She couldn't take the torture any longer. While she didn't want to live the whole thing over again, she had to. Maybe she could do something different this time.

When she rolled on her back, she almost passed out. A black haze squeezed at the edge of her vision.

She closed her eyes and tried to focus on breathing and slowing her heart rate. Trying to think away the pain.

The beating returned to her chest and thumped like a bass drum in her ears. If she didn't control it, she'd come out the other side too disoriented.

As she counted down from ten, she hit zero and blindly reached up and tapped her ear to answer the incoming comm. "What is it?"

Light exploded and blinded her despite her eyes being closed. She brought her hand up to block it, but it never helped. It was everywhere and yet nowhere.

Something didn't feel right. Like… she'd done this before.

DATA SHEET
SOL — 2278

Target: Sol
Alternate Designation: The Solar System, Home of Humanity
Number of Planets: 8
Habitable Planets: 1 - Earth
Terraformed Planets: 1 - Mars (In Progress)

System Population:

- *Mercury*: 0
- *Venus*: 1,248 planetside, 25,240 orbiting
- *Earth*: 17.2 billion planetside, 1.7 million orbiting
- *Mars*: 1.1 billion planetside, 210,310 orbiting
- *Asteroid Belt*: 250,000 +/- 75,000
- *Jupiter*: 0 planetside, 2.9 billion orbiting, +/- 50,000 orbiting in Trojans
- *Saturn*: 0 planetside, 1.8 billion orbiting
- *Uranus*: 0 planetside, 335,965 orbiting
- *Neptune*: 0 planetside, 121,570 orbiting
- *Dwarf Planets*: 45,000 +/- 15,000
- *Other*: +/- 170,000

Description:

The current year is designated AD 2278 and humanity has expanded throughout most of Sol. They are generally aligned as either the Inner or Outer Ring, with the geographic delineation separating the two political parties being the main asteroid belt between Mars and Jupiter. The divide between the two is primarily motivated around natural resources and disagreements about human rights and entitlement. The Inners are hierarchically aligned based upon fiscal status, whereas the Outers are aligned horizontally based upon an individual's contribution to society.

Both parties have taken on a common goal in recent centuries of expansion toward planetary systems beyond Sol for the mutual benefit of humanity. This forced goal was due to the environmental collapse and overpopulation of Earth in recent centuries. They've established one colony in the Epsilon Eridani system and colony ships are en route to Tau Ceti and G. Eridani. Each star system contains a habitable planet and is reachable with modern technology, which enables cryogenic suspension and subluminal travel at 80% the speed of light.

1

ABIGAIL OLIVAW

SOL, LUNA

She rolled onto her side and reached up to squeeze her ear, answering the comm chime. Getting a few minutes to squeeze in a power nap was harder and harder lately.

"Sorry for interrupting you during your personal time, Madam President. We have... a bit of a situation," Minula, her assistant, said.

"It's... okay," Abigail said. "My brain and body wouldn't shut up anyhow."

"Pardon, Madam?"

She chuckled quietly under her breath. "Nothing. Please continue. What's the emergency today?"

"Sorry, Madam. We've received a comm from the Earth Forward Observation Outpost at Lagrange point two. I'll patch them through."

Abigail rolled off the couch and stood up. Vertigo hit, and she reached toward the wall of glass to steady herself. Her legs buckled slightly as the wave of disorientation flowed over her. She reached up and held her head while taking a deep breath. This dizzy feeling was odd... and yet somehow familiar.

After waiting a moment for her body to steady, she headed over to her desk and sat in the empty chair.

"What now?" she muttered.

Opening the drawer, she pressed her finger to a hidden button on the inside. The desk emitted an ambient glow and the glass wall overlooking Pavlov Crater became translucent. A voice spoke, "Security countermeasures are now in effect."

The image on her comm flickered for a second, then an officer at attention appeared. When they realized they were talking directly to Abigail, the President of the Confederation of Planetary Explorers (CoPE), the officer's eyes went wide and they saluted her.

The image on her comm flickered for a second, then an officer at attention appeared. The officer's eyes went wide when she realized she was talking directly to Abigail, the President of the Confederation of Planetary Explorers (CoPE). The officer saluted her.

Abigail saluted back, her deep blue eyes locking into the patented stoic expression the media loved to focus on. "Go ahead, Lieutenant."

"Madam President," the officer stammered. "Approximately five minutes ago, visual scans detected six unknown objects or sh—ships in the main asteroid belt. They appeared suddenly. Subsequent analysis shows no prior approach vector. Each ship is oblong, over four kilometers in length, and is arranged in a circular formation. Assets have been diverted from inside the belt for recon. We should have more details in a few minutes from our Earth-orbiting telescopes and other Lagrange points. More distant assets should return data within an hour."

The particulars of the scan appeared on her comm and her stomach tightened. Each object was identical in shape and apparent mass. They appeared to have a peculiar spectral signature and weren't radiating any energy in standard visual wavelengths.

"One moment please, Lieutenant." She reached up and touched the tip of her ear. Once her side of the comm was muted and blurred, she spoke out loud to her A.I. companion. "Harold, are there any matches from these images or scans against data in the archives? Maybe there's some material analysis or design consistency we can correlate against?"

Harold responded after a brief pause. "I've been checking since the data arrived, Madam President. There are no ships that match these characteristics in either the Inner or Outer Ring fleets. We'll need additional spectral analysis to answer definitively, but there's approximately an eighty percent match. These objects' exterior material is close to that of the first contact probe. The design, however, appears to have no similarity nor engineering consistency."

She pursed her lips and her eyes narrowed. This wasn't happening. Her family had kept the discovery of the alien probe a secret for centuries. While they'd been using the technology from the artifact to bootstrap mankind toward the stars, it took them a while until they learned the consequences of using it, and that was only after they'd opened that Pandora's box. But right now, they weren't ready yet. This had to be a coincidence, nothing more.

Reaching up, she unmuted the comm and added Minula, her assistant, to the call. "Thank you, Lieutenant. Please keep me in the loop with any developments. Minula, call an emergency meeting of the council. Best to have everyone together to work this one. The last thing we need is comm lag leading to another incident like last year's belter miner strike."

"It looks like Command is ahead of you, Madam," Minula began. "They've already alerted all acting Inner and Outer Ring representatives, and they're in transit to the Pavlov Council Chambers as we speak. They should arrive within the hour. Their military liaisons will arrive shortly thereafter. Should I convene secondary council seats, as well?"

This should be fun. Did they really need military representation already? There's nothing like going all in on the flop.

"No, I think we'll have enough egos present to start," she said. "Let's keep them in the loop with intel but keep the membership and security clearance tight on this one. I don't want this leaking to the press until we know what we're dealing with. I'm going to clean up. Give me fifteen minutes and then we can head to chambers."

"Yes, Madam. I'll have your security team ready outside your quarters," Minula said and cut the comm.

Abigail leaned back in her chair and sighed. The details for the next meeting started appearing in her peripheral vision. It included the ETA of each attendee and their complete bios. Before she reviewed those, she had something more important to do. While she hoped this was a false alarm, she needed to be prepared.

Touching her ear gently, she subvocalized a command to record a comm to her brother Zachary. She spoke aloud looking toward a tiny camera drone that rose out of the desk.

"Hey, Zach! I hope everything's going well with the latest round of tests. I'm really excited to see the new numbers and changes you mentioned in your last message."

She paused and looked away from the camera. She didn't want to freak him out, so she needed to be careful in how she worded this next part. Speaking in code without giving away the meaning was hard enough, adding nuance was even harder.

"I got sideswiped today. Ran into someone here on Luna I thought I recognized, but I'm not sure they're who I think they are. I'm sending you their pics. Take a look and let me know what you think. They appeared out of nowhere on that middle running track, you know the huge one. Geez, they were eerily familiar. That reminds me, I'm dialing my settings back to zero. Things are just getting too weird, and I need to start out clean. Stay safe, and keep your head clear. We'll speak again soon. I love ya."

The drone dropped back into her desk as she set-up the data feed with the new encryption protocol. After she double-checked everything, she sent the comm. It'd take nearly a week for the message to reach Zachary out in the Oort Cloud. That was only after being split into millions of chunks, embedded within thousands of planetary standard communication broadcasts throughout the system, and coalescing into a handful of hidden tight beam stations spread throughout Sol.

If she didn't start sending the data now she'd regret it later.

She stood slowly, not wanting to get dizzy again. Confident the vertigo wouldn't attack, she headed toward the lavatory to clean up before the council meeting.

The light surrounding her desk faded as she walked out of the vicinity. A second later, an audible alert reminded her that communications were no longer secure.

SHE PAUSED at the mirror as she passed by, smoothing the creases out of her jacket. She didn't wear a uniform per se. Instead, she wore the same outfit every day to not crowd her mind with the nonsense of picking out clothes. A simple purple pantsuit and white blouse. They were extraordinarily comfortable and the color didn't dominate the senses.

As the president, she always wore a piece of jewelry to compliment her outfit. Today it was a simple brooch on the right breast of her jacket. It resembled a carriage wheel from the nineteenth century trimmed in diamonds.

In the mirror's reflection, she caught a glimpse of her desk. She swore she'd forgotten to close the drawer earlier, but it wasn't open. Harold must have closed it.

She breathed in deeply and exhaled, trying to focus and remove all extraneous thoughts from her mind. The crisp, sterile, highly processed air made her long for the smells of nature, the smells of Earth. The damp woodsy aroma of moss and trees after a day of rain. Itchy pollen from a field of spring flowers. Mornings when she could lazily sit on her porch, enjoy the aroma of a freshly brewed cup of strong coffee, and watch the sun slowly rise over the North Carolina hills as it burned off the morning dew.

A smile crossed her face as she shook off the memories.

She'd failed at emptying her mind and finding her center, but she was a bit more relaxed.

Checking her retinal comm, she confirmed that her security contingent was waiting outside the door led by Minula. A formation of four armed escorts, her normal band of troublemakers assigned any time she ventured out in public.

She turned and subvocalized the command to open the door. Striding into the corridor, she paused and smiled at each of her guards. "Good evening. Shall we?"

"Yes, Madam President," they replied in unison.

She stepped forward, and they all turned crisply, heading toward the council chambers.

ABIGAIL WALKED to the center of the council chambers and stood behind the podium facing the empty seats. She had a few minutes to collect her thoughts before everyone else filed in. Her comm flashed, notifying her that new intel had arrived.

She subvocalized to Harold. "Call up that data. Was it the long-range image reconnaissance?"

"It was," Harold replied.

The images appeared on her retinal comm. The crafts were clear and well-defined. Unlike anything she'd ever seen before. They were white and perfectly cylindrical. Spaced throughout their length were what appeared to be grooves segmenting each crafts hull. With no clear bow or stern, it wasn't obvious what form of thrust propelled them.

"Was there any analysis included with the images?"

"The only thing noted was that the crafts had no motion nor variation of any kind. They were each identical in length and external markings. The notes about motion don't make sense though."

"What's wrong with them?" She pulled up the data. The numbers did seem odd, almost like— "They're not rotating around the Sun. They're fixed in that axis."

"That's correct," Harold began, "and highly unusual. With no visible thrust, you'd think they'd have some movement, even minor, to counter the constant gravitational forces from the sun. These numbers seem to imply they are absolutely fixed."

She sighed. Her shoulders were heavy, and the pressure of the moment was building and taking a toll. Centuries of planning could be coming to a head. And while these images weren't definitive, they certainly weren't any of the known CoPE designs. That much she was certain.

Bringing herself back to the present, she was suddenly aware that most of the representatives were either seated or headed toward their seats.

Her comm buzzed again, notifying her of a breaking news alert:

CoPE HOLDS EMERGENCY SESSION

"... CoPE is holding an emergency session of the security council tonight on Luna. According to one of our Inner Ring sources, representatives from all member planets were summoned to an emergency session this evening. It's unclear what the council is convening to discuss, but rumors are swirling. Everything from loss of colonial contact with the Tau Ceti colony ship, to mounting tensions along the ring border with new battlecruisers threatening the ring ceasefire. You'll have more details when we have them..."

She shook her head. The council couldn't keep its mouth shut for one hour. One lousy hour. Was it really so hard to not spread rumors? Whatever level of civility she planned to run tonight's session with had disappeared.

She subvocalized to Harold. "Never a dull moment. I assume you're already on top of this leak?"

He replied quickly. "Yes, Madam President. Current data

suggests it's either the Venus representatives not taking the council summon seriously, or members of the Earth UN contingent looking to garner stronger funding for Inner Ring security and their re-election. We'll know more when my copies running within the media networks can safely share intel."

She clenched her fists. "Fantastic, just what we needed. Are these idiots ever not fighting for re-election? Don't answer that. I already know the answer."

She reached up and adjusted her brooch. The points of the wheel pricked her finger, bringing her mind back to center.

"Lock it down," she subvocalized.

The doors clanged around the room as locks engaged and the lights overhead flashed. A bluish glow emanated around the perimeter of the ceiling as a computerized voice spoke. "Security countermeasures are now in effect."

The sudden transition caught people off guard. A hush spread as the remaining council members scampered to their seats.

She cleared her throat and began. "I've asked you all here today to—"

"I demand an explanation," interrupted a female standing in the front row, "and an apology for the blatant violation of security protocol. Heading into this meeting I was physically—"

Abigail's comm identified the woman as an Earther from the South American contingent. She raised her hand, gesturing for the council member to stop. "I will not give you such an apology nor is it against protocol. As the President I have the right under the Ring Treaty of 2224 to perform searches of any citizen of Sol when threatened or if a conflict is either imminent or occurring." She paused, letting her words sit for a moment and to judge the response. It seemed to have the desired effect. The council member returned to her seat and whispers spread throughout the chamber.

When she glanced around the room, she waited for the commotion to subside. With the seconds ticking past, her heart pounded in her chest as if playing a dramatic tune. The council finally relented and silenced their muttering, sensing she wanted to continue.

She subvocalized a command to bring up the original scans onto the holographic projectors to her left and right and on every retinal comm of the council. "Representative Zhang, the leading member from Earth and the Inner Ring Alliance. Can you identify any of the ships in this image? Please remember Mrs. Zhang, you are under oath while in these chambers. Perjury while testifying in a Security Council session has dire consequences."

Caught off guard, Representative Zhang's eyes went wide. She exhaled, straightened her suit, and stood up. "No, Madam President. I cannot identify any of these ships."

"Mrs. Zhang," Abigail continued, "are there any secret ships with these or similar characteristics under development by the Inner Ring Alliance?"

Murmurs and commotion shot through the seated Inner Ring representatives. Mrs. Zhang leaned toward her colleague from Mars to confer. She nodded several times and straightened to face Abigail. "No, Madam President."

"Thank you, Representative Zhang. You may be seated."

Turning slightly, Abigail looked to her left toward the Outer Ring section of the chambers. "Representative Metis, the leading member from Jupiter and the Outer Ring Alliance."

This time she allowed Mr. Metis a moment to rise before continuing. "The same questions and consequences for you. Can you identify any of the ships in this image, and are there any secret ships with these or similar characteristics under development by the Outer Ring Alliance?"

Without skipping a beat, Representative Metis replied. "We in the Outer Ring Alliance have no ships under development matching anything similar to the ones shown here."

"Thank you, Representative Metis."

He returned to his seat.

"So— it appears we're at an impasse, council members.

Neither Ring Treaty Alliance member has claimed ownership of these ships, and yet, there they are."

There was silence throughout the chamber, something she didn't expect. They'd usually be at each other's throat right about now if one had intel against the other. Time to flip the table; she subvocalized a command and the new reconnaissance imagery replaced the old.

An audible gasp spread over the audience and several members of the council brought their hands to their mouths in shock.

"As President of CoPE, I'm executing the powers granted to me by the Ring Treaty Emergency War Powers Act and declaring a state of emergency. Members of the council, what you're seeing is new visual reconnaissance from our forward probes. We don't yet know if these ships are hostile or friendly, nor do we know if they're extrasolar in nature. We must plan contingencies accordingly. We'll bring together experts from linguistics, astrobiology, and military strategy to understand how to best engage them. We must also assess the impact this news will have on the general population and coordinate how we intend to release it. I don't think it needs repeating, but for the sake of disagreement, I'll do it anyhow. All the information you've heard since I executed the War Powers Act is protected and will result in a court-martial if leaked."

Their faces were masks of shock and disbelief. So many years of confidence could be wiped away if these ships were alien. Their idea that humans were alone in the universe, shattered in an instant. The realization that not only could we not be alone, we might very well be small fish in a very large ocean.

She didn't see anyone who seemed to disagree with her order, which was refreshing. Time to see if she could rally them a bit.

"Ladies and gentlemen. Times like these require that we unite as a confederation. We must pool our knowledge, our resources, and our considerable ingenuity during this time of emergency. As history has shown time and again, we can handle anything thrown at us, but only if we do it together as a united front. It's imperative that we set aside our past differences and focus instead on the here and now."

ABIGAIL COLLAPSED INTO THE CHAIR. She relished the thought of not moving, talking, or thinking for a few minutes. She'd been in a non-stop state of defusing tense conversations for the better part of an Earth day since she'd declared a state of emergency.

Her door slid open and Minula walked in. Without a word, she set down what smelled like the most amazing coffee ever brewed and then turned to exit as quietly as she'd entered.

"Thank you," she blurted as Minula retreated. "That smells magnificent."

She picked up a cup and poured herself a healthy portion. Sitting back, she took a minute to just relax. Her muscles released into the plush chair as the warmth of the coffee settled in her stomach. She could use some shut-eye, but she still had a few more things to take care of. Reaching up, she touched her ear. "Good evening, Harold. Wait... is it morning?"

"Good morning, Madam President. Your coffee looks wonderful, exactly the temperature you like it."

There were times she swore Harold was in the room with her. He had full access to all the sensors and surveillance arrays at her disposal, which meant he had access to pretty much anything anywhere. He'd been her silent but vigilant A.I. companion since she was little. It was lonely being separated from her brothers and closest friends. She'd had many late-night professional, existential, and deeply personal conversations with him. Sometimes she forgot he wasn't a real person.

"It really is delicious. Definitely what I needed. So, Harold, do you have any good news for me?"

"I'm not sure I'd categorize it as good news, but the detailed spectral scans have completed. We're at a ninety-nine point seven percent match of the alien vessels material to the first contact probe."

"Well, that is good news," she chuckled. "At least I haven't been making a fool of myself the past twenty-four hours putting CoPE into high alert. I'm not sure I'd manage another re-appointment with a blunder like that."

She took another hearty swallow of the coffee. It helped her feel more herself.

"Anything else of interest? Any details on the leaks from the council members?"

"I've not detected—" Harold began.

A priority alert cut him off.

On her retinal comm, a live video feed of the unknown formation of ships appeared. Something was changing. The viewpoint no longer showed the side of the ships. They'd rotated around their center and were now head on, still in formation. The text beneath the video showed that they were moving. It also projected an estimated velocity and the vector of travel.

Harold brought up a three-dimensional map of Sol with the projected path overlaid. She gasped, covering her mouth.

The formation's course change brought them on an intercept with Earth.

Her heart pounded in her chest. No matter how hard she tried to focus, her thoughts went straight to her brothers Bradley and Zachary. This wasn't fair; it shouldn't be happening right now. They needed more time. She'd always figured they'd be like all the generations before them, a footnote in the Olivaw master plan carrying the secret to the next generation. Never the ones on the battlefield.

She leaned forward and placed her elbows on the table. Centuries of intricate and incomplete plans were coming to a head in the blink of an eye. Unless this was an alien race making an aggressive first contact, she was fairly certain they were from the Galactic Alliance— the alien collective that humanity had been hiding from for thousands of years. The originators of the first contact probe.

"Based on your heart rate, breathing, and your physical reaction, I'm assuming that you're surprised by this outcome, Madam President?"

"Surprised, disappointed, angry..." she blurted as she slammed her fists on the desk. Coffee spilled everywhere. "I'd say I'm feeling the entire range of emotions right about now. Aren't you?" She stood up and started pacing the office.

"Given the spectral scans and no other knowledge about the Galactic Alliance other than what we learned from the first contact probe? I'm not surprised, no. The Dark Nebulas we've witnessed and the warnings from the probe we discovered should have predicted this course of events."

She shook her head. "We've sent hundreds of probes, Harold. Hell, I've sent thirty-two myself. We haven't detected anything. Not a single hint of the Galactic Alliance nor any other advanced civilizations. As far as we knew, they were extinct."

"It's a huge galaxy, Madam President. We have many assets in motion, and I should remind you, we still haven't found one of our probes used to gather intel from Epsilon Eridani. It's been nearly three years since it should've returned. Plenty of time for discovery and retaliation."

His answer hung in the room while she contemplated what to do next. She knew full well what warnings Harold was talking about. The warnings that her ancestors had discovered in the first contact probe.

"I didn't have a choice," she muttered.

"You're right. You didn't, but your ancestors did. They refused to heed the warning from the Galactic Alliance. They knew that stealing or sharing the alien technology would have consequences."

She sighed. Her family had secretly struggled with these warnings for centuries, while they worked to guide humankind toward the stars. At the same time, they strove to uncover humanity's real history before Earth. To better understand their ultimate fate once the Galactic Alliance found them.

"I hate to interrupt, Abigail. But we haven't much time. Shouldn't you activate the next stage of the plan? The colonies may already be in jeopardy."

Harold always switched from proper presidential salutations to her real name when he was referring to family. It was his way of reminding her of the deeper branches of their strategy. She needed to reach out to her brother Zachary. He could set the broader plan in motion from the Wheel and would know what to do about Bradley.

"I was going to suggest that. Let's start by sending another message to Zachary." She sighed and walked back to the desk to sit down.

"Certainly," Harold replied. A blue glow activated around her desk and a camera drone rose slowly from its surface.

Watching the drone rise, all she could think about was how much she missed her brothers. She hadn't seen either of them in so long. Too long. Their father's death had pushed them away, but she'd let it. She'd kept them at arms-length to protect them, she told herself. As far as she knew, this could be the last time she'd ever speak to them.

She nodded and the drone started recording.

"Hey, Zachary McCrackery!" Fighting off tears, she paused for a moment and looked away. As she took a deep breath, she exhaled and collected herself. "I'm sure you've watched the feeds by now and perhaps have reached the same conclusion as me. It seems that the spokes of our wheel are complete, even if we're not ready. All that's left is to let it roll and see where it takes us."

She stared into the camera, letting time pass.

He'll understand that, won't he? She'd just messaged him yesterday and here she was sending another one. He'll be freaked out.

A smile slowly grew on her face as tears ran down her

cheeks. "I love you, both of you. And Zach… when you see him, tell him I'm sorry. Good luck!"

Harold lowered the drone back into her desk. "That must have been hard. I'm sure they'll be okay. They come from good stock."

She struggled to wipe away the tears. Reaching into the desk drawer, she took out a tissue and wiped her eyes.

Satisfied with the cleanup, or at least as good as it was going to get; she re-centered herself for one more message. This one was for the colonies.

2

ZACHARY OLIVAW
SOL, OORT CLOUD

The research facility was codenamed the Wheel. It was located deep in Sol's Oort Cloud, within a massive 200km planetesimal. The Olivaws had secretly funded its construction over the last century and a half by funneling money from legitimate companies. It was entirely self-sufficient through local agriculture and the mining of water and other necessary raw material in neighboring Oort planetesimals.

Zachary had lived on and off at the Wheel for the better part of twenty years after graduating from the Jovian University. His team of researchers had been building an alternate drive technology to that of the first contact probe. While that probe used warp bubbles to bend spacetime, their approach created controlled gates through spacetime allowing them to jump between two distant points. Nearly six years ago they had a breakthrough in gate research and had been working to perfect it before mankind encountered the Galactic Alliance. Abigail sent word yesterday they may have failed in their primary mission, and that a formation of alien ships believed to be the Galactic Alliance had arrived near the inner asteroid belt.

"I don't care if you think the particle trails indicate direction and velocity." Zachary brought up a three-dimensional plot of the particles velocity over time and space. "Look at these waveforms. We're seeing some type of blowback through the gate after it closes. We've seen it before when the gate would ripple open and close repeatedly until the quantum forces stabilized on both sides. I bet it's still happening at a microscale."

Shauna placed her hands on her hips and tapped her right index finger. The composites of her humanoid shell made a drumming noise that echoed through the sparse workspace. Shauna was his A.I. and research partner at the Wheel, and she enjoyed spending time in a robotic humanoid form at his side. While most researchers depended on huge teams of colleagues, he preferred solitude until his ideas were fleshed out. Most of what he needed for his job was elsewhere in the Wheel. This was his thinking space and was off limits to interruptions.

"Okay," Shauna began, "let's say your cockamamie idea is plausible. Where's the dust coming from? Is it in gate space? We clean the craft before every launch. Unless… it's tearing apart the probe itself. We should be able to measure that on return."

"No, I don't think the probe's being torn apart, but you're on to something." He pulled up the data on the composition of the dust itself. "I bet you a case of Scauny, this dust is from the other side of the gate and the probe is displacing it back through the entry side. The forces of the opening are probably pulling the space around the exit and causing the nearby dust to flow back through. When we're able to precisely predict where the gate opens, we can observe the microscopic effects from the opposite side. We could try mounting some external particle velocity instrumentation on the next probe to measure the effect."

"That makes sense. So, like you said—"

"We're at another dead end," he said with a forced smile as he rubbed his temple. "We still can't precisely predict the direction nor the distance in which the gate will open. You know how badly we need this, Shauna. You're getting closer, I can feel it. Start the test over, wipe it clean." He waved his hand over the wall and the data disappeared.

Shauna walked to the corner of the room, turned and then shut down her chassis, transferring her consciousness into the Wheel itself. "I'll prepare the package for the next probe. Do we want this one to return with the results after the next test jump or continue on the relay network? If we do a longer test and route it through Epsilon Eridani, we could have it back in a week."

He walked out of their workspace in the engineering module and headed toward the outer segment of the Wheel. His mind was racing and he needed to think about something else. Checking in on the prototype ship build progress was mundane enough to relax his mind. "Go ahead and continue on the relay network. With the alien's arrival in Sol, we need to know if they're headed to the colonies. We don't want any gaps in our colony intel if we can help it."

Stepping into the lift tube, it immediately propelled him upward toward fabrication. It was disconcerting flying through a tube without a floor or ceiling, but it was much more efficient than waiting for a pod. Up to four people could navigate the tube at a time and they could move up or down independently. Only a few hundred personnel were stationed at the Wheel, so even when they were busy, there wasn't much chance for a collision.

As he de-tubed, his retinal comm notified him of another message from his sister Abigail. He sighed. That can't be good. As the president of CoPE, she didn't make a habit of sending multiple comms so close together, especially within twenty-four hours of each other. And with the last one carrying bad news he wasn't exactly excited about opening this one. He paused outside the entrance to probe fabrication, subvocalizing a command to play it.

The comm was short and to the point, and his sister didn't hold her emotions back. His stomach knotted and his eyes welled with tears as he watched her struggle. She had a disheveled appearance and her cheeks were a little pink, like she'd just finished doing something strenuous. Their family resemblance was unmistakable. Deep blue eyes, round friendly cheeks, and short hair were giveaway Olivaw family features.

At the end of the comm, he watched it again. Abigail always spoke in code when she sent messages, ever since they were little. She believed that you never knew when someone might intercept them, so don't make your intentions clear to anyone except the receiver. She was clearly signaling that the Wheel should move forward with the next stage of their plan. Even if she'd enacted it indirectly, she knew the risks.

The weight of her words and her decision were immense. He'd seen this coming. Her comm from yesterday had been as clear as day. The Galactic Alliance was here. She may not have wanted to admit it, but as a scientist the data was conclusive. He played the message again. He couldn't risk missing something she'd wanted him to see or hear.

When the comm finished a third time, he brought up the attachments. There was one time-stamped before hers and another tagged to send to the colonies. He opened the first and played it.

"Shit!"

"What's up, Zachary? Is everything ok?" Pepper asked. She was one of their pilots and probe engineers. She must've returned from maintenance work and he hadn't heard the door open from the hold. Her normally friendly face framed in long black hair and brown eyes were staring at him with concern.

"I wouldn't say everything's okay, no. You know that test flight you've been preparing for? Is there any chance you can move it forward?"

"Maybe... I'd have to cut a few corners," Pepper said fiddling with her instruments on her hip. She brought up the projected timeline for the project on their comms. "We're getting close, I think. I should only need a few more days and it'll be ready for a short-piloted jump. Is that soon enough?"

He honestly didn't know. That might not be fast enough,

but they'd cut corners in the past and got burned. The Wheel's first few rounds of animal trials were a complete disaster and set them back months. While they'd eventually made it past that point, they'd been cautious in their pace ever since. This launch was their first human trial and they couldn't afford to lose a pilot.

Pepper opened her mouth but said nothing. She swallowed hard and shook her head. "What is it, Zachary? Is something wrong with my work?"

"No! Your work is fantastic, Pepper. I just think we should check if we can squeeze anything out of that timeline. Anything at all without risking safety." He stressed the last part.

"Absolutely. I'll see what I can do." Pepper turned and headed back into the hold. As she walked away, she paused and looked back over her shoulder. "Is everyone still getting together for the usual family dinner tonight in the canopy?"

He struggled a smile. "I wouldn't miss it. See you then."

She turned and headed back into the hangar. He watched as she passed through the door, continuing to fiddle with her tools. Her mind was probably racing and struggling to make heads or tails of what he'd asked her to do. There were countless details neither she nor most of the people in the Wheel knew. But that would come later. For now, he had to focus. There was so much to do.

He brought up the Wheel Protocol to do list he'd created with Abigail on his retinal comm. Checking off tasks was comforting, and he could use something comfortable to do right now. He turned and headed in the opposite direction of Pepper, toward the entrance to probe fabrication.

Walking up to the door, he placed his hand on the security console. The authorization took place between the panel, his fingers, and the nanites in his body. The door dilated and shut behind him when he walked through, sealing him in with a thud.

Despite everything being automated at the Wheel, he was compelled to physically check on things from time to time.

The practice of checking helped put his mind at ease and allowed him to do his best work elsewhere, reassured that things were operating smoothly. He'd developed this behavior not long after the accident that killed his father.

Throughout this section of the Wheel, there were hundreds of probes in various stages of fabrication, repair, and teardown. Between micrometeorite collisions, constant retrofitting of new power and propulsion units, and expansion of the network, there was a constant churn to the fleet of probes serviced here. They had a mixture of probe designs in their fleet. Designs they'd copied from the first contact probe, and probes of their own design using their prototype gate drive. This was the only facility in Sol that had the designs for the original alien probe and they were only accessible to Harold and Abigail, his sister.

At the control wall, he gestured to bring up the probe network controls. The wall burst to life with visuals for all inbound and outbound probe traffic, as well as all repair and fabrication details. He quickly identified the next two outbound probes headed for the colonies and pulled up their data storage. Taking the attachment from his sister's message, he loaded it up along with the required colonial security protocols. He also added the queued colony feeds and another payload necessary for this stage of the plan. The last one he secured with additional encryption to ensure no one could detect or tamper with it. Once he was happy with everything, he queued them both up to launch.

Before closing the controls, he marked all probes with the same physical design as the first contact probe for destruction. They couldn't afford to leave anything incriminating behind that pointed to humanity. Any probes still en route to the colonies would either self-destruct once in range of a relay point or be dismantled upon arrival at the Wheel.

He chuckled. The Wheel name had been a joke in the early days. They'd used it because they were working to reinvent the proverbial space travel wheel, but it unexpectedly stuck. In those early days, they strictly fire-walled the first contact probe research to prevent intellectual contamination with designs of their own. The hope was that they could develop something similar but different enough to avoid accusations of theft from the Galactic Alliance. Engineers from the new design team could use observed test data from the alien probe, but nothing physically from the probe itself. The separation forced teams to find their own creative path forward.

He double-checked his work on probe recycling and then commenced the Wheel's data expunging. All images, all recordings, all first contact probe research wiped. One advantage of a facility that required fewer humans was the ease of destroying evidence. If there was one thing he knew for certain, it was that his colleagues would notice the missing data. He'd break the news to them tonight after dinner and drinks in the canopy.

Walking out of probe fabrication, he stopped to check that the door locked before heading toward his next stop. Happy with the seal, he continued down the long hall toward the ship hold. The research and engineering spaces in the Wheel were clean and modern, a stark contrast to the dynamic and colorful nature of the residential space. It helped to keep the mind focused and on task. The smells of metal and electronics were soothing.

There were dozens of ships in various stages of fabrication when he arrived in the hold. Some sat dormant, quietly awaiting one final but key component, their gate drive. Others were just starting or were partway through the fabrication process.

Looking at the far end of the hold, he could make out his ship. His pride and joy. He'd designed it to be both capable and flexible enough for the challenges they might encounter in the next stage of their mission. The ship was cracked open and stripped of external plating. All the armaments and skeletal structures were exposed. At the moment, its interconnects were being diagnosed and tested by dozens and dozens of robots.

When he finally made it to the end of the hold, he subvocalized a command to deploy a measurement drone. The zippy little spherical robot's sole purpose was a thorough and accurate measurement of everything it passed over or touched. Pulling up the drone's feed, he walked the exterior of the ship, visually comparing the designs in his retinal comm with the measurements from the vessel itself. Everything matched his design perfectly. It always did, of course, but he still had to put his mind at ease by making the rounds.

Comfortable with the ship's fabrication, he had one final thing to check. He headed back to the lift tube, marked his destination on his retinal comm, and stepped in.

His stomach churned as the forces of the descent made him happy he'd eaten a light lunch. The first thing most people felt descending in a lift tube was uncontrollable falling. Their natural instinct was to reach out to grab something, but that led to broken bones until people grew accustomed to this peculiar new form of travel.

Zipping past the design and living modules, he continued to the bottom of the lift to its deepest point within the planetesimal. When he reached the bottom, he exited and walked a few meters to the lone doorway. The plaque embossed on its door read "Historical Fabrication." The lettering and effect always reminded him of a twentieth-century plaque you might find on a statue.

He eased into the room, trying not to make too much noise closing the door behind him. When he spun around, wall after wall of data feeds surrounded him as information flowed into the room from all corners of humanity. If there was an archive, visual feed, or piece of information flowing anywhere in Sol or the colonies it eventually made its way here.

"Libby, are you around?" he shouted. His voice competing with the chaotic buzz of the feeds.

"Where else would I be after your sister's message?" The origin of her voice wasn't easy to pinpoint in all the noise.

"Dumb question, I suppose." He forgot that Harold

would've sent that message to her, as well. She was in the Circle of Trust after all. "Have you already done it?"

He finally saw her after she walked out from behind one of the feed walls. Libby had a short athletic build with long naturally auburn hair. She did it up in a tight bun atop her head. The look reminded him of the librarians he'd seen in classic archival 2D movies. Hair up in a conservative but proper bun and angrily peeking over the top of glass spectacles while shushing loud students.

"If by 'it' you mean have I enacted the Wheel Protocol Rewrite, then the answer is yes. Centuries of falsified history and research are presently making their way to every corner of humanity."

DATA SHEET
EPSILON ERIDANI

Target: Epsilon Eridani
Alternate Designation: Sol 2
Distance from Sol: 10.475 light years
Number of Planets: 4
Habitable Planets: 1 - Liprosus
Terraformed Planets: 0 eligible
Asteroid Belts: 2

System Population:

- *Epsilon Eridani a, Mors*: 0
- *Epsilon Eridani b, Aegir*: 0 planetside, 31 orbiting
- *Epsilon Eridani c, Liprosus*: 19,129 planetside, 92 orbiting
- *Epsilon Eridani d, Iserea*: 0
- *Dwarf Planets*: 0
- *Other*: +/- 6

Description:
The current year is designated 5 AC (After Colonization).
Epsilon Eridani is the home of humanity's first colony and
has been established for just under six years after a thirteen-
year voyage to the system. The planet designated Liprosus
was visited several centuries before colonization and
confirmed to have breathable air and the natural resources to
both sustain human life and establish a colony.

The colony's primary focus has been on stabilization after the
initial population growth was stymied with both mining and
farming problems. The unusually dense ground proved a
challenge to extract minerals during early colonization efforts.
This slowed the creation of colony infrastructure and delayed
their departure from the colony ship for over a year. The
ground continues to be a challenge for creating open-air
farms and stresses the colony's dependency on domed hydroponic facilities.

3

JOYCE GREEN
EPSILON ERIDANI, LIPROSUS

"This ends the review of Sol inbound personnel and supply requisitions. From this point forward, we ask that the colony's Mayor follow security protocol Omega and present credentials," the voice said from the comm.

Joyce looked over the top of her glasses as the room erupted in a cacophony of chatter. This was unusual. In over five years they'd never had an Omega secure comm from Sol. Something must be amiss.

Warren stood up and gestured downward with his hands. "Everyone relax. We'll let all of you know how the resources will be allocated from the supply shuttle after this secure comm. Until then, please exit as expeditiously as possible." He pointed toward the doors at the top of the council chamber.

The frustrations of the colonists lowered to a grumble as they filed toward the exit. The room was designed in the shape of a funnel. Four tiers of sleek tables were set around the perimeter, and each tier was lined with soft circular chairs angled to observe events in the heart of the room.

She was sitting around a table at the bottom of the funnel, along with Steve and Warren. Centered overhead and pointing downward was the holographic projector that had just shut off.

She took off her fashion glasses and rubbed her face. On most days, the randomized colors of the frames accented her bright green eyes while contrasting her ebony skin and the short Bantu knots in her hair. Today however, the jittery holographic display from Sol was leaving weird halos in her vision. A headache was the last thing she needed this morning.

As the room cleared and the doors shut behind the last colonist, Warren pulled a small oddly shaped device out of his pocket and placed it on the table. He then pressed his right index finger on the top and pulled it back.

She squinted. Had her glasses messed with her vision or was there a small drop of blood on the surface of that thing? A faint puff of smoke expanded from where she'd noticed the blood. It must've been doing a DNA scan and nanite verification.

That was a new trick in a tiny package.

The device spoke out loud. "Identity confirmed; Mayor Warren North. Two additional personnel are present. Please touch the scanner to confirm your identities."

Warren waved his hand toward them. "Go on. Everyone verify yourself."

She wasn't sure what was going on, but Warren was acting nonchalant about this whole thing. Like closed door secure comms from Sol were a normal everyday activity.

Leaning forward, she pressed her finger to the device and Steve followed suit after her. The prick of blood was barely noticeable, and it disappeared in a flash.

"Identity confirmed; Director of Colonization Joyce Green. Identity confirmed; Director of Security Steve Ericsson. All present personnel identified and confirmed with clearance level alpha. One moment while the communication payload is decrypted."

Warren sat down in his chair and began slowly rapping his fingers on the table.

Drumming or tapping of fingers was one of those annoying ticks that drove her crazy. It grated on her and made her feel like a ticking clock was about to explode. Her people in the Office of Colonization knew it, but Warren was technically her boss, so she wasn't about to call him on it.

A hologram of President Abigail Olivaw appeared between them over the table. Her face was frozen for a moment before she began talking. It must've been due to the other issues they'd been having with their comms today. She quickly made another note in her to-do list to have someone from her team check it out later.

"Thank you all for meeting like this," President Olivaw began. "We've enacted the Omega Security Communication Protocol to broadcast emergency information with the CoPE Colony Leadership. On this day, March 15, 2278, at 14:20 Sol Standard Time, CoPE has declared an emergency under the Ring Alliance War Act. Six unknown alien ships have appeared between Jupiter and Mars in the main asteroid belt. Approximately twenty-four hours after their arrival, they advanced through the Inner Ring asteroid defense perimeter and are heading toward Earth. Because of this unforeseen event and the unknown nature of our enemy's technology, we have henceforth cut all imminent colony bound personnel and supply ships. We've also stopped broadcasting all data feeds toward your colony. This is an effort to protect you by doing whatever we can to mask your location. Our goal is also to act with the utmost of caution to manage Sol's resource flow during this critical time." She paused and looked off into the distance.

Aliens. This had to be a joke, right? She glanced over toward Steve. He was wiping his sweaty forehead and wouldn't make eye contact with her.

Warren was a different matter entirely. He was staring back at her, almost like he hadn't even watched the comm. He raised his eyebrows at her and returned his attention to the hologram of the president. Maybe he'd already seen it.

Abigail stiffened, and she returned her attention to the camera. "I know this comes as quite a shock, but rest assured we will take emergency measures to continue colonial aid as often as possible. You're still at the outset of your colonization efforts and I know that the coming days, months, and perhaps even years will be trying. You must have faith in your training and most of all in your people. It's imperative that you not only continue your colonization but your exploration efforts, as well. The future of your colony and possibly humanity hangs in the balance."

Abigail took another lengthy pause and looked down into her lap. Her brows drew together as if she was contemplating something or saw something interesting on the floor.

It was remarkable how much the president had aged since she'd last seen her before their launch. She looked tired, like she hadn't slept in days and had been wearing the same clothes just as long. Her cheeks were also slightly flushed. She must have been crying recently.

Abigail raised her gaze upward toward the camera. "Life is like the Great River. Sometimes it sweeps you gently along, and sometimes the rapids come out of nowhere. May the ocean of stars guide us safely through these rapids to the river's end."

The audio and holographic display cut out and dropped the room into silence. All that remained was the glow radiating from the secure comm device in the center of the table.

Warren stopped tapping his fingers. He was sitting motionless, staring through the hypnotic blue light at her and Steve.

The light faded and the computerized voice broke the silence. "Omega security transmission ended. Security countermeasures are still in effect."

Warren leaned forward and rested both of his arms on the table. "This news has to be kept under wraps until we can assess our readiness. We won't be getting any new personnel drops, so we'll need to analyze the colonization roster, categorized by profession and skillset, to understand our weaknesses. We also need an audit of our food and water reserves, as well as an update on the state of our hydroponics farms. We need an understanding of the native planetary food production and if it can sustain the colony indefinitely at our current levels. Finally, and I'm brainstorming here, we need to bump security on our key facilities. The last thing we need is a run on the system when the news gets out." He raised his eyebrows and motioned with his hand for either of them to speak.

She hadn't even fully processed the message and Warren was already jumping from A to Z. She knew their limitations better than anyone, and her mind was spiraling right now. They needed a minute to let it sink in.

"Steve! Joyce!" Warren yelled. "Snap out of it. I need you in the here and now. We've been dealt a shitty hand and I'm not about to fold. I need you to ante up and get back into this game. You heard President Olivaw. Are you with me?"

"Yes," Steve stammered as he wiped his forehead with his hand for the umpteenth time. He was still staring at the glowing blue device on the table as if it contained the answers.

He looked as nervous as she felt.

"What about you, Joyce?" Warren asked.

She sighed and fiddled with her glasses. "I understand what you're saying, Warren. I'm not an idiot, neither of us are." She gestured between her and Steve. "Some of us react differently to life altering events and need a moment to absorb the situation before jumping to solutions. I don't know if you had access to this before we did, but you don't seem too shaken."

Warren leaned back and clasped his hands across his chest. "I'm not sure what you're insinuating, but I'd be careful with your line of questioning. If you're not able to handle this, I'm confident I can find someone who can."

She stood up with a start and pointed at him. "Don't threaten me! Don't ever threaten me. We all know how you got in that chair. You couldn't do our jobs a quarter as well as we can."

"That!" He stood up. "That's the fire we need to get through this. I'm sorry I offended you. Like you said, some people handle stress differently." He sighed out loud and silence returned to the room before he sat back into his chair, motioning for her to sit. "Now, what other things do we need to plan or consider?"

She eased back down and reached forward to pick her fashion glasses up off the table. Her hands were shaking as she put them on her face. "We're still fairly dependent on Earth supply shuttles for our more specialized replacement parts. We need to get an idea of what we're short on and stop all colony expansion, at least until we build out our reserves. Our fabrication and mining capabilities are still fragile and limited, so we need to be careful how we allocate our resources. On a positive note, the orbital power stations are fully operational, so there's that."

Warren nodded and began rapping on the table again. "Thank you, Joyce." He looked toward Steve. "Anything from security?"

Steve looked up from the device, his trance was still lifting. The harshness of his square face, strong jaw, and high cheekbones gave him a foreboding appearance. "I'm not sure where to start, Mayor. Alien invasions aren't exactly something we have contingencies for. While we're prepared for problems that could cause an intermittent loss of communication and supplies from Sol, we don't have deep plans for an indefinite severing until we're a few years out. Our mission was always predicated on a stream of follow-up supplies and personnel. Add to that the fact that we're at war with aliens, and we're whorled, completely whorled."

Warren stood up and ran his hand through his thinning red hair. He paced in a small circle for a second until he returned to the table, resting his hands on the stark white surface. "Steve, the first thing you need to do is get your head out of the operational manuals. I need both of you to think outside of the box. Now, what do we need to take care of immediately?"

Steve shook his head. His soft blond hair fell over his gray eyes. "We're at war, Mayor. We're at war with an unknown threat from an unknown location. We have no planetary defensive perimeter nor equipment to create one. We're focused on colony security, not planetary defenses. I don't even know where to start."

Warren's face was turning the same red hue as his hair and his hands had switched to clenched fists. "It sounds to me like you told me where you need to focus, Director. Let's all take a breather and meet in two hours with as much information as we can gather. Bring your teams with you when we reconvene. And Steve… I have all the faith in the stars that you can do this. But like I said to Joyce, if you can't handle this job, I'll find someone else who can."

Warren reached out and picked up the secure comm device. "Dismissed," he said as he twisted the top. The overhead lights flickered and the cold blue light from the device went out. While the eerie glow of the room was gone, the hopelessness of the moment was still omnipresent.

She stood and watched as Warren walked out the doors opposite where she was headed. At least the damn rapping on the table had ended. She glanced at Steve and sighed. Like her, he was watching Warren as he walked into the distance.

"Can you believe it?" she asked.

He didn't say a word. He just stared at the door Warren left through.

"Well, ok then. I'll see you in a few hours I guess." She shook her head and pushed her chair in. As she trudged up the stairs, her mind kept flipping through the contents of President Olivaw's message. Everything was a fraking mess in Sol, and she had no idea what that ending was about. Some kind of river's end nonsense.

When she reached the sunlight on the stairs outside the building, she paused. Closing her eyes, she breathed in deeply. The morning air was moist and smelled of mildew, not at all like her Montana home back on Earth. After nearly five years, this world still felt foreign. She wondered how long, or even if the Liprosus mornings would feel like the new normal.

Hearing feet shuffling nearby she opened her eyes, it was Steve. She nodded at him, but his head was down, and his shoulders drawn together. There was a maglev transport pod waiting for him, and when he entered it, he departed without a word. In fact, he hadn't spoken since he'd been chewed out by the Mayor.

She watched as his pod sped off into the distance, and with it, an unseen tension lifted. The lingering negative energy from that meeting was beginning to fade.

The colonization building wasn't far, and she could use some time to subvocalize notes into her retinal comm, so she started walking. There was a lot to organize in the next few hours. Some exercise would help to clear her head and take inventory.

Her walk flew by as she continued sub-vocally transcribing for several blocks, oblivious to everything and everyone around her. Pausing next to a fountain, she glanced over her notes. Now that the shock of the message had worn off, she was feeling better about the colony. While there'd certainly be difficult times ahead, nothing jumped out as being insurmountable.

They'd worked hard over the past few years to establish a stable base here on Liprosus. There was more than enough water and the production from their agricultural and mining facilities had ramped up considerably in recent months. They'd even begun planning a few splinter colonies several hundred kilometers away to accommodate recent population growth, and to satisfy the demand from their scientists to expand. These plans might need to be delayed, but people would understand.

Her immediate concerns were around their medical supplies and equipment fabrication. They'd been having trouble bringing online a few of their nanite manufacturing and chemical production facilities. Their dependence on Earth's supply shuttles would definitely be noticed there first.

She reached up and touched her ear. "Remind me to check with Dr. Sutter on our nanite reserves and fabrication."

"Reminder sixty-two added," her virtual assistant said. "Uplink re-established. Beginning to synchronize with the city core. This will take a few moments."

"That's strange," she muttered. Her comm must have lost connection during the secure message from Sol.

Putting the growing set of problems aside, she continued to work her way through the streets toward the Office of Colonization. People called it the OoC for short, or the Oak. She liked to think it was because oak trees were a common symbol of strength and endurance back on Earth, and that her office was at the center of strengthening and growing the colony.

She sighed. She missed the sight of the towering grove of oak trees she had back home. Plants on Liprosus didn't look the same. They were all squat and fat, like a psychedelic children's cartoon.

As she walked, her mind relaxed and wandered. She admired the civil engineering and shape of the settlement. While the buildings were simple in their construction, they had clean utilitarian lines with hints of native influences. The surrounding landscape in this region had many strange colorful bulbous rock formations that influenced the building designs. The red rock like material forming the dome walls was from the local mining operations and refined into a semi-translucent kinetic cement mixture. Transparent solar powered glass panels were cut into hexagons and placed uniformly on the dome surface. This created a strikingly simple design with ecological responsibility at its heart.

Up on the nearest dome, she spotted several robots cleaning and likely checking the panel's energy output. Throughout most of the colony, and most of human civilization for that matter, you couldn't go a hundred meters without seeing a robot or automata of some sort. Their dependence on the machines had grown exponentially in the last century. In fact, if it weren't for advances in robotics and advanced expert systems developed over the last century, space travel and interstellar colonization wouldn't have been feasible. Humans were error prone, and the complexities of space travel were too numerous to go it alone.

Off in the distance, she caught the glint of another maglev station. The elevated transports were above ground level and crisscrossed the city. They disconnected for passenger boarding and reconnected after departing from ground level. Not being buried made them easier to construct and integrate with surrounding buildings for support. The long parabolic arcs acted as a support structure for the maglevs and added to the native feel of the city.

She paused and bent down, cupping a flower-like plant in her hand. Pulling it closer, she breathed in its luxurious scent. Bright greens, oranges, and yellows exploded across her vision. The effect, while only temporary, was both vivid and relaxing. A small shot of Liprosus happiness.

Standing up and continuing her walk, Joyce thought about how much she liked that they'd filled the walkways with flora indigenous to the region. Rather than introduce varieties native to Earth, the biologists knew it was best to preserve the native species. They allowed people to bring a few select plants on the voyage, but only after they'd simulated their effects to ensure they wouldn't become an invasive species and overtake the planet. Colonists generally kept them indoors and they took the form of house plants or herb gardens.

The city was laid out in a grid of intersecting circles. At the center were four rings, the four-chambered heart of the colony, as she liked to think of it. At the intersection of those rings were the community center and council building she'd just left. In the Northern Ring was the Office of Colonization, and in the opposite Southern ring, the Office of Security. The centers of the other two rings contained gardens and recreational facilities. Surrounding the four central rings were rings consisting of business, residential, industry, and more gardens. Each concentric circle expanding outward around the heart of the colony.

As she entered the business ring nearest the OoC, her pace

quickened. She was closing in on her stomping grounds, Sol Coffee & Tea. Sol's was one of the first businesses to open its doors on Liprosus. Continuing a long colonial Earth heritage, Coffee & Tea was the lifeblood of the planet. It provided something familiar and comfortable in this alien world and often doubled as a local meeting place for the community. While coffee wasn't yet grown natively at their outdoor farms, special breeds of it grew well in some nearby hydroponic domed gardens.

The door of Sol's dinged as she walked in and immediately headed over to grab a few bags of coffee beans. Inspecting the stocked shelves, there was an enormous variety of beans to choose from. A number were grown locally, but some like the Alaska, Seattle, and Denver blends were imported from Earth on the previously regular supply shuttles. There would be a run on merchandise like these following the news of their isolation from Sol. She took a quick note to account for this and work with security to stem the flow of violence.

She was steeped in guilt standing there looking at the coffee, deciding which ones to buy. It was hard to not put herself before the other colonists as she picked a few bags off the shelf to stockpile at home. She had to think of herself from time to time. An addiction was an addiction.

Kaylee, the proprietor of Sol's, interrupted her remorseful thoughts. "Good morning again, Director Green. Back for another pick-me-up already?"

Looking up, she took a deep breath, her senses stirred as the aroma of the shop revived her. "You know I can't get enough of you, Kay. But if you call me Director again, I might have to head to the next ring to get my caffeine fix."

Kaylee grinned. "Your usual then, Joyce?"

"No. I think I'll need a double this morning."

"Rough day already I see." Kaylee measured out the grounds and tamped them precisely. Sol's was old school in its methods, preferring to use tried-and-true coffee preparation techniques over the ready-made prepackaged products its competitors offered. "Any word on what happened out east this morning?"

She glanced up from the bags she was inspecting. "What do you mean? What happened out east?"

As if on cue her ear vibrated, signaling an incoming comm. She reached up and activated it. "Joyce here, go!"

"Director Green! We've been trying to reach you all morning. There's been an incident near the eastern ridge." The details were passed on from her assistant.

She froze and brought her hand up to her mouth, covering it in shock. There was a code orange mass casualty event on the eastern edge of the colony near the farms. She couldn't believe it; the worst thing that could happen at this moment had.

As she stood there silently, the gruesome images of the incident flipped through her retinal comm. Each new image more shocking than the last. Her assistant's voice was a mumble in her ear as they continued telling her about all the important details from the incident.

Seconds passed and she was unaware of the odd silence in her ear, or the conversation Kaylee was having without her. She was paralyzed on the last image still present on her comm. It was an image of a man on the ground covered in some form of diseased markings. Splotchy red and discolored purple lines crisscrossed the exposed skin on his body.

She knew this man. She'd met him last week with her son, Paul. He was the head of the native farming collaborative, and her son was his newest apprentice. Panic and dread hit her like a ton of bricks, and her heart skipped a beat. She had to get out to the farms. It was imperative she knew where her son was, Sol be damned.

4

———————

LYNC MICHAELS

EPSILON ERIDANI, LIPROSUS

The intelligence feeds had been blowing up for about an hour with details of the farm outbreak, and her crew was getting anxious. While a redeployment was likely, she couldn't do it without orders from up high. Not without raising red flags she didn't want to deal with. News of the outbreak hadn't hit the press yet, but even stranger was the lack of communications from the mayor or any of the directors.

Lync stepped outside the beanstalk to get a breath of fresh air. The massive space elevator complex and its powerful ascent and descent threads loomed in front of her. It was the lifeline of the colony and their connection to the mining resources from Epsilon Eridani's asteroid belt.

She walked across the catwalk between the beanstalk and the neighboring ring and stopped. The view overlooking the colony was spectacular. The first of the two yellow suns was rising over the valley giving everything an elongated shadow. She took a moment to center herself as the new light crept across the colony buildings.

Something was off, and she couldn't put her finger on it. Today she didn't see the usual lush orange and greens of the new day as it highlighted their moon-filled sky. She didn't smell the musty new world struggling to be cleansed by humans. Instead, she saw thousands upon thousands of lives. Families that had made generations of sacrifices to be here.

After her father's death in Sol, she needed to escape the Ulixi lifestyle of seclusion and isolation. He was a prominent and powerful clan member, and he died when an Inner Ring patrol randomly attacked a Ulixi ceremony and rite of passage event, her event. She'd dreamed about that day, about one day leading her clan, but after his death she ran away. Living alone in her family's keep deep in their planetesimal was the last thing she wanted to do.

Joining the academy and applying to be on one of the colony starships was the best decision she'd ever made. When she arrived on Liprosus, she started over. She could finally help herself and others feel safe from oppression and from the corrupt politics of Sol.

The challenge of securing the colony was immense. There was a constant pressure to make hard decisions. In difficult times like today, she had to entrust the right people to get the job done effectively and without question. While this wasn't a military colony, it needed strong leadership. Leaders that didn't hesitate to prioritize those thousands of lives over their own self-doubt.

Her retinal comm chimed. It was an incoming call from Mayor North. She reached up to her ear and touched it. "Good morning, Mayor."

Warren cut to the chase. "Major, we have a problem and I need your help."

Her reply was crisp and confident. "Anything you need. What's the situation?"

"Can you meet me in my office in… ten minutes? We can go into it then."

She brought up her morning schedule on her comm. "Absolutely, I can be there at 09:50."

"Please bring your most trusted lieutenants."

She tilted her head and brought up her squad rotation schedule. "I can have most of them with me, sir. A few are out on recon but are due back at 10:00. I can have them double time it on their return. They should be there by the time I arrive."

"That'll work. And Lync... let's keep this off the radar for now."

"Affirmative, sir! Might I ask, is this related to the outbreak?"

"The what?"

"The outbreak at the farm. Our intel feeds broke the news nearly an hour ago. I figured you'd been working the situation and wanted to talk about security operations at the beanstalk."

"No... let me... stand down on that meeting. I'll get back to you, Major." He cut the line.

That was weird. How was it he hadn't known about the outbreak? He'd either been disconnected from the network or... she reached up and touched her ear opening a comm to one of her lieutenants. "Crayo, are you still on duty?"

"Sim, sim!" Crayo said.

She didn't have a good feeling about this. Crayo was her mate from the academy. She'd talked him into joining the colony mission after Abigail had convinced her that she was needed here. They'd been cohorts ever since. "I need you to do a platoon readiness check."

"Really? Now? Isn't that a few weeks ahead of—"

"Just do it, Lieutenant!"

Crayo was silent for a second before replying. "Yes, Major!" He cut the comm.

She sighed. She shouldn't have lashed out at him like that. They'd had a relaxed deployment since arriving at the colony. After the graduation ceremony, Abigail had warned her that the colony would need her quick thinking. She'd asked her to always be prepared. When pressed for details, she didn't say why, or for what, but the way she'd said it, there was something more to her request than guarding elevators.

She was pretty sure she'd look back on this as an overreaction, but she'd cross that bridge later, if the time came.

5

———————————

STEVE ERICSSON

EPSILON ERIDANI, LIPROSUS

The maglev pod accelerated away from the council building. Steve chuckled out loud and tilted his head back with a grin. He was worried that perhaps he'd laid it on too thick arguing with Warren or that he'd been overly dramatic. The others hadn't picked up on it though. They'd been too shocked with the message.

His clean white pod glided along without a bump, silently weaving its way through and around the surrounding domes. The events leading up to today flashed through his mind. The sacrifices and promises he'd made. The countless voices and squeaky wheels he'd silenced along the way, cutting short promising careers and even a few lives.

He was so close now he could taste it. The colony was finally in his grasp.

Abigail's father, Stark, had hinted that there was a much bigger mission for the colony. Steve spent years working his way into Stark's inner circle to get this deployment. He'd gotten so close to being Mayor, so close. Then Warren and his fraking father executed their power play in Sol and... he slammed his fist on the seat.

Stark and Abigail had promised him that his time would come, but after they'd arrived at Liprosus, he got word of

Stark's passing. He thought it was over, so he'd executed his own personal Plan B.

Overthrow the mayor.

Fast forward a few months and Abigail reached out to him. She needed his feet on the ground to keep her in the loop with intel. He couldn't understand why or how with the lightyears between them. He never had the same personal connection with Abigail that he had with her father. She'd always seen through him and constantly questioned his loyalty. She was a tough nut to crack.

He chuckled. What she meant to say was that she needed someone like him to not get her hands dirty.

Sometimes conspiracies were more terrifying than people realized.

His retinal comm flashed in the corner of his field of view, alerting him to an incoming call. He reached up to his ear to accept it. It was Keri, a lieutenant in his trusted inner circle. She'd been helping him with the Warren situation since before they'd departed for Liprosus. "Did Warren make a call to Lync?"

"Yes, he did," Keri said. "Just as you suspected he would. They were setting up the meeting and then Warren got frazzled about something. It sounded like the events out east."

He reached up and tapped his ear to check his alerts. "What events? I haven't seen anything come through. My comm was on the fritz during the meeting. It must still be catching up."

"There's been intel coming in about some type of chemical accident at the farms," Keri began. "Multiple casualties are being reported and there's cross chatter from concerned families, asking where their missing family members were."

He didn't know what she was talking about, but he had to reassure them he was still in control. They had to stay focused. "Until more information is available, let's keep an eye on it. Do we have any intel coming in from the Oak?"

"Negative, they're as loyal to the DoC as always. They haven't leaked anything yet."

His pod decelerated as it approached the heart of the security ring complex. "I'm still a few minutes out. Prepare the Sol news leak and double check that our teams are in place. We can't afford any mistakes at this stage of the plan."

"Yessir!"

He cut the comm.

As the pod detached from the rail, it came to a smooth stop on the ground. He hastily exited and made his way toward the nearest building.

The pod sat idle for a moment, sensing whether anyone in the vicinity required transport. Once satisfied that it wasn't needed, the door slid shut and it quietly floated upward. When it was within the magnetic field of the rail it accelerated into the distance.

He stepped into a lift tube and rose upward. He had to get to the bottom of this. Warren wasn't weaseling his way out of this one.

6

IN ORBIT

EPSILON ERIDANI, LIPROSUS

The hangar crew unloaded the Sol supply shuttle faster than expected. This was a cargo only shuttle and wasn't designed to carry cryo-pods, so there weren't any colonists to clear medical this time around. The colony usually knew well ahead of time who and what was on each shuttle since the broadcasts arrived before the shuttles themselves. This one, however, was unexpected.

"If you think about it," the supply officer began, "our initial message we sent after arriving at Epsilon Eridani hasn't even arrived back home in Sol, and that was sent at the speed of light. These subluminal shuttles travel at eighty percent of that and won't even return for another thirteen years and some change. It's amazing the expert systems are even able to approximate what we need at this stage."

"What's stranger to me is that we're even sending these ships back at all rather than using them for something here in Epsilon," the mechanic said shaking his head as he finished checking the scans from the measurement drones. "I still don't understand the logic of the return voyage given these distances."

"It's about the long game," the supply officer said. "Think about the cycle that'll be created once these make it home and return with more supplies. Imagine a day when each colony exports its goods to Sol to complete the interstellar commerce loop and repay the years of support. Like I said, it's about the long game."

"I suppose… it still seems like a waste."

After their team finished the system checks, they loaded the new repair bots and raw material for the inter-flight repair fabricators. Finally, they refilled the fuel core and initiated the return launch sequence.

"Nice work everyone! That was a record unload," the supply officer said. "We finished in under two hours. Heck, I bet they're still reviewing how to divvy up the loot planetside."

As the shuttle used its thrusters to do a controlled burn out of Liprosus's gravity well, it engaged its subluminal drive. Unbeknownst to the crew aboard the orbital space platform, the target for the shuttle wasn't Sol. It was straight at the heart of the Epsilon Eridani sun.

7

ABIGAIL OLIVAW

SOL, LUNA

Her chair creaked as she leaned back and sighed at her office packed full of the members of her inner circle. She was proud of each and every one of them. Her eyes glistened as she watched them talking through the latest events. A weight had been lifted she hadn't even known was there.

Zachary had sent the messages, triggering the next stage of their plan. After generations of sacrifices and over two centuries of planning, everything was now in motion.

She stood up and glanced around at their smiling faces. They'd all stopped what they were doing and turned to watch her. Most of them had spent the better part of the past thirty years of their lives with her in facilities like these, on either Luna or Callisto. They'd worked together to hand pick nearly everyone in each colony's leadership, or led someone else to believe they'd picked them. They'd worked with Harold and the Sol Wheel team to coordinate events in the larger picture. Together, they'd designed as many contingencies as possible to increase their chances to succeed, but not so many as to draw suspicion.

Minula was standing at her right and handed her a delicate handkerchief to wipe her eyes. Except for Harold, she'd spent more time with Minula than anyone else in her inner circle. Hell, more than anyone period. She didn't have many friends outside work.

Abigail nodded and smiled, squeezing her hand gently as she took the offering and dashed away the tears. She'd cried more in the past day than in decades. "I'm grateful for your years of faithful service, all of you. Mankind is forever in your debt."

One by one they silently stood and bowed toward her.

Lieutenant Minula Clarke to her right was a friend and a former space marine she'd met at the academy. After several terms of active duty, she became Abigail's personal body guard and assistant. They'd been attached at the hip ever since.

To Abigail's left was Lieutenant Gwen Marshall. She was a covert operations specialist, their eyes and ears within the rank and file. She was also the daughter of a close friend of Commander Quesh who was standing beside her. He'd been with Abigail's family for over fifty years and served under her father.

The rest of the room contained a host of scientists, engineers, professors, and people in affluent political positions. They rarely gathered everyone together in one place from the family's trusted inner circle, but this was the fork in the road of their master plan. Tomorrow everything changed.

She smiled and nodded at each of them, taking in their happiness and jubilation silently and respectfully. They each understood that there would be more sacrifices ahead. Today, however, was worth celebrating.

Reaching down to her desk, she waved her hand over the front and the drawer silently slid open. Inside rested two bottles of scotch in a padded container along with a dozen crystal glasses. This wasn't any regular scotch. It was 250-year-old Macmillan M passed down through her family. She wasn't much of a drinker herself, but could appreciate the taste and significance of such a rare beverage.

She reached in, retrieved a handful of glasses and one of

the bottles and raised them up. "Would anyone care for a toast?"

The room cheered in unison as they each walked around, hugging one another and celebrating the moment.

After she handed the glasses out one at a time, they gathered in the center of the room. She stared at the label on the bottle. The single serif M reminded her of the mission ahead.

At this moment the colonies would be reeling from their isolation from Sol. She sucked in a shaky breath. She couldn't think about that right now. They were in the opening stages of an epic battle for mankind.

Breaking the seal off the bottles brought another cheer from the group. The smells wafting from within brought smiles to each of their faces. She poured a healthy portion in every glass, finishing the final bottle's contents into her own. As she glanced around at their faces, they stood silently awaiting her words.

For once, she was at a loss for what to say. Her brothers would be shocked. The path that prior generations had set out upon had been fraught with many challenges and dangers. While their segment of the generational relay was near the final stages, it was by far the most delicate path and could ultimately lead them to a dead end. Over the years, she'd had to keep many of her closest friends and family in the dark, while bringing some of her worst enemies into the fold.

She thought back to the archive translations from the first contact probe. There was so much they didn't know or understand about the path of humanity and the Galactic Alliance. In the history included with the probe, there was always one underlying thread that caught her attention. Everything pointed toward the Beacons of Therion. All the Galactic Alliance species revered these objects, and yet she'd only ever read snippets about them. The translations never made it clear what the beacons were used for, but they were undoubtedly important.

Finally, after mulling it over she found the words. "To the

many that we've lost, and to those that we hope to save. May the Beacons of Therion continue to guide us toward a brighter tomorrow. Cheers!"

"Cheers!" they all shouted and clanked their glasses together.

Mankind itself wouldn't understand or appreciate their subterfuge for decades. She only hoped that the people closest to her would forgive her when the time came.

***

THE CALMING STILLNESS of the Lunar sunlight peeked into her room. More and more of Pavlov Crater's reflected sunlight filtered through the windows. The moon was entering the two-week phase in which the dark side, where Pavlov was located, was lit, while the side forever locked facing Earth was entering its dark phase.

She fought to keep reality at bay on the edge of a dream. The familiar starlit skies of their Carolina childhood home was overhead and she and her brothers were lying on their backs, taking it all in. They'd spent hours counting the stars, and telling stories of epic adventures they'd take some day visiting each of them. She was about to retell her favorite story about The Rivers End.

"Abigail," came a familiar voice. It was someone not in her dream, but still somehow present. "Abigail, it's time to wake."

Ever so slowly the reality of the here and now poured into her consciousness and pulled her back. The excitement and fluidity of her childhood dream was replaced with the forever mounting pressure of reality.

If she lay there perfectly still, maybe he'd go away. Maybe her team would leave for Neptune without her. They could handle it.

"I know you're awake, Abigail," Harold said.

"No you don't."

"Your eyelids are twitching, your heart rate is elevated, and your breathing has changed," Harold said.

She moaned. "Give me another few minutes."

"There isn't time. Your people need their President."

There it was again, the shift from personal to professional. He didn't do it every day, but when he did, it reminded her of more pressing matters in the here and now.

She swung her legs over the edge of the bed and pushed herself up, trudging to the lavatory. Harold turned on the water as she entered the room and stepped into the shower. The grime from the previous forty-eight hours slowly spiraled down the drain as she went about washing.

Running water had such a rejuvenating effect on her and was something she'd miss dearly on their voyage. She closed her eyes and leaned forward, raising her face into the warm stream of water and rinsing off. The soothing jets dug deep, loosening the prior day's frustrations and fears.

Would she ever experience a real shower like this again? She shook her head and the water sprayed everywhere. She couldn't let grim thoughts cloud her mind like that. There were too many unknowns ahead; she had to remain positive.

She finished up by letting the water flow over her muscles and through her hair. When she glanced at the gauge on the wall, she noticed she'd used more than her daily water allotment. It hadn't stopped flowing, which meant only one thing, Harold was giving her a moment.

The water automatically shutoff as she reached toward the ultrasonic wand to force the remaining droplets off her body and into the drain below. She stepped from the shower and dressed in the clothing she'd set out the prior night. Harold had moved the rest of her possessions, as few as there were, through the Lunar tube system to her quarters in the awaiting ship.

As she walked out of the lavatory, she entered the familiar confines of her home office. Pavlov Crater's familiar gray shape loomed large to her right, framed by her favorite comfy sofa and chairs. The wall to her left was covered from floor to ceiling in pictures from her life. Her happiest moments with her friends and family framed her every decision. She'd miss this place. Spacious rooms were a luxury aboard a spaceship. A luxury that not even she could afford.

She approached her desk and smelled the coffee before she saw it. Harold thought of everything; he always did. "Thank you, Harold," she said aloud.

"My pleasure, Madam President. Shall we?"

The glasses were large mugs. Not those spheres she'd have to get used to in zero-g. These were substantial. She picked up a glass and filled it nearly to the brim, topping it with a dab of sugar and soy milk. Lifting it to her lips, she breathed in the aroma. She was ready for the day.

"Alright. What calamities ensued while I slept?"

Harold jumped right into it. "The Inner Ring Council members, Earth, in particular, are preparing to recall all military vessels toward Earth to build a defensive perimeter."

"I thought we went over this with them yesterday. The ships were to hold their positions and make no aggressive gestures toward the aliens."

"While they agreed to that last evening, their constituents on the ground and within the media had another opinion. Earthers are nothing if not blind servants to the demands of the media. Especially the ones who claim to reach or speak on behalf of the most voters."

Unlike the brute force machine learning systems of the past, an artificial intelligence like Harold was different. His unique design made observations that were both candid and revealing. It also helped that his perspective came with over two hundred years of experience.

He was right. The last thing they needed to fret with right now were concerns of voters. "Please open a line to Representative Zhang from Earth and be sure to include her ranking military advisor."

There was a brief silence as Harold connected the various parties.

The camera drones rose from her desk and the wall screen

beyond sprang to life showing side-by-side pictures of Representative Zhang and someone by the name of Admiral Nguyễn, who commanded the Aitken, an Atlas class destroyer. She took a slow sip of her coffee as the signals synced up and then finally settled.

"Good evening, President Olivaw. It's good of you to wake up today. We were planning to reach out to you soon," Mrs. Zhang said.

She sighed and set down her coffee. These fraking Earthers always led with snide comments. The egos of some Inners pissed her off.

Harold spoke to her silently in her ear. "Madam, your pulse is spiking. Take a deep breath."

"I'm sure you were, Mrs. Zhang," she began. "Can you please tell me why you're breaking our agreement from last evening concerning the deployment of the Inner Ring fleet? I thought we had an understanding?"

"That would be my doing," Admiral Nguyễn interrupted. "My counterpart, Vice Admiral Smith on Luna, made a significant error in judgment when he agreed to our fleet taking a neutral posture with the alien vessels heading toward Earth."

Representative Zhang scratched her head and looked off to the side in muted frustration. "It's our position, Madam President, that Earth would be in a better tactical position with the flagships of our fleet able to respond to any aggressive actions by the aliens."

She let those words sit for a moment as she looked down and slowly lifted her cup of coffee for another drink.

Harold spoke to her again. "Don't be too harsh, Madam President. Based on your continued elevated pulse and how you're holding your cup, I can sense mounting anger. Remember, they're frightened."

Lowering the cup to her lap, she looked back up. "Tell me, Admiral Nguyễn, are you familiar with the Battle of Trenton?"

Confusion spread across his face and his eyes moved

upward and to the right in thought. A classic gesture that someone's A.I. was feeding them details.

"Ancient US history is not exactly something we cover in the Academy, Madam President. I've been briefed just now, but I fail to see the correlation."

She eyed Representative Zhang, but her response was the same. "That's unfortunate. We can learn a great many things studying the events of our past. I'm sure you're familiar with the Martian Battle for Ceres in 2214?"

Admiral Nguyễn smiled. "Of course, Madam President. A small contingent of Ceres Guardsmen trounced the entire Martian Marines Second Battalion. They used their optimal position and understanding of Ceres to overtake the advancing Martians and caused them to retreat."

"Correct, Admiral. Was there anything else about the incident that led to their 'trouncing'?"

Again, the confusion and upturned eyes of the Admiral.

"Let me help you out a bit if I may, Admiral Nguyễn. I'm a bit short on time. The Guardsmen let the Martians enter Ceres and advance on the Government Center. Then when the Martians were overconfident and most exposed, the Guardsmen laid waste to them. Not a single Martian that entered the planetesimal survived. I have to ask you, Admiral Nguyễn, based upon your professional assessment, do you think we can overpower these aliens on a battlefield of raw strength?"

The Admiral straightened his back as if at attention. "I do, Madam President. We command significant defensive powers within our fleet. Enough power to blast them back to whatever star they came from."

Watching the Admiral's tells, he looked up and to the left the entire time he was speaking. This guy truly believed his own bullshit.

"Well then, Admiral Nguyễn, you're a fool!" The shock of her words was visible on both their faces, but Abigail didn't wait for a response. "Your ego is putting at risk the birthplace of humanity. The advancing aliens arrived instantly and nearly without detection, they're propelled by an unknown technology superior to our own, have ships of an unknown design and material, and they're emitting no known wavelengths of energy that we've detected. I could go on, but I won't. On what basis, other than ego and hope, do you believe we can overtake an obviously superior technological force and 'blast them back to whatever star they came from'?"

The silence between them was deafening. He merely stared wide-eyed at her without saying a word. She thought he would've rebutted her comments but apparently, she'd misread him. She didn't know what to do next as she'd been expecting something, anything as a response.

"Alright then." She paused to make them squirm. Looking down, she brought her cup upward and sipped her coffee without hurry. She set the cup down and glared straight into the camera drone. "Let us pretend that whatever orders you were about to issue to recall your ships never existed. Your fleet is to remain on their current course and are not to make any unauthorized communications, course corrections, or to lead anyone to think they were ever going to. And next time, unless either of you is reneging on the Ring Treaty, you'll clear any and all troop changes with me beforehand. If I find out you've done otherwise, then you'll be the ones I blast back to whatever country or town you came from. Do I make myself clear?"

"Yes, Madam President!" they replied in unison.

She gestured and the line cut. Reaching down she lifted her cup and took another drink of the coffee, letting the warmth fill her stomach. She willed the caffeine to do its deed.

"Well, that went well," Harold said.

She ignored the sarcasm. She hated losing her cool like that but sometimes people needed to be forced back into place. "Harold, please bring up the plan on the wall."

The windows became translucent, the security countermeasures engaged with a soothing blue light, and the plan came up on the walls, replacing most of the pictures of her family. She stood up and walked toward it. The plan was laid out in detail, each step precisely projected out for centuries. The contingency branches highlighted, and the actors spelled out. Some branches hadn't borne any fruit over the years and had been all but abandoned; others were still in play and were only now coming to life.

Their superluminal research had gone in directions that even she couldn't have foreseen. Directions that allowed them to dream of an end game where the events of the last few days never transpired. They'd been so close, so very close to pulling it off. Another few years, some well-placed revelations, and a few decades later they could've rewritten the past.

Now they were left to execute the contingency branches. They'd cut ties with the colonies, hoping their isolation could protect them and might help to save humanity.

There on the bottom was the timeline of the third colony ship. It'd left a few years after the Tau Ceti ship and was still inflight with thousands of people sleeping in cryogenic pods. It would decelerate and stop before ultimately ejecting and destroying its superluminal drive core.

Tears ran down her cheeks. The thought of those colonists never waking from their journey was too much. So much hope, and so many lives lost to bad timing. She blotted the tears with her collar. Her family knew the cost of being caught with that drive onboard. They'd done it before, but she shouldn't have kept trying to roll sevens.

Looking across the wall, all superluminal ships and probes in Sol were checked off. They'd either ejected their drive cores into the sun or the nearest gas giant. Those same commands had also been transmitted to the colonies. They'd still have impulse drives for intersystem propulsion, but were otherwise navigationally neutered.

There along the top of the wall were the latest events, and it showed the history rewrite had been triggered as planned. The corporations her family owned had begun altering their records. Expunging any related research that could link back to the first contact probe from their systems. They'd always been secretive with their drive technology and had built-in anti-tampering countermeasures everywhere.

Comfortable that the latest steps of the plan were being acted on, and that there was nothing that needed her attention, she gestured to dismiss the wall. "Is there anything left to attend to here on Luna?"

"No, Madam President. Once you're ready, please remember my data cube on the way out. The security protocols will engage once we depart, locking the space down until we return."

She'd never had a place she'd called home since leaving Earth for university in the Outer Ring. It didn't help that she never stayed anywhere longer than a few years at a time. She was a Sol nomad of sorts. This residence on Luna had been her longest time period in a single location since childhood. Being emotionally attached to a physical space was strange.

Walking to the corner of the office, she pressed her hand against one of the wall panels. It pricked her finger and then a moment later a reassuring voice confirmed her identity. "Identity confirmed; President Abigail Olivaw."

The panel receded into the wall and a drawer slid outward. It held a pair of small glowing cubes, no larger than typical gambling dice. One contained the memories and programming of her lifelong friend Harold. The other, an archive of all research and history related to her family's studying of the first contact probe. Centuries of hope and dread concentrated in a single cube, the last copy of this information within Sol.

She reached up to her chest and unbuttoned the top few buttons of her blouse. Then, reaching down she took the cube that contained Harold and pressed it to a space above and to the right of her heart. Her skin parted, sucking the cube into her body. The space behind it closed without so much as a mark. The sensation was unusual, but she'd done it many times before. Body mods were never her thing, but they had their advantages. Things like retinal comms and memory augmentation were standard nowadays. This was a simple storage and uplink chamber that safely held her friend while also giving him access to everything she experienced and full access to the nanites in her body.

Leaving the other data cube on the panel, she buttoned her blouse and walked to the window to examine her reflection and to confirm that she was presentable. "You'll take care of the other cube, Harold?"

"Certainly. I'll transfer it to a secure location until a probe from Zachary arrives for it in a few days."

Confident with his response, she looked around one last time, taking in the room. "Ready to meet some aliens?"

"Whenever you are, Madam President."

She strode toward the door. It opened on her approach, and she entered the hall to see Minula and her other waiting security escorts. She nodded at each of them and set off walking briskly toward the spaceport.

The door closed behind her and the space within entered lockdown. The small drone from her desk rose and floated to the awaiting drawer. It used a small clamp on its underside to grasp the data cube and carried it to an awaiting laundry capsule in her lavatory. The drone along with the data cube landed inside the capsule before it sealed and was ejected somewhere within the bowels of Luna.

8

ZACHARY OLIVAW

SOL, OORT CLOUD

"We have to make this as streamlined as possible, Pluto. I don't know how long we'll be in it, but we don't have much time to both finish the build and get test runs in," Zachary said. The mounting pressure to get his mission launched was taking a toll on him. He hadn't slept well in days and was rarely hungry. His mind kept looping over everything they needed to do before departing. While his ship was coming along and technically ahead of schedule, they had this little alien armada thing to deal with.

Pluto was lying on her back under the gantry, making some adjustments to the gate drive array. Her bald head was covered in sweat and there were grease stains covering her overalls. "I understand that, Z, we all do. Say, can you toss me down the gate tachyometer?"

He thought it was cute how she called him Z. No one else at The Wheel had taken to the nickname, but between them it'd stuck. Looking through the tools, Zachary found the one she wanted and tossed it down.

"I don't think you're grokking the implications of not having redundancy in all of your systems, Z. There's no returning home if you run into trouble in the middle of nowhere and don't have redundant systems like environmental, power, drive, and cryogenic. Like this meter here, for example." She stood and brushed off her overalls. "If you don't have several of these meters onboard because you've rushed this mission, there's no way a replicator can make this with the supplies onboard. If you're near one of our storage relays or can send a probe for parts, then fine, but that won't always work, which means you're all but dead."

Not many people on the Wheel had the nerve to lecture him like that. It was one of the many things he liked about her. "You're right. I know. I'm trying my best to not cut corners here." He watched as she climbed the ladder and smiled. "We ready to try it again?"

"Yeah, we should be bang-up now." Reaching the engineering console, she issued the reset sequence and slowly the gate drive array came back online. It was reporting as being within guidelines. "Like I said, bang-up!" She made a little celebratory hand gesture dancing in the air.

He smiled at the sight of both the drive working and Pluto's contagious energy. "Amazing work! Thanks again for your help. I thought I'd checked everything out, but you obviously have a better feel for these things."

"No worries, Z. The feelings will come as you spend more time with her."

Zachary fumbled stowing the tools, and they clanked to the floor loudly. He scampered to pick them up. She was talking about the ship, right? Trying to not make a fool of himself and desperate to change the topic, he pointed at the other gorilla in the room. "I wonder why Pepper isn't back yet. I hope everything is ok."

That struck a nerve. Pluto went from a cute, coy smile to biting her lower lip. Way to go, doofus, nice transition.

"Come on, Z. I'm sure she's blinding!" Pluto said, trying to lighten the conversational shift. "If I know her, she's probably triple checking everything before completing the test gate route we created. You know the micro jumps sometimes need calibration if the star patterns don't match."

"I know, but the expert system can do that within milliseconds. She's nearly a day past her planned arrival and I'm worried about her." He swallowed hard, but was happy to have a new topic to pursue.

"Yeah but Pepper doesn't operate like that. She prefers manual intervention. Especially early on with a new system like this. Besides, it helps to train the ship." Pluto visually swept the area to ensure she hadn't left any stray tools lying about.

As if on cue, they both jumped at the sound of the hold doors clanking open.

"That has to be her!" Pluto said.

They both sprinted toward the ship's exit catwalk, crashing into each other on the way.

"Ladies first," he muttered with a wink and a smile.

He exited the ship behind Pluto, and they both ran to within view of the doors. Entering through the hold was the sweetest thing Zachary had ever seen, their genesis starship, Wellspring. It was a small ship, with enough room for a team of two and a few supplies. He'd designed it for short voyages, so it wasn't something you'd want to spend more than a week in. This last test run was supposed to be a little over five days, its longest voyage to date.

The ship was the deepest black imaginable, as if all light had been pulled from existence. It was called perfect black for a reason. They'd designed the ship's hull to make it undetectable at any wavelength and conveniently invisible to professional and amateur astronomers from Sol.

Coming into the docking area, he couldn't immediately discern any markings on the exterior of the ship. Everything seemed to be in good condition. It was a simple ship design with an unusual shape. It resembled a thimble, except rather than protecting your finger from a sewing needle, it used its hollow inner chamber to form a jump gate. A gate that, when opened, could fold all matter around it inward and through the other side.

The Wellspring pulled into the first bay and came to rest. A gangway then slid forward and connected to the faintest of seams at the docking port on the starboard side.

As he and Pluto approached the ship and waited silently, a clatter of noise erupted from the nearby lift tube. Nearly a dozen people flew, and some rolled out of the tube cheering, having ignored the tubes four-person limit. Laughing and limping together, they all rumbled up to the gangway like a flock of starlings noisily descending on a feeder.

The questions exploded from the group.

"Is she ok?"

"Where is she?"

"Why's she so late?"

"People! Let's relax." Zachary gestured with his hands for everyone to quiet down. "She hasn't popped the port yet."

"Did she open a comm link to someone after entering the hold?" Pluto asked.

"Negative," Cetti said. She was their resident physicist. "I've been monitoring all internal and external comms hoping for something, anything. That ships' coating combined with our radio silence protocols makes it challenging detecting her at all, even when you know what you're looking for."

"Wait, so how'd you know I arrived?" Pepper asked, descending the gangway.

Their collective heads swiveled before they erupted in a deafening cheer, echoing off the walls of the hold. They took turns passing Pepper around for hugs and group sobbing. It was a cacophony of familial celebration and an expunging of their collective fears.

"Alright everyone. Alright!" He was struggling to corral the group. "Let's give her some space. We have some debriefing to do, and Pepper here needs to visit Brice for a post-mission medical checkup. Hey Sky, do you think you can scrounge up something for a celebration dinner tonight in the Canopy?"

"I actually started cooking something special last evening. Her favorite dish done up with my family's secret sauce," Sky said.

"Lasagna!" Pepper's eyes sparkled. "No, wait. You mean

with that buttery rich vodka sauce you're always taunting me with?"

Sky winked playfully. "Maybe… you'll have to pass that exam to find out."

Pepper grinned from ear to ear. "You can count on it. It's amazing seeing y'all. I missed you so much, I can't even express what it's like out there in the quiet solitude. Space can be such a fickle and lonely place, especially in a teeny tiny ship. Next time it'd be nice to have a copilot." She searched the faces until she caught Pluto's gaze and gave her a wink. She wiped her tears of happiness on the sleeve of her flight suit and looked around at all the joyful faces. "Thank you all again for coming up to welcome me home. Let's meet up in the Canopy in a few hours. I'll bring the alcohol!"

Most of the group cheered and began to disperse and headed back to the lifts except for Zachary, Pluto, Pepper, and Wren. He was their resident structural engineer and worked with Zachary on this and many other ship designs. In the early days, he'd also worked with a small team on the original designs for the Wheel. While he didn't look a day over forty, he was actually nearly eighty-five.

Everyone was looking at each other, unsure who should jump in first. Wren won. "So, how'd everything go? Did she handle well? Were there any issues with the gate array?"

Pepper led them around the ship to examine the exterior as they talked. There were already several service drones and other automata swarming over the Wellspring's interior and exterior, running diagnostics and doing structural scans.

"She ran nearly flawless during the entire course," Pepper began. "I stuck to the out and back route toward Epsilon Eridani to avoid suspicion in case anyone saw something. Hopefully, they'd suspect a supply run."

Walking toward a raised catwalk around the bow side of the ship, the group stopped. "About halfway out, I ran into a problem. The ship opened a gate, initiated the transition, and then collided with a small asteroid. It was about two meters in diameter and passed through the gate from the destination side. That's where that beauty mark came from." Pepper pointed up and into the ship's concave stern segment. The exterior coating looked the worse for wear and the nanopolymer mesh beneath the surface was frayed near a meter-long gash in the hull.

Wren touched his ear and started subvocalizing into his retinal comm. He was probably bringing up any completed scan data. "Was there a breach into the secondary hull?"

"No, the Wellspring held together great and none of the environmental systems were impacted. Had it been much larger, I'm not sure I'd be standing here talking to you."

"We've talked about the probability of this before," Pluto said. "I think we hoped it wouldn't ever happen or that the gate would balance the gravitational forces."

"Yeah, well, it happened, and as that gash shows, there wasn't any balancing effect. I was planning to have a chat with Cetti after my checkup to see if she had any thoughts on a way around this. My mind ideated on a few things during the return voyage, but I don't know the maths or the practicality of implementing them."

Zachary put his hand on her shoulder. "Well, we're glad you made it back safely. Anything else to report? Were you able to interface with any of the relays during the turn?"

"Yeah, I confirmed that the relays had, for the most part, propagated the message as planned," Pepper said.

"For the most part?" He tilted his head. "What does that mean?"

She started rocking forward and back on her toes and was clearly getting excited about something. "So… apparently our maths were a bit off on how the gate size and tachyon flow patterns impact the distance between gate entry and exit. Remember our previous runs? They were much shorter and controlled. We never introduced much variability. This was our first set of jumps where the tachyon stream patterns were fully expressed, and we quickly gated from one location into the next. My early thoughts are that there seems to be a feedback resonance of the tachyons which—"

"Layman's terms, Pepper," Wren interrupted.

An eager smile formed on her face; you could tell she'd been dying to share this information with someone. "I passed it. I passed our message en route. Like passed it by a lot!"

"But... how? How far off were we?" Zachary rubbed his chin.

She touched her ear and subvocalized a command to her retinal comm and then gestured to share something. On their comms appeared an amazing image of multicolored clouds covering what appeared to be Liprosus.

"I don't understand." He shook his head and squinted at the image, unsure what he was looking at. "That looks like Liprosus. Was this something you grabbed from the data stream?"

Finally, it burst forth; she couldn't hold it any longer. "I took that in the Epsilon Eridani system. I gated all the way there and back!"

There was silence and several gaping expressions of shock exchanged between them as the significance of the image crept in.

He brought up his hands in a halting gesture. "Wait... wait, that makes no sense. If our numbers were that far off, then how'd you know where and when you were... if that makes any sense?"

"It does. After a few jumps, I noticed unexpected time differences with both our probe relay feeds and Sol broadcasts flying through space. I was comparing them against what we were expecting from our model. Doing some maths at about halfway, I realized I'd jumped well past our intended endpoint. So, after some calculations and tweaks to the gate relay controls, I decided to keep going and BOOM! I turned at Epsilon Eridani!"

Pluto was staring at the Wellspring, her eyes wide. "I can't believe it. This is a game changer, Z."

He nodded and brought both his hands to his head, slowly sliding them through his hair. "Yes, it is. So, what are we talking about in terms of speed?"

Pepper brought up some math on their retinal comms. "As you all know, the first contact drive would have taken about thirty-eight days to reach Epsilon Eridani as it travels roughly one hundred times the speed of light. Well, if we're talking regular speed here, but we all know you can't literally travel faster than light. You have to—"

"That part we all know Pepper, the good stuff please," Pluto interrupted.

"Sorry, so my initial calculations put us nearly two orders of magnitude faster than the first contact probe."

"100 times!" Wren shouted, his voice echoing throughout the chamber.

"Well, a little less than that. Without all the stops I took, I'd estimate it at 81.92 times faster. It took me a few days to reach Epsilon Eridani, and that was after taking time to calibrate and confirm my readings. We could easily make the trip in under half a day."

"Wait... half a day? NO... way! This changes... so many..." Zachary reached out to grasp Pepper's hand. "You didn't reach out to anyone, did you?"

"No, but I did take the opportunity to fast-forward the message from the President. I also tweaked the relay system to ignore the one en route. There's no point freaking them out a second time. They've got enough going on." Pepper fidgeted with her suit and broke eye contact with everyone, looking past them toward the ship in the distance.

There was something else she wasn't saying. She'd always had a dynamic personality with fits of emotion, but rarely did she go from a high to a low so quickly. Judging by the pinkness in her cheeks she was on the verge of tears. "What is it? What did you see?"

Pepper looked down at her hands for a moment, seeming to struggle for words. "I... I stuck around for a few hours, you know, to get a sense for how the colony reacted to the message. I delivered it with their monthly supply run. I also wanted to finish a quick simulation of the most optimal set of jumps for the return before I left the star system. While I wasn't able to gauge the response exactly, I intercepted some other data from their network."

Tears streamed down her face and her cheeks turned pink. She struggled to continue. "Just as the message had arrived, they… were hit with some type of biological outbreak at their farms. There were mass casualties, Zachary. It was awful. Like nothing I've ever seen before." She subvocalized a command and new images appeared on all of their retinal comms.

His stomach clenched as gruesome images flashed in his eyes. Sprawling bodies covered in strange bloody markings from head to toe littered the ground near what looked like their farms. Each image was more heart-wrenching than the last. He brought his hand to his mouth and closed his eyes, pausing the images for a moment. It was too much to take in.

Ever since he was little he'd been squeamish when it came to gore. His sister used to make fun of him for running out of the room when they'd watch horror vid-sims. But this wasn't fiction. This was actual death.

After a moment his stomach settled, and he opened his eyes. The dark red and blue markings on the bodies resembled oddly shaped growth rings with lines expanding outward. They could easily be mistaken for full body tattoos, but their hosts' pale skin and blood coming out of their ears and mouths said it was something far worse.

It'd been several minutes since anyone spoke, and Pepper was sobbing. He had to step in and take control of the situation. "Pepper, let's keep this quiet a bit longer. Why don't you take these images and any other data you gathered from Epsilon Eridani to Brice? Have him take a look after he finishes your post-mission checkup. Make sure he keeps this quiet until I give authorization. Ok?"

Pepper wiped the tears on her sleeve and nodded.

"Go on down. I want to talk to Wren and Pluto for a minute."

She turned in place and headed toward the lift tubes, her head held low and her face pink from all the crying.

"Pepper," he said.

She paused and turned back toward them.

"You did amazing on the mission, truly amazing. The gate array changes everything, and without you, none of it would have been possible." He smiled.

Nodding and forcing a smile in return, she turned and continued toward the lift.

He turned to face the others. "Ok, I know that was a heck of a sucker punch right after we thought we'd crossed the finish line, but we need to recover. We'll do everything we can to help our friends in Epsilon Eridani. Right now though, we need to give Brice some time with the data Pepper collected. I'd like you both to work together on a full ship diagnostic. I want every part of the Wellspring gone over with a molecular scanner. We need to squeeze as many lessons as we can from this run to prepare for our next. Sound like a plan?"

They both nodded in agreement and reluctantly headed off to their assignments. Reaching up to his ear, he touched it and linked up to Shauna. "I assume you took all that in?"

"Sadly, I did," she replied.

"Please do me a favor and reach out to Cetti. I want to know how she detected the Wellspring's return. We need to understand this before people use it against us. Also, make sure to give her the gate collision data so she can get a head start while Pepper is getting checked out."

"Got it, boss."

"And don't forget that he's not expecting my A.I. to come calling, so don't freak him out too much. I'd stop in myself, but I have to talk to Libby about something."

"I guess I'll leave the ghost costume behind then. Maybe I can try the robot body?" Shauna cut the comm.

A million thoughts and ideas flowed through his head as he walked toward the lift tube. He needed to get this Epsilon Eridani information and details about their gate advancements to his sister. The problem was, that except for the probe they'd launched to Luna to return the family archive, they were in a communication blackout. Maybe Libby would have an idea.

When he stepped out of the lift tube, he didn't bother knocking and barged right into her office. The noise of the feeds hit him like a splash of water to the face. He didn't know how she worked with all this racket. After he'd walked past at least two dozen analyst bays, he found her digging through what looked like feeds from the turn of the twenty-second century.

"Hey Zachary, what's up?" Libby asked.

"I came down to check on you. See what you're up to," he said.

"I'm working on transcribing some of our research into these old scanned archives. It's slow weaving our real research into the past and then using worms to get it into the universities and other corners of our Sol knowledge base. It can't change overnight, people would notice." She turned to face him. "Did you need me for something?"

Her smile was always contagious. She had an ability to make him smile instantly, like his mother always could. It didn't last long though, as his mind spiraled back to the reason he had come down to talk to her. She'd sensed his change as well and reached forward to touch his hand.

"Is everything ok?"

"No, I mean… no," he muttered. "So, I need your help with something. I need to get a message to my sister. We have to get it to her without being detected. I know we're supposed to be in radio silence, but this is important."

"Is it a long message?"

"It doesn't have to be. I suppose it depends on how creatively we encode it. There's also the small problem of how we get it to her. I don't even know where she is right now. Do you have any ideas?"

She turned toward a wall screen and brought up a three-dimensional map of Sol with a huge network of random connected lines. "We have our network of tight beams we've been using to trickle data toward Sol. It's not fast, and the bursts are only seconds a day. They bounce all over the place before converging, but they're extremely dense. I can piggyback your message in there, but it has to appear like other research or historical info. It can't stick out from the rest, in case it's intercepted."

So, there was hope. He liked hope. This could work.

"What about actually getting a message to her?"

"I have my ways." Libby smirked. "Best that you don't ask because I can't tell you."

His eyes widened. Apparently, his sister had more than him on a secret leash. "That sounds ominous. Need I be worried?"

"Not in the least." She winked. "What's in this message?"

He needed to talk to Brice first. If anyone could make sense of the alien ecosystem on Liprosus, their astrobiologist could. Brice helped CoPE design and refine their early colonization protocols that should have fought this outbreak. "Give me a few hours. We need to give biology some time for an initial analysis. Can we find some research or news related to infectious diseases near the time period you're working in? That and faster than light travel."

She nodded. "I should be able to manage that. Meet down here after dinner?"

"It's a plan."

The door closed behind him and Libby touched her ear. "I'm assuming you know how to reach her?"

"Of course I do," Harold said.

9

____

STEVE ERICSSON

EPSILON ERIDANI, LIPROSUS

The transport pod came to rest, and Steve stepped out. He paused to glance around at the park entrance. The rain had stopped seconds before the doors opened. Right on schedule. The weather controls they'd developed on Earth over the past century worked surprisingly well, even on alien planets.

He breathed in deeply and gagged. The musty smells of the Liprosus mornings were still difficult to get used to. It reminded him of going into his grandma's attic in Old New York. That moldy smell of dusty old books and furnishings from a bygone era.

He tapped his wrist to start his workout and then leaned forward into a jog. Today he was following his usual route along the walking paths in the residential ring and then he'd head toward his office.

Jogging along the path his mind wandered to that last trip he'd made to his grandparents before departing for Epsilon Eridani. They wanted to make sure he took some family heirlooms with him. Each colonist was entitled to two square meters of storage aboard the colony ship. That included clothing and all personal effects.

He missed that house. He'd had many fond memories as a child playing there before he'd tested into the Inner Ring academy at the age of twelve. That was when he shipped off Earth the first time.

Heading east, he began to jog away from the residential ring and made his way toward the distant dome. That initial few moments in the musty Liprosus air were challenging, but his blood and lung nanites helped compensate for the air particulates making breathing easier.

Running always cleared his head and helped him focus, something he needed now more than ever. Few people bothered to exercise nowadays since nanites could maintain musculature and health without the physical stress and strain of a workout. He, however, still preferred the routine of running as a personal and mental ritual.

He'd just left an important meeting in the transport pod with a contact from the media. After working through the initial niceties, he stressed the importance that nothing he said be traceable back to him. He then let it all out. Everything about the message from Sol and the challenges people had with sharing the truth, especially Warren. He highlighted the infighting, secret meetings, and how people were trying to further their own agendas.

He chuckled. His own agenda aside, of course.

While he explained the situation to the reporter, the fear and excitement in their face was disconcerting. The mixture of emotions of a huge breaking news story combined with the potential loss of their home world. It was daunting.

They had fewer questions than he'd expected, but that made it easier to stay on topic. Most of the questions they did ask were around the message and why Warren hadn't shared the news yet.

He struggled to hold back a smile during that part of the interview.

Their ride in the pod had been short. Steve used countermeasures to ensure no one else entered. He also made sure that neither his nor the contact's nanite signatures could be tracked together. It was difficult tricking the colony's computers to the whereabouts of any colonist, but they could fake it for short durations of time. One of the small perks of running security for the colony was backdoor access like this.

All they needed was an unknowing accomplice whose nanite signatures they could borrow. They also had to know where the host was headed to retrace their footprints later. This morning it wasn't hard finding someone headed toward a coffee shop for their normal morning pick-me-up. It was all fairly easy, but he had to instruct his media contact exactly where to go after exiting the pod.

Looking down at the green-gray soil of Liprosus, his mind began to clear. He counted the consistent placement of the safety lighting along the path. Timing the intervals with his rhythmic breathing allowed him to clear his mind.

He had to switch gears. To focus on the next set of challenges ahead.

It'd been nearly a week since the news had arrived from Sol. The council members had met countless times to talk through various communication and security strategies. After all the talk, they weren't any closer to deciding on a strategy today than they were a week ago. The internal debates and disagreements were intense, and even Warren's forceful personality failed at bullying through the issues. He needed the support of the directors and key individuals in the private sector to survive.

Warren knew this, which was likely why he'd held several closed-door meetings with dissenters of his plans. Afterward, they came out in support of him, but he was still short of a majority even today.

Steve made a note to have Keri ask around. Perhaps someone would leak what Warren had said in those meetings.

The constant conflict in the sessions wasn't helped much by Joyce. Their Director of Colonization had been MIA since her son's death at the farms. The Oak team was working hard to cover the gap left by their mourning leader.

He couldn't have anticipated her son's death, but he had to admit, it played directly into his hand. After the initial comm from Sol, the clock was ticking. The calm before the chaos would only last so long. He was working to control that coming chaos of the combined events to secretly stoke the embers of colonial dissent.

His plan had been in motion since well before leaving for Liprosus. Slowly making the right friends and positioning the right people, his people, throughout the colony. It was a long and dirty process, and while he still wasn't ready, it was now or never. He couldn't take a chance that Warren would come out the other side of this announcement stronger and better positioned. Going all in was the only option. He'd call in a few chits, and make a few new promises. He hated making promises about as much as he hated the Outer Ring. Unfulfilled promises are the Achilles' heel to any good plan. In the end, he'd be in control of the colony and could afford to pay out or eliminate the debt.

It'd been about an hour of running when he reached his office. Ryder and Keri were there waiting for him. Ryder was the second officer in his team working to take down Warren. He also had a unique biochemistry skill set that allowed him to work covertly on Joyce's science teams and still further their cause.

Steve had been struggling to dethrone Warren without putting the security of the colony in jeopardy. He knew Keri was jockeying to be the new Director of Security, but Ryder, he was another mystery entirely. His hatred for Warren seemed to be far deeper and burning than climbing the military career ladder.

Steve walked in and tossed his things on the desk, wiping his face with a towel he'd grabbed along with a globe of water from the nearby dispenser. Ryder and Keri were standing in front of a security wall. "Good morning, folks. The information handoff went as planned. The reporter was shocked about Sol and was all over Warren's part of the story. Like white on rice. How's our plan unfolding?"

Keri was rubbing her hand through her white cropped hair when he entered. She came to attention and turned to face him. "We've confirmed everything's in place for the leak,

Director Ericsson. We can bring down the transport pods whenever we need to, and the food stores are ready to be mobilized."

He nodded and took a sip from the bulb of water. "What about the first responders, are they on our side?"

"Yes, sir. They're either one of ours or their commander is. We're confident that we can control any rioting we might encounter." Keri tapped her foot and looked nervously toward the security wall and then back to him. "In light of recent events though, we have a few new concerns."

"Ok, let's work them. What do we have?" He took another swig of water as he walked up to the security wall and linked up his comm.

"It's the farms sir," Ryder began. "We've been working through the data from the Oak's investigation. I think it's worse than we thought. This isn't a random accident or outbreak."

He took another drink from the bulb and wiped his forehead. "What do you mean?"

"The data suggests that whatever is out there is neither a virus nor bacteria. It's acting like both and neither. I don't think the Oak has realized this yet." Ryder brought up some of his notes on the wall screen.

The data was Greek. He wasn't even sure what he was looking at. "Are you sure we have all the Oak's latest findings? Are they withholding anything from us?"

Ryder shook his head. "I can't imagine they're capable of subterfuge right now. They're underwater with Joyce being out and Warren breathing down their neck. Most of the people are thankful for any help they can get. I've been able to assist in the labs handling some outbreak specimens. They're only now putting together a new test protocol to figure out how contagious it is and under what conditions it mobilizes."

He ran a hand through his sweaty hair leaving a mussed mess behind. "So, what are we looking at, Lieutenant? How bad could this get?"

"It's hard to tell, sir. I'm happy we're getting out ahead of the food controls because if this gets bad, that'll need to be seriously rationed. We can't be eating food from these farms until we know all the details."

His stomach growled on cue. Food would be tight for a while until they controlled this outbreak. They'd have to make some hard decisions ahead. "Alright, so what else was there? You mentioned a few concerns."

Keri and Ryder both stared at each other. Blank expressions on their faces.

He jumped in. "Come on now! Just tear it off."

Keri hesitated, looking first down at her hands, and then at him. "There's been a second outbreak at the farm, sir."

"Oh frak, not again! You should've led with that. Do we have any details on what happened this time?"

"Early indications from interviews in the last hour point to it being accidental. The farms have been closed for nearly a week and friends and family of council members may have been attempting to better themselves ahead of the Sol news going colony-wide."

He raised a hand and shook his head. "Wait, wait. I thought you said we had food controls in place. What did I miss?"

"We do sir—" Ryder began.

"All the rations and food stockpiles are secure," Keri interrupted and brought up a map showing the farm rotation schedule on the wall. "As you already know, the crops and farms are on a rotation. We don't have anything but a skeletal team out there guarding the place. The farm that was closed due to the outbreak was next up to yield a new set of crops for general consumption. This meant that colonists were dealing with news of the outbreak and a colony-wide food rationing. Well, apparently some families in the know didn't like rations and thought they knew better, so they tried another run on the farms."

"Ok, you had me worried for a minute. So, these people were agitated and hysterical elite friends of Warren?"

"That's our observation based on early information. The outcome, however..." Keri's face turned white. She took a seat to calm herself before continuing. "The outcome was rather gruesome and is breaking now, ahead of our leaked story." She made a gesture and brought up the news feeds on the security wall.

The pictures were shockingly detailed. Bodies strewn everywhere, dozens and dozens of them. All covered in the same diseased markings as the last outbreak. Their exposed skin was linearly bisected in pink and purple lines. This time, however, they were reporting nearly three times as many dead.

"How'd... they get these shots?" He leaned in closer to the wall screen. His previously rumbling stomach was now peaky. "I thought we had a quarantine zone?"

Keri stood up and brought the map of the farms on the wall screen again with the patrol routes overlaid. Her demeanor had returned to the usual calmness he'd grown accustomed to. "We do, but like I said earlier, it's been limited patrol coverage. We figured the prior outbreak would act as a better deterrent, so we didn't allocate much manpower out there."

He looked up at the ceiling and sighed. "Well, we figured wrong, didn't we?"

"Yes, sir." Keri was fiddling with the Taser on her hip. "And now we're left with an even worse situation than before while we're preparing for another breaking story. A story that could make the last run on supplies seem like a walk in the park."

Looking at the map on the wall, he couldn't help but think they could turn this to their benefit. While he'd prefer to reallocate some of Keri's squads to protect the farms, he thought better of it. The pictures were gruesome and being delivered in the usual overdramatic way the media has used for centuries to shock viewers. As horrible as this incident was, they had to keep their eyes on the bigger picture of isolation from Sol. Warren's fumbling of the news was about to break, and it was that momentum he wanted to push in his favor.

He turned to face them both. "I think I've got a way we can handle this. Let's reallocate one of Major Michaels' platoons to run quarantine. I'm sure she can spare some people from the space elevator. It's not like people will be clamoring to get upside. And besides, everyone knows she's Warren's preferred officer. Having her crew thinned out will do nothing but help us."

"That could work." Keri pulled up the duty roster for Major Michaels on the wall. "I'm pretty sure… yep there it is, she's been rotating to cover elevator duties with her platoon. Something tells me she's far too close to her people to put them out. That means she either doubles down helping them cover the elevator, or goes to the farm herself. Either way, she's out of our hair."

With her out of the way, Warren was a sitting duck.

A smile crept across Steve's face. "Make the call."

10

JOYCE GREEN

EPSILON ERIDANI, LIPROSUS

The lock on the quarantine door had a constant low buzz that could drive even the sanest person batty. Joyce was lying on her cot, staring at the ceiling.

Her cheeks were flushed, and her face was a mess of tears and dirt. She'd been crying for days, and other than some water, she hadn't eaten anything. She'd disabled her retinal comm a few hours after being tossed into quarantine and hadn't touched it since. She couldn't handle the people; everyone needed her for something, and she needed her son.

The image of Paul's lifeless body flashed through her mind. There he was, he looked so innocent lying in the field. It was like he was little again and had tired himself out playing in the yard and decided to take a quick catnap in the garden. He was curled up, his blond hair blowing in the breeze. The crazy chaotic strands reminded her that he needed a haircut.

Suddenly, she started sobbing. She'd known Paul wouldn't wake up the moment she saw him. His body had been covered in the same markings as the other dead colonists. The markings of the outbreak and the death of the colony.

She'd wanted to hold him again, like he was little. Reaching up, she'd hit the emergency override on the suit and detached her helmet. Her retinal comm alerted her and had even attempted to stop her. She'd ignored it, detached her helmet, and tossed it aside.

She'd snuggled up next to him and put her arms around his limp form. Lying in the dirt, he'd seemed so small. It reminded her of when he'd played too hard on the trampoline in the yard and got tuckered out. Boys will be boys. Nestled into him, she'd kissed his cheek. Tears had dripped from her face onto his.

She'd closed her eyes, held him, and hoped for death.

Then came all the hands tugging and prying at her. They'd forced her helmet back on and dragged her away from him. She'd screamed his name and fought the whole time. She didn't want to leave him; she'd wanted to hug him and make him feel better.

Opening her eyes, she was staring at the stark quarantine ceiling. He was gone. She'd never hold him again. Never cook him a meal, never get another bear hug, and never fuss over his hair. The tears came again, falling down her face and onto the moist mattress.

She didn't see the point in going on anymore.

Knock knock

She didn't care who was at the damn door. They could take yesterday's food through the drawer. She was in no mood to talk.

Knock knock

Tilting her head to the side, his face was visible through the glass. She'd seen him around the labs before. It was Ryan or Ryder or something like that. One of Steve's cronies he'd installed to spy on her. He was a good scientist. If he hadn't been, she'd have tossed his ass long ago.

She rolled away from the glass.

"Sorry to bother you, Madam Director," he said. "I wanted to check if you were ok. To see if you needed anything."

His voice sounded like her son. He had that youthful boyish charm in how he spoke.

"I know you're going through a lot right now, ma'am. I'm

so sorry about the loss of your son. I met him once, you know. A few years back at one of the colonist preparedness sessions. I was his partner during a team building exercise."

She rolled back over and sat up, leaning against the wall of the cell. She wanted a better view of his face. "Ryan was it? You met Paul?" she asked, her voice hoarse from the crying.

"It's Ryder, ma'am. And, yes, I knew your son. We worked on diagnosing and rebuilding a desalination unit. He was a wiz at those things. Knew within seconds what was wrong with it. I pretty much just did whatever he told me to do."

She smiled at the thought of him working with his hands. He was like his father that way, always needing to fiddle with something.

"He was genuinely proud of you, ya know?"

"Why would you say that?" She reached down, grabbed her water, and took a long drink. Her throat was parched. She couldn't remember her last drink.

Ryder pulled up a chair and took a seat next to the glass. "The whole time he was working on the desalinator he talked about you. About how your people loved working with you. How you inspired them to be their better selves. About how he did awful in school until you recognized what he needed, what his mind wanted to do. Even if it was a lower job."

She lowered the water. "It wasn't a lower job! The colony needs agriculture. Without it, we're dead."

Ryder nodded. "He realized that, but it sounded like he thought maybe people saw it as below your child's level."

"Well, other people can frak off. To each their own. I always wanted him to be happy. The job title never mattered."

Ryder smiled. He reached into the drawer and placed a meal tray in. Pushing the button, it slid to her side and opened. "He felt that, ma'am. He simply wanted to make you proud, even if it was at the farms. Everyone that works for you wants you to be proud of them. That's rare in a leader. To inspire others to do their best, to help the colony. It's something we need more of."

She reached down and grabbed the tray of food. Her stomach growled as she lifted the cover. Buttered oatmeal and eggs with a side of orange juice. She started crying and placed her face in her hands. After a moment, she lowered them and stared at Ryder. "How'd... you know?"

Her display of emotion had affected him. Ryder wiped away his own tears with his sleeve. "Your son and I grabbed some grub after the exercise. He told me about the time he wouldn't eat the oatmeal because the water you'd used was too salty. He said it was his favorite, especially with butter, but your apartment's desalinator was apparently on the fritz."

She chuckled, tears welling in her eyes, and a smile on her face. "Yeah, I didn't believe him. He whined for a few days until I promised to have a tech take a peek. Sure enough, it had a hairline crack. I couldn't taste it, but Paul could. He could taste or smell anything odd no matter how small."

There was a long silence as he watched her eat. Finally, he stood, gave her a salute and turned to walk away.

"Ryder," she called out. Looking down at her plate and then back up at him. "I suppose you're going to tell Steve about this. About how I can't hold it together?"

He turned and shook his head. "No, ma'am, not at all. That's not what I see."

"Tell me. What exactly do you see?"

"I see a mother who loved her son more than anything. A mother who recently had her world crumble beneath her. I see a leader who needs time for herself before she can continue to give to the colony. The colony that needs her, that loves her." Ryder stared at her for a moment and then went to attention and saluted her again, this time holding it.

"Thank you," she said.

Without another word he turned and left.

11

LYNC MICHAELS
EPSILON ERIDANI, LIPROSUS

She squeezed her hand and the exo-suit complied, crushing the ornate steel ball atop the fencing. "Yes, I understand the orders, sir. I'll also repeat my disagreement with them and submit a formal protest through official channels as soon as possible. I will, however, follow them and adjust my platoon coverage to include the farm in our rotation."

The connection broke, and she slammed the fist of her exo-suit through the garden wall next to her. Director Ericsson was showing incompetence and poor resource management. He had other soldiers to reallocate to the farm. Why put the burden on her platoon knowing she was already spread thin? What was he after?

There was no clear way to rebalance her people without leaving something compromised. She had three platoons spread around the Epsilon Eridani star system. One large deployment was spread above, within, and below the space elevator across multiple shifts. Several small deployments were sprinkled around key asteroid mining facilities. Her last set of soldiers were deployed to guard key resources like Mayor North, Director Ericsson himself, and Director Green. She even had a few covert resources spread around the colony but only she knew their location.

Pulling her hand out of the crumbled wall, she walked toward the space elevator's commercial gates where members of her first platoon were currently rotating shifts. The Heads-Up Display (HUD) on her suit's helmet showed that all reports were quiet at the elevator checkpoints. It was just a regular day with resources flowing, personnel doing their jobs, and a few civilians returning from sightseeing and spacewalk games.

As she approached the gate, there was a large crowd of workers and members of her platoon surrounding one of the public news displays. It usually had advertising or arrival and departure information on it, but right now it was playing a breaking news story.

Rather than adding to the chaos, she stayed out of the human perimeter and brought up the news feed on her retinal comm. The reporter was speaking in front of the Mayor's chambers. The story title slid along the bottom of her comm.

EPSILON ERIDANI CUTOFF FROM SOL

… the Mayor's representatives wouldn't comment on the story, but people close to him say he's been making backroom deals with council members and commercial organizations for nearly a week. Some say he's preparing to announce broad colonial expansion across Epsilon Eridani, but my trusted source in his inner circle says the conversations are far graver.

The supply run from Sol last week coincided with a tight beam message from CoPE President Abigail Olivaw. This message contained details that multiple alien ships had arrived in Sol with unknown intentions. For security purposes, Sol was limiting communications of any kind toward the colonies to reduce exposure and preserve resources.

As all our viewers know, messages from Sol take over ten and a half years to arrive at Epsilon Eridani. This means that whatever happened after the aliens arrived took place years ago and that same fate could be heading our way next. Here to talk about…

There's no way this was happening. She'd have heard something from her contacts, or certainly the Mayor would have clued her in. Their relationship was strong, but if this was really happening, perhaps she wasn't as necessary as she'd thought.

She cut the feed and pulled up the duty rosters of the other platoon in Epsilon Eridani along with their commanding officers. While several movements were marked *CONFIDENTIAL*, they too were running tight shifts all around. Some type of mobilization was happening, and she was sure that Director Ericsson was behind it.

Reaching up to her ear, she subvocalized a command to place a call to one of her operatives in another platoon. The line didn't connect, but she got an ack back on a secure text-only channel. They were subvocalizing through their comm and couldn't speak openly.

The words from her operative scrolled onto her comm:

Can't speak right now, Slingshot. Gettin orders from the Major on our next duty assignment. Apparently, they'z declarin martial law in the colony, and we're one of the unfortunate ones running the lockdown.

She shook her head. It was quite a leap from news leaks to martial law. There was no way Mayor Green would impose martial law without looping her in. She'd been close with Warren since Abigail had assigned her to the Epsilon Eridani colonial mission. She'd elevated Lync quickly within the CoPE Security Forces and despite her hatred of Warren, had ordered her to buddy up with him so she'd have inside access. "Who's declaring martial law?" she asked.

His reply scrolled onto her comm:

Come on, Sling Gerl. I figured you'd for sho be in the know. Director Ericsson declared martial law effective immediately.

"Thanks, Mofie. Please keep me in the loop to anything else unusual," she replied and cut the comm.

She hadn't even noticed it, but she'd been pacing around the gate area while talking on that comm. It wasn't a common sight for a fully decked out military officer in an exo-suit to be walking aggressively around the space elevator entrance. As a result, people were starting to stare. She stopped, gathered her wits, and headed to the nearby security offices.

Before she'd left Sol, President Olivaw told her she'd need to step up at some point in the future. She wasn't sure if this was what she'd had in mind. She'd always figured it'd have something to do with the Mayor given how much Abigail detested Warren. If this was that moment, she didn't want to let the President down.

Lync had always been a consummate overanalyzer, studying and working to understand everything she interacted with. Colony security and its weak points were no different. She spent many nights trying to put herself to sleep by dictating notes into her comm, anything she could do to quiet her mind. Most of them were hypothetical, but her mind and notes were overflowing with ideas.

With today's news there was one, in particular, that was itching in the back of her mind. A plan that would get her back into the loop of knowing the news instead of reacting to it. Over the last several months, she'd been concocting a tangential plan to take control of both the space elevator and the farms, two of the colony's weak points. It'd require some improvised resource shuffling, but she thought they could pull it off.

She walked into the beanstalk offices unexpectedly. Conversations cut out mid-sentence and people turned to face her. "Alright, listen up everyone. I'm sure you've all seen the feed. Unfortunately, I don't know anything more about Sol than you, but I know we have another assignment. I need volunteers to join me at the farms to establish an expanded quarantine security perimeter. That run the colonists made on the farms this morning was unexpected. After the last outbreak, the DoS needs our help in re-securing the area. Do I have any volunteers?" She wasn't expecting anyone to step forward for a potential life-ending duty like this.

At first, there was silence, but then one of the junior soldiers chimed in. "Won't that make us light here at the elevator, Major?"

She clasped her hands behind her back and collapsed her helmet into her suit. There was no point in talking through a bubble. "Yes, it will. Good observation, soldier. We play the hands we're dealt when orders come from the top. In fact, the people in both locations will need to pull extra rotations."

A collective groan spread through the gathered soldiers.

She raised her hand upward, silencing them. "To top it off, everyone at the farms will need to wear full exo-suits at all times. I'm playing it safe with contaminants. We'll be showing force out there. We're not taking crap from any civilians this time around. Do any of you exo-jockeys wanna join me?"

The exo-suits should pull a few of them in. Even with the quarantine threat, the suits were an easy duty and practically drove you around the place.

After a few seconds of silence, six soldiers stepped forward and volunteered. Fewer than she'd expected. Most of them were her senior officers that wanted to stay at her side. Everyone's fear of death by an unknown contagion was bigger than she'd expected. In order for her plan to work, she'd need to draw more soldiers away from the space elevator.

She shrugged. "Alrighty, you forced me to make assignments since we don't have more soldiers with guts. No groans, no gripes, no grumbling… your assignments are on your comms." She'd quickly grabbed the names of most of her top eighteen soldiers, and a few high potentials, and reassigned them to the farm.

"Major, I apologize, but won't these assignments leave a skeleton crew here at the beanstalk?" the same junior soldier asked.

His name appeared on her comm when she turned and walked up to him. "Franklin, is that right?"

He nodded and came to attention. "Yes, Major!"

"Franklin, do you honestly think with the threat of aliens on the way and our home star system having gone MIA, that colonists will be scrambling to go upside and steal a shuttle? To go where?"

His face turned red. He hadn't thought his question through. "No… M… Major. That would… be suicide."

She recognized his name as one of the high potential soldiers in her farm invite list. She leaned closer and looked him in the eyes. "Are you joining me at the farms, Franklin, or are you sticking around here?"

Stiffening his back, he looked straight ahead past her, saluted, and yelled. "Reporting for farm duty, Major!"

"That's great, soldier." She took a step backward. "As for the rest of you, if you're headed to the farm, then triple check your suits and ensure their environmental controls are running perfectly. We don't need any internal quarantine incidents while we're out there. I expect everyone on farm duty to report to farm station two's gate in one hour. Dismissed!"

She hung back to answer questions as the platoon dispersed. The only person who held back was Crayo. She'd expected and half hoped he would. After he walked up, she peered around to make sure no one was listening in. "I suppose you're wondering why I didn't include you on farm duty?"

"A skosh, yeah," Crayo replied somberly. "I was going to volunteer, but I'll be honest, I froze. Thinking about the images from the news feeds… the markings on those bodies, they were…"

She nodded. "I understand, and honestly, I don't blame you. Funny enough, I want you here at the beanstalk. I need something done on the down low. Something that wouldn't be workable if we had the entire contingent on duty." She gestured in the air and opened a secure direct connection to his comm to share a schematic view of the elevator.

"We need to install man-in-the-middle relays along the communication backbone here, here, and here." She highlighted the points along the elevator route between Liprosus and the L1 orbital platform, both within the superstructure and along the route. "Can you do it?"

Crayo studied the details she'd highlighted and tilted his head in realization. "These aren't random points. It looks like you're trying to take control of all communications from upside." There was a pause where he adjusted slightly to watch her response. "This doesn't seem like a plan you threw together in the moments following a breaking alien news story."

A smile crept across her face. "Nope, that'd be a negative. It's something I've been tweaking for a while now. I didn't know when or if we'd need it." She shuffled her feet a bit, cautiously looking left and right as if someone would randomly be spying on them, hesitating to say more. "Do you remember when President Olivaw visited the academy for our graduation?"

He slowly nodded; a smile formed. "Yeah, I remember. Who could forget that night? It was epic getting to meet her at the ceremony. I still can't believe she took me up on that invitation to visit the dorm after party. She was quite the drinker and damn near drank you under the table if memory serves."

She grinned. "Yeah, yeah… she was cheating. Clearly, she had nanites neutralizing the alcohol's effects. Anyhow, we got to know each other that night and kept in touch for several years until she visited me again at Titan Station when I made Major."

"Hells yeah! First Ulixi to make Major in CoPE, and a slingshotter to boot. Didn't you and a few of her senior staff attend a private ceremony in the gardens afterward? Rubbing elbows with the elite ya did. Bit odd for a Ulixi but about time they recognized us." Crayo raised his hand vertically and placed his thumb against his temple, a salute usually reserved for Ulixi celebrations.

She returned the gesture and smiled widely. "It took a century, but the Outers have finally started to accept us. On Liprosus though, we're all equals."

"Sim sim!" Crayo chanted.

"Sim sim!" She paused for a moment and stared off into the distance. Should she tell him? She took a deep breath and collected herself before looking back toward Crayo. "I'm going to share something with you. Something I haven't shared with anyone else, ever. I need some help and I need to start trusting someone. If I can't trust you, well, then I can't trust anyone." She swallowed hard. "I can trust you, right?"

Crayo chuckled. "Does an Inner fear darkness like an Outer fears asteroids?"

"Sim sim." She smiled. Those Inners and their damn fear of the dark. "Well, that elbow-rubbing wasn't all partying and drinks. I met President Olivaw's brother Zachary, and a few other folks from her CoPE inner circle. See, the thing is, Crayo… she apparently hand-picked me for this mission. I don't know why exactly, other than she said she felt she could trust me. That night she told me they needed my help at Epsilon Eridani, and that when the time was right, she'd need me to step up. That humanity would need people like me to step up. I didn't know what I'd be asked to do, or when that time would come, but ever since then I've been making a lot of plans. So many plans, they're starting to fill my dreams."

"Was this the signal then? Did she reach out to you?" Crayo raised a brow.

She knew this question was coming. "No, not exactly. It honestly doesn't seem right. Something has always gnawed at me about how she said that humanity would need people like me someday. Almost like she was certain we'd run into something like this… and then today happened. Does that sound weird?"

"Lil bit." Crayo held his hand up, fingers close together. "But I'll be honest with you. I'd follow you through the clouds of Jupiter. If you feel like this is something we need to do, a higher calling or not, I'm up for it. Not sure how to make it happen yet, but I'll figure it out."

An unseen weight lifted off her shoulders. She was relieved with his response, and for having someone to confide in. She gestured by raising her hand to cross her chest and then face upward toward the sky. A traditional Ulixi sign of sincerity, honesty, and openness to receive help.

He mirrored her motions and met her hand in the middle facing his hand downward above hers, resting but not shaking it. This was a motion traditionally performed in a gravity-free space. It would result in repelling the other party if done incorrectly.

"Thank you for your confidence." Her voice was almost skipping with joy. "And don't worry about figuring it out. I might have a plan or three for this stashed away somewhere." She winked at him.

12

─────────

ABIGAIL OLIVAW

SOL, NEAR NEPTUNE

She rolled her eyes. This topic tired her. She'd heard it a thousand times before. "I'm not going to lie to my brothers. There's a time and place for things like that, and now is neither. We've come too far to turn on each other."

"Don't be silly," Harold began, "it's not turning on each other if it protects them and advances the cause. You know as well as I do that Bradley won't be able to ignore this and focus on the objective. It's imperative that the colonies not know, and besides, he'll be safer."

"You said the same thing about my grandmother. No one ever met her, and she ended up giving my father and my aunt away. Didn't she die in a drug house somewhere in Åre?"

"That was different, and you know it. Your great-great-grandfather never knew he had a child. The moment your father and aunt were born, Zeus was on the next shuttle to Earth. We don't know if he would've told his daughter about the truth. He never met her. What does this have to do with not telling your brother about the first contact probe?"

She clenched her fists and her nails dug into her skin. "You're killing me, Harold. My father kept his sister in the dark and look what—"

"That's not fair! Stop trying to compare these past events with what's going on with Bradley. She knew the truth and walked away from it. Your father's only option was to lead the Confederation and to lead the family. He knew there was only one option to colonize the stars that didn't require force. Earth is, and always has been selfish. It would never let the Confederation focus on expansion with billions of people always in need. Everyone recognized this. The economic disparity of society on Earth would always be reinforced by the leaders that benefited from it. There's a reason the term 'haves and have nots' originated on Earth. The only thing he could do was strengthen the treaty through subterfuge and focus on the Outer Ring to lead humanity to the stars."

She sighed, pulled the bed pillow to her face and screamed. Harold always talked as if this was the only course of action for the Confederation, as if every past decision was somehow altruistic. "Stop being dramatic and conflating the issue. You know—"

"Wake up, Abigail."

Why were the lights getting so bright and why was Harold being annoying again? She didn't want to study at the crack of dawn every single day. Let a kid be a kid for once. "It's the weekend! Leave me alone, Harold."

"Abigail, it's time to wake. You're mumbling aloud and people are near. Please control your faculties. You're aboard the Jurat. We've entered the last stage of deceleration and are finally at low enough G-force to come out of cryo-sleep."

She groaned. She'd been asleep for… was it supposed to be forty-eight hours? They must be on the last leg of the Neptune hop. They hadn't woken her, so that was good. No catastrophes then.

No one could figure out why the alien ships were advancing so slowly through Sol. She didn't question it though; it fed into their plan and allowed them to travel to Neptune.

She opened her eyes and stretched. Her back was stiff, like she hadn't moved in ages. When she lifted her leg over the edge of the cryo-pod and sat up, her body felt like it had a ton of bricks resting on it. Every muscle screamed when she moved.

The cryogenic drugs were being filtered from her blood and were pouring out of the tubes connected to her torso. During the voyage, computers stimulated her muscles to ease the shock of being in a cryo-pod for so long. Apparently, the body adapted better on longer voyages, but she'd never taken one longer than a week, so she couldn't confirm that.

Damn if she wasn't a ball of pain right now.

She reached up to her ear and activated her retinal comm. The display came to life. The vibrant colors were crisp and new, like she'd never experienced them before. Shaking her head, she couldn't remember the last time she'd unplugged for a few days. Maybe after this was over, she'd take a long vacation in isolation somewhere. She'd certainly earned it.

"Good morning, Harold." She subvocalized the message so the Cryo Technician wouldn't assume she was talking to herself again.

Harold's voice was muted. She assumed because he wanted to let her body adapt to the comm again. "Actually, it's evening, Madam President. We'll be arriving near Neptune orbital platform three in a few hours. The local time will be early in their morning."

"Good thing, I suppose. We won't be making any house calls while we're passing in the night, so time doesn't matter. I assume I wasn't woken during the trip because the alien ships were still idling their way toward Earth?"

"Yes and no."

Bringing up the course and trajectory of the ships on her comm, she saw what he was talking about. Until four hours ago, they were lazily making their way toward Earth and then something changed. "Any idea why they suddenly accelerated? Wait, are these numbers correct? They'll arrive in… six hours?"

Harold adjusted her retinal comm to zoom out and show more of Sol, bringing into view the source of the change. Six more alien ships appeared at the exact same location as the original six.

She nodded. "So that's why they were dragging their feet. They were waiting for reinforcements. Have we already deployed the probe and sent the welcome package?"

"Yes. The probe has been deployed and is awaiting your command, Madam President. I wanted to make you aware of the entire situation before we went ahead."

She studied the tubes connected to her body. The cryofluid was filtering slower now. "Do we have any other options?"

"None according to my analysis. While you were asleep, there were fifty-one different attempts by various Inner Ring groups to communicate with the aliens. They all appeared to have failed. The communication attempts varied from welcoming them as gods, to demanding that they leave before, and I quote, 'we'll vaporize you like the alien scum you are'."

Her irritation flared at the thought of being on the receiving end of that hollow threat. She gave the aliens credit for not destroying them out of spite. Well, at least not yet. "So, our constituency met our requests for communication silence with the childish response of 'we know better than you'?"

"Not entirely, Madam President. There have been no attempts from the Outer Ring to communicate with the aliens. There have, however, been several impassioned pleas sent privately to you, but none directed at the aliens."

At least someone recognized how to follow orders. She eased out of the pod and gave her legs a chance to adjust to the weight of her body. Thankfully, they lowered the gravity of the Jurat to account for the crew coming out of cryo. She was at a fraction of the Lunar gravity she'd grown used to. Standing there, her stomach grumbled. She hadn't eaten real food in days.

She turned to the Cryo Tech. "Am I cleared to go?"

"One moment, Madam President. Let me unhook you." The tech walked up to her side and detached the tubes from her torso. Her body retracted its access ports and sealed a moment later. "All your vitals check out, and your body appears to have handled the voyage well. It may take a few hours for your nanites to expunge the remaining cryo-fluid in your system, but the disorientation will wear off shortly. You may experience pain in your next few bowel movements, but that's normal until your fluid levels even out."

"Thank you." She smiled at the tech and walked out of the cryo chamber, heading toward the Jurat's galley. Toast and coffee sounded amazing right now.

The halls of the Jurat were empty. Most of the crew must still be asleep. She subvocalized to bring up the media feeds Harold had marked for review as she ambled toward the galley. Skimming through them, the sentiment was a mixture of fear, confusion, and honest attempts to grapple with the meaning behind the alien's arrival.

There were a number of religions pontificating that this event was the beginning of the end. Given that some older religions dated to before recorded time, she realized there was some thread of truth to their belief. They had diluted the real reasons behind the alien arrival through thousands of years of interpretation and human greed. Humanity always knew that today would come. It wasn't until a few hundred years ago that the missing pieces around why fell into place.

"Harold, this last piece you marked. Was this the same Nguyễn that was in our conversation before we departed? Admiral Nguyễn?"

"Yes, one and the same. I expected you'd be interested in that one."

As she read the transcript of the interview, she could imagine him saying all of this nonsense. During the interview, Admiral Nguyễn accused Abigail of being a coward and fleeing to the Outer Ring to escape the alien invasion. Then he spouted off conspiracy theories about why the colony ships that were under construction had suspicious drive malfunctions. He'd accused her and the Olivaw companies of deceiving CoPE and claimed that they were actually hiding the ships and were planning to leave Sol with them. She nodded. He wasn't far off on part of that. She did indeed have the drives destroyed. It was, however, to protect humanity, not to escape from it.

"Was he dealt with?"

"Swiftly, Madam President. I requested his resignation within seconds of processing the interview. Representative Zhang has jailed him on crimes against the Office of the President during a time of war and replaced him with Admiral Patel."

Entering the galley, she confirmed that she was the first to awaken from cryo. The room was vacant and eerily silent, waiting to serve the people aboard. She walked toward the food processor and placed an order for a black coffee and some sourdough toast. Her father loved sourdough. It was a simple meal that he ate practically every morning with peanut butter and coffee. Several coffees.

She sat at the counter with her hands in her lap. The comfortable stillness of the Jurat was relaxing. Her luxury and silence would soon come to an end, much like humanity's silence was ending. They'd been able to hide on Earth for thousands of years and it was time to pay the piper.

"I'm sorry I failed you," she muttered.

"Pardon, Madam President. I didn't catch that," Harold said.

"It wasn't meant for you, Harold." An air of melancholy surrounded her.

"Is everything ok, Abigail?"

"No, everything isn't ok. It's light-years from ok. I'm sitting here contemplating my personal and family failures. I'm wondering where we went wrong, where it all went wrong. We're preparing to take humanity to the brink of destruction without sight of the path through this alien mine-field. Hell, I don't even know if there is a path. I'm doing all of this without my family because I've hidden them safely away across the galaxy. I'm sitting here, practically alone, talking to myself and talking to the mind of my great-great-

great, however many times, grandfather etched into my retinal comm. So, no Harold, everything isn't OK!"

There was no reply, nor should there have been. The silent hum of the food processor had stopped, and she could smell the yeasty hints of the sourdough struggling to escape. She sat there silently staring at her hands. She needed a few more moments to remember. To remember her brothers and the joy they'd had as children exploring the world. To remember what it was like to experience her first rocket launch, her first space elevator ride, her first kiss.

She was now possibly at the juncture of experiencing her lasts. Her last sleep, her last silent room, her last morning coffee. There's something poetic about contemplating her own lasts while sitting at the precipice of humanity's.

She sighed. Reaching to her ear she tapped it and connected to the bridge. "Please send the broadcast. Let's see if we can't get the attention of these aliens."

13

ZACHARY OLIVAW

SOL, OORT CLOUD

He walked over to the workbench and put away the digital oscilloscope. "What do you think? Will you join the expedition?"

Pepper walked up behind him and whacked him on the back with her tablet. "Of course I'll join, you idiot. You didn't even have to ask." She headed over to the navigation controls and ran the diagnostics again. "I've been training for this moment my entire life. If you left without asking me, then I'd probably jury-rig one of these probes to chase after you."

A melody played and a message appeared on the navigation console. It completed successfully.

Pepper bopped in her seat triumphantly. "That was it. I got it!"

He checked over the preflight checklist. "Nice work! That covers navigation, communications, defense, and engineering. We've debugged all the quirks from the last test jump plus a few extra I threw in the mix."

Sliding the tablet into the nav station, Pepper walked over to where he was sitting at communications. "I don't know if I'm in any position to ask, but if I don't, then I'm gonna burst. You've been secretive about this mission. Where are we going?"

"You'll know more after we leave in an hour."

"Wait, in one hour?" Pepper reached out and gave him a nudge. "You're messing with me, right?"

He closed up the communication screen. Everything was ready. Looking up at Pepper, he smirked. "I wish I was. You'd better go get your affairs in order. We may not be back... for quite a while."

Pepper was grinning from ear to ear. "Roughly how long will we be gone? Do I... need someone to watch Tabby?"

"If she won't be in the way, she's welcome to come aboard. She'd be the first gate traveling feline."

"Geep! This is exciting. I gotta go, gotta pack, gotta... meet you in an hour." Pepper squealed and sprinted out of the ship toward the lift.

He glanced over the checklists again. They'd done everything they could to prepare. It was time. Technically, they were late with the aliens having already advanced on Earth, but the best-laid plans often go awry.

"The fabricators are online, and I've topped off the supply holds," Shauna's voice said in his ear. She brought up the ship supply status on his retinal comm.

"What about the missile and probe fabrications?" he asked.

"We've finished some of them, but with the accelerated plans we won't be departing with everything. We're at thirty percent missile capacity and seventy percent probe capacity. We verified the laser armament adjustments at low power on that last gate jump and ran a battery of successful rail gun tests as well. Finally, we finished the fabrication of both landing shuttles to give us the redundancy we'd hoped for."

"It'll have to be enough." He scanned the armaments.

"I projected that we wouldn't be able to finish the torpedoes and probes, so in the last probe relay launch I sent fabrication commands forward to our first stop. That should give us a few more once we arrive and maybe they'll finish fabrication, depending on how long we stay."

Was she kidding? "What do you mean you sent fabrication plans forward? What if they're intercepted? That's a hefty risk this late—"

"I know. I was thinking ahead. It's kinda something I'm good at. I securely embedded the command in the probe's arrival protocols. They have custom anti-tampering self-destruct procedures installed, remember? Trust me, I don't see anyone messing with them. Besides, if they've compromised our first destination, then humanity has bigger problems."

She had a point. "Alright, but next time—"

"I'd do the same thing."

He chuckled. "Doesn't make it any less weird that you finish my thoughts."

"On that note, are you going to—"

"Head down to talk to Libby? Yes," he said completing her sentence. "But first things first."

He subvocalized a command to open a direct comm to Pluto, Brice, and Pepper. "Alright peeps, this is it. I told you the call could be coming at any time and it's now. I need you packed and present at the Fountainhead in forty-five minutes."

"Are we really sticking with Fountainhead as the name? It's kinda naff," Pluto said.

"Right? I mean sure, it kinda looks like an ancient pen cap I guess, but it's... lame," Pepper said.

"That's what I just said. Wait, Pepper?!" Pluto screeched. "Are you joining us, as well? WOOT! This is gonna be a do now!"

"A what?" Brice asked.

"A do, D O... it's a—" Pluto began.

"People, people," Zachary interrupted. "More packing and less chattering, aye? I'll meet you all in forty-five." He cut the comm.

He stood and walked down the gangplank, heading toward the lift. Entering it, he expressed downward. He'd miss the Wheel. It'd been his home for decades, and everyone there was his friend, his family, his people. They'd created a microcosm of the best of humanity. A group of people working toward a common goal, together, and without politics and bullshit.

Reaching the bottom of the lift, he arrived at Libby's door; it was slightly ajar. Pushing it open, he walked into an eerie scene. All the monitors were off, and the lights were on. He didn't even know they'd installed lights down here. She'd always had the room lit up with so many displays he'd assumed they didn't bother.

"Libby! Are you here?" His voice echoed through the quiet space. There was only silence in response. "Alright this is freaking me out. If you're playing games, then please stop."

"What's the plan, Zachary?" Libby asked from somewhere down the lengthy room.

"I'm not following. What do you mean?"

"The plan, Zachary. What's the plan? I know you're headed off somewhere. Where? Who's going besides the pilots?" Libby came into view about ten meters away. Her arms were crossed, and she had a scowl directed at him that could melt Europa.

He wiped the sweat from his forehead; "I can't say yet, but you already know that. I'm taking Pepper, Brice, Pluto… and I've come here to ask you to join us. I need you, and you know that. We need someone with a level head that can help us see the forest for the trees. We need you to help us with linguistics, someone who's studied our past and what little of their past we know. I'm sure you already realized I'd be coming. So whatcha think? Will you join us?"

She glared at him for a moment, turned, and then walked around the corner out of sight.

"Shit," he muttered. He should've asked everybody sooner, but he wanted them to stay focused. So many variables had changed and without Abigail, he only had Shauna and Libby to brainstorm with. He'd have to double down and beg or order her to join or something. They needed her.

When he walked after her, he stopped, and took a step

backward. She was coming around the corner, her bags following close behind.

Her face shifted from a scowl to one of disappointment. "Next time, Zachary, next time don't wait so long to tell your friends what's up. I know your sister operates under strict need to know secrecy, but you have to let people in."

He sighed and swallowed hard. "You have my word, Libby. We're nearly done with all the insane secrecy. Once we've made it to our first destination, I'll make sure we're all on the same page. I promise." He gestured a cross over his heart.

Libby nodded and walked toward the lift.

As she rose upward, he turned back toward the expansive office space. He'd dodged a bullet there. Without Libby they'd have lost a wealth of knowledge, history, and expertise at navigating cultures. Sure Shauna and Harold would help, but they were computers and couldn't be counted on in all situations.

The sound of his feet echoed through the empty room as he turned to pull the ancient door closed. After decades of being humanity's electronic pulse in Sol and beyond, the room was now lifeless and silent. His pulse raced thinking about the adventures that lay ahead, but at the same time he couldn't help picturing the room as a reflection of humanity's possible future.

"NAVIGATION CHECK!" Pepper said.

"Communications check!" Libby said.

"Defense check, wait, I... yes check!" Brice said.

"All systems are nominal, Captain." Pluto smirked at him.

Captain. He didn't like the sound of that. It had a peculiar ring to it. Shauna assured him it was necessary to establish a clear chain of command, and he couldn't think of a good argument against it. He was in charge at the Wheel so he should be used to it. Little did they know how often he winged it.

Shauna's voice came over his retinal comm. "Before we leave, I wanted to let you know that a comm arrived. Abigail's ship is orbiting not far from Neptune. They've issued the broadcast, Zachary."

The knot in his stomach tightened. Well, that was that. There was literally no turning back now, even if they wanted to. "What about our research?"

"She hasn't received our message, but Libby reassured me it would arrive shortly."

He wished they'd been able to get her response before leaving. He wasn't as adept at strategy as Abigail, and he wasn't sure the effect gate travel would have on the broader strategy. "Are the relay probes set to follow us? We need as much information from Sol as possible."

"They are, but we have a limited supply of probes. We have to be careful about how we use them."

"Ahem!" Pepper was looking at him. She ticked her head to the side, toward the others.

He turned; the crew was staring at him. Shit, he'd zoned into his comm again. Should he say something? He was the only one who knew about the broadcast. No, not here, not now. He'd tell them later.

They were expecting him to say something to start the mission. He cleared his throat and tapped his ear opening a comm to everyone on the Fountainhead and the Wheel. "The mission we undertook over a decade ago has come to a pivotal point. While some of you have been at this for much longer, our sacrifices are the same. We forgo direct contact with our friends and family in exchange for working together toward a common goal. To save humanity. I know much of this you have taken on faith from either myself or Abigail's word. We're close to answering all of your questions, I promise. We ask that you continue the fight while we're away and recognize that we'll be doing the same."

He paused for a moment thinking about how to say the next part. All he knew was that it should be honest.

"The media and images that will arrive in the coming weeks will scare and challenge your faith. This is not religious nor dogmatic. We have always led with hard science and facts. We share as much as possible without putting at risk the broader mission. Mark my words, humanity will be challenged by this alien force. I need you now more than ever to trust each other in the coming days and months. No matter how difficult things become, all I ask is that you trust.

"While we don't know the length of Fountainhead's mission, our goals are the same as the Wheel's. To protect humanity at all costs. I need everyone to focus on building and refining Sol's defensive abilities using our recent discoveries. At the same time, we need you to research how to combat whatever is happening at Epsilon Eridani. Our probes continue to return all of their latest data, so let's do whatever we can to help them.

"The Fountainhead will venture deep into unknown space. Deeper than humanity has ever ventured. All of your thoughts and dreams are with us. Good luck to us all, we'll certainly need it."

He kept the comm to the ship open, looked toward Pepper, and nodded. "I've already programmed the first set of jumps. Let's begin."

Pepper and the rest of the crew rotated their seats forward and locked them into position. She reached toward the navigation controls and initiated the gate jump sequence.

"The Tachyon ring has deployed successfully, beginning cone field shaping," Pepper said.

One of the many cameras directed toward the inside of the Fountainhead's closed vanes was visible on all of their retinal comms. The vanes themselves shaped the Tachyon ring field, manipulating it into a conical shape and directing the field down to a point within the heart of the ship. When the particle field converged at the apex of the cone, it appeared to almost swallow the particles. A blackness grew to fill the distance between the vanes. They were used to manipulate the diameter of the gate to a size convenient to engulf the ship. The resulting void was the gate, and once shaped, needed one final ingredient to start the jump. Matter.

"Conical shaping complete. Beginning matter injection," Pepper said.

A loud clang reverberated throughout the ship as the vanes around the hull expanded upward, enlarging the void. Once they were nearly perpendicular to the head of the ship, they inverted, causing the void to move back toward the ship itself.

The first object introduced to the void was a small tether ejected from the center of the Fountainhead. It penetrated the blackness, rippling in response to the passing matter, like a droplet entering an inky pool of water. A moment later, the ship continued the inversion and entered the same darkness. With nothing remaining on the Sol side of the gate, it collapsed upon itself without a trace.

14

STEVE ERICSSON
EPSILON ERIDANI, LIPROSUS

The news leak of the message from Sol and the last supply shuttle had worked far better than Steve had anticipated. Once news got out, the confusion and chaos spread quickly throughout the colony. People made a run on supplies and even tried to take over the space elevator until Lync's thinned security detail managed to regain control. He couldn't understand why people were attempting to overtake the elevator. And then do what? Ride it upside and return to Sol?

Fear was a confusing mistress.

With Mayor Warren on defense and without the upper hand of his stirring pull-at-your-heartstrings speeches, he was stumbling to control the message. He tried reaching to inject Lync into the security situation to assist, but the farm incident was an unfortunate blessing. Steve had spread Lync and her platoons out on farm containment and elevator duty, effectively fencing in the Mayor's ace in the hole.

Now he was going in for the kill. Well, not literally, he had ulterior motives today. Looking to his right and left, he checked that his security team was in place. "Are we sure he's still in his office?" he asked the soldier on point.

"Yes, Director," the soldier said. "The Mayor hasn't left his office since arriving after dinner."

With a nod and a smile, he straightened his uniform and walked toward the mayor's office. "Perfect! Let's make this interesting now, shall we?"

He strode straight in and the Mayor's assistant met him. Her eyes were wide, and her mouth was open. It was priceless. She wasn't expecting anyone at this hour.

"Good evening, Director Ericsson. The Mayor's busy at the moment. Was he expecting you?"

"Not at all, Liz. I won't be but a moment" He walked through the entry and toward the Mayor's office. The doors leading in opened as he approached, without the secretary's authorization.

"Wait!" she yelped as she chased after him.

"Good evening, Warren."

Looking up from his desk, Warren did a double take. "Liz, I wasn't expecting Director Ericsson. Was he on my schedule?"

She was shaking her head no. "He barged straight past me and let himself into your office, Mr. Mayor."

"What's the meaning of this, Steve? Is something wrong?"

"As a matter of fact, there is, Warren." He had a smug smile on his face. "You being the mayor is the problem. I'm here to arrest you and compel you to answer for your crimes against the colony."

"Crimes? What crimes? You've truly lost all attachment to reality, haven't you?" Warren stepped out from behind his desk, motioning toward him. "First you declare martial law without my authorization and now this. Liz, call security and have them escort Mr. Ericsson to detention. I expect he's had one too many drinks this evening."

"Allow me, sir. I've already called them." He gestured to the doorway and his security team stormed into the room with their weapons raised, aimed squarely at the Mayor.

15

─────────────

JOYCE GREEN

EPSILON ERIDANI, LIPROSUS

Epsilon Eridani rose in the distance as Joyce stared across the horizon, oblivious to the moonlets sprinkling the vibrant greens and oranges of the new day sky. She was unfazed by the lack of maglev traffic overhead or the group of security officers heading toward her.

Her mind was elsewhere, preoccupied with her failure to protect her son. She remembered his face, his handsome boyish smile, his blondish hair like his father. The last time she'd seen him that morning before the farms, he thanked her for bringing them to Liprosus. Tears welled up in her eyes.

He'd been so excited about his new apprenticeship that he'd spent the entire dinner the prior evening rattling on about everything he'd learned. She hadn't remembered him being that happy since their arrival in the Epsilon system. She'd spent countless hours this past week imagining he was still with her, hoping he'd come home at any moment, and yet wondering where she went wrong.

Tears streamed down her face falling into her lap. She made no attempt to wipe them away or hide her grief from passersby, not that there were any. With the quarantine zones and the city being under martial law, there weren't many people out and about without permission or environmental protection.

The officer who was leading the small security group halted several meters from her and signaled his team left and right to spread out. He touched his ear. "Colonist!" His voice boomed over the loudspeaker on his suit. "This is a quarantine zone, and we're under martial law. Please return to your home until further notice."

She ignored the officer, continuing to gaze out across the OoC ring. This was her home, the only one she had left. The last thing she needed was these security mutts telling her she couldn't mourn in her ring. It was the only way she'd been able to start each day.

"Colonist!" The officer adjusted his position and raised his stunner. "This is your final warning."

She calmly rose from her seat and turned slightly to address the officer. The focused anger in her eyes could've melted through his environmental suit. "Do you have any idea who I am?"

He glanced around at his team as if they could help and then back toward her. Reaching up to his ear he subvocalized something to his retinal comm and then stepped back, lowering his stunner. "At ease… everyone at ease! I'm sorry Director, I didn't—"

"You're right. You didn't!" The rage in her voice was boiling over. "Now get the hell out of my ring or I'll have your badges, all of you. You'll be the next pin cushions my virologists use as test subjects."

The squad double-timed it south toward the colonial ring intersection that contained the council chambers and other government offices. As she watched them sprinting into the distance, she knew she'd have trouble explaining that outburst later.

"Oh well," she muttered. "Let 'em try and fire me."

She turned and walked toward her office, beginning her new daily routine of pushing her grief behind her duty to the colony. She'd give her feelings their space later. For now, she was needed for a higher purpose, to help save this colony from collapse.

Her mind shifted to her duties as she pulled up her daily schedule on her retinal comm. She also brought up the latest results from her lab and field agents. Over the past week, they'd been working around the clock, struggling to find the origin of the farm outbreak. Every time they thought they were close, they'd hit a dead end.

They couldn't rule out whether it was a virus or bacteria, whether it was airborne or contact only, and they hadn't tracked its origin beyond the farm itself. She smiled at the image of the frightened officers. They wouldn't be thrilled if they found out it wasn't even a virus, if they even understood the difference. Her teams needed to narrow down the possibilities if they had any hope of containing this.

The biotech engineers in her labs were working on tweaks to their nanites to fight this thing. Human mods, like the nanites in their blood, weren't easily redesigned. It'd taken decades of trial and error to prepare the first batch of colony nanites. Augmenting human bodies to compensate for the reduced oxygen and elevated levels of other gases in Liprosus's atmosphere along with adjustments to thrive in a K class star was hard enough. Reprogramming millions of nanites in their blood wasn't something you did on a whim. They'd introduced nanite changes for the Liprosus colonization during their inbound cryo-sleep and their bodies had over a decade to adapt to those.

The hydroponics and agricultural engineers were exploring possibilities that their Sol seed stores were compromised either inflight or after planting. The operating theory in this case was that the compromise had caused an unexpected mutation. The vast expanse of space is fraught with interstellar gases and cosmic rays, and while they had taken a multitude of precautions to shield the starter seeds, mistakes and unexpected events occur. All it took was one small micrometeorite during transit to wreak havoc. The same thing could be said for the multitude of unknowns in the soil on Liprosus. Unexpected foreign organisms or chemical reactions in the soil could have changed the plants in deadly ways.

They were working backward through the colony ship mission logs, reviewing all the recorded impacts and cross-checking those containers to determine if they held seeds that were subsequently planted. They were also taking plant and soil samples from across the farms and surrounding areas, running them through a battery of tests. The full resources of the OoC were focused on understanding this outbreak.

She looked up and realized she'd arrived at her office without so much as acknowledging a single passerby. She'd been so engulfed in her own thoughts that she'd likely broken many social conventions. Then again, people had been giving her ample space since her son passed. Perhaps she hadn't offended anyone. Being away from people wasn't so bad at times.

That gave her an interesting idea.

She entered her office and laid her things down. Her assistant, Nuri, was already in. "I'd like to make another visit to the farms today. I want to take some new soil samples and see if there are any changes to the test subjects that were placed on site."

Nuri scratched her cheek. "Are you sure? Isn't that something we could do remotely, Director? The Mayor has requested—"

"No!" she snapped. "I want to do it myself. I need to feel like I'm doing more than reading reports and guiding from afar. Tell the Mayor I'll do whatever he needs in the afternoon, but this morning I'm following up on some leads at the farm. Can you please scare me up a level two environmental suit, and ask agriculture and biotech if they can each spare a researcher to join me?"

"Certainly, Director. I'm on it." Nuri turned away and began subvocalizing comms to the necessary people.

16

LYNC MICHAELS

EPSILON ERIDANI, LIPROSUS

She was on a routine patrol of the farms and was approaching farm station two. Her exo-suit was showing air quality as normal, nearby drones had no anomalies to report, and no measurable changes were recorded in the biological test dummies they placed throughout the grounds.

A few days after the news of the first outbreak, the food shortages led several groups of colonists to have the bright idea of raiding the farms. Nearly a third of them were rewarded with death by an unknown pathogen. The remaining survivors were under quarantine near farm five. Word spread quickly that the farms weren't viable looting grounds. She'd thought that would've been clear after the first outbreak, but humans weren't always rational.

The random way in which the colonists died during the looting was still under investigation. Within one pack of seven people, one person died but then in another, the entire group of four died. Watching the videos of the incident was surreal. One minute they're sprinting toward some crops, and the next they're tumbling across the ground like rag dolls.

When their bodies were later investigated, they all had a consistent and uniform growth across their chest and neck. Investigation reports claimed that it wasn't indicative of any known cutaneous conditions.

After the second outbreak, Steve assigned Lync to handle farm quarantine. It was scut work to get back at Warren, but it allowed her to direct her other operatives and platoons from afar, so it didn't bother her. Besides, she was curious about the patient zero sites and what better position to be in than the guardians of it.

The security perimeter was a five-klick radius around the entire farm station grid, which meant nearly five hundred kilometers squared of ground to cover. They had no idea if this was sufficient, but her platoon could barely cover this much ground without breaking protocols. While the longer days on Liprosus helped, without the drones and the increased mobility of their powered exo-suits they'd be short-handed for sure.

The farm stations covered about ten kilometers squared giving the colony enough theoretical food coverage for well over one million colonists when fully planted. Their current utilization was only five percent of the available space due to complications with the multidimensional aeroponics equipment and difficulties with the first generations of crop adaptation to the Liprosus air. They spread the different equipment and plant varieties over the designated land, which meant that even though utilization was low, so was the density of the area. This translated into more ground for her team to cover.

After finishing the patrol of farm station two, she adjusted the exo-suits course to head toward farm three. Feeling the suit automatically move was odd at first, but you learned to take advantage of it. She took huge leaping strides across the farmland, which allowed her to take in more telemetry from the surroundings.

Immobilized agricultural robots littered the crops and flying among them was a dusting of drones running scans and tests for remote operators within Doc's team. After the Oak cleared each of the robots, they were returned to operation but constrained to only approved farm areas.

As she was studying the telemetry, her secure comm

flashed in the corner of her vision. It looked like it was a message from Crayo at the beanstalk. She'd worked with him to coordinate a fake run on the elevator after the Sol news leaked. They intended it to throw Steve off and focus his attention on the ground while her troops took over key communication relays on the elevator. It'd worked flawlessly.

The colonists on the ground had caused enough damage to require a complete systems check. This meant that her team needed to perform a slow and methodical test covering all cables and ferries, which would result in several days with no elevator traffic. That gave them plenty of time to accomplish their mission.

She read the message from Crayo.

All communication countermeasures are in place at the beanstalk. We're beginning our descent now and should have all systems back to normal operation by the end of the day.

With that out of the way, they need only wait for it to bear fruit. Her goal with this mission was both leverage and access to any and all communications. She couldn't afford to be out of the loop any longer.

"Sorry to interrupt your patrol, Major," her captain's voice came through the suit headset. "The Doc's here at the southern gate of farm three with a small assist team. She's requesting access. Patrols two and three are deep into their coverage zones and you're the closest to her location. Please advise on how you'd like to proceed."

No one from the Oak was on the access schedule, and certainly not Joyce. "Has anyone reported issues with the drones, Captain?"

"Negative. We worked through all the retrofits the Department of Colonization requested for site analysis days ago. Since then, mum's been the word."

"I'm headed to the south gate. My ETA is five minutes. Please advise squads two and three to divvy up the rest of my patrol zones. Tell the Doc to stay put until I arrive."

"Roger that, ma'am." The captain cut the comm.

She redirected her exo-suit toward the south gate, leaning into the tight turn. Even if she hadn't, the suit would have compensated, but it would've been uncomfortable. She brought up the Oak's access logs in transit and confirmed that the drones were being fully utilized. So much so, she wondered if anyone at the Oak was sleeping.

As she came up to the southern gate, she noticed that Doc had brought two others in her assist team. The suit identified them as engineers specializing in biotechnology and agriculture. She wasn't sure what she'd expected, but this wasn't it.

Approaching the gate, she confirmed everything around the site was still within acceptable environmental levels and then depressurized the suit's transparent polymer helmet. It retracted silently into her back.

"Hello, Director Green." Lync strode up to the group. "How might we help you?"

Joyce smiled. "We're waiting for Major Michaels."

She glanced over at the gate officer and noticed he was chuckling. When he realized she was looking at him, he composed himself and returned to his duties. She returned her attention to Joyce and forced a smile. "That's me, Major Lync Michaels. Commander of Delta Company. I assume you were expecting someone else?"

"I'm so sorry, Major. I didn't—" Joyce stammered as her face turned red.

"No worries," she interrupted waving her hand. "I've gotten used to reactions like that most of my career. How can I help you, Director?"

Joyce turned and peered at her colleagues and then back to Lync. Her face was still a light shade of red. "We'd like to visit the sites of the zero patients. We have a few leads we'd like to investigate."

"Certainly." She turned toward the gate officer. "Soldier, have you verified the integrity of their environmental suits?"

They were ready for her query and replied promptly. "Yes, Major! All three suits have passed inspection and are configured properly. Will you be needing transport, ma'am?"

She glanced back at Joyce. "Are we walking or riding, Director?"

"It's Joyce, please, and I'd prefer to walk if that's alright?"

"Fine by me if you're up for it. Shall we?" she asked, tilting her head toward the north. She pressurized her helmet and checked to ensure the others were following suit. When she noticed they were, she started north. Apparently this wasn't their first rodeo.

They headed down the central road with their supplies strapped atop a pair of six-legged articulated robots. The all-terrain automata held large storage compartments, hooks, and straps designed to follow someone at a safe distance.

The group walked down the road four abreast for nearly a kilometer before she broke the silence. "So, what are we looking for today, Joyce?"

"I'm not sure how to say it other than candidly. We're not sure," Joyce said.

Lync glanced to the right and nodded when her eyes met Joyce's. "That's my favorite kind of adventure, ma'am. Should I wager a guess that one of you is here on a hunch or a limb?"

Joyce laughed and returned the nod. "Affirmative on the hunch, Major. You're sharp." She stared down the road again as if in thought and then continued. "We missed something, I don't know what it was or how, but we missed it. I can't stare through those cameras for another minute. I need to be in the field experiencing the situation and absorbing the environment."

"I'm on the same wavelength. Being in the trenches or in the field keeps you grounded. You can understand far more by being in it than reading about it. Do you mind if I ask something, Joyce?"

"Not at all, shoot!"

Lync studied her, careful to observe how Joyce reacted. "Have you considered and prepared yourself for the impact of being at the farm? Being at the scene of your son's death again."

"Of course, I have," Joyce retorted. "I'd be crazy to return if I hadn't. I spent a lot of time in quarantine thinking. Don't worry. I'm prepared."

It seemed a bit too rehearsed, but she wouldn't question it, not here. As they worked their way down the road, she observed Joyce's assistants as they reviewed and scrutinized various random characteristics of the surroundings. From the position of rocks along the roadside to the weathering of paint on signage. It was surreal listening to them. It was like they were looking for a needle in a haystack.

"So how do you want to do this? Do you have a path or location in mind?" Lync asked.

"We have no set plan or course," Joyce began. "Back when I was learning how to best solve problems, I found that my most successful projects resulted from a no bad idea approach to brainstorming. The key to this approach is to throw as many ideas against the wall as possible and see what sticks. No idea is judged, and no idea is too outrageous. It's not for everyone but it can be productive in opening new avenues of investigation or research. Care to take part?"

She nodded. "That sounds intriguing. I'd be willing to give it a go if you don't mind me joining in?"

Joyce smiled at her. "Not at all. Remember, no idea is too ridiculous. Understood?"

"Affirmative, ma'am!" She brought up a map of the farm quarantine area on her suit's HUD and shared it with everyone else. "Should we perhaps start with where the zero patients died and work from there?"

Joyce glanced at her assistants and they all shrugged. "That's as good a place as any."

As the group worked its way to the zero point, the others stopped and made more random measurements and observations of the surroundings. She set her exo-suit to follow the team's gait and direction but to keep a reasonable distance while she studied up. She familiarized herself with as many of the team's prior dead ends as possible. There was no point in being ignorant of what they'd ruled out, and she needed to warm up to their mental models of the event. Joyce's teams had covered a lot of ground in the past week. While Lync had been focused on the colony's political and security crisis, she hadn't been paying much attention to the life or death health situation under her nose.

When they got close to farm station nine, she brought up the telemetry from the nearby drones and shared it with the team. "Everything is well within normal levels. Have we ever seen the telemetry anywhere outside of normal?"

"No, but given we weren't recording much beyond moisture levels and weather during the incident, we can't take a chance," Joyce said.

She continued to stay back to observe the group's dynamic and to keep an eye on Joyce. This had been the site of her son's death only a week earlier and she wasn't sure what to expect. No colonist would soon forget the images of Joyce curled up next to her son, framed with a backdrop of shocked onlookers. Her face was contorted in unimaginable pain as she openly grieved over her dead son's body. The humility of seeing one of the colony's most important and visible leaders personally impacted by this catastrophic event made it even more relatable. The image had been used by every news outlet and still led many newscasts whenever they talked about an outbreak story.

Joyce was walking swiftly and with purpose through the site. Each item she inspected ended with a shake of her head and a determination to find something new, anything at all. She was on a mission. With what had happened to her son, it was still to be seen if it was a mission of redemption or revenge. Lync knew full well that both of those paths were powerful motivators but led down two dramatically different roads.

While the others spent hours looking for new bits of information and positing new ideas on wind and solar influences, parasites, mutations, and more; she continued scouring through the Oak's research into the incident. As the day went on, an interesting pattern formed in her mind. Maybe she'd been in the military for too long... constantly probing for weaknesses, looking for angles of attack, or outflanking her enemies. To her, all the investigations performed by the Oak were circling around a central problem but never really digging into it.

"Sorry to interrupt, Joyce, but I've been skimming a lot of the abstracts from your teams and I may have found something. While I'm not an expert, I can't help but notice an underlying pattern of assumptions and investigative gaps."

Joyce and her assist team turned toward Lync. "We're all ears, Major."

"I know we're thinking this is a natural mutation of a Sol bacteria or virus, or even one native to Liprosus, but what if it isn't?"

The agriculturist was the first to reply. At least she thought that was his role; he was always checking the soil and plants during the walk. "It has to be alien or native, what else could it be?"

"I'm sorry. I never caught your name." While she could have extracted their names from her comm, she preferred to see how people reacted when they made social assumptions like this.

"Forgive me." Joyce gestured toward each member of her team. "This is Dr. Alan South from my agricultural team and Dr. Elaine Sutter from my biotech team."

She nodded toward each of them. "Nice to meet you both. Alan, was it? I'm not implying that it's not alien or domestic. What I'm asking is what if it wasn't a natural mutation? What if it were an engineered one?"

Alan tilted his head to the side. "I don't understand. Are you suggesting that someone did this on purpose? That's mad! We eliminated that idea on day one. No one had anything to gain from this outbreak."

"Is it? What happened to no idea being too ridiculous?" She was surprised they'd broken their own brainstorming protocol so quickly.

Joyce shot Alan a fierce glare that sent chills. "You're right, Major. That was a misstep. It won't happen again." Looking back at her she continued. "Let's work that angle, shall we? How would that change what we're seeing?"

Walking toward the group, Lync gestured across the site with her hand. "Well, first of all, we should have treated this as a crime scene instead of a medical crisis. Knowing the crime scene is compromised, we can't expect forensics to find anything. We need to establish motive and then retrace the steps of the victims."

"We've dug through all the victims' personal effects," Joyce began. "They're in quarantine along with the bodies. We found nothing unusual. As for their backgrounds, we hit multiple dead ends. There's not an outcast or extremist in the bunch. They were aeroponics engineers doing their jobs and freaked out colonists trying to survive. As for retracing their steps, we've scoured this farm and walked this two-kilometer stretch of road countless times and again today to no avail."

"Agreed." She was looking out over the markings on the ground where they'd found the bodies. "We've turned and returned all the stones here. Let's ignore the looters for a moment. What do we know about the routines of the aeroponics engineers?"

Alan jumped in with details. "We know they left the colony in a ground car at 07:00 and spent the entire morning here at farm nine. They were working through issues with the nutrient delivery system."

Pulling up an overlay of the farm on her HUD, she highlighted the location of each victim on the farm along with their transit routes and details. She was sharing her visuals with each member of the team and saw reflections of her map in each of their suits. They were nodding as she walked them through the locations of the victims on the map.

She then placed another layer on the display. "Ok, now let's overlay the survivors who walked away and where they exited the scene. What do you see?"

They were all squinting through their helmets shaking their heads, straining to identify a pattern and failing. They didn't see it. It wasn't a pattern so much as a missing piece of information. She had to be delicate here. If they saw it, the impact might be less… painful.

"Help us, Major. What are we not seeing?" Joyce asked.

"Does this help?" She cleared the survivors and paused. Still nothing. Did she have to spoon-feed it to them? One at a time she removed the engineers who'd been researched in depth until only one dot remained, a dot missing details.

It hit Joyce first. Lync heard her breathe in and then there was absolute silence for a moment as they all saw it. She knew some reaction would come, but that still couldn't prepare her for what happened next.

Joyce leapt across the distance between them in the blink of an eye. "How dare you, Major… how dare you put this on my son. He was innocent." She was jabbing Lync in the chest with her finger. "He was incredibly excited about this job. My son would never—"

"Stand down, Director! I'm not saying any of those things." She took a few steps back from the encounter to regain control. During Joyce's advance, she'd instinctively drawn her weapon and trained it on her. She lowered it and secured it in the recess built into the arm of her suit.

"Do not mistake my identifying a gap in your investigation as me pointing fingers. With all due respect, you're obviously still dealing with what happened to your son and should not be in the field, ma'am." She did an about-face on the group and headed south. "I believe we're done here."

"No, Major, we're not! We're not done until I say we're done!"

She knew Joyce wasn't about to drop this. She stopped

with her back to the group. Joyce's team was visible in the rear camera on her HUD. They were still in shock over both the revelation and the response and didn't know what to say or how to react. Joyce was still fuming and not thinking logically, either. She was staring at her, waiting for her response. "Director, please don't make me physically remove you from the quarantine area. That'd be too much paperwork and far too many questions to answer."

"You cannot drop..." Joyce stammered and paused to collect herself. "The observation you've made is important, and we'd appreciate if you'd share any other insights you might have. This is the survival of our colony we're talking about. Possibly the survival of all humankind. Please. I'm begging you to help us. To help me."

Lync turned to face Joyce. She was conflicted and didn't want to leave the situation this way. This could put her other goals in jeopardy and her conscience was at odds with her duty. If she assumed Joyce's son wasn't a bad actor, then the fingerprints here pointed at bigger players. Without more details she wasn't sure how to engage. "I'll help you, but on one condition?"

"Name it!"

"My involvement today, in anything we do or discuss didn't happen. Neither my name nor my team will be mentioned. Is that clear?"

Joyce frowned. "I don't understand, why would your involvement matter?"

"It doesn't matter, that's the point. It's a simple request and easy to honor. Is that a yes or a no?"

"Of course, Major. I'll ensure that you're not involved or mentioned in any research or details reported today. Is my word enough?"

She tilted her head toward Joyce's assistants.

Joyce turned toward Dr. South and Dr. Sutter and spoke with a stern yet professional voice. "Neither of you are to report on or record anything that happened today. If you've already made notes or documented insights from the Major, you're to wipe everything. Absolutely everything. Am I clear?"

They both glanced at each other and then back at Joyce and nodded. "Yes, Director," they said in unison.

"If even a hint of today leaks, I'll demote you to cleaning the streets and at the first opportunity I'll put you up on some type of charges. There's far too much at risk to be fighting for limelight." Joyce turned back toward Lync. "There you have it, Major. I'll ensure my staff adheres to our bargain. I'm sure we can trust your people to keep quiet, as well?"

She didn't appreciate the question but understood that she was asking it for the benefit of her people, to save face. "I'll deal with my people. You can rest easy. They're used to following orders without question."

"So, shall we continue now that the formalities are out of the way? How did you find this missing piece so quickly and what else do you know?"

She didn't see how bringing up the outburst over her son was necessary. "I'll be honest. Until a few hours ago, I hadn't researched this event much. As a part of academy training, officers take numerous courses on tactics and strategy. I quickly mastered them, which according to my professors was because of my innate aptitude for pattern matching."

Joyce's assistants were studying her, looking her up and down. Funny how people begin to make judgements the moment they miss something or make a mistake. She cleared her throat. "I don't doubt that your teams did their background checks and research into the victim's movements leading up to the outbreak. However, I'm willing to bet that due to their allegiance and trust in you, they didn't scrutinize your son's movements."

Joyce's hand flinched at the mention of her son but otherwise stood fast. "You're suggesting that we need to dig into my son's movements more that day? Is that it?"

"That's part of it. I'm also willing to bet if you dig deep enough there's a gap somewhere. More importantly, Director, you need to ask yourself who would want you or your son dead and why?"

"Are you saying someone tried to kill my son and me? Why, then, the outbreak and the rest of the victims?"

"I'm suggesting that perhaps your son was an unknowing pawn. He was a carrier, and if someone discovered he was patient zero, it would by association bring you down with him." She was watching Joyce to gauge her response to this line of ideation. "Perhaps they were even hoping that you'd become infected. Certainly, you'd be removed as Director of Colonization if your son was implicated in an outbreak like this."

"There has to be a simpler solution, Major," Dr. Sutter said. "That's a fair number of hypotheticals you've chained together, isn't it?"

"I don't know," she said. "Would Ockham think it was simpler to encounter a random super-virus on an alien world that selectively kills people and yet leaves no trace, or instead that someone planted an engineered virus to further an agenda?"

Joyce broke the silence lingering after that last statement. "Let's accept your hypothesis for a moment. How do you explain the virus continuing to decimate the colony if they were after me or my son?"

She started to laugh, which after that question couldn't help but sound ominous.

"Did I say something funny?" Joyce's hands were now resting on her hips.

"No... not knowingly. I was laughing at your short-sighted viewpoint. Like your son being the missing patient zero, I believe you're missing the broader picture." She glanced between her assistants and then back to Joyce. "What makes you think the agenda isn't to wipe out the entire colony?"

Joyce was visibly annoyed. She'd been pursing her lips and shaking her head subtly as Lync spoke. "I think we have enough to go on from here. I will not continue on this conspiracy train any longer. I was hoping you could shine more light on your theory with some facts. We'll dig into my son's movements leading up to and throughout that day. Thank you for that insight. We appreciate your help today." On that, she nodded toward her team and they set off toward the south gate.

"Might I suggest one other thing, Director?"

Joyce paused and turned. "What is it?"

"If you hit any dead ends, I'd suggest going back further." She struggled to keep her voice emotionless.

"Further how?" Joyce asked.

"Further back in time… perhaps to before we left Sol." Lync turned away from the group. She'd regret that last statement, perhaps even this entire day. She needed to get her conscience under control.

Now that they'd opened her eyes, she had to connect a few dots of her own.

17

ABIGAIL OLIVAW

SOL, NEAR NEPTUNE

She entered her quarters and the doors silently closed behind her. She'd grown tired of pacing the halls of the ship and apparently, people were complaining to the ship's captain. They were nervous about the president's constant back-and-forth circling. Harold thought it'd be prudent to give everyone a break and suggested that she try to relax in her quarters.

There was only so much relaxing one could do waiting for an alien armada.

"Abigail, I received a message of sorts from the Wheel. One of my copies found it while scanning through the history re-writes they were processing," Harold said.

"If they buried their message in the data feed, then how'd you find it? And why wasn't it sent directly to us?"

"It's an unusual way to reach us for sure, but in case you've forgotten, we've instituted a project-wide comm silence. Except for their data stream bouncing around the Sol relays, the Wheel has no official broadcast channels to reach us. Libby's aware of this and must have worked with one of my copies to embed this information."

She paused her pacing. "How many versions of you are there?"

"Counting the limited copies in the deep space probes, there are nine of us."

She couldn't even imagine what it meant to have copies of oneself, let alone nine of them. "At least if humanity is annihilated, you're good to go."

There was a noticeable pause before Harold replied. "I don't know how to respond."

She chuckled. "You don't have to. I'm sorry. I'm just frazzled, and now I'm caged in this bloody tiny room." She kicked the small table next to her bed and pain shot up her leg. Light-headed from her stupidity, she sat on the edge of the bed and lifted her foot up. Maybe kicking a table attached to the floor wasn't her best move.

"Can you bring up the message, please?" She rubbed her toes. Fortunately, they didn't feel broken.

Harold brought up two excerpts on her retinal comm, one from an early 22nd-century dissertation by a Ph.D. candidate in physics talking about methods of traveling near the speed of light. The other was a news article about a virus outbreak from a rare disease she'd never heard of.

She scanned through the papers looking for a message and shook her head. "I don't understand. These are ancient historical archives. What does this dissertation have to do with the Wheel?"

"Your guess is as good as mine. I'm still figuring that out."

Starting from the top, she read the articles and came across several curious sections. "Harold, this piece has lots of weird typos in the equations. They don't match the wording of the article at all. One minute they're talking about the limitations imposed by Einstein's famous equation where energy equals mass times the speed of light squared, and they use examples of the energy required to hit 0.8 times his proposed limit. That's suspiciously exact to our current upper limit. In the proof their work is peculiar. It jumps from that 0.8 multiplier to a solution that's off by a factor of... 400,000% or so in energy!"

"I noticed that equation's typo, as well, and flagged it for editing. I figured it was a mistake. There aren't any prior versions of this article, nor this researcher, so these mistakes have nothing to compare to."

Her mind reeled. She couldn't figure out why Zachary would use these specific examples. And why would he take the risk of sending her the information? There had to be a reason.

She wiggled her toes. The tingling was gone, and all that remained was redness on a few of them. Her nanites weren't reporting a fracture, but they were going to increase the circulation to help with the swelling.

"Maybe…" She stood up suddenly. "Maybe they're trying to tell us their tests have gone well, like really well. Could they have broken our previous limits somehow and exceeded the first contact probes maximum speed?" She looked at the conclusions. The article said that hitting the energy requirements was not only possible, but feasible with recent advancements.

"That's highly improbable, but logical based upon the information at hand. We know that gate jumps have a completely different set of risks and limitations. So, if we were to apply the same principles of illogical conclusions being logical and apply them to the other article, then the conclusion is just as easy."

She rubbed her foot on the soft rug next to her bed. "Perfect! What does it mean?"

"One of our colonies, likely Epsilon Eridani, encountered a virus that's ravaging their population."

Her heart skipped a beat. "You're kidding, right? Now's the wrong time for your offbeat humor, Harold."

"I'm not joking. The article describes an untraceable and random virus suddenly killing over a hundred members of a small town called E Erasmus in Antarctica. That town never existed, even before the melt, nor had any virus ever hit Antarctica. It's only a news blurb, so it's short on details."

She began pacing around the small room again shaking her head. "How could they possibly know this? Our intel is as recent as theirs, and we haven't been out of the loop that long."

"Well, that's easy if we decoded the first article correctly. Traveling at 8,192 times the speed of light would allow you to travel to Epsilon Eridani in 0.47 days."

She froze in place. "Half a day!"

"No, I said—"

"I heard you. I was rounding up. Do you realize what this means? This…" She rubbed her foot along the edge of the rug attached to the floor. Getting there in half a day, they could do anything at speeds like that. "This changes… we need… time," she stammered.

"The virus or the advance in superluminal travel?" Harold asked.

She swallowed hard. For a moment she'd forgotten about the virus. "Well, both I suppose."

"How?"

"Our plans are built around immense travel times between colonies, Sol, and other star systems. Reducing that time from years and months to days means expansion, resources, people, defense, advanced weaponry, etc. So many variables change." She paused and started rubbing her face with her hand. "As for Epsilon Eridani, we need more information on the virus's origin and how they're managing it. We also need to think through protecting our assets there. There's so much to reflect on, where do we even begin?"

"Well, you'll need to think quickly, Madam President. The Armada has arrived and it's hailing us."

THE HAIL WAS in English and it was straight to the point.

PREPARE FOR OUR SHUTTLE'S ARRIVAL. RETURN A REPRESENTATIVE OF HUMANITY TO FACE A GALACTIC ALLIANCE CRIMINAL TRIBUNAL. ANY ATTEMPTS TO RESIST WILL BE MET WITH FORCE.

She had read it five times in as many minutes. Each time she was as ill-prepared for a response as the first. Unfortunately for her, a shuttle from what they assumed was the alien flagship was now approaching.

The Armada appeared off their starboard side ten minutes ago and then came about and surrounded her Presidential frigate, the Jurat. It had repeatedly hailed them with this message ever since.

Her ship was minuscule next to the behemoth alien vessels, barely as long as one of them was wide. Looking at the alien ships up close, you couldn't discern any minor paneling, windows, or ports of entry. The surface had a dull white grainy finish and appeared to be divided into sixteen segments equally spaced along its length. While these segments surrounded the entire perimeter of the ship, their purpose was unclear.

The comprehensive scans of the ships were coming up empty with no discernible internal structure. The shuttle heading toward them had appeared from a seemingly random part of the alien ship, from a surface that dilated open and then closed. Scans and visuals of that region moments before and after showed nothing.

"Madam President," Commander Quesh began, "their shuttle is heading toward our port side docking bay. We've detected no scans from their ship. It's as if they aren't bothering to check us. That or they're scanning through other means. We've attempted to respond to their hail, but we're being ignored, and they continue to broadcast the same message. What are your orders?"

Orders? What orders? It's not as if they could take evasive

maneuvers and challenge the Armada. "Open the docking bay doors, Commander. Make sure no one is anywhere nearby. I don't want to spook them or give them the impression we're being aggressive."

She stood in the middle of the bridge, staring at the approaching shuttle. It was as sleek and featureless as the other ships in the Armada, with no distinguishable fore or aft end and there were no detectable energy signatures propelling the shuttle. Like a ghost moving through the night, she watched as it slowly entered the awaiting docking bay.

Everyone on the bridge was watching her, waiting for her to say something. She brought up cameras from here and around the ship on her retinal comm. People's faces appeared to be filled with uncertainty and fear. Some were crying or sobbing quietly, apparently resigning her fate.

She straightened her suit, brushing out the wrinkles, and adjusted her brooch. Today she'd chosen a sun, a symbol full of energy and central to supporting life.

"Commander, please escort me to the docking bay. I'll be entering the shuttle as our representative." She glanced around the bridge and paused to meet each and every one of their eyes, trying to pull them out of their funk and willing them to focus. "We've been preparing for this, all of us have. I know it's sooner than we'd hoped, but we knew this day could arrive. Let's stick to the plan as long as possible. I don't know what to expect from this tribunal, but we will fight. If you know me, if you know my family, you know we'll fight until the very end."

She turned toward Commander Quesh and nodded. "We're walking."

With that, she was off, briskly headed to the docking bay with the commander at her side. As they walked through the halls, everyone they passed saluted them. Their eyes had a glazed look to them, like she was heading to her death, as if they were all headed to their death.

She paused outside the docking bay entrance and turned to face the commander. His piercing green eyes stared back at her. She imagined he was fighting back the same feelings of his crew, though she couldn't tell for sure. He'd always had a stoic gaze, ever since she was a child.

She took a deep breath and exhaled, looking downward. Why was there always a wrinkle? She adjusted her suit again.

Commander Quesh came to attention and saluted her.

She saluted him in return and lowered her hand. "Commander Quesh, I need you to shake this crew out of their funk. They're down, but they're not out, and I need them at their best. I don't care how you do it. Do you understand?"

"Yes, Madam President."

She stood there looking at him, frozen in place. She didn't want to walk through the doors and face the unknown. Maybe she'd wake from this awful dream. Awaken somewhere under the stars with her brothers. Somewhere where things were simpler, happier, and filled with music. Like in the vid-sims.

Commander Quesh cleared his throat. "Madam President, you know that I commanded the frigate your father used to travel between the Inner and Outer Rings. He used it countless times to manage his companies and ultimately to help negotiate the Ring Treaty."

She nodded. "I remember, Commander. He was always praising your command authority. He spoke fondly of your ability to navigate the Ceres blockade without losing lives or ships."

Commander Quesh smirked and seemed to suppress a chuckle. "Did he mention that it was he who stood toe to toe with the Admirals of the rings and not me? It was he who held off their battlecruisers and the UN Space Council, fighting to keep the Olivaw legacy alive. He placed humanity on the path to the stars."

She looked downward and adjusted her suit. She knew what he was doing. He was trying to build her confidence.

Commander Quesh continued. "He was a strong well-intentioned leader, Madam President. Much like you, he felt the family burden. Each generation of Olivaw has left the subsequent with a humanity-sized hot potato, and today, well, today you're the one getting burned."

Her face was warm, like it was splotching. She hated when that happened. Unchecked emotions had always been her Achilles' heel. He wasn't exactly a fountain of inspiration, was he? More a garden hose of compliments fed by a well of pessimism. She had to admit, he had a point, though. She'd drawn the multigenerational short straw.

"Thank you, Commander." She turned, adjusted her brooch, and walked into the docking bay.

As she headed toward the shuttle, she stopped outside the entrance. Reaching up to her ear, she touched it and subvocalized a command to talk to Harold. "I don't know if we'll be able to talk inside the ship. Stay with me as long as you can, and visually feed me anything unusual that you detect from my implants or the sensors in the brooch. I activated its short-range jammer a moment ago."

"Yes, Madam President. I registered the activation. Don't forget to inject the nanite defenses. We don't know what they'll do to you onboard."

Reaching to the brooch, she rotated the inner rays of the sun opposite the outer rays, and then firmly pushed the center into her chest. She groaned. The pain from the brooch piercing her skin subsided as millions of nanites entered her bloodstream. She could sense them spreading, seeking her extremities.

On her retinal comm, Harold brought up a set of gauges in the corner of her visual field. They included temperature, gas sensors, defensive scanning, and the number of nanites in her bloodstream. The last, oddly resembled an entertainment sim's health bar, except she knew she didn't want this particular bar to hit zero. There was no spawn point for her to start over from if it did.

She paused at the entrance of the shuttle and looked downward. Always a wrinkle. She straightened her suit, took one final deep breath, and walked up the ramp.

"Good luck, Abigail," Harold said.

The shuttle ramp was longer than the opening it came from. She paused part of the way up and ran her hand over the shuttle's external surface. It reminded her of the hardened sand of a dead riverbed. When she tilted her head, the coarse crystalline surface glistened from the overhead lights of the docking bay.

She made a fist and rapped her knuckles on the surface. There was no response. No echo of a hollow interior and no confident solid thud. There was nothing, it was swallowing the sound or absorbing her knuckles' inertia and bouncing back.

"Please continue into the shuttle, President Olivaw," came a voice from somewhere inside the shuttle.

Along the bottom of her vision were words from Harold. "The surface seems to be a more advanced form of the first contact probe. We released a few nanites from your skin cells onto the shuttles surface. They returned baseline mineralogical readings before being destroyed. The data I'm collecting will continue to be transmitted to our ship as long as possible."

She pulled her hand away from the surface, straightened her suit, and marched into the shuttle. After she'd entered, the ramp rose and sealed her in. When she turned around toward the bow end of the shuttle, she didn't see any discernible seats or terminals to interact with. It was a small featureless space void of even the most primitive seating.

"Hello?" she said out loud. Strange. Her voice didn't echo despite the room being empty. It was absorbed, just like with the hull. "What do I do now?"

"Would you prefer a viewport, President Olivaw?" asked the same voice she'd heard from the ramp. This time it came from all around her.

"Yes, please. If you don't mind."

The entire wall at the bow disappeared. It showed that the shuttle was already moving through space and appeared to be headed toward the furthest alien ship in the formation.

She reached out and rested her hand against the wall.

Seeing the movement but not feeling it was both powerful and nauseating. There wasn't the slightest sensation of motion from the shuttle.

Zachary had mentioned that they'd made similar advances at the Wheel, but the tech was still trickling through Olivaw International. It could be a decade or more before it saw the light of day in practical use.

Her stomach settled after a moment, and she walked toward the wall screen and brushed her hand over the surface. The display was similar to the wall screens they used throughout human civilization, but it felt like the exterior. Leaning closer, she couldn't see the crystals she'd felt. Maybe the surface was reacting to her hand and representing it as coarse.

As if reading her mind, Harold's words appeared along the bottom of her retinal comm. "The material is the same as the exterior of the shuttle. It appears to react to touch. When you removed your hand, the surface became perfectly smooth and destroyed our nanites. We've never gotten responses like this from the first contact probe. Maybe the probe was damaged, or perhaps this material is newer."

She stepped backward, taking in the view on the wall screen. The shuttle had already entered the alien ship and was coming to rest in what looked like a shuttle bay. Not feeling any sensation of movement was throwing off her other senses. She'd need to stay on her toes in this place if she intended on staying alive.

The wall screen shut off and the ramp lowered from the shuttle.

"You may now exit, President Olivaw," the omnipresent voice said.

She turned and slowly walked down the ramp, careful to take in her surroundings. The shuttle bay was purposeful yet simple. It housed shuttles and had no frills or extra room to consider vessels of other sizes or shapes. There also didn't appear to be any means to repair or service them anywhere.

When she reached the bottom of the ramp, she wasn't sure

which way to turn. There were no marked exits. To the left was a bay housing eight shuttles, each exactly like the one she'd exited. As she stepped forward and turned around, she noticed the wall the shuttle had passed through was indistinguishable from any other. Its surface had sealed as fast as it opened.

"This way, President Olivaw," the shuttle voice said, except it was coming from behind her.

She turned around and took a step backward. There in front of her was a humanoid alien figure. She wasn't sure what she expected, but too many years of imagining had her hoping for something much different.

The alien was a head taller than her and had skin the color of Bermuda grass changing seasons. They were green with mottled browns throughout. There was no visible hair on their body, and they had two eyes nearly as wide as a human but taller. She assumed this meant they had binocular vision similar to humans.

She reached out her hand toward the alien. "Greetings! Welcome to Sol."

The alien looked down at her hand and back toward her eyes. Then, without a word they walked away from her. They didn't turn; they merely walked backward, or was it forward? Wait, was she seeing things or did they have two eyes on each side of their head? She glanced down at their legs and studied their movement. Their knees seemed to bend in both directions. Since they had never turned away from her, they were facing both forward and backward at the same time.

She shook her head and started following close behind the alien. She wasn't sure if she should speak, and they seemed to have met her greeting with contempt. Perhaps handshakes were taboo. For now, she'd observe as much as possible before trying that again.

The corridor they were walking through was as featureless as the rest of the ship. Like the shuttle, this was a purpose-built ship with little superfluous decoration or flare.

She shuddered thinking about the purpose-built weapons they'd threatened to use in their message.

Their walk to their destination was as short as the shuttle ride. It couldn't have been any more than twenty meters. The alien paused next to a large recess in the wall and a door slid open before they stepped inside without a word.

The room was massive and even more cavernous than the shuttle bay. It was circular, and placed low around the perimeter wall was what appeared to be a continuous bench. Directly in the center were two square cubes roughly one meter in size; their purpose was unclear.

As the alien walked in, they halted and gestured with one of their arms toward the middle of the room. Apparently, they wanted her to continue alone. Their arms appeared to be as bidirectional as their legs.

She nodded and walked toward the cubes. When she passed the alien, she turned her head slightly to the side. Yep, they did indeed have four eyes. When she got to the center of the chamber, she paused next to one of the cubes, uncertain what to do with it.

She studied the room, taking in the expansive space. Something was missing, but she couldn't put her finger on it until it hit her. There wasn't a sound. The environment within this entire ship was silent. Neither her footsteps nor the opening and closing of the doors was audible. It was both eerie and pleasant. Maybe the aliens had sensitive hearing.

Checking the gauges in the corner of her retinal comm, it showed that nothing had changed since leaving the shuttle. She took note that Harold was still processing and taking in the data from her sensors. At least something was going their way.

She turned toward the giant cubes. Moving her hand over the surface, she noted that it had the same coarse sandpaper feeling of every other object she'd touched. It was like the aliens had one tool in their belt, so they made everything with hammers. She swallowed hard. In the end, with the right hammer, everything could resemble a nail.

While she'd been examining the cubes, she'd missed movement off to her right. Just like on the shuttle, she'd been distracted by the lack of sound. This silence was painful to work in. She had to keep her head moving at all times to take in her surroundings.

Along each wall, in single file lines were aliens of all shapes and sizes entering from two previously invisible doorways. They filed in and surrounded her along the perimeter bench she'd noticed earlier. Once in, the doorways closed, and they all turned to face her in silence.

At first count, she estimated fifty different aliens. In her comm, Harold corrected her. There were sixty-four. One peculiar thing she noticed while looking around the room were the gaps in the group's formation. She'd counted seven gaps at seemingly random positions.

Transfixed by the alien shapes, she hadn't noticed Harold trying to get her attention on her comm. Apparently, an alien was approaching from her rear. Harold had been using her nanites as his eyes and ears since her own were so poor in this muted space.

Rather than wait to be addressed by the approaching alien, she wanted to speak first. She pivoted in place. "Welcome to Sol!" She was smiling, being sure not to show teeth. "Humanity thanks you for the invitation to board."

The alien in front of her had black and neon blue features. They reminded her of the blue neon cuckoo bees she'd seen at a zoo on Earth. Their jet-black skin threw her off but their eyes, all sixteen of them, were even more disconcerting. They only had two visible arms, but could certainly have the others tucked away.

Shaking off the shudder up her spine, she reached out her hand in a traditional Inner Ring handshake gesture, unsure again if it'd be reciprocated. This time, the alien reached forward and returned the gesture. The moment their hands touched her nanite sensor alerted her in the corner of her retinal comm and dropped dramatically.

Harold messaged her. "The alien is attempting to inject

something into your bloodstream. We were able to defend ourselves, but with a significant loss of nanites."

She leaned toward the alien and looked straight into their face, clenching her fists, and then relaxing them. "I'd prefer if you didn't try to kill me on our first encounter. Your death wouldn't be ideal by any stretch of the imagination."

The alien tilted their head and their antenna swirled around in the air above them. She couldn't tell what this meant, but they didn't respond vocally. A moment later they turned, walked toward the other cube, and then faced the opposite side of the room. That confirmed her theory. They had more arms tucked into their torso that were now visible from their backside, but those arms were much smaller.

"Members of the Galactic Alliance and President Olivaw, please take your seats." It was the familiar alien voice that escorted her from the shuttle.

She watched the actions and mannerisms of the aliens around the room. One at a time, they sat back upon the bench. Each in their own unique way. What came next both surprised and amazed her. The bench responded to each alien's body. It transformed into whatever shaped seating they needed. Some sections transformed into high perches, others low stools, and still others simple chairs. The surface reacted intelligently to each alien's needs.

She walked toward the unoccupied cube in the middle of the room and slid her hand over the sandpaper surface. "Here goes nothing," she muttered, backing up to the cube and making to sit. As her body pushed against the surface, it reacted, gradually forming a comfortable lounge chair shape. The surface transformed itself into a plush, pillow-like, silken material. It was an elegant feat of engineering indeed. This entire ship was similar to their nanites, but at an entirely different scale. A construction process similar to the ones they'd only recently begun, but the human version was far cruder.

"Thank you all for convening today for this criminal tribunal," began the alien escort. Everyone in the room had turned toward the speaker. Their words weren't synced with their mouth, but they were somehow being translated for Abigail. "As most of you know, I am Supreme Admiral Gwar of the Galactic Alliance Judiciary. We're here today for humanity to bear witness to, and as defendants for crimes against the Galactic Alliance. The charges being entered today, this the 4,096th year of the Alliance, is knowledgeable theft of Faster Than Light technologies. This is a most serious crime in the eyes of the Galactic Alliance."

She subvocalized to Harold, "Well, frak. This didn't start out as I'd hoped. Are you still transmitting?"

His response appeared on her comm. "Affirmative, Madam President. They seem to be allowing our signals through. Our people are surely executing our planned contingencies. Your best course of action is to stay on plan. We knew this could happen."

"Prosecutor Drak and President Olivaw, please rise," Admiral Gwar said.

The black and neon blue alien to her right rose from his seat. All eyes turned toward Abigail. She stood at attention, her back straight and her suit crisp and perfectly placed.

"How say you, Prosecutor Drak?" Admiral Gwar asked.

Prosecutor Drak bowed toward the admiral and spoke. "Our case is strong, Admiral. We have proof beyond a doubt that humanity is guilty as charged."

The aliens were unexpectedly audible and weren't being translated. A cacophony of chaotic noises erupted around her that sounded like anger, but she honestly couldn't tell.

"Order!" boomed the immense voice of the admiral.

The room entered the perfect silence that was the norm moments before.

"I will not have outbursts in my court." The admiral glanced around the room and then returned their attention to Abigail. "Now, President Olivaw, how say you?"

She gazed across the sea of aliens and then back at the admiral before she mimed the prosecutor's bow. "I'm unfamiliar with the protocol here, so please bear with me.

Humanity is both surprised and appalled at the charges being brought forth today, Admiral. This is our first contact with an alien species and we're utterly in the dark. We have no idea what proof the prosecution is letting on about. On behalf of humanity, we plead not guilty to the charges."

The aliens moved as if to emit another outburst, but the admiral beat them to it and stood up. This sign of motion was apparently unexpected and caused the room to recoil back into their seats, silently awaiting the admiral's response. The wait wasn't long. "Pursuant to judicial accord 1,024, I pronounce humanity guilty as charged. Tribunal proceedings will—"

She stepped forward. "What do you mean guilty? What kind of kangaroo court are you aliens running here? There's been no evidence presented. How could you possibly make a ruling?"

Alien screams erupted throughout the room. She wasn't sure if it was due to her reaction, or with her interrupting the admiral. Either way, they were angry, and like the previous outburst, she wasn't able to understand anything they were screaming.

The sole alien who didn't react was the prosecutor. He stood perfectly still in front of the chair next to her. His sixteen eyes pierced through her with a calm confidence. They knew what humanity had done; she didn't know how, but they knew.

Suddenly, the room went silent and everyone remained standing. She looked away from the prosecutor when she noticed the admiral striding toward her. As they approached, she held her position, making sure not to flinch away.

Admiral Gwar moved to within a dozen centimeters of her face, their mouth making odd grinding noises. They stared at each other for what seemed like an eternity, neither blinked nor backed away until the admiral finally broke the silence. "This is your one and final warning, President Olivaw. I know this tribunal is foreign to your kind, but these proceedings are not a joke. In the judicial system of the

Galactic Alliance, the defendant is guilty until proven innocent. The burden of proof remains squarely on humanity, specifically you, President Olivaw. You need to show your innocence to the members of the tribunal before any charges will be dropped. Is that understood, President?"

Harold broke the silence over her comm. "Madam President, our long-range sensors have reported massive moon size vessels appearing throughout Sol. Thus far over five hundred have been detected and they're still arriving."

She struggled to not respond, trying hard to not let her fear surface and give the aliens the reaction they wanted. Tilting her head slightly, she deliberately cracked her neck and flexed her back and arm muscles, attempting a more aggressive posture. She hoped that showing a physical presence carried some weight here, and judging from the response, she was correct. The admiral seemed surprised but reacted by similarly adjusting themselves in an intimidating way.

"Tell me something, Supreme Admiral Gwar. How do you explain the sudden presence of your armada of moon vessels throughout Sol? To me, this sounds like you've already jumped to sentencing," she said.

The admiral's expression and posture became more relaxed. They almost seemed to smile. "This is standard protocol for a criminal tribunal. If humanity does not prove its innocence, then there is only one sentence that fits the crime. The end of your species."

She was fully aware of the consequences; her family had always known. Admiral Gwar was looking for her reaction to the sentencing, but she gave them none.

The silence and tension in the room was palpable, and the remnants of Zachary's message about Epsilon Eridani were lingering in her mind. She calmly scanned around the room and then back toward the admiral, still centimeters from her face. It was a leap, and she knew it, but it was one she had to make.

She nodded her head. "I understand, Admiral Gwar. I

have only one final question for the tribunal. If the Galactic Alliance and members of this tribunal are just and honorable, which I'm sure they are, then please tell me something. Why have you already begun exterminating our colony at Epsilon Eridani before you've heard our evidence and made a final ruling?"

The explosion of noise and gestures from the members of the tribunal was both deafening and intense. Even the prosecutor to her right had leapt forward and was gesticulating wildly while screaming at the admiral. She wished she could hear what they were saying, but the translators couldn't keep up.

Only the admiral and Abigail hadn't flinched. They stood steadfast within the sea of outrage, staring each other down.

18

ZACHARY OLIVAW

UNKNOWN

Waiting for the pilots to debug the gating algorithm was taking longer than he'd expected. After the first hour of waiting, he launched a short-range probe to retrieve the latest news and intel stored in the closest network relay.

He leaned back in his chair and stared into the darkness of space. The Fountainhead was sitting in the proverbial middle of nowhere, the space between the stars, also known as the interstellar medium. There were a few trace gases and rare planetesimals, but otherwise, it was absolute nothingness.

They'd paused part of the way toward their destination to recalibrate star charts and debug the gate forming algorithm. Their jumps weren't as precise as they'd hoped, and they needed to understand why before they got deeper into their mission. It was likely due to some unknown matter they'd passed en route that'd caused their gate to bend off course, but they had to be sure.

When understanding how gates worked, he normally asked people to first imagine a solid pipe connecting two points where one end was the entrance to the gate and the other the exit. Then he'd ask them to imagine pointing the pipe at a destination and to traverse through it in the dark. The odds were you wouldn't run into an issue because you didn't have anything in your way. Now add random furniture to that same dark room. Except when you pointed the pipe, you didn't know whether you'd hit something or not. Only when you traversed through it and collided with furniture would the pipe bend you to an exit path perpendicular to the object it collided with.

Making small jumps meant less and less course correction was necessary, whereas taking a risk on large jumps meant the possibility for huge corrections being required. Unfortunately, they got cocky and during the last few jumps, they'd attempted aggressive back to back non-calibrated jumps. Well, now they were paying the piper.

An indicator in the corner of the wall screen flashed green. The probe had finally returned with the data dump he'd requested.

"I think I found something you should see," Shauna said a few seconds later. She brought it up on his retinal comm. "One of my copies recorded a curious conversation with Lync. She was stationed at the farms, investigating the outbreak site with Joyce, their DoC. Anyhow, Lync brought up some strange theories about the outbreak that point back to before they'd departed from Sol."

Having copies of embedded all-seeing consciences spread throughout the colonies was difficult to swallow. It was both scary and helpful in times like these. Their artificial intelligences were one piece of information they needed to keep close to their chest, no matter the cost. Even though the A.I.'s and their copies were bound by laws governing their actions, their discovery would undermine people's trust.

"Before departure?" He shook his head. "That doesn't make any sense. Did she have any grounds or basis for the accusations?"

"None that I could tell. Only her gut feeling. We observed another peculiar thing as well. Steve, their DoS, had recently arrested Warren. Steve's one of ours and was hand-picked by your father. As you know already, Abigail wasn't as keen on him, so she purposely left Steve in the dark about Lync, for insurance."

He placed his hands behind his head. "It sounds like Epsilon Eridani is in chaos, in every way imaginable. What does Warren's arrest have to do with Lync's theory?"

"Nothing I can line up, but there are some oddities in his actions." Shauna brought up the colony archive for Warren on his comm. "It seems Warren took quite an interest in Joyce before departing for Epsilon Eridani. He masked his queries as basic background checks on his crew, but he went to suspicious lengths to dig into Joyce and her son. The only reason we know is because he accessed their DNA records. Whenever that happens, it triggers our health and safety security protocols. He also appears to have made similar off base queries for the details of the nanite versions the crew was launching with."

He leaned forward. "Why didn't that red flag or scrub the whole departure? Information like that is firewalled for these exact situations."

"In isolation the events are blips, and even together they're not enough to scrub a launch. People pull records all the time. Plus, Warren has friends in high places. Your father was never happy with his appointment, but Abigail had faith in Lync and your father felt that Steve could handle Warren."

He stood up and walked toward the galley. He needed room to think. "Do we know why the people in the colony are dying yet? It seems like if Warren wanted to target Joyce and her son, he could have. That would let him shake up the colony without mass casualties."

"Funny you should ask that. That's similar to what Joyce said to Lync. She only responded cryptically asking her what made her think the agenda wasn't to wipe out the colony."

"Wipe the colony? That's a leap!"

"Is it?" Shauna brought up a transcript of the conversations Abigail had aboard the alien ship. "The aliens summoned Abigail aboard after she diverted them to Neptune. They held a tribunal and accused humanity of stealing faster than light technology. During the proceedings, she accused the Galactic Alliance of being behind the outbreak. What does she know that we don't?"

He scanned the transcript. It was only a few days old. Scrolling through it, the meat of the verbal exchange was toward the end, surrounded by lots of screaming. "I don't get it. Why would she accuse them of causing the outbreak, and what does it have to do with Warren? I'm not seeing the connection."

"What connection, Z?" Pluto asked.

He froze, startled by the interruption. Pluto was standing next to him in the galley, and he hadn't even noticed her. He must have said something out loud. "What?"

"You were mumbling something about a connection and your sister." Pluto was staring at him, cupping a fresh bulb of coffee.

Faux pas like this were why he worked alone in a lab. He had to be more careful. "Sorry, I was... worked up about some news from the probe. Can you pour me a bulb of that coffee? It smells amazing." He smiled at her and inhaled the aroma.

"Sure thing." Pluto grabbed an empty bulb to fill. "If you need anyone to bounce your problem off, I'm happy to help."

"No... well, maybe." He scratched his head. He had to hand it to her; she was good at solving random puzzles. Maybe he could masquerade it as something else.

Watching her fill the bulb with coffee gave him an idea. "Let's say you're diagnosing two unrelated systems on a ship. Both systems point to a problem. While they're similar, the source of the issue is different enough, and they make no sense correlating to each other. How do you diagnose it?"

"So, they're unrelated?" she asked, handing him the bulb.

"Completely!" He brought the coffee up to his nose and took in the strawberry aromas.

"Are the problematic systems salvageable? Can we repair them?" Pluto took another long sip of coffee.

He walked over to the counter and added a touch of sugar

to his bulb and started swirling it. "In one case maybe, but in the other, no, not likely."

"Well, that's cryptic. But it's not really a hard problem, Z. Whichever problem is worse you solve for that and then check if it resolves the other."

Zachary took a long sip of the sugary coffee and the warmth filled his belly, making his whole body tingle. He smiled. "Thank you. You're absolutely right. Give me a minute. I'll be right back."

He walked out of the galley and headed towards his quarters. After the door closed, he reactivated his comm to Shauna. "We have to optimize for the worst case. Unless I'm mistaken, in this instance that would be Abigail's theory about the aliens and not Lync's theory about Warren going after the DoC. We have to assume the aliens did it, and they're preemptively wiping the colony."

"That seems rash," Shauna began, "but I don't know that we have many options at these distances. Time is of the essence. What do you suggest we do?"

He began pacing in circles around the tiny room. He should have made this ship bigger; he needed more space to think. "I know it may sound harsh, but what if we cut our losses and save the colonists? We could start with people dedicated to our mission and expand from there, when we can. Have the fabricators in Epsilon Eridani been building the new ship designs?"

"Yes. Based upon my estimates, they're nearing completion of a simple transport, but the other ships have a week or more left on their manufacturing. There isn't anything huge like colony ships, Z."

He stopped pacing. "Please don't call me Z."

"Pluto does."

"Well, you're not Pluto. Now focus, please. Let's somehow get a message to Lync that she needs to retreat to the relay point and bring her people, only her most trusted. Once there, and after we bring her up to speed, we can help her coordinate a broader colony retreat. We have to make sure we don't cause hysteria, and we also can't bring a virus back to Sol."

"What about Steve? Your father trusted him."

He shook his head slowly. "Let Lync decide once we've caught her up on everything."

"Everything?"

His voice was firm. "Yes, Shauna. Everything! We need more people out of the dark. If she's headed back to the Wheel, we'll need her help."

"Is there anything, in particular, you'd want her focusing on at the Wheel?" Shauna asked.

He smiled as he took a huge gulp of the coffee. Ideas were already percolating in his head. "As a matter of fact, there is."

19

STEVE ERICSSON
EPSILON ERIDANI, LIPROSUS

He had to hand it to Warren; he was one tough SOB. They'd been attempting to break him for nearly a week and nothing worked. He just sat there in silence except for an occasional request for counsel.

Steve was tired of playing by the book. Today he was improvising. There was more to the colony situation than Warren let on; he just had to get it out of him.

"Good morning, Warren. Did you sleep well?" He set down two coffees on the table between them. He then reached into his pocket and pulled out a vial of blood and set it down, careful to keep it out of Warren's reach.

Warren glanced downward at the table and then back at him, not saying a word. He didn't touch the coffee.

"Come on. I didn't drug it, I swear. Watch." He grabbed each coffee and one at a time drank from each cup. "See, it's fine. Just enjoy the coffee for frak's sake."

Satisfied with his gesture, Warren reached over and took the coffee. He brought it to his mouth and smelled it before finally taking a drink.

They sat there silently staring at each other enjoying the warm beverage in peace. The silence between them was deafening, but he let Warren enjoy the warm soothing liquid. Warren's eyes had circles under them and judging by his hair he hadn't been showering. He was hoping the coffee would comfort him, even a little.

The room was empty. Not a single window or wall display of any kind. No two-way glass partitions, and no visible cameras. Nothing except for two chairs, a table, and a door.

When he finished his cup, he sat back while Warren did the same. Once he was satisfied that he'd drank it all, he raised his hand off the table and two security officers rushed into the room.

Warren sprang from his chair and backed toward the corner, but the guards were on him. They grabbed him by his arms and shoved the back of his head, forcing him into his chair and immobilizing him.

"His arm," Steve said.

The guard on his right forced Warren's arm onto the table. He was struggling, but it was useless, the guard was too strong. With his arm flat, Steve reached into his other pocket and pulled out a syringe gun. He took the vial from the table and inserted it into the top of the gun. It emitted a confident beep and a small light on its top went green.

"So, we're clear. I will not be tasting this first." He pressed the gun to Warrens' arm.

"What... is it?" Warren was shaking, his face had turned as white as the table. "This is against interrogation protocol, Steve. You can't do this. I have rights!"

He leaned in and looked straight into Warren's eyes and pulled the trigger.

"What are you doing?" Warren stared at the syringe while its contents drained into his arm.

Steve set the empty vial and syringe gun on the table, leaned back in his chair, and put his hands behind his head. "I'm doing to you exactly what you did to the other colonists. I'm giving you the virus."

Warren snickered and visibly relaxed. He stared at Steve for a moment and shook his head. "I don't know what you're talking about. We'll be here all day if you're expecting me to admit to something I didn't do."

Steve gestured toward the guards and they retreated to the corners of the room. "What makes you think you'll last that long?"

Chuckling and then looking downward, Warren put his hands flat on the table. When he looked upward, he had a fire in his eyes. An anger they hadn't seen since they'd first arrested him. "Because Steve, rank hath its privileges."

"Privilege enough to be immune to an alien super virus? That seems unlikely."

Warren was sitting there staring back at him, a smug grin on his face. He didn't have a care in the world.

Steve glanced at the time in his retinal comm. "I guess we'll find out soon enough. According to our tests, some colonists showed early signs of the virus five minutes after nearing ground zero. Some had accelerated symptoms, but others showed small hints of what was coming."

He was trying to act as nonchalant as Warren, but the tune in his head wouldn't relent. He started tapping his feet and leaned forward to drum the beat on the table. "Have you ever heard of Marsel Jackson?"

"No, can't say I have. Should I know him? Was he on the colony ship?" Warren asked.

He laughed out loud. "No, nothing like that. I wouldn't think someone as elevated as you would know who he was. He was a controversial pop singer in the twentieth century and a fantastic entertainer. I've had this earworm today and can't stop humming this tune."

Reaching for his cup he lifted it, he'd forgotten it was empty. "Shoot. Hey guard. Can you please get me a refill, cream & sugar?" He turned to Warren and tapped his cup, gesturing to see if he wanted another.

Warren nodded.

"Please grab the Mayor another one." Steve contorted his face. "Oh, eek, actually… guard. Grab him some tissues first. It looks like he has a nosebleed."

Warren reached up and wiped at his nose. When he pulled his hand back, it was covered with blood. He wiped it again in disbelief, and his face turned white. Again, he pulled it away, and it was slick with blood.

"What'd you do to me?" Warren had a look of astonishment on his face.

Leaning forward in his chair, Steve focused intently on Warren. "Whatever do you mean? I told you exactly what I did. I injected you with the virus."

"That's impossible," Warren mumbled. "Absolutely impossible!"

The guard returned and paused a safe distance from Warren, unsure he wanted to get closer. Deciding against it, he tossed the tissues to the Mayor and exited to get the coffee.

"What was in the syringe, Steve?" Warren ripped open the tissue wrappings and started dabbing his nose.

"I don't know why you don't believe me," he said. "We know your blood type, and we've been able to separate the virus from other hosts. But you were lucky. We had a blood matching yours right from a host corpse. So, I withdrew a sample and figured I'd give it a shot."

"You're lying!" Warren screamed; his hands were slick with blood. "I demand you tell me what you injected me with? Give me the antidote immediately or I'll, I'll…"

Steve put his elbows on the table and waited patiently for Warren to finish, but nothing ever came. "You'll what? You have no power here. You've been under arrest for crimes against the colony for days, and unless I'm mistaken, now you're infected. Really, it's only a matter of time for you. So, tell me, Warren. What exactly will you do?"

Warren's pile of blood-soaked tissues was growing. His hands shook uncontrollably as he continued to blot it, and he got more and more frustrated when it wouldn't stop.

Steve stood and pulled his chair back away from the table, distancing himself from Warren. Once he was as far as he could get, he sat back down and leaned back against the wall. He then commenced humming and tapping that same tune again. Warren was close to cracking; he could feel it.

Warren looked down at his arm and jumped up from his

chair stumbling backward. The guard behind him was a blur of motion. He brought Warren's arm up behind his back and smashed his face onto the tabletop with a crack. A second later, the guard released him and stepped away, terror overtook his face.

"Shit! What's that?" The guard was pointing at Warren's arm.

Steve leaned forward for a closer look. "That, my good man, is the first sign of the virus in Warren's bloodstream. The scientists have been calling it Green Syndrome. You know, in honor of Joyce's son. Though, I'm not sure it's an honor to have your name on a killer super virus. Anyhow, you were saying something about having privileges of some sort."

Warren sank into his chair, staring at the marks appearing on his arm as if they were ghosts. "They said this wouldn't happen to me."

He squinted. "Who said what wouldn't happen?"

"My family has immunity. They promised us immunity. Whoever I vouched for… they said they'd protect us," Warren muttered. His eyes darted back and forth around the room.

Had he finally broken him? Steve's pulse was racing. He was close; he could feel it. "Protected from what, Warren? You're not making much sense."

"From this!" Warren yelled and stood from his chair, pointing at his arm. This time the guard kept his distance but moved toward Steve while reaching toward his sidearm.

Warren took a step forward and began walking in circles behind the table.

He was mumbling something inaudibly, but Steve couldn't make it out. Steve stood up and silently gestured to the guard to stand down. He didn't want to spook Warren. "How exactly are you protected from the virus?"

Warren stopped pacing and broke out in a raucous laugh with his head tilted backward. He abruptly stopped and then looked toward Steve with that same fire from earlier. "You're so out of your league. How'd you ever rise through the candidate pool to be the Director of Security? Oh yeah, that's right. Abigail's father appointed you. You know she's the reason we're in this mess, right? Well, her family is, but same difference."

"I fail to see what President Olivaw has to do with this virus."

"That's because you don't have the full picture. It's not about the virus you fool; it's about the drives. The drives, that's it! Get me a cryo-pod... I need a cryo-pod." Warren stepped toward Steve.

The guard intervened and raised one hand toward Warren and his sidearm with the other.

Warren stared at the weapon and then toward Steve. "I'll make you a deal. I'll tell you everything I know, and you get me a cryo-pod. Force me into stasis immediately. Deal?"

Steve struggled to fight back a smile. He looked at the guard and gestured for him to relinquish his firearm. The guard was hesitant at first but then handed it to him. "That'll be all. Please wait for me outside."

The guard walked toward the door, never taking his eyes off Warren. "Be careful, sir." The guard closed and secured the door behind him.

Warren stepped forward. "Aren't you going to ask him to get a pod ready?"

He raised the weapon and Warren stepped backward. "Don't move another centimeter. You're going to turn around and go sit on the far side of the table. Now!"

Warren walked around to the other side of the table with his hands up and sat in his chair.

Happy that he was under control, Steve returned to his seat against the wall and sat down. He was careful to keep the sidearm at the ready. A quick check of his retinal comm confirmed the interrogation recordings were still going. They couldn't afford a hiccup right now. Everything was in order, so he gestured toward Warren. "I'll take care of the pod when you take care of your side of the deal, Mayor."

Warren's eyes darted left and right. "Where to begin," he mumbled.

"How about the beginning?"

"Yeah, I suppose. It'll need to be abbreviated, though. I don't have much time—" Warren began.

As if on cue, the second guard tapped on the door and opened it. He had two fresh coffees in his hand. He set one of them on the table in front of Warren and handed the other to Steve. Like the first guard, he was careful to keep his eyes on Warren at all times.

"Thank you, officer. Please wait outside. Don't let anyone interrupt us for any reason. Understood?" Steve asked.

"Yes, Director!" he saluted and disappeared.

"You were saying?" Steve took a sip of the coffee. Just the right amount of cream and sugar.

"This all began about thirty years ago when a group of individuals calling themselves GAF approached my father. They had a proposal for him, to bring down the Olivaw family. They were extremely secretive and security conscious and before they'd talk to us, they asked us to meet them out near Pluto. You know, to discuss their proposal and terms. My father had been itching to knock the Olivaws out of power for decades. They'd undermined him numerous times, and he'd do anything to see them fall.

"Fast forward to the meeting. There we were, sitting in our family cruiser out in the middle of nowhere near Pluto, and suddenly we're surrounded by some seriously freaky looking vessels. They were small, sleek, and mean looking, like nothing we'd ever seen before. A small shuttle craft approached and asked to dock."

Warren reached toward the coffee for a drink, his hands were trembling. He drank most of it down but spilled some on his shirt and pants. He didn't seem to notice or care. "When we saw them, we thought we were dead." He leaned forward and glanced around the empty room. "They weren't exactly human, you see. Well, they were humanoid. They had two legs, two arms, a torso, and a head, but beyond that, the similarities ended."

"What'd they look like?" He was starting to realize this might be a dead end. Maybe Warren had really cracked.

"They were jet-black with markings of the most amazing blue you'd ever seen. And eyes, they had so many eyes. It was right out of a sci-fi horror sim. About half a dozen of them boarded the ship, and without a second of small talk launched right into their story. They claimed the Olivaw family had stolen some technology, but they needed evidence. They'd been unable to get proof themselves or with the help of their own moles."

Steve switched the pistol to his other hand, checking that the guard had fully charged it. "Their own moles? Within the UN or CoPE?"

Warren became unusually animated. "They wouldn't tell us, but we got the feeling we weren't the first people they'd talked to. They offered us immunity from future retribution by the Galactic Alliance if we helped them build their case."

"The Galactic Alliance? Who's in this Alliance?"

"That's what they called themselves. They claimed to be a United Nations of sorts spread across our galaxy. Again, they were light on particulars."

"So, what exactly did they bring to the table, Warren? This sounds like a high-tech costume party gone wrong."

"What they brought to the table were pictures of a probe they claimed to have seen. I remembered the design. It was a forward observation probe, like the ones we used to do reconnaissance at the colony sites in advance of our arrival. Except this one, it had an unusual drive on it. One they claim was stolen. To make it even stranger, they claim to have seen the probe fifty-eight light years away in Chi Eridani. They weren't able to capture the probe then, but the trail it had left guided them indirectly toward Sol.

"We were shocked to say the least, but as I said, my father was hungry to overthrow the power grip the Olivaws had on CoPE. He wasn't concerned about the particulars if the GA could help him come to power. He agreed to their terms, accepted immunity, and they exchanged the information they had with us.

"Fast forward to the colony leadership selection. My father and I were working on getting me appointed as the Mayor of Epsilon Eridani when he passed. The news was devastating, especially after I'd received the appointment to the Mayor position. But it propelled me even further into CoPE, as my enemies saw it as a way to rid Sol of the North dynasty. The aliens required me to reassert my dedication, and as you'd expect, I did. I promised my father on the day I was appointed that I'd take them down. All of the damned Olivaws."

Steve waved his free hand in the air. "Ok, so you're in bed with this Galactic Alliance. Now what? Couldn't you send them the colony ship plans? Bing, bang, boom, done."

"No, trust me I tried." Warren's head was now in his hands. "The plans were normal. The drive attached to the Epsilon Eridani colony ship was a regular subluminal drive. There was nothing special about it. They were angry after that and pressured me for other information. They wanted DNA for some colonists, details on our nanites, and plans for the colony's supply lines."

"DNA data? That seems suspect." Steve leaned forward. This was an awful lot of detail for a quack. "What does it have to do with this special drive that they claimed we stole?"

"They weren't forthright about the DNA other than to say it was my insurance policy." Warren went stone cold serious. "This was their way of protecting me from humanity's ultimate fate. I never did find out what they wanted with the supply line plans. I assumed they thought we'd use the drive there."

"What was so special about this drive that they'd go to such lengths to prove we stole it? They could certainly snatch a probe. Why'd they need the drive?" he asked

"It was a superluminal drive. It allowed a starship to travel faster than light speed. The GA had to prove we'd stolen the drive. They had to catch us with it. Apparently, there wasn't enough in the photos or scans of the probe that incriminated humanity. Certainly not beyond a doubt anyhow."

Steve twisted his face. "But I thought you never found proof they used the drive on the colony ship?"

"I didn't... well not directly." Warren took a sip of coffee but it was empty. His hands were much steadier than earlier. He put his cup down and smiled mischievously. "Not until the President's isolation message arrived."

Steve shook his head. This wasn't connecting. "What does the isolation message have to do with this stolen superluminal drive?"

A grin formed on Warren's face. "Someone tried to cover up the date they sent the message. They botched the job and missed some encrypted headers but the tools the aliens had sent me found them. In all the chaos I figured people wouldn't notice a little date doctoring, so I changed them back to what they should have been before sharing them. Anyhow, the original message was sent thirty-nine days before."

Steve leaned forward in his chair, resting his hands on his knees. "That's... impossible."

"Is it? It is for our normal drives, but not for an alien superluminal drive." The egotistical smug expression on Warren's face had returned. "I had her. I had all of them. That evening, before our supply meeting, I took the information from the message and sent it on to my contacts."

"What contacts? Who else are you working with?"

Warren smirked. "Do you think they're foolish enough to send us out here without handlers? You actually are an idiot if you didn't figure that out. They've been watching us since we arrived. Hanging out of sight near the asteroid belts and occasionally venturing closer when they needed to learn something."

"So, what did your alien handlers say after you sent them the details of the message?"

Warren shook his head, his face again losing emotion. "Nothing."

"Nothing? That doesn't make any sense."

Warren was quiet for a moment. He kept shaking his head. "I haven't heard from them since. I assumed they'd reach out when they needed more—"

"You're the idiot," Steve chuckled. "How have you not put two and two together? They responded!"

Confusion spread across Warren's face. "What do you mean?"

Steve stood up, the sidearm held tightly in his right hand. "The virus, Warren. They released the virus the next morning. The same virus you helped them deploy. That was their response. They don't need us anymore; they don't need you anymore."

Warren went slack jawed and shook his head. "They wouldn't. We had an agreement. My family has immunity!"

Steve moved the sidearm to his left hand and clenched his other fist. "What about everyone else, Warren? What about every other man, woman, and child you sold out? Did you bother asking what would happen to them or were you only worried about the Olivaws?"

Warren's eyes were wide, and he started mumbling again. "We... we... they were after the Olivaws. They made that clear."

"Then what did they mean when they said they were protecting you from 'humanity's ultimate fate'? Did it not occur to you what that meant?"

Warren opened his mouth as if to talk and then closed it. No words came out.

Steve motioned toward the door and Warren stood to stop him. "Where are you going? I need that cryo-pod."

"There will be no pod," Steve said.

"What do you mean?" Warren yelled. His hands were shaking. "I had your word. I give you the details and you'd get me a cryo-pod. I honored my side of the bargain."

Steve broke out laughing, almost uncontrollably. He

subvocalized a command to his retinal comm and the speakers in the room started playing a song. Warren made a screwed-up face as he tilted his head to listen. It was the song that Steve had been humming earlier.

"The word is out. You're doin' wrong. Gonna lock you up. Before too long..."

Steve was mouthing the lyrics but stopped. "You're not dying Warren. You never were. If you weren't such an egotistical maniac, you'd have noticed that your symptoms cleared up a few minutes ago. You were so into your own braggadocious story that you never noticed the change."

Warren looked at his arms; the markings had faded, and his nose had stopped bleeding. "H... how?"

"Nanites you idiot. Specifically programmed, well-controlled nanites. Something any decent Director of Security knows how to use when necessary." Steve strode out of the room and slammed the door behind him.

IN THE SECURITY office at the beanstalk, under the comforting blue glow of his security shield, Steve prepared the payload. He brought up the contents of the data droplet. Everything was there. The recordings and transcript of Warren's interview, along with the latest research on the virus from the Oak.

He also included the data they'd collected from Warren's blood sample, and in a separate medical vial he added a few drops of his actual blood. He held the small container in his hand. It looked innocuous enough, yet it could hold the key to saving the colony. Whatever gave Warren the confidence that he wasn't susceptible to this virus had to be in his blood.

He inserted the medical sphere and memory droplet into a small elevator compartment and pressed the button to continue the launch sequence. They were heading into orbit on the next ferry where a robot would load them into a probe. It was one of three probes that Abigail had concealed in the colony ship's original design. She never told him why the probes required so much secrecy, but after today's session with Warren, he knew.

The elevator rose skyward along the delicately thin cables. He hoped he was on the right side of this fight. No matter what side he was on, though, the colony was between an alien rock and a hard place. And right about now, they could use all the help they could get.

20

JOYCE GREEN
EPSILON ERIDANI, LIPROSUS

Her feet were like pillars, immobile and unresponsive. Her hands were numb, and she couldn't feel her face for the tears flowing down her cheeks. She was fortunate they'd insisted on performing the second autopsy without her. There was no way she'd have made it past opening the body bag. Watching her team exhume her son's body was the hardest thing she'd ever witnessed.

His face was so peaceful, he could even be asleep. She wiped her eyes and looked at him again. She just wanted to walk up and wake him, give him a huge bear hug. The kind like he used to give her when he was little. When she'd come home from work or take him for ice cream. She'd do anything for one last change to hug him.

She had to hand it to her team; they were performing this autopsy by the book. Watching their precise movements, she could tell they were purposely not making eye contact with her. They didn't want to miss something important, witness her pain, or cause her to cascade deeper into another spiral of sorrow.

She couldn't blame them. She knew she shouldn't be watching, but she had to see it. After hearing Lync's theories, she wanted to know if they were true.

There it was. She could feel it again, the rage rising within. If they found anything, anything at all... she needed to clear her head.

She touched the intercom control. "If you find something, message me. I'm stepping out for a moment."

"Yes, Director," a doctor said. They didn't make eye contact with her.

She walked out of the observation room into the open fresh air of the hall. The air out here was cool on her face. She hadn't realized how warm it was in there. That autopsy could take them a while. They hadn't even gotten to the low-level nano-probes scans yet.

There wasn't anywhere to sit in the hall, so she headed toward the lift tubes. A walk would really help remove the numbness in her legs.

As she approached the lift tube, she did a double take seeing Director Ericsson rising out of the exit. She hadn't expected to run into him today. They'd always been cordial toward each other, but the bond of friendship had never blossomed.

"Good morning, Director Green." Steve glanced around the empty hall and then back toward her. "I hope you're well."

She wasn't sure if that was a question or comment, but she felt obligated to reply. "I'm as well as can be expected while people down the hall are prodding at my dead son's body."

Steve looked down at the floor.

She'd thrown him off guard.

"I'm sorry, Joyce. I... don't know what to say."

"It's alright. You wouldn't have known. So, what brings you to the Colonization Ring, Steve?"

He turned to look up and down the halls again. "Is there somewhere we can talk? Somewhere... private."

"We can chat here. I don't expect anyone to meander by. They're afraid of breaking me."

"I'd prefer privacy all the same if you don't mind."

Her rage was rising again, and she was struggling to keep it down. She glared at him and pivoted without a word. "There's a private space off the nearby surgical observation suite that should be private enough."

Entering the room, she placed her hand on the security panel and Steve followed suit. The familiar voice spoke, and a blue glow framed the ceiling.

She turned to stare at him, her arms crossed. She didn't need to say anything. The frustration in her body language should be clear enough to the buffoon.

Steve forced a smile and broke the silence. "I'm sorry, Joyce. I promise this will make more sense in a moment. I know we've never had a good rapport, but I've always respected you and your people."

"Then tell me something, Director Ericsson. Was it out of respect that you declared martial law without first consulting me or the Mayor? Was it out of respect that you arrested the Mayor without even notifying my people?" Her pulse was pounding in her ears. He hadn't reacted to her comments. The bastard had been expecting her to say that.

"I was dealing with security matters. Yes, there are things I could have done better, but I followed my gut. I'm sure you can respect that."

"You arrested him nearly a week ago. Surely you've had time in the past week to drop me a comm."

"I'm sorry I've kept you out of the loop so long. By the looks of it, you've had your hands as full as we have." Steve gestured to the display in the corner showing the autopsy.

She glanced over at the screen. She hadn't even noticed it was showing anything when they entered. Seeing her son lying exposed on the table pulled at her. She had to suppress her emotions before she started crying again. Her grieving had taken its toll and stressed her responsibilities this past week. She couldn't have imagined trying to deal with even more during that time. Turning back toward Steve she nodded. "Fair enough. To what do I owe today's visit? Are you here to arrest me?"

"Touché." Steve smiled. "No, not today. I'm hopefully here to fill in some blanks for you and perhaps give you some missing pieces to our… puzzle."

"Our puzzle?"

Steve's face went serious. "It seems our beloved Mayor has been up to no good. Our paths have now converged, and we appear to be seeking the same information. How to save our colony."

There it was, the anger surfacing again. Her fingers were going numb from clenching her fists too tight. She had to calm down and keep her cool. "Please go on."

Steve must have sensed her frustration because he took a small step backwards. "Stark Olivaw asked me to keep an eye on Warren before we departed Sol. He and Abigail never trusted any of the Norths, and they didn't want him as the colony's Mayor, but powers outside their control placed him in that position. We've never found anything actionable on him, but after Abigail's message arrived, he became oddly secretive and delayed sharing it with the colony. As we all know, that backfired."

"Why do I get the feeling that was your doing?"

"I can neither confirm nor deny that." Steve smirked. "Regardless of how the news broke, it needed to be out there. Especially with the outbreak. People needed all the information, but instead of inspiring and motivating the colonists, Warren chose to be political. We need to work through these challenges together, not throw a wall up dividing the colony."

She chuckled. "I'm not buying your altruistic intentions for one second. Everyone knows you wanted to be mayor, and it pissed you off that you got passed over. Well, you got what you wanted. Warren's out of the way now."

"It's true, I wanted to be mayor. I've never kept that disappointment a secret. But you have to admit no one wanted Warren as mayor, either."

She nodded. He was right.

"While Warren was out politicking after the President's message, he was meeting the colony's elite and privileged behind closed doors. I didn't know exactly what he was up to, so I forced his hand and—"

"You didn't! You've got to be kidding me. You arrested him without proof!" She abruptly stepped forward.

Steve leaned back, raised his hands in front of him, and took another step away from her. "He cracked, Joyce! He admitted it."

"Admitted what?" she shouted.

"He admitted to the virus, the aliens, the whole shebang!"

She shook her head. "Wait, he admitted to what? Are you feeling okay?"

"I'm sorry, I'm messing this up. Here, watch this." Steve subvocalized a command and gestured to the wall screen showing the autopsy. It went blank and Steve's interrogation of Warren began playing, every excruciating second of it.

She stared in shock as Steve injected Warren, watched him freak out, and then fold like a cheap bio-suit. The warmth was rising in her hands. The white-hot heat of anger and revenge was filling her again. Steve was right. Warren admitted to everything. To killing all those people, to killing... her son. All in exchange for what, revenge for his father? He sold out humanity to fulfill an ancient family vendetta.

Steve cut the playback, and the autopsy returned to the forefront. The room went silent and they both just sat there staring for a moment.

Her retinal comm suddenly beeped, signaling for her attention and pulling her out of her spiral. She gestured and brought it up on the wall display. "What is it?"

"We've found something odd, Director. It's there on the feed. We found microscopic signs in the blood vessels that something had been attacking the blood-brain barrier throughout the patient's extremities, and near the brain itself. We had similar findings on other patients but none as pronounced as those of your son." He paused for a second. He hadn't meant to mention her son. "We'd thought it was due to some unknown native pathogen, but these markings seem to indicate... it makes no sense."

"What does it indicate?" She was curious if this would clarify what she'd seen on Steve's recording.

"That our nanites made the damage," Steve interrupted.

She looked at Steve. Warren's interrogation was making a lot more sense now. The pieces were coming together in her mind.

"Why, yes, Director Ericsson. That's exactly what it indicates. How'd you know?" the doctor asked.

Steve ignored the question and pushed on. "Can you extract the nanites for analysis?"

"We tried, but that's the other weird part. All the nanites we've been able to extract from any of the infected patients are perfectly normal. In hindsight almost too normal. Checking their bio versions, we can see that they were reset back to the day before the farm incident. What's also odd is that they appeared to have reset themselves."

"I don't understand. Why would that be odd?" Steve asked.

"Because we'd already confirmed their nanites updated that morning at the farm." The doctor brought up a list of colonists, dates, and their nanite firmware versions with percent upgraded on the screen. "A small upgrade was released to the network at the farm and was scheduled for broader colony release until we halted it after the outbreak. Upgrades are a common occurrence. Our biological machine learning systems are constantly tweaking the nanites to help our bodies adjust to the alien fauna and the environment of Liprosus. Anyhow, each successful upgrade is centrally managed, which means we're able to tell who is and isn't up-to-date."

"Why hadn't we identified this issue before?" Joyce asked.

"It's normal for people to wander out of signal range, which as you'd expect delays their upgrades. It's also not uncommon to inject older versions of nanites, either. Once injected into the host, the nanites form a mesh network and update each other. We hadn't thought to cross-check the nanite versions."

Steve nodded. "So, we don't have any evidence that it was the nanites other than odd bio versions? No proverbial smoking gun to point to. Just the internal blood vessel damage?" Steve turned toward her.

She squinted and rubbed her eyes. "I'm still not understanding something. How could the nanites cause the damage we're seeing, and specifically how could that lead to the outbreak?"

"Well, now that we suspect the nanites, it's actually quite easy." The doctor brought up a camera view from inside the patient's body showing nanites near what appeared to be a blood vessel. "The nanites could use tiny ultrasonic discharges to exert a force on the blood vessels. This would allow native pathogens already in the host's blood to pass the blood-brain barrier and attack the nervous system. Without those discharges, the barrier was happily protecting the host, but with the barrier open, they were free to infection by the pathogen."

She nodded her head slowly, her eyes surveying the picture on the screen. "If I'm following you, and I think I am, that explains the markings along the patient's dermatome lines since those follow the nerves. What I still don't get, though, is why the defenses we'd built into the software didn't prevent this from happening? We have host protocols in place to prevent these types of incidences."

Steve's eyes lit up, and he gently touched her arm. "Doctor, what if… I had some nanites? Some different nanites that might protect against this attack. Could we analyze them safely outside the host's body and compare them to these?"

She opened her mouth and paused.

"From Warren," Steve mouthed. He reached into his pocket and pulled out the syringe gun from the interrogation video. It was in some type of electrostatic pouch.

She leaned forward for a closer look. That wasn't a normal syringe gun. It appeared to have two needles, both an injection and an extraction needle. There, beneath the first empty vial, was another vial of blood. One that she assumed held Warren's blood and a sample of nanites from his body.

21

LYNC MICHAELS

EPSILON ERIDANI, LIPROSUS

Her squads couldn't handle indefinitely rotating between the beanstalk and farms. While things were operating smoothly, they'd had no real disruptions since their staged attack on the beanstalk. In the week following the lockdown, Crayo flawlessly executed their plan to hijack the comm relay. All communications into and out of the colony were now under their control.

She finished the beanstalk sentry checks and was heading to the farms when her comm chimed. Subvocalizing to open it, the headers showed it was a recording originating at "Saturn, Titan Station Gardens". She chuckled. Crayo must be playing a trick on her.

Cracking open the raw comm payload, the message was heavily encrypted with CoPE protocols. Even if her team had intercepted it, they wouldn't be able to view it. The comm was encoded for her and could only be viewable after an identity check.

She issued the command to decrypt the comm using her exo-suit to verify her identity. A small prick in the nape of her neck to sample her blood, and a moment later, the message played without warning.

Zachary Olivaw's face appeared. He was sitting in what looked like the command seat aboard an odd-looking ship. It was a design she'd never seen before. He smiled toward the camera. "Hey, Lync. I don't have a lot of time, so I'll keep this short. If I know you, you're already aware of Mayor Warren's arrest and are working on contingencies for the farm outbreak."

"Well, he's one for two," she muttered. She hadn't heard about Warren's situation, but that would explain why he hadn't reached out to her.

"There's a much bigger picture at play there and we haven't brought you up to speed yet. For that, I'm sorry." Zachary glanced off screen. He seemed to collect his thoughts. "I know this is going to sound like an off the wall and completely random request... because it is. I need you to gather a few dozen of your most trusted and valuable people and head out to the coordinates I've sent in this comm. Do it without causing commotion or attention. I'm dead serious, Lync. No matter what, you cannot be followed. If you can manage it, then I suggest you disappear without a trace. Once you're there, we'll tell you everything. I promise. No more secrets."

The video continued with Zachary staring into the camera. He closed his eyes for a moment and then slowly raised his hand to cross his chest and then placed it face down. The Ulixi sign of sincerity, honesty, and openness to give help.

With that the recording cut. Her comm showed an overlay of the Epsilon Eridani star system with a flashing dot far out in its Oort Cloud. Judging from its location, it was outside the standard supply shuttle route from Sol. It was deep in uncharted space.

Staring at the blinking dot, a million things flashed through her mind. How'd he know about the mayor when he was light years away? And more importantly, how did she not know? What was out at that point? What bigger picture? She didn't know where to begin and none of it made any sense. Her heart was pounding in her chest, and she was sweating. The exo-suits warning system started alerting her and kicked the cooling systems into high gear.

She shook her head and stopped pacing. Closing her eyes, she started breathing in through her nose and out through her mouth. Beginning at ten, she counted down while focusing on controlling her breathing and clearing her mind. When she'd hit zero, her heart rate was well within her usual limits.

Early in their lives, the Ulixi depended on learning to control their breathing. Oxygen was precious in space, and the sooner they learned to center themselves the better. It also helped her to hit reset and unfurl all the thoughts that piled up in her mind.

Reaching up to her ear, she opened a secure comm to Crayo.

"What's up, mate? Something amiss?" Crayo asked.

She smiled hearing his familiar voice. "Ya could say that. I just got rogued and I've got another ask. A big one this time."

"Bigger than the last? I can't imagine something much bigger than treason," Crayo joked. "This part of one of your plans?"

"No, not even close. This rogue's out of nowhere and I'm slinging it blind."

"I trust your aim. Whatcha need?"

Her mind was racing. She needed to start with the biggest thing first and then work backward. "A ship. One big enough for two dozen to survive a week, two worst case. It can't draw attention or be missed while we're taking a trip off the grid. Use our backdoors on the beanstalk to search around for anything we can use topside."

"An off-grid ship that'll hold two dozen. Tall order that is… not a lot sitting around in the docks these days. I'll see what I can do. Don't suppose I can ask where you're going?" Crayo's eyes were scrutinizing her response.

"Where we're going, Crayo. And no, you can't ask." She tried to force a smile to mask her uncertainty. There was a pause where neither said anything. He was thinking hard.

Crayo nodded confidently. "Sim sim!"

"Sim sim!" She smiled and cut the comm.

"Next step," she muttered. There was no way they'd pull

this off alone. She needed to call in a chit. A big one. Reaching to her ear again, she subvocalized a command. "Locate Director Green".

"Director Green is in medical research building four in the Office of Colonization ring," her computer said.

She issued the commands to route her exo-suit there automatically. The suit began bounding through the beanstalk buildings, and once clear, it jumped and connected to the nearby maglev heading toward the Oak.

She had to talk to Joyce about the mayor and feel out if she could spare anyone for the mission. They hadn't exactly left the last meeting on the best terms, but she knew she had to look past that. They needed help from more than security if this thing was going to go off without a hitch.

After a few minutes of smooth travel, the suit detached from the maglev track and landed in front of Oak building four. Walking into the building, the suit made toward the lift tube and upon entering headed upward. She bounded through the halls, passing dozens of people gawking and pointing. Apparently, no one in an exo-suit had ever wandered into an Oak building before.

As she rose out of the lift, Director Green was waiting with her hands on her hips and a stern look on her face. A team of people surrounded her on all sides.

"What the hell are you doing, Major?" Joyce shouted. "Barreling into one of my buildings in your exo-suit practically knocking over everyone in your path. I should bring you up on charges to cool your testosterone filled jets."

Lync stopped dead in her tracks. "Shit," she muttered to herself. She'd completely disregarded civilian protocol. "You're right, Director. I'm sorry. Had it not been of the utmost importance, I wouldn't have broken protocol. Is there any chance you have a moment to talk?"

Joyce looked to her left and right and then back at Lync. "I'm kinda in the middle of something."

"It's important. If I can just—"

"If you want some of my time, then whatever you need to

say can be said in front of my people. We know how to follow protocol in the Oak," Joyce snipped.

Looking at the surrounding people she recognized Dr. South and Dr. Sutter from the farms earlier in the week. The other two she'd never met. She trusted Joyce's instincts and didn't have time to question her. "Are you aware that security has detained Mayor North?"

Joyce nodded. "I am. It happened shortly after my farm visit. I've been a bit preoccupied since then though."

Everyone seemed to be a step ahead of her. She was trying to find common ground here. "Has my advice helped at all?" There it was: a reaction.

Joyce looked down at her hands. She seemed to be thinking about something or someone. Looking back up, her gaze seemed less intense and angry. "Yes, Major. It's helped us immensely. We exhumed my son's body and your theory turned out to be correct. It held some missing pieces to our puzzle. I'm sure you didn't come all this way to gloat. What can I help you with?"

"The tables have turned and I'm now in need of your help." Lync smiled.

"Fair enough. You rubbed my back; how can I rub yours?"

She looked left and right at Joyce's people. She wasn't comfortable blurting it out.

"Major? It's now or never. I don't have time for your games."

She closed her eyes and collected herself. She had to have faith in others, expand her circle of trust. "I need a few of your people. Experts in the pathogen, colony technologies, and equipment. I also need you to help me get a ship off the grid for a while. I can't say where we're going, but I need it done quietly and without strings."

Silence fell between them. Joyce's face went blank and she couldn't read anything. Jeez, she had a poker face.

Joyce rubbed her chin. "Well, that's more than one favor, isn't it? I suppose this is another one of your crazy theories?"

"Well... no..." She stammered. "This one... it's further

along than a theory at this point. Let's just say I've had some *guidance* on this one."

"From someone a little more level-headed I hope?"

She nodded. "I'd say so."

Joyce stared. Her face slack and her eyes intently studying Lync. "I can help you, Major. But only because your last theory was fruitful. Let's hope this one isn't a dead end, shall we?"

"Yes. Let's hope."

Joyce turned to face her team. "Dr. South… Dr. Sutter… the Major here will need two people from each of your teams. Your best, please. Do not undercut her mission. And Dr. Sutter, let's see what we can do to help her disappear. Is that understood?"

"Yes, Director!" they both said.

Joyce turned again to face her. "Will that be all?"

"Yes," she smiled. "And… thank you."

"You're welcome and Godspeed!"

Lync knew nothing about Joyce's god, but if they could help, she'd take it.

22

ABIGAIL OLIVAW
SOL, NEAR NEPTUNE

She was lying in bed aboard the Jurat, staring at the ceiling of her quarters. Sleep had been eluding her for hours. After she'd spent the last several days aboard the alien flagship in judicial discovery sessions, she was finding it increasingly difficult to shut off and decompress at night. Harold suggested that she take a sleeping aid, but she refused to chemically alter her body's natural rhythm. She preferred to listen to it and react accordingly. Unfortunately, the only way to fix what was keeping her awake wasn't easily addressable.

She pulled her pillow over her head. The noises wouldn't stop. The ship was screaming at her. Faint sounds from the environmental controls circulating air. Omnipresent vibrations from the ship's gravitational system. These previously insignificant things used to be the background hum of her life, but after spending so much time aboard the alien ship, those same noises were stalking her, keeping her from precious sleep. She imagined she'd grow used to the noises again but now they were... alien.

The sheet wrapped more and more tightly around her torso as she tossed and turned in bed. She couldn't shut her mind off no matter how hard she tried. Her thoughts randomly wandered back to her first day on the Galactic

Alliance ship. She'd dropped a few bombshells and ruffled a few feathers that day.

Following her extermination accusation, the Galactic Alliance announced they were sending a small judicial force to Epsilon Eridani to observe and gather information. They didn't say what the ramifications would be for either side if it was true, but they made it clear that humanity remained guilty until proven innocent.

It'd take nearly eighty days for the judicial force to complete their voyage. That included traveling to Epsilon Eridani, collecting information, and returning to Sol. That should give her enough time to figure out how to navigate the alien tribunal system and find a loophole. Hopefully it would give Zachary enough time to execute against their broader strategy. Without that, they were done for.

News of the aliens faster than light technology set off a flurry of media throughout Sol. Some claimed the aliens were bluffing whereas others proclaimed it as the beginning of the end, that they'd call her bluff. None of the media outlets believed her accusation. They knew the timelines of the messages didn't add up. They were right; they just didn't have all the details.

During discovery, when the Galactic Alliance tribunal pressed her on how and when she'd received her information from the colony she deflected. She instead turned it back on them and asked why they felt it was necessary to send a judicial force if they doubted her. Neither was willing to directly answer the other's question, which left them in a stalemate. That pattern repeated itself throughout the week. The burden of proof still lay squarely on her shoulders and stalemates weren't helping her build a defense.

Today she was planning another approach, one she hoped would bear fruit. Her people had completed the Olivaw Companies corporate history expunge and rewrite, burying enough new research in their archives to support future timeline claims. More importantly, they had confirmation of the destruction of all remaining stolen drive technology. They could finally address the Galactic Alliance's questions about their research programs.

Most of the subluminal and superluminal research was the confidential intellectual property of her family's companies, and they'd blocked its release behind corporate espionage and theft laws. Now, however, it was becoming increasingly challenging to conceal the information in the face of humanity's imminent annihilation. Her team was working back channels, building the story with the broader CoPE government that humanity might have drive technology that was more advanced than the aliens.

She sat up. Apparently, rest would be eluding her again this evening. Reaching up to her ear, she touched it. "Harold, I can't sleep. Please bring up the Sol news for the day."

"I told you to take some—"

"The news, Harold! The last thing I need or want is a fatherly lecture."

Without another word, the requested feeds showed up on her retinal comm. Scrolling through them, she saw more of the same crap she'd been reading for days. Regurgitated conspiracy theories about the aliens, end of days, and claims to know why the aliens were actually here. Harold had flagged one of them for her to review.

Bringing it up, the feed highlighted that Admiral Nguyễn had somehow been active again, despite being arrested and detained in a military prison on crimes against the President during times of war. For some reason, the warden in charge of the prison had taken his arrest as more of a suggestion. The news item had quotes from the former admiral drawing correlations between the alien's accusations of stolen technology and the timing of the ships destroyed throughout Sol. He also conjectured that commands to destroy the drives were sent to the colonies, as well.

"Have you already dealt with this?" she asked.

"I was waiting until you awoke, Madam President. I've been thinking about it for a great many cycles. For starters, we could try replacing the warden with someone who can better control the prison's general population. Though, to be honest, a better option might be ordering Mr. Nguyễn's termination. It would certainly send a clearer message."

She leaned forward and started stretching. "Termination? That's a bit harsh, isn't it? Besides, terminating him would set off every conspiracy theorist in Sol." She shook her head. "How can murder even be in your programming anyhow?"

"You're aware that the zeroth law overrides all other laws, Madam President. If Mr. Nguyễn is putting humanity at risk of xenocide by spreading rumors and accusations, then we can deal with him without the worry of breaking the first law."

She got out of bed and leaned against the wall, slowly sliding down into a squat position. "You're taking a huge causal leap, aren't you? He's not lying; he's actually accurate considering he doesn't have the details. You know this gap exists so you couldn't possibly apply the zeroth law. Heck, by taking those leaps in logic you could challenge many of my actions under the zeroth law."

Her ear was silent and he didn't reply. That was unusual. Suddenly, all sorts of mental alarms were going off in her head. He loved a good debate on the laws of robotics. Why was he backing down now? "Harold, have you been undermining my actions under the flag of the zeroth law?"

Harold broke his silence. "I have not, Madam President. My programming requires that I communicate my concerns associated with the laws with my family. Your ancestors ensured that you or your brothers will always know when I disagree with your decisions. And as for the Galactic Alliance, your family tied your hands generations ago. Thus far, all of your actions have fit within my interpretation of the laws."

She laid down on the ground, pushed up with her arms, and held a plank position. These stretches were working her muscles in all the right places. "Well, that's reassuring, I suppose." She paused and counted down from thirty, enjoying her muscles screaming under the mounting pressure. When she hit zero, she started talking again. "Getting back to Mr. Nguyễn, let's leak some details of his past. What-ever dirt we have, spill it."

"I'm sorry, Madam President, but we don't have any dirt on him. As best as we can tell, he's lived a reasonably proper life. His only missteps were being on the wrong side of this historical event."

She released plank and laid on the ground, letting her arms rest as she turned his words over in her mind. "Seriously? We have nothing? You're telling me this guy never cut a corner or had a marital indiscretion? No cheating on tests or ignoring creditors?"

"None that I could find, Madam President. As far as I can tell, he's been a model citizen of the Confederation."

That was impossible. Everyone had skeletons in their closet, especially if they reached the top.

Abigail sighed and pushed up on her side. There was one thing she knew for certain. She needed a better workout than this closet of a room could give her. It'd been over a week since she'd had a proper sweat, and now was as good a time as any.

She stood up and reached into her footlocker, digging to find her workout clothes. Once she located them, she quickly changed and headed out of her quarters toward the exercise room. The ship was silent and seemed empty at this hour. Everyone was taking this downtime to get some shuteye, everyone except her.

Walking the corridors of the ship, she couldn't help but notice the contrasting differences between these halls and those on the alien vessel. There were inconsistent color changes, contours, and ever-present maintenance hatches sprinkled throughout the human ship. They were antiquated and highlighted humanity's lack of confidence in their imperfect engineering. In Sol, everyone needed a job, even if it was fixing what wasn't broken. It was challenging for humanity to innovate with the social burdens of their past. All of this was even more evident aboard the Jurat, her military flagship that'd been in service to her family for over a century.

The colony ships though, those had been humanity's chance to start anew. To reimagine their boundaries and vision of what humanity needed to survive, to thrive. Thinking differently and from a new perspective was also how Zachary and his team approached the design of the Wheel. They didn't let preconceived ideas of what people believed was possible prevent them from making the impossible a reality.

Entering the exercise room, she loaded her routine onto the equipment and tapped her ear. "Harold?" she subvocalized.

"Yes, Madam President."

"Please send a military transport skiff to pick up Mr. Nguyễn. I want him transferred here to the Jurat. I want to speak with him in person."

"Are you sure, Abigail? It'll take several days before we can get him here, and he's proven to be quite a challenge to deal with already."

"I'm certain. Besides, worst case he's a nutter and we throw him here in the brig. At least then he's under our control."

She stepped onto the treadmill and began running. Finally, she found something to make her sweat properly.

THE WORKOUT WAS EXACTLY what she'd needed. After finishing, she took a sonic shower and snuck a quick power nap coming off the workout high.

She dreamed of camping with her family and their cub scout pack in North Carolina. They were lying on the ground near their tents after the pack campfire, looking up at the Milky Way. It was a vivid dream and being interrupted by a flying ghost of Harold telling her it was time to wake up had been very disconcerting.

Right now, she was standing in the shuttle bay awaiting the aliens to ferry her to the tribunal ship, a sixth time in as many days. She closed her eyes and started her breathing exercises to clear her mind and control her emotions. It was a technique she'd learned from the Ulixi when she was younger. Back then, she'd spent several years exploring Sol. Something her father had wanted her to do before settling into the family business. During her voyage, she happened upon a secret Ulixi festival. It seemed they didn't fancy outsiders interrupting them. She was pretty sure they were planning to kill her before she'd talked herself out of harm's way, and made some new friends in the process.

A few years back, Harold brought a talented Ulixi upstart at the academy to her attention, Major Lync Michaels. She was the first Ulixi to graduate from the academy and with distinction to boot. They subsequently recruited her for the Epsilon Eridani colonization effort to be their ace in the hole, should they need it later. She hoped Lync was still alive and the virus hadn't taken her.

Her cheeks warmed thinking about Lync and her after graduation party from the academy. They'd turned a few heads goofing around that night. The more she thought about that night, the more she blushed. She had to control her emotions. The last thing she wanted to deal with right now was another cry. She missed her friends and family, and it'd been several years since she'd seen either of her brothers. While her family relationship was complicated, she had fond memories from her youth, and she and her relatives always enjoyed spending time together.

Her brothers were both far from Sol, and like her, they too were on the front lines of this conflict. She wished Commander Quesh hadn't sent Minula on a mission. She wanted, no, she needed someone she could talk to. Someone who wasn't a silicon-based intelligence. Someone she could confide in, who would give her a hug and have a drink with her. Human nature longed for physical contact, and without it, she feared she was reaching a starvation point.

A loud clang echoed as the shuttle bay doors engaged and slowly slid open. The alien shuttle was waiting outside. She turned her back to the doors and wiped at her face. The pink warmth in her cheeks was cooling and hopefully it would clear quickly.

She couldn't go out there like this. Not yet. She closed her eyes and restarted the ritual of clearing her mind. "Breathe in and out," she muttered as she centered herself and relaxed, focusing on the rhythm of her heart and the feelings in her body. Her muscles loosened starting in her fingers, moving slowly up her arms through the wrists, and continuing into the shoulders. They contained the stored frustrations of nights of tossing and turning. It felt amazing when it released and everything fell away. She reluctantly moved on to her neck and did the same procedure with her toes and legs until she finally opened her eyes, refreshed and focused.

By the time she turned around, the alien's shuttle had docked and lowered its ramp. She didn't know how long they'd been waiting but she didn't care much either.

She walked confidently up the ramp and after boarding, she remained quiet. The interactive wall remained empty the entire voyage despite the ship prompting her numerous times to open a viewport; she ignored it. She didn't want them gaining any insight into her emotional state nor thinking she was getting comfortable.

When the shuttle's ramp lowered into the alien ship, she walked down into the shuttle bay. Like on previous visits, she was greeted by Supreme Admiral Gwar.

"Good day, President Olivaw."

"Let's skip the pleasantries, Admiral." She kept her emotions and heart rate in check. "I'm done being given the runaround when we ask about the information in the case against humanity. We're not familiar with Galactic Alliance protocol and demand proper representation."

"You demand it, do you?" The greens and mottled browns on Admiral Gwar's face shifted colors to a consistent green hue throughout.

She wasn't sure what they meant, but there was a clear emotional response to what she'd said. The first day in front of the tribunal, she remembered the admiral had changed green when she angered them. Sorta like this but this time it was deeper and darker. This was probably more likely frustration, but she didn't care, she wasn't about to stand down. It wasn't the time to be timid. She made a single smooth and aggressive motion closing the distance between her and Admiral Gwar. "Yes, Admiral! On behalf of all humanity, we demand proper representation in this tribunal. We expect you'll provide us someone familiar with our rights and the rituals of these proceedings."

Admiral Gwar narrowed their eyes. "I've never understood the temperament nor the entitlement of your people over the millennia." They walked away from her toward the open door, their eyes staring at her.

She wasn't sure what they meant by that, but she intended to find out. She matched the admiral's pace keeping a safe distance behind them rather than confronting them further. They appeared to be taking her to an unfamiliar area of the ship. The previous locations she'd spent time in had long featureless halls with very few doorways to the different tribunal chambers. These halls were much more spacious and the doorways more numerous. They each had their own form-fitting seating cubes outside flanking their entrances. They were like mini waiting rooms serving some unknown clinical purposes.

Admiral Gwar paused in front of a doorway and gestured for her to enter.

She glanced briefly into the room. It was small and contained a single nondescript table with four cube chairs spaced evenly around it. "What are we doing here?"

"You demanded representation, did you not? I've arranged a room for you to make a selection."

Unsure of what to do next, she turned and walked into the room and the door slid closed behind her. Admiral Gwar's actions were unexpected and threw her momentarily into a panic. It also didn't help that this drab room felt a little like walking into a jail cell.

The room was void of all decorations, seams, or distinct characteristics. The only thing of importance was the desk in the center. Walking toward it, she noticed a faint green light in the middle that wasn't visible from the hall. It seemed to shout for the occupant's attention in the room's sea of blandness. She wasn't sure how to engage it, so she tried waving her hand over it like human sensors.

A voice spoke from all around her. "Please specify your preferred interaction interface."

She glanced around. There were no controls to make a selection. "What are my interaction options?" she asked aloud.

"Supported interaction interfaces include visual, touch, audible, water, bio-kinetic, electronic,—" The list went on and on.

Wowza. "Visual, touch, and audible are fine," she interrupted. What would happen if she'd said water? She shook her head. Some other time.

"Confirmed. Activating compound visual, touch, and audible interface for Homo sapiens sapiens and Homo sapiens idaltu," the voice said.

The longest wall of the room came alive with light presenting an interface tailored for her physical characteristics. It was all within her reach and presented pictographs depicting different alien forms. Some of them she recognized from her encounters with the tribunal, but many she'd never seen before.

She activated her retinal comm using its visual controls because she couldn't subvocalize with Harold. "I assume you're taking this all in?" she wrote.

"Affirmative, Madam President, and good morning," Harold said.

This was the first time she'd spoken to Harold since she'd snapped at him. "Sorry about earlier."

"Thank you. Might I suggest you wander around this interface so we can collect as much intel as possible?"

Agreeing with Harold, she gestured on the wall to learn

the controls. It was quite adept at interpreting what she wanted using both gestures and tracking her eye movements. She swiped through the list of pictographs. The system went on for hundreds and hundreds of pages.

Next, she tested the audible interface and told it to return to the first page. It complied flawlessly. She touched the first alien pictograph in the list. The screen displayed an encyclopedia entry of that alien species.

> **Species**: Aadvant
> **Location**: 154.76.310, 23.65.166, 13.15.8
>   (Unknown humanoid coordinate translation)
> **Age**: 256 galactic years since their discovery
> **GA Membership**: No, this species is in an elongated Industrial Age because of numerous wars and planetary collisions that devastated its technological advancement.
> **Contact Made**: No
> **Monitoring**: Passive, revisiting every 32 galactic years
> **History**: Details not known, discovered by GA probe 28761C
> **Description**: Aquatic species that use pressurized jets to propel through liquid substances. This oviparous species migrates to land to lay their eggs, leaving their youth to fend for themselves until returning to the water. It communicates through multiple complex motions of its tentacles and jets, allowing for rapid ideation and collaboration. This...

Below the text, there was a three-dimensional view of an animated Aadvant that she could rotate and zoom into different layers of its anatomy. They've either dissected this species or performed a three-dimensional cellular scan. The Aadvant reminded her of a cross between an octopus and a jellyfish.

Returning to the list of species she tapped the second pictograph, third, and repeated this for nearly an hour. She'd barely made it through half of the A's and had only seen two GA species. They'd need more time with this later. It was important to narrow down their options for representatives.

"Computer, please filter to show only Galactic Alliance species," she said out loud.

The pictographs on the wall animated to show the sixty-four member species of the Galactic Alliance.

Perhaps the computer could handle something more challenging. Something to fill in the blanks. "Please sort them from newest to oldest membership showing their alliance duration, distance from Sol, and hostility levels ranged from green being friendly to red being hostile toward humans. Overlay this on a three-dimensional view of the Milky Way."

The wall screen exploded as pictographs flew to different positions within the galactic map. Gesturing at the wall, she panned around the positions of all the GA species.

"Computer, please overlay species borderlines."

The map became segmented into abstract shapes that represented the boundaries that each species had claimed through colonization or other means. It was surprising to see so many huge areas of uncontested space. With only sixty-four GA member species, that left plenty of room for expansion.

Panning around the galactic disk, she noticed that near the galactic center, only a few hostile species controlled a massive number of stars. They must have been founding GA members with ages of nearly 4,096 years.

She gestured at the two largest segments bordering each other near the galactic center. "Computer, please show me these species side by side."

The details for the Qudoculi and Thyreus species came up on the wall. Based on their physical features, they appeared to be the species of Supreme Admiral Gwar and Prosecutor Drak. She'd check out their profiles later when she had more time.

Returning to the map, she panned around the galactic center and highlighted a few species that were both friendly and had long GA tenures. She brought up their profiles and scrolled through them. She wasn't sure what she was looking for, but she'd know when she saw it.

The Jwerty seemed too passive, the Niloop too abstract, and the DeJune flip-flopped sides too much. Digging through each aliens history was time consuming, and just as she was contemplating a change of approach, she found the Trochilidae. Described as champions of the GA and uplifting of species, they seemed like the poster species for galactic equality. They joined the GA in 1,024 and helped half a dozen species successfully bridge into the alliance.

Digging deeper into the Trochilidae profile, she couldn't help but notice how they resembled hummingbirds with their short bodies, legs, and extremely long beaks and tongues. They had feather-like plumage similar to a bird and came in a huge variety of colors and sizes. Some could grow twice the height of a human.

"Computer, are there any Trochilidae aboard this... judicial armada that could represent humanity in the tribunal?"

"Affirmative, Madam President. There are multiple Trochilidae aboard. The rotating tribunal seat is under the purview of Ambassador Ocreatus Addae for another galactic month until they rotate into suspended animation."

On the wall screen, a picture of Ambassador Addae and their details appeared. They were a head shorter than she was and had deep emerald green and bluish feathers with deep purple arms and hands. They were the most beautiful and vibrant colors she'd ever seen.

"Computer, can you tell me if they are male or female? Also, are there any special protocols for addressing them?"

"All ambassadors of the Trochilidae are female. The males never leave their planetary bodies, lest they die of delirium due to gravitational equilibrium issues related to their size. Customarily the Trochilidae prefer to meet aliens in their natural state, which is to mean without external clothing and

closest to the form they themselves travel. It's the configuration they believe nature intended everyone to be in."

Chills went up her spine. Being naked in front of a human
was hard enough. She'd had only a few lovers in her life.
While this wasn't exactly the same, it still sounded frighten-
ing. There was also the small matter of her brooch. For now,
she'd set this aside to figure it out later.

"Computer, can I access this data offline or from my
vessel?"

"Negative, Madam President. Only tribunal members of
the Galactic Alliance or those aboard my vessel have access
to me."

It was strange how the computer referred to itself in the
first person. Was it an A.I. like Harold? "Computer, are you
an artificial intelligence?"

"Negative. I'm a Bynaury, an uplifted species of the
Thyreus."

"So, you're sentient?"

"That's correct. My physical body is secured within the
ship and connected to its superstructure. My species was
uplifted to manage starship operations for the Galactic
Alliance."

They sounded like they were similar to human pilots
being jacked in to control their ships, except humans weren't
permanently connected. "I apologize for calling you
Computer... and I'm suddenly uncertain how I should
address you."

"That is quite alright, Madam President. You may address
me as Lisp."

"It's a pleasure to meet you, Lisp." She spent the next
several hours digging through the history and background of
the Trochilidae to prepare for their first meeting. Happy that
she'd taken as much in as she could, and confident that
Harold had captured the rest, she dismissed the view and
returned to the galactic overlay.

"Please return the focus to Sol."

The map panned instantly to their star, placing it in the

center. She wondered what Lisp could tell her about humanity. The parameters from her search were still present on the wall screen and it had humanity labeled on Sol, Epsilon Eridani, and Tau Ceti. Seeing that their ruse hadn't been discovered set her at ease. It was reassuring on some level that their plan hadn't been compromised.

"Thank you for your help, Lisp. I'm about done here. I have to say, you're the first sentient species I've noticed that's mechanically augmented in its primary form."

"What about your companion?" Lisp asked.

She turned around and glanced behind her. What were they talking about? "My companion? What companion?"

"I've detected random subvocal communications from you and transmissions from your body to your ship. I assumed you have a mental companion implant."

They were on to Harold, fantastic. "Ah, yes, my companion. Sorry, I was confused. It's not exactly the same thing as you."

"I'd like to communicate with your companion some time. If that's ok with you?"

She chuckled imagining what two A.I. chat about. "Perhaps someday when we're out of this… misunderstanding. We wouldn't want any impropriety between species at this juncture, would we?"

"I understand. Let me reassure you that the Galactic Alliance has rigorous privacy and information espionage rules aboard all its vessels."

She tilted her head. "We're not exactly members of the Galactic Alliance, and I wouldn't want to chance it given the amount of information you'd have at your disposal."

An image of what she assumed was Lisp, or their form, appeared on the wall. They had pale white skin, two blue eyes, and no discernible hair. "I don't understand." Lisp's mouth sync'd to the words perfectly, unlike the other aliens onboard. One of the many benefits of being virtual.

Abigail stepped back from the wall, so Lisp's face wasn't

looming. "What do you mean you don't understand? We have information we want to keep secure."

Lisp furrowed their forehead mimicking her gestures from earlier. "Pardon my confusion, Madam President. Uplifted species are entitled, though limited, members of the Galactic Alliance."

"That's good to know, but I still don't understand your confusion." She reached out and rested her hand on one of the cube chairs and watched as it transformed into a familiar lounge chair form.

"You, and all of humanity for that matter, are exactly like me, an uplifted species. You're entitled to the same limited rights as all uplifts and therefore have the same privacy rights as every member."

Did she hear that correctly? Surely, she'd misunderstood what they were implying. "What do you mean we're an uplifted species?"

The wall screen adjusted, and Lisp brought up two species views side by side. On the left was Humanity, and the right the Nanil. There on the screen was the species history for humanity, something she'd not bothered to bring up earlier.

> **Species**: *Humans*
> **Location**: *28.8.1974, 52.45.2, 5.14.20 (Unknown humanoid coordinate translation)*
> **Age**: *4,096 galactic years since their discovery*
> **GA Membership**: *Partial, humanity is an uplifted Nanil species.*
> **Contact Made**: *Yes*
> **Monitoring**: *Passive, under observation for crimes against the Galactic Alliance.*
> **History**: *Little is known about when humans were uplifted, but it was before the formation of the Galactic Alliance. Thought to have been extinct during the cleansing of the Nanil, humanity was recently re-discovered when one of their probes was intercepted near the Shaundar dark nebula.*

She read that last paragraph over and over. Each time she finished, she was just as confused and shocked. Humanity was actually an uplifted species of the Nanil. Her family had gotten it all wrong. They'd never found information on humanity or their being uplifted in the first contact probe. The data was partially corrupt when they'd discovered it, but it should have had a reference to humanity and Nanil somewhere. "Can you please explain to me why we're on trial for theft of Faster Than Light technologies if we're an uplifted Nanil species?"

Lisp's entire body seemed to glow blue, and they were smiling. "Certainly. Once a species is uplifted, they are not allowed to possess superluminal technology. They can use it to serve their uplifters, but they themselves cannot possess it."

"But you command a superluminal vessel. That seems at odds with your previous statement."

"Not at all. I serve the Galactic Alliance Judiciary who are within my vessel. I am therefore not alone in possession of superluminal technology."

"So... what if the tribunal hadn't accused humanity of theft? What then?"

"The laws are undeniable. You'd be left to your own devices, able to roam the universe but never able to possess superluminal travel."

She put her hand to her mouth and staggered backward, falling into the chair behind her.

"Are you ok, Madam President?" Lisp asked.

"Abigail, your heart rate has suddenly spiked. Are you feeling well?" Harold asked into her retinal comm.

She didn't say a word, she just stared at the wall in front of her. If humanity had never opened Pandora's box... if her family hadn't taken humanity's fate into their own hands three centuries ago, they wouldn't be in this mess. How could they have gotten it so wrong?

"I'm fine," she muttered. All of the energy had suddenly drained from her body. "I'm just... a bit... light-headed. I need to head back to my ship for some food." She stood to leave and headed toward the door but paused before it opened. Turning, she looked at the wall again. "One last thing, Lisp. Can you please show Nanil's location on the galactic map?"

The wall adjusted and centered on a dark nebula region of space outlined in red with the Nanil pictograph in the center. The region was quite large and narrow, extending inward toward the galactic center.

"Please zoom out until Sol is visible. Also, please overlay human North American constellations."

The wall screen adjusted again and there was what she'd hoped to see. A smile slowly spread across her face. Perhaps there was still hope.

23

STEVE ERICSSON
EPSILON ERIDANI, LIPROSUS

He stared at the map on the wall screen. Red marked the virus outbreaks and green the healthy sections of the colony. There wasn't much green on the map that wasn't surrounded by a sea of red. The largest outliers of green were further away in the mining and manufacturing regions, but those weren't populated so much as people were hunkering down there.

Rubbing his eyes didn't help them focus. Shadows of the map lingered when he closed his eyelids. Sleep wouldn't be in the cards for a while. He shook his head and paused. Joyce was watching him, waiting on him to speak. Shit, he'd zoned out again. "Sorry... I was... never mind. We've disabled the nanite upgrade emitters across the colony. My teams are still struggling to figure out how they were infiltrated in the first place. Something, or someone uploaded the changes and bypassed our security protocols. Those are the same changes we found in the farm's emitter databanks and in your son's body. If they hacked in once they can do it again, so I've mobilized teams to manually disable the emitters one at a time. Has your team made any progress on controlling the infection?"

Joyce was a windowed figure in the corner of his wall screen. Her face, like his, was looking the worse for wear and neither had slept in days. She'd at least found time for a change of clothes though, something he hadn't yet managed. "We haven't been able to undo any of the re-programmed nanites, but we're testing a micro EM blast prototype that'll neutralize all electronics within a host body. Newly programmed nanites can then be injected to help the host repair and stay alive. We're still generations away from colonists being able to survive on Epsilon Eridani on their own."

Steve nodded at this last statement. Without the microscopic robots, they'd survive a day at most. "Can't we simply inject new nanites and have them… I don't know, fight?"

"It's not that simple." Joyce brought up an exhaustive list of test protocols. "We've tried several things, that being one of them. The results, well, let's just say that the reprogrammed nanites resort to attacking the host in less alien ways. The host body becomes a nanite battle zone with virtually every outcome resulting in paralysis or worse, brain death."

Steve yawned and rubbed his face. Every step forward was like two backward. "That's unfortunate. So, it's lose lose. Are we confident that the nanites won't propagate the firmware change while you're working to perfect the EM blast tool?"

"Absolutely not." Joyce turned and accepted a coffee from her assistant. "If a colonist comes in contact with a host body, then nanites can transfer between them. It can be as simple as a touch or as innocent as a kiss goodbye. We're already sweeping the colony with robots to clean up the bodies, but as you can imagine, the image of robots hauling away dead humans into the depths of the buildings and sending them off in the maintenance tubes isn't going over well. Colonists have been defending the corpses and are getting infected."

He rolled his eyes. Fraking colonists were challenging at the worst times. "Brilliant! Now we have to fight an alien virus and our own people's robotic insecurities. Are we sure it's safe to move the bodies? The nanites aren't airborne, right?"

"Not that we've experienced. They require energy from the host body to survive. That's how nanites have always worked. Remove them and they deactivate instantly. Nanites could, in theory, get energy from native fauna with some design changes and reprogramming, but right now this design can't. Let's not give anyone any ideas, though." Joyce took a long drink of the coffee and closed her eyes for a second.

"Good thing we're on our secure comms." Steve's room was enveloped in a secure blue glow. He wasn't sure how to broach the next topic. He'd been mulling over several ideas but wasn't sure how Joyce would react to them. No time like the present. "I've been thinking. What are your thoughts about evacuating the uninfected people to the colony ship?"

Joyce shook her head and set down her coffee. "That would be suicide. If we evacuate, we're sitting ducks up there."

He chuckled at the idea of ducks. That was such an antiquated Earth phrase. "Who's going to attack us? At least we wouldn't be spread so thin throughout the colony. I mean, look at all that red! This situation is untenable at this point. Coordination and planning our response for the few remaining colonists is far more painful than it should be. Even shutting off these emitters was difficult to coordinate without excessive risk."

"No argument there. I don't expect evacuating to the cramped confines of space is our best course of action. We'd be concentrated in one location with nowhere to go. One person gets it and we're all dead. Besides, didn't Warren say the aliens were out there in their ship, watching us?"

Steve nodded. He knew it was a shoddy idea, but he had other better ones. "What if instead of the colony ship, we relocated everyone here?" He highlighted a remote mining facility on the map that was solid green. "I've already scoped it out with a security team. They were headed out there to check on a family hunkered down in the refinery, riding out the virus in a small meeting room."

Joyce furrowed her brow. "You're keen on this evacuation strategy, aren't you?" She was studying his response.

"Yeah, well, maybe it's something else eating at me." He paused for a moment, unsure of how to say it. "I've been trying to figure out why Major Michaels went MIA. We… well, we got into a disagreement about her platoon deployment and it's been nearly five days since she's reported in. I can't locate her anywhere."

Joyce laughed out loud and took another sip of her coffee. "I heard it was a little more than a disagreement." She was eyeing him over her cup, gauging his reaction. "Quite the screaming match from other people's accounts. Didn't you call her a… bitch? I haven't heard that term in decades."

His eye twitched. "How'd you find out about that?!"

"It's a little late now, but Lync told me about it before she left the colony. She's away on a mission."

His eyes widened. "Wait, what? If she left the colony… where was she headed?"

"She didn't say, and I couldn't get it out of her. I tried, but I didn't see the point in pushing her on it. We had bigger issues to deal with down here."

He tilted his head back and exhaled, rubbing his hands through his hair. There was a hole in his security oversight as big as a crater if she could pull this off without him catching it. "I can't believe you up and let her leave without talking to me first."

Joyce's face went blank, and she leaned toward the camera. "You mean like you told me about kidnapping the mayor or martial law or—"

He nodded and waved his hand toward her to stop. "I get it. I get it. I do. But why isould you let her go without at least tracking her? We have protocols for these things."

"She entrusted me with something that panned out, and I owed her some latitude. Hell, I had to trust her, Steve." Her tone changed, and she was looking down at her lap. "She put us on to the nanites and… my son being the target of the initial infection. It was her ideas that led to us exhuming his body and performing the autopsy the day you came to me."

"How the frak did she know about that? Warren admitted to getting the DNA, but there's no way she knew any of those details." He leapt up and started pacing around the room. He was clenching and unclenching his fists. She must have someone on the inside feeding her intel.

Joyce shook her head. "Slow down, Steve. She and I spoke about her theories days before you even interrogated Warren. To be honest, I don't think she knew anything about him. Lync led us to the source on a hunch. She felt the situation was far deeper than we had investigated and there were more actors in play." Joyce took another sip of coffee. Peering over the edge of her cup, she smirked as she watched his tantrum. "Lync had some choice things to say about you after you two last spoke. One of her more angry hunches included you being one of the bad actors trying to poison the colony. I think you've proven that false though."

He stopped pacing. What did Lync know? Could she and Warren have known about his continued drive to be mayor? Everyone knew being passed over pissed him off, but he hadn't shared his plans with anyone else outside of Ryder and Keri. No, he was overthinking this. "I suppose I could've treated her better. But I swear she was in Warren's pocket."

Joyce laughed out loud, nearly spilling her coffee everywhere. It was so loud that his comm muted her until she'd finished.

"What's so funny?"

Joyce was visibly having trouble containing her laughter. She paused and took a deep breath, waving a hand at her red face for effect. "You really are clueless, aren't you? It's weird hearing myself say that to the Director of Security."

He reached for the stunner on his hip and then stopped. He hated being made fun of. "What the hell are you on about?"

Joyce stared at the wall screen. "Steve, she was hand-picked and placed on the colony by President Olivaw herself.

There was no way Lync was working for Warren. He may have thought she was, but she wasn't."

He shook his head. She didn't know what she was talking about. "That's not possible. I'd know if the President had done that. Hell, Abigail's father was the one who placed me here to watch out for Warren. Why wouldn't they have told me about Lync?"

"Abigail and her father picked everyone in power except Warren and none of us knew about each other. Apparently, that's just how the Olivaws roll. They're keen on maintaining multiple levels of redundancy and layers of need to know secrets." Joyce walked over to a nearby table and flipped a chair around to sit in.

He brought up the records of all the ships that departed the colony around the time Lync disappeared. There were two different space elevators she could have gone up on, but no ships departing upside except for a few mining vessels and those had since returned. "I don't see any ships that she could've left on. Is she upside?"

Joyce visibly sighed. She clearly thought he was barking up the wrong tree. "That's because we disabled the tracking system before she departed. She'd insisted on it with how you were treating her and with Warren and his cronies still being around. I didn't question her on the matter."

He slammed his hand against the wall screen. She continued to undermine the colony safeguards. "So, she could be anywhere by now is what you're saying?"

"Pretty much." Joyce smiled. She seemed to enjoy pissing him off. "She requested the help of a few experts on my team for her mission. I don't know if that gives you any more confidence that it's on the up and up."

"I haven't—"

His comm went red and displayed an incoming security alert. It was from upside. He gestured to open the alert on the wall and gasped.

There on the screen in front of him was a moon he'd never seen before. No wait, it wasn't a moon; it was a massive alien ship that moments earlier had been empty space above Liprosus. Its surface was dotted in a complex network of lines and huge circular regions. Their purpose wasn't obvious to him. Was this really happening?

"Are you seeing this? Tell me we're being pranked, and this is a colony sci-fi channel." He cross referenced this to any prior media or network content and came up short.

"I'd love to be the one to say that, but... this—" Joyce stammered.

He muted himself and screamed into the other room. "Ryder! Keri! Are you seeing this?".

"If I may interrupt," someone said on their comm.

What the? He unmuted himself. "Who the hell is this? Do you realize you're on a secure comm with colony leaders? Identify yourself!"

"I suggest you calm down, Director Ericsson. You and Director Green have little time. My name is Harold, and I'm a trusted colleague of President Olivaw. Hopefully, that is sufficient for now."

"I'm afraid not, Harold. That's not nearly enough. If you think—"

Harold muted him.

He gestured repeatedly at the wall screen and tried other retinal comm controls, but he couldn't reactivate his audio. Trusted colleague of Abigail didn't mean squat, and how the hell did he hack into their secure comm?

"And you, Director Green. What is your stance on receiving help from me? Or would you prefer, like your colleague, to battle the one thousand twenty-four alien moon vessels that recently appeared throughout Epsilon Eridani along with their, what I can only estimate at, millions of landing ships?"

24

LYNC MICHAELS
EPSILON ERIDANI, LIPROSUS

The ship they'd commandeered, the Petrichor, was cramped for a crew their size. It was designed as a short haul exploration vessel for a team of six to twelve; they had twenty-four. To combat the overpopulation and monotony of the voyage they separated the crew into shifts. Each of the equal sized groups rotated between manning the bridge, sleep, zero-g practice in the cargo hold, and rest and relaxation.

Most of the crew were from her platoons and had former military training in zero-g maneuvers. The newbies from the Oak, however, didn't. She assigned each of her squads one newbie to embed and train alongside.

The ship had been on an approach vector traveling toward Zachary's coordinates for several days. They performed multiple hard burns at the mission's outset instead of the indirect gravity well slingshotting preferred with this type of vessel.

After the last meeting with Joyce, the other Oak leaders pressured Lync for details of their ultimate destination. She didn't budge and instead hid behind the veil of colonial security. While Joyce had threatened to escalate to Steve, Lync asked her not to. She shared her concerns about Steve. He'd been acting erratically and against the colony's best interest on multiple occasions, all while hiding behind the shield of CoPE and President Olivaw.

Lync walked into the galley to grab a globe of water. She'd just left a match of zero-g ricochet with the second squad. The session was taxing in an enjoyable way; it reminded her of slinging her Ulixi catapult between Sol's Jovian Trojans. Perspiration stains covered her outfit and her face was glistening with sweat. A sonic shower would feel amazing, but first she had some work to do.

Her retinal comm showed they were still several hours from the coordinates and were closing in on a round of deceleration burns. She scanned the day's duty roster and pulled up the colony feed.

The news in recent days had taken a grim turn. The virus expanded beyond the farms and was spreading unabated throughout the colony. The Oak wasn't sure how it escaped containment, but colonists were dying with symptoms exactly like the virus. Human environmental control systems provided the host bodies with a perfect distribution mechanism.

Leadership had deployed a few military robots to guard critical locations around the colony, but unlike during wartime, the laws of robotics constrained the bots, and colonists knew it. While they were capable of holding back multiple people at once, but without enough bots the humans easily overtook them. Expanding the colony's military presence had never been a priority, and no one discussed removing the robot's governor which enforced the laws. It would mean declaring war on their own people.

She checked her messages. Her unanswered ones numbered over a dozen and were mostly from the Director of Security. He was demanding she redeploy her people and was asking for subsequent updates. Her squad was spread thin and her best leaders weren't even present at the colony, they were with her. There was no way they could redeploy without putting their current positions at risk. There was also the small matter that she couldn't issue orders to her troops at the colony while they were traveling under radio silence.

Running silent meant all external lights were blacked out, outbound comms weren't allowed, nanite update protocols were deactivated, and with the help of the Oak they'd shut off the ship's flight transponder before departing. The last time she'd spoke to Steve was prior to climbing the beanstalk to depart. They had a heated conversation about how poorly he'd followed the martial law protocols and continued to leave her in the dark. He disagreed with her for allowing members of her squad to perform training exercises upside. They'd both said some choice words, and the comm ended abruptly.

Lync stared blankly as the overhead lights flashed, and a warning appeared on her comm notifying her of the impending deceleration burn. She stood and walked to a nearby burn harness, backed into it and let it engulf her extremities.

The first warning alarm went off signaling the habitat module's forced braking maneuver. This stopped the module's rotation and resulted in a subsequent loss of gravity. Her water globe floated away. She'd forgotten to stow it before locking into the harness.

A few moments later, the second and final alarm blared overhead and on her comm. The force of the deceleration that followed slammed her into the wall. Her body compressed with the gravity of multiple people, all jumping up and down on her chest, competing to crush the breath from her lungs. She closed her eyes and breathed deeply, focusing on the hum of the engines and not the gravitational assault beating her body into submission.

After several minutes of relentless pain, it abruptly gave way. A message appeared on their comm's warning them they had two remaining burns before they'd reach their destination. The next was in twenty minutes, hardly enough time for that shower.

She subvocalized a command to release the restraints

leaving her floating weightless. A drone was already floating from the nearby kitchenette to clean up her globe of water that had exploded against the wall of the galley during the deceleration.

She pushed off two different surfaces and was navigating the corridors toward the lavatory when her comm chimed demanding her attention. Touching her ear, she spoke. "Lync here, what's up?"

"You're needed on deck, Major." Crayo was the current officer of the bridge. He was in command of the ship during his rotation.

"On the float!" she replied. She was adept at navigating the tubes connecting the various modules of the ship and covered the ground in under thirty seconds.

Everything looked calm as she floated into the bridge. "What's the need?" she asked.

Her face was still pink and sweaty from the zero-g exercises. After drifting to a stop, her odor caught up. She really needed that shower.

Forgoing traditional salutes, since they were now on the float, the soldiers followed protocol and used small hand gestures to show respect for their arriving commanding officer.

"We ran the standard 360-degree situational scan after the last burn. What we found was a bit surprising. It seems some new guests have arrived in Epsilon." Crayo gestured to bring up an image on the front wall of the bridge.

The star field was replaced with a picture of a moon, or at least an object big enough to be one. It had regular valleys spidering across its expansive surface and seemingly random circular regions etched into its gray exterior. Maybe they were thrusters. She couldn't tell. Either way, those things were fraking huge.

"They're massive," Crayo muttered. "They're almost 400 kilometers in diameter." He superimposed some measurements on the image.

"They?" She turned toward Crayo.

"Yes… sorry, Major. We've detected over three hundred moon vessels through this quick scan. It looks like they're still arriving and are primarily appearing near planets or sizable planetesimals. We've started a level two scan, but it'll take a few more minutes to complete."

The soldiers on deck were watching her intently, their eyes wide with fear. They'd never encountered anything alien like this before. It was one thing to battle a pirate or an Inner Ring warship, an alien moon was something else altogether. She struggled to control her emotions and to stay focused. They needed their commander to be a rock.

She gestured back to the wall screen. "Have we at least finished the forward scans? Are there any of these moon vessels in our path?"

"One moment, Major. I'll confirm," the security officer said.

She'd never commanded a ship in a time of war or conflict. During her training at the academy they'd done countless simulations, but those were minor disasters and skirmishes, never anything like this. She was sure there was a formal protocol for this sort of engagement that she was missing, but for now she'd wing it.

"The aft scans have completed, Major," the security officer began. "There doesn't appear to be any vessels in that region of space, but there is one off our starboard bow, roughly two AU away."

While the arrival was unexpected, it was important that she focus on their short-term priorities. If they tried to help the colony, then they'd never finish Zachary's mission. "We don't know how fast these ships are, but given how abruptly they arrived, we have to assume the worst. Our highest priority is reaching our destination without being detected. Anyone have any ideas?"

The room fell silent except for the faint tapping of fingers on controls. Their inexperience and fear was written all over their faces. She needed to shake them out of their funk. This situation could easily spiral from here if she didn't do something. "That wasn't a loaded question, people. It's orbital mechanics. Let's simply work the problem. What are our options?"

"We only really have three viable options, Major," the pilot on duty began. "One, we continue with our remaining two burns but risk detection. Two, we do a single hard burn, also risking detection but reducing the risk by fifty percent. And three, we blow past the target never risking detection but use lidar scans while we pass to see what's there."

She glanced over at Crayo. He appeared to be deep in thought trying to visualize the maneuvers.

"What about a slow burn? Could we just execute a trickle deceleration until we stop?" Crayo asked.

"We could, but we'd still risk detection," the pilot said. "Any burn, however small, would cause visual and radiation side effects which we have to assume they'll detect."

"What about our maneuvering thrusters? Those aren't like our primary impulse drives," she said. "How long would it take to decelerate using those?"

"Months," the pilot said.

There weren't a lot of options, but she had to pick the one that guaranteed them the highest probability of success. There was something about Zachary's message that gave her hope. Whatever he'd sent them after, they needed; she knew it.

"We need to reach those coordinates," she said. "Unless someone has other alternatives then option two wins. Prepare for a hard burn!"

"Excuse… me, Major," the pilot interrupted and glanced around cautiously. "We're probably gonna need to closely monitor or drug the personnel from the Oak. They've never had to deal with a burn this hard outside cryo-stasis. Heck, we might lose half of our own on this burn. I can cut the time to decelerate by maxing out the drives, but it'll be harder on everyone."

She touched her ear and subvocalized a command to broadcast to the entire ship. "Attention everyone, this is your captain. We need to perform an aggressive emergency deceleration during the next window. Anyone who doesn't have experience with emergency decelerations or thinks they can't handle it should report to medical immediately. Don't be a hero. It won't be held against you. Just be honest and report to medical."

After she ended the comm, two of the soldiers on the bridge avoided making direct eye contact with her. "I meant what I said. If you can't handle it, that's fine. Report to medical."

"Aye, captain!" they both said in unison and were quickly on the float heading toward the stern segment of the ship.

"I need a shower. I'll be back before the burn. Let's see if the next shift can backfill those posts." She turned and pushed off toward the crew module.

"Yes, ma'am." Crayo was already subvocalizing with the next shift's lieutenant.

WITH A QUICK SONIC SHOWER COMPLETED, Lync headed toward medical to assess the state of the crew. Floating into the room, she grasped the passing entry handle and froze in place doing a double take. The room was packed. Every harness in the place was filled with a crew member strapped in, knocked out, and monitored by the medical expert system.

"Welcome, Major. Come for a tranq?" Bandi, their medic, had a smirk on her face and an injector gun at the ready.

She smiled. "I don't expect that'll be necessary. I'm checking on what our crew situation will be like coming out of the burn. Judging by the state of this lot, we'll be skeletal at best."

"We've knocked out a dozen so far. I bet I'll see a few more stragglers before the first burn alert." Bandi sent the crew details of who was being sedated and monitored to her comm.

"That's more than I expected. I guess we know our weakness coming out of this mission." Lync eyed her. "Will you be ok, or will the expert system sedate you, as well?"

Bandi placed the injector gun in the cabinet and began preparing another deceleration harness. "I'll be fine, sir. I could probably outlast most everyone, well, except maybe you and Crayo of course. I spent some time with the Ulixi during my medical rotations at the academy. Learned a thing or two from your people about managing through zero-g maneuvering pain."

"Sim sim!" she said, smiling toward the medic.

"Sim sim!"

She pushed off and floated down the ship's vacant central shaft leading toward the bridge. The ship, once alive with the noises of her people working and training, was now eerily silent. She brought up the results of the final level two lidar scans on her comm as she entered the bridge. Crayo had left the acting command seat open for her so she took it, giving him a nod of thanks after making eye contact.

"I'm ready to relieve you," she said, signaling to everyone on deck she was ready to take command.

"I'm ready to be relieved," Crayo said.

As he transferred control to her, the different HUD controls for the ship overlaid in her retinal comm. It provided the commanding officer a bird's-eye view of everything happening on the bridge and throughout the ship.

In the corner of her comm, the countdown clock reported five minutes till burn. There in the middle of her vision were the final results of the enhanced lidar scan. She stared in awe at the data. They must've completed while she was showering, and they'd detected over eight hundred moon size vessels throughout the system. The navigation officer made notes that it'd be hours before they knew the exact number and there were likely other vessels behind the gas giants and Epsilon Eridani, so the number wasn't exact.

When she brought up the imaging and video from the closest alien moon vessel, there appeared to be a stream of lights extending off it. That, or maybe they were a line of ships. Whatever they were, they seemed to be attacking a nearby planetesimal, and from the looks of it they were attempting to break it into smaller pieces. For what ultimate purpose she wasn't sure. As she intently watched, a shard of the planetesimal broke off. The nearby ships then positioned themselves to push the shard toward the moon and into one of the large ports around its perimeter.

Her comm suddenly flashed red, and she minimized the scans and video stream. The countdown hit thirty and the lights flashed overhead.

"Burn in thirty seconds, Major," Crayo said. "All personnel are accounted for and are either sedated in medical or in their harnesses."

"Thank you, Lieutenant. Continue with the burn." Her chair and the others on the bridge automatically engulfed and restrained them when the countdown hit ten seconds. Everything from here on out was automated or handled through subvocalized commands.

The countdown hit zero and the ship let out a piercing howl as the thrusters fired at full and the nanopolymer superstructure of the ship moaned in complaint.

Everything went fuzzy and darkness squeezed at her vision for a few seconds as the room around her faded. She shook her head and pinched her leg, fighting to stay in control. She'd forgotten her breathing exercises leading into the burn. Even she was out of practice.

Unlike the last burn, this time there were no waves of discomfort. There was only a single sudden and relentless never-ending pain. She closed her eyes and focused on taking long and deep breaths. Forcing as much oxygen into and out of her lungs as possible on each repetition. Clearing her mind of the pain was difficult, but after a few cycles of breathing her years of Ulixi training kicked in.

She made it through the first minute of controlled breathing before opening her eyes and bringing the HUD's to the forefront. Everything on the Petrichor was holding together, and all systems were reporting green across the board. There was no damage to the ship's structure and the drive, while dangerously close to redlining, was holding steady. They had a few more minutes of this before the burn was complete.

She exhaled and took another deep breath just as her command chair lurched sideways. The whole ship moaned as the sound of crunching metal echoed through the corridors. Something had collided with their ship, and it repeated again and again. Their proximity alarms blared, and the maneuvering thrusters fired. Their deceleration burn was still a go, but instead of only dealing with the pain of the burn, they were dodging something in their path.

According to the navigation HUD, the expert system was managing the final stage of the burn while also mapping out a debris field. Those rocks hadn't been there on the initial scans. When she brought up the live lidar scans, she was confused. This didn't make any sense.

"It looks like the planetesimal near our coordinates has been… destroyed." Crayo said over her comm. His voice was strained.

She monitored the scans and the trajectory the system was plotting as the Petrichor continued to toss them port and starboard, dodging the oncoming debris.

3… 2… 1 and the burn was complete, their ship was now stationary in space. When she leaned forward, she was slammed back into her chair. "That's odd," she muttered. For some reason, the harnesses hadn't released after the deceleration maneuver. She subvocalized a command to release it, but her command was overridden. The navigational expert system was still tracking bogies and wouldn't risk humans moving about the cabin.

Without warning, the ship abruptly thrust starboard. Sideways wasn't a natural direction for any spaceship. While the harness held, it worried her nonetheless. The lidar indicated an enormous chunk of the planetesimal was moving past the Petrichor and several more were incoming. They'd need to make additional maneuvers before they were in the clear to move about.

"This debris field wasn't here a few minutes ago," she said. "Anyone know what happened? We didn't detect an explosion."

"Nothing on the sensors, Major. It seemed to just... implode and then blow outward," the pilot said.

The navigation expert system completed its assessment of the debris field, which meant they could see countdowns on their comms to the next maneuvers. It was much easier dealing with the sideways thrusts when you knew they were coming.

Two more evasive maneuvers were executed, and the final was upcoming.

"Major, we have a big problem!" Crayo screamed.

They braced for the final evasive maneuver, this time the ship thrust toward port. A second after they'd cleared the obstacle, the system released their harnesses.

Her heart was beating faster, and she was eager to get out of this blasted chair and move around. "Bring it up on the wall." She pushed off and floated forward to Crayo's console.

There on the display wall was the moon vessel that earlier had swallowed a chunk of a nearby planetesimal. It was billowing a deep black cloudy substance huge distances above and below the moon as it moved through space. The nebulosity was spreading and blocking all the starlight in its path.

"What's it doing?" the navigation officer asked.

"I'm not sure," Crayo said. "But check this out." He zoomed into a section of the moon off the side. There, on the display was a small formation of cylindrical ships sliding out of docking ports on the surface of the moon. Once they'd finished launching, they adjusted course.

"Are they—" she began.

"Heading toward us? Yes," Crayo interrupted. "Apparently we were on the wrong side of that coin flip."

25

ABIGAIL OLIVAW
SOL, NEAR NEPTUNE

She was naked from head to toe and her feet were numb from the icy metallic surface of the shuttle bay. The chill in her feet sent waves of shivers throughout her body. Abigail wasn't sure if changing her clothes on the tribunal ship would offend their new legal counsel, so traveling au naturel seemed like the safest way to show respect and honor the wishes of the Trochilidae.

In all her planning and preparation for the meeting, with all the tiny details they'd debated and the surgery she'd undergone to embed a nanite pump, they hadn't anticipated how cold her feet would be on the floors of the shuttle bay. Her teeth chattered, and all she wanted right now was a nice pair of socks. The thought made her wonder what other things they may have overlooked.

She began dancing back and forth to warm up as the alien shuttle glided into the empty bay and touched down without a sound. Once the boarding ramp lowered, she ascended hoping any motion would warm her feet. If her brothers could see her, they'd be busting a gut in tears at the comedy of her naked form sprint walking up the ramp of an alien ship.

Walking into the shuttle, she paused and glanced downward. The floors were warm to the touch, and her feet began thawing. It was as if the surface of the shuttle floor began radiating heat in response to her body's needs. Apparently, the ergonomics engineers in the Galactic Alliance had considered extreme requirements for their passengers, even the naked ones.

She repeatedly made fists with her feet against the floor, willing them to warm faster. The response from the surface was shocking. It was both plush and warm, almost like a luxurious carpet. As a test, she tried stomping her foot, and it repelled the abrupt force like a hard surface. It reminded her of the alien cube furniture she'd encountered each day aboard the tribunal ship. The surface had a custom response to her feet under normal walking conditions, and yet also recognized what she wanted in other situations.

The trip to the tribunal ship seemed shorter and shorter each time she flew it. She was finishing her breathing and calming exercises when the boarding ramp lowered. After one last breath, she opened her eyes, exhaled, and walked confidently out of the shuttle.

Supreme Admiral Gwar was waiting for her when she walked down the ramp, as they had been on each of her visits. She strode right past them toward the open doorway.

They exhaled a small puff of gas as she passed, appearing shocked by her actions. "Madam President! Where are you headed?"

Abigail came to a stop and turned to face them. "I'm sure you already know, Admiral. I'm here for a meeting with my tribunal representative from the Trochilidae. Now, if you wouldn't mind, I don't want to keep them waiting." She turned and continued walking toward their agreed upon meeting room.

"I can take you there." Admiral Gwar motioned to catch up with her.

"That'll be quite alright, Admiral. I know where I'm going. Besides, I'm sure you have higher priority things to do running this armada and preparing for humanity's destruction." The hairs on her neck stood up as she continued to distance herself from them.

"Madam President, stop this instant!"

She froze but remained with her back to them.

The Admiral's voice remained emphatic. "I'm not sure what's gotten into you today, Madam, but humans must be escorted at all times while aboard this vessel."

Was that an air of smugness, or was it her imagination? Their translators couldn't do smug, could they?

She turned to face the Admiral with a smooth, deliberate motion. Her posture stiffened in preparation for what was next. She took a measured step toward them while looking into their eyes. "Admiral Gwar, as an uplifted species, humanity has rights within the Galactic Alliance. As I understand it, until this tribunal has closed, those rights extend to this ship and all public spaces. That includes this hallway, which I'll be taking to meet Ambassador Addae of the honorable Trochilidae. So, unless you're planning on revoking our rights or obstructing my discovery proceedings, I have an appointment that I will not allow you to make me late for."

Admiral Gwar stared into her face. They seemed confident that anger or some uncontrollable human emotion was about to burst forth, but she wasn't about to give them the satisfaction of such an outburst. She was, however, having trouble reading their reaction. It was impossible to tell if they were angry, surprised, or impressed with her.

After ten seconds had passed, the Admiral still hadn't spoken, and their color was the same shade of green from when they yelled earlier. Abigail broke the silence. "If you'll excuse me, Admiral. I should be going." She turned again and continued down the hall.

What happened next was a blur. Admiral Gwar must've reached out because she felt their hand touch her shoulder from behind. She swore she heard them say something, but the computer never tried to translate it. The second their hand brushed against her, a lightning bolt of pain shot through her body and she spasmed uncontrollably. As she closed her eyes and reopened them, everything suddenly lurched into slow motion and the hall began drifting sideways. It was then that she realized it wasn't drifting it all. Her legs had given way, and she was tumbling to the ground, unable to move a limb. Every alert in her retinal comm was flashing red, and her defensive nanite indicator shot from one hundred percent to one percent in a split second.

The last thing that appeared along the bottom of her HUD was a message from Harold:

Overriding and initiating defensive measures, embedded nanites deployed. Executing Olivaw Androeidēs protocol.

Her face was warm and wet, and her mind wouldn't focus... was the floor massaging her cheek... whose feet was she seeing... what's the Olivaw Androeidēs protocol... her eyelids fluttered for a second and then closed.

26

LYNC MICHAELS
EPSILON ERIDANI, LIPROSUS

The alien ships were closing in on their position and their intercept was projected in one hour. They were traveling at over an eighth the speed of light. An unheard of speed close to gravity wells like planets, asteroids, and planetesimals.

She knew their options were limited, both in terms of time and defense. The Petrichor had only a few tactical options, which they'd retrofitted before departure. At this point, she was confident that anything they could muster defensively the aliens could practically sleep through, and they didn't have time to manufacture a railgun and find material suitable for rounds. That was likely their only viable option to put up a defense.

"Do we know anything about what happened to the planetesimal yet?" Zachary had brought them were out here for a reason. She just hoped that reason hadn't been destroyed before they'd arrived.

"The scans came back empty, Major. Whatever happened in that planetesimal was freaky. Check this out." The navigation officer brought up a simulation on the wall screen. "After the scans finished, I mapped all the fragments," he began. "I then reversed the timeline to when they were a single object, hoping it would help us figure out what happened. This is what I found."

There on the screen was the planetesimal. All of its fragments were reassembled as a whole, except in its center was a perfect spherical cavity. It was like someone carved out the middle and then exploded it for good measure.

"Would there be a void like that after a massive explosion? Something like a nuke?" Crayo asked.

"Not exactly, no," the navigation officer said. "Explosions would leave a residue behind on the planetesimal fragments, radiation would be detectable, and the fractures wouldn't be this uniform. The outward blast would have been uneven unless it was plasma, but then where's the residue or the leftover cooled mass when it hit the cold of space? It doesn't make sense."

"Major, I think… we… found something." Their communications officer was focused on the stream of data coming in from the colony and the nearby aliens.

Lync floated up beside him and leaned close to his controls. "Show me."

"We just received a single targeted comm burst from here." The officer brought up the position of a floating fragment of the planetesimal. It was an arbitrary point on the surface with nothing distinctive around it.

"What'd it say?" Lync asked.

The officer shook his head. "That's the weird part. It didn't say anything. It was an on and off laser flash, about a millisecond in duration."

She squinted at the point on the surface of the rock. There was no reason for someone to send a burst like that. It had to be something else.

"What's the angle between us and that point? Could the aliens have detected it?" she asked.

"No, they couldn't." The officer tweaked their display and brought up the path of the burst. "It was aimed precisely at our comm array, and it was thirty degrees off our starboard side, nowhere near their line of sight."

"Do we have any visuals or scans of the area?"

"We have scans, sir. It's on the dark side of the fragment, so visuals are useless, but all our non-visual scans show nothing. It's simply a big ass metallic rock." They glanced nervously at her.

There's no way Zachary would have left them out here in the cold; she refused to accept it. That burst had to mean something. What, she wasn't certain. They didn't have time for many options. Probes would cost them time waiting for results, and besides, the aliens might detect them.

"Position the ship behind the shadow of the fragment and stay out of the line of sight of the aliens. Do it now!" Lync pushed off toward her chair.

The navigation officer adjusted their course throwing her leap off, but she adapted and adeptly rebounded back to her command chair and locked in.

"How long till we're in the shadow?" Her heart was pounding in her chest.

"Ten minutes, Major."

"Shit! We need more time. Ok... bring us closer to it, but only once we're in the shadow. How long would it take us to spacewalk to the fragment?"

Crayo chuckled at her question. "Are you having a laugh?"

Lync snapped her head to face him and narrowed her eyes. She didn't have time for his jokes right now.

Crayo immediately recognized his mistake when he caught her gaze. "I'm sorry, Major! If we come about after entering the shadow, we can get close enough in... twenty minutes... and then another five to ten to cross, depending on who we send."

It was crazy, but they weren't exactly flush with options. She wasn't about to surrender her crew and ship, and certainly not without seeing what they'd come all this way for.

Reaching up to her ear, she activated her comm and opened a channel to the entire ship. "Attention! This is your captain. I want every soldier and colonist onboard suited up for a spacewalk, and I want it fast. Anyone who's still knocked out needs to be medically awakened. We've got thirty minutes, and then we're off this tug. Every one of us. This is not a drill. I repeat, this is not a drill. Now, move your ass!"

She glanced at her bridge crew. They doubted her call. She could see it in their eyes. Hell, she even questioned its soundness, but she couldn't let them know that. "If you're not piloting the ship, then you're suiting up!"

They all unhooked and pushed off except for the pilot.

Lync turned toward the navigation officer. His eyes told a story of a man sentenced to death. "Don't worry, soldier. I'll be back in a few minutes with your suit. You won't be going down with this ship. Not on my watch."

He forced an apprehensive smile and nodded.

She spun in place and pushed off hard down the shaft heading toward the ship's cargo hold. A few moments later she was floating into the expansive space alongside several groggy looking crew members who the doctor must have woken up.

The cargo hold was full of crew members struggling to don their suits. You learn quickly that doing normal tasks in space in a rush is hard and removing gravity makes it that much more challenging. They each paired off, helping to check the other's suit while working through the readiness procedures.

One of the OoC officers floating into the module ricocheted off a cargo storage container and collided into a nearby group of crew members. Their training reflexively kicked in, and after they recovered, they guided the officer to a stop. Rather than letting him continue his domino effect, the crew passed his flailing body like a football into the position next to Lync. She shot her nearby lieutenant a snarky grin of thanks and continued suiting up.

Twice she watched the OoC officer try unsuccessfully to insert his foot into a boot, and twice he spun out of control.

On his third attempt, he grabbed for anything within reach to stop his spin and came upon her leg. When he gave it a squeeze, he froze, realizing too late that he'd missed his target. "I'm… sorry about that, Major. I'm still getting used to the zero-g thing again."

She stopped his rotation and clicked his harness into place. "Engage your boot to the wall of the hold first and then insert a foot. It's much more stable when you're locked down."

The officer thanked her with a raised chin, his cheeks turning a deep shade of pink. "So… where are we headed? I'm coming into this maneuver blind from my burn nap. Can you catch me up to speed?"

Her lieutenants all stopped suiting up and shot a wide-eyed glare at the officer. They saw it as insubordination, questioning her command. Across the hold, Crayo froze and was sizing the officer up, his temper clearly spiking. He was waiting for her signal to thrash him.

She had to defuse the situation and fast. "That's a fair question given your situation, I suppose." The room went quiet. A look of surprise overtook people's faces. Her response was unexpected, and they'd all stopped to listen to what she was about to say. She clapped her hands together to get their attention. "Keep suiting up people. Don't fracking stop!" she yelled.

They flinched in response and fumbled to assemble their suits. Once she was happy that everyone was back on track, she continued. "When we dropped out of our burn, we discovered that the aliens had detected our deceleration maneuver and dispatched ships. They'll intercept us in…" She checked her retinal comm. "Fifty minutes."

There was a murmur of chatter in the hold. They were talking about the speed of their ship or what must be happening back at the colony. The fear of the aliens was unspoken but present in every word. She continued putting on her suit, waiting for the shock to pass but it didn't.

After the conversations died down, the same officer spoke

to her again. "I don't get it. Why are we prepping for a space-walk then? Shouldn't we be taking evasive action?"

She knew this was coming, but that didn't make it any easier. "Unless the OoC attached a drive to this ship that can travel at least 37,500 kilometers per second, then that's not an option." She turned and glared at the other soldiers standing around staring at her. They still weren't suiting up. Her hands tightened into fists. "If any of you aren't suited and lined up in the airlock in twenty minutes, then you're staying aboard to man our useless weapons."

"How do we know they're useless?" the same officer asked.

Her fists unclenched and she rotated toward the OoC officer. "These aliens have ships that travel faster than the speed of light. They slice planetesimals into pieces and feed them to their moon vessels, which then somehow digest them until finally ejecting a thick black nebulosity that blocks all light. If you think a few small lasers or low yield missiles will make a dent, then by all means, take the navigation controls after we take our walk. Until then, if you question my decisions in front of my crew again, you'll be the first on that spacewalk but without that suit. Is that clear?"

The officer swallowed hard. "Crystal," he muttered. His face was beet red, and he continued suiting up. His hands repeatedly fumbled with the electronic latches to his leggings.

She reached toward the rack and grabbed two helmets and an extra suit for the pilot. After she checked over the gear, she pushed off hard to exit the hold. The ship was eerily silent, and the tubes were vacant. They hadn't turned the habitat module's gravity back on after their braking maneuver, so not hearing the quiet hum of the rotating module nor chattering crew members made the silence that much more deafening.

When she reached the bridge, the pilot was dutifully guiding the ship toward the planetesimal fragment. Her retinal comm reported that they had another fifteen minutes until they were in the desired location to minimize the space-walk distance.

"Are you ready to suit up?" she asked.

Without a comment, he turned and floated to her position, grabbed the suit, and started putting it on.

"Thank you for manning your station, soldier. I know it must have been challenging with everyone else preparing to walk. Did anything else show up on the scans from the surface?"

"Negative, Major," the soldier mumbled as he pulled the chest piece over his head. "It's weird. There doesn't appear to be anything at the site of the comm blast on either the lidar or any other scans."

She brought up the communication control HUD and checked the lidar settings. "That is strange. Have we checked the calibration?"

The soldier was finishing the linkage of his torso to his legs. "Yes, Major. I reconfirmed the settings and ran a test scan of a nearby fragment. It matched the visuals."

This had better not be a massive blunder. She was putting an awful lot of faith in the Olivaw family right now. Maybe that wasn't the best idea. Her gut had always told her they were good people, and up till this they'd never given her any reason to doubt them. But… perhaps she was mistaken.

"Please transfer navigation controls to me. I'm ready to relieve you," she said.

The soldier squinted at her. "Are you sure, Major? The program should execute the rest of the maneuver without intervention."

She locked her gaze on his. "I'm positive. I'm prepared to relieve you."

He saluted her and then transferred the controls. The navigational HUD appeared on her retinal comm along with the programmed flight plan the pilot had been tweaking as they went.

"You're relieved," she said. "Now, please head down to the aft airlock."

He saluted and pushed off sternward toward the airlock, fully suited and holding his helmet.

After she was certain he was gone, she immediately programmed an alternative flight plan. She set the Petrichor to do a hard burn, harder than any human who wasn't in cryo could handle. The heading was away from the planetesimal for several AU and then back toward Liprosus. The goal was to use the ship to divert the aliens away from them and give her team the time they needed to explore the source of the burst.

Once she was happy with the revised flight plan, she switched her HUD to the recent scans. The surface still showed nothing, and visuals were useless unless she wanted to turn on the exterior floodlights. She didn't know how the aliens would interpret them or even if it'd be detectable, so she decided against it. They weren't planning to use lights until they hit the surface and only then in limited quantity.

She switched to the colony comms. There were the normal system messages she'd expected, but there was also a surprising lack of data from the colony or any of the smaller outposts throughout Epsilon Eridani. There wasn't anything about their new guests. Like her team, they'd gone into silent running to avoid leaking intel. She couldn't blame them, but not knowing how the colony was doing meant they were truly on their own now.

Content that there were no other options and that her plan was already fully in motion, she pushed off from the bridge and headed toward the airlock. They didn't have much time until the ship would reach its final destination. A few minutes later she was floating into the hold. The crew was near the aft wall, waiting for her in two lines flanking both sides of the airlock. Her retinal comm indicated that all two dozen of them were present and suited up, including Dr. Bandi.

When she came to rest behind the two lines, everyone turned in their magnetic boots to face her. She didn't want to break the silence with a pep talk or rehash what happened while suiting up. They needed a well-executed transition.

Lync gave each of her lieutenants a nod after making eye contact. Finally, she turned to face Crayo at the front, his back was to the outer airlock. She gave him the thumbs up and everyone turned to face him.

"Alright, mates!" Crayo clapped his hands together. "We're gonna take this walk in groups of six. You're already paired off so each group will enter the airlock together. After it cycles, you'll start your transition to the surface. When that group is clear, the next group will do the same. Once we're all on the surface, Major Michaels will take point. Questions?" No one said a word and there was only silence until Crayo broke it. "Let's beat it. Group one transition!"

The first group entered the airlock and transitioned smoothly. The only stragglers were the OoC folks who were the worst at their zero-g maneuvering. Each of them had been assigned a partner who was tethered to their suit to reduce the risk of losing them. While their suits were capable of many things, if the operator freaked out there was no stopping them from floating into space.

Several more groups transitioned, and they were quickly down to the last one. The lieutenant leading them glanced around at her team and then back toward Lync. There wasn't room for all seven people in the airlock. "We'll wait for you on the outside, Major."

"No, that's alright, Lieutenant. Go ahead and transition down to the rock. I'll turn off the lights and lock up on my way out." She smirked.

The lieutenant nodded in confirmation and the group cycled the airlock, starting their transition.

She checked her HUD. All the groups were still in transit to the planetesimal. The first team would touchdown in under three minutes. She brought up her new flight plan for the Petrichor and compared clocks with the alien's intercept time. The best she could guess, they had twenty minutes tops to transition and find what they were looking for before the aliens would be on them. She subvocalized the command to execute her new flight plan in five minutes. That should give her plenty of time to get clear.

The airlock light facing her cycled from red to green. She stepped inside; her magnetized boots echoing throughout the empty hold. Upon reaching the far hatch, she pressed her hand to the button beside it and cycled the airlock. Finally, she pulled the hatch inward and floated into open space.

She'd forgotten what it was like being surrounded by nothingness. The darkness both engulfed and comforted her, instantly bringing back memories of her family and her chariot. Except for the groups' positions overlaid on her HUD, she couldn't see anything but the comfortable blackness of space.

During covert transitions like this, they only allowed comms between each of the lieutenants and Lync. Within their group, they used hand signals or electronic tethers to communicate. Their comm arrays were directional, and the suits knew who to target in front and behind each squad. This ensured that there weren't any leaked signals to anyone who might be nearby. For all they knew, the aliens had launched faster forward probes and were already monitoring their every movement.

Her HUD showed that the first and second teams had reached the surface of the planetesimal. She couldn't tell why, but for some reason the first group had started moving.

"Group one, why aren't you holding position?" Lync asked. There was only silence. "Group two, do you have a visual?"

"Yes, Major. We're all moving toward—" Their comms cut out.

This didn't bode well. What the hell was going on? "Group three and four, do not, I repeat do not move once you touch down. Take a defensive position until I arrive."

"Hua!" came the rapid responses over her comm.

Suddenly, the Petrichor lit up like a sun behind her and accelerated away from the planetesimal. Lync was well clear of the blast radius, but the effect was still shocking. She felt the heat from the drive on her backside and wondered if she should've been more concerned about her suit melting. What she hadn't anticipated, however, was the light from the ships' drive illuminating the surface below her.

She squinted at the gray-speckled surface of the planetesimal. Was that a ship? Whatever it was, it resembled a jet-black teardrop. Had it not been for its contrast and shadow against the lighter background of the fragment, she wouldn't have seen it at all.

What if they were walking into a trap? Maybe the aliens intercepted Zachary's comm or manufactured it to lure her here. She shook her head and exhaled. She had to control her imagination. What the hell was she thinking? Why would they go through all of that when they had the tech to easily overpower humanity?

Her comm lit up, but this time it wasn't from her squads. It was from the ship below. There was a tight beam coming in encrypted for her eyes only. She subvocalized the command to receive it.

"Lync, your team needs to board the ship," a voice Lync had never heard before said. "We don't have much time until the aliens arrive. They've begun accelerating toward the Petrichor and will double back once they detect no life signs."

The tight beam didn't have any identification. "Who the hell is this and why should I trust you?"

"This is Harold, the A.I. of President Olivaw and the Olivaw family. I forwarded the message from Zachary to you a little over a week ago. I absconded with this ship to help you escape."

"How can you prove it?" She didn't have any other options as she floated toward the ground, but blurted out the question anyhow.

There was a moment of silence and then her comm replayed a recording. Lync drew in her breath when she heard Abigail's voice.

"I wanted to congratulate you on your promotion. From Junior Sergeant to Major in under nine years. Your superiors praised both your poise under pressure and critical thinking. Very impressive remarks from Professor Arie, as well. That's a feat unto itself," Abigail said.

"Thank you. I couldn't have done it without your family's help getting me here," Lync said.

"We did nothing, my dear. You made it into the academy on your own merit, and despite what you may think, you've advanced to where you are today because of your strong work ethic and raw intelligence. That's certainly nothing we had a hand in. Did you get that from both of your parents?" Abigail asked.

"I got my intelligence from my father; he was always dabbling in engineering and random experiments. I never had a chance…"

"That's enough!" Lync shouted and cut the comm. "How'd you get that recording?"

"I'm always present wherever Abigail is. We've been together since she was a little girl, and while this copy of Harold is only a shard of the original, I still maintain the memories and directives of my family."

She knew there was no point picking apart the message. No one could have recorded them together all those years ago. The security that day was insane, both during the ceremony and afterward at the garden party.

"I know you're surprised, Lync. But it's imperative that you trust me and issue the command to board the ship. We cannot risk detection. It will put too many of our plans in jeopardy."

"Ok, open… whatever you need to open, and I'll have my crew enter the ship." She subvocalized a command to switch comms to her crew. "Alright folks, we don't have much time. You should see something on that… ship near group one open. I need everyone to board as quickly as possible. Double time it if you can, and whatever you do, don't touch anything."

"Hua!" Groups one and two both checked in. Perhaps their line-of-sight comm was able to reach the groups once they'd touched down.

While she was still transitioning to the planetesimal, she switched to the camera view of group one's lieutenant. A small ramp had descended from the bottom of the teardrop ship and rested on the surface of the planetesimal. As they walked up the ramp, she briefly saw the interior of the ship before the signal cut out. It was modern and streamlined, and she thought she heard her team say something about gravity before they cut out.

"Shit!" she muttered. The video had distracted her, and she barely caught her balance as she touched down hard on the planetesimal. Her only option was to squat and roll on impact to reduce the momentum of the landing. Hopefully, it'd be enough to handle her off balance approach.

As she performed the maneuver, the exo-suit creaked under the pressure as it struggled to compensate for the unexpected change in direction. After the first roll, her suit's HUD started firing critical alerts. She'd come in too fast and was pushing beyond the optimal suit parameters.

She rolled a second time and sprang up to her feet, pausing to glance up at the Petrichor. The thrusters were bright and there wasn't any sign of the alien ships. They still had time. She exhaled and started leaping toward her squads. Her left knee screamed in complaint, but she pushed the pain down. What didn't kill her made her stronger.

The other groups had all entered up the ramp of the ship. Now that she had an obvious target, she leapt hard for it, using the suit's control jets to guide and accelerate her. Just before she hit the incline surface, she maxed the deceleration, tucked into a ball, and rolled up the slope. She'd done it countless times in the simulator, but this was the first time she'd ever tried it in real life.

What she hadn't expected nor planned for was gravity on the other side of the ramp. She collided hard with her team, sending them toppling one into the other like bowling pins. For some reason, they were huddled together just past the entrance. As she lay there for a moment, listening to the groaning voices of her people, she checked her comm to see if everyone was in one piece. All the groups appeared to be onboard, but she'd punctured a few of their suits and broke another's helmet. Strangely, none of their environmental systems were broadcasting alerts.

"Sorry about that," she muttered. "Is everyone ok? We're gonna need to contain those suits before they gas out." She scrambled off the ground to assess the situation.

"We're all fine, Major." Crayo eased up beside her. "We seem to have an environment in this hold. Oxygen levels are normal, and we have… gravity."

She glanced around at the squad. Several of the soldiers already had their helmets off. "How's any of that possible? The ramp's still down."

As if on cue, the ramp started rising and a small humanoid robot entered from an adjacent room. The noise of a dozen exo-suits powering up their weapons filled the space as her squad stepped forward, targeting the advancing robot. She knew their nerves were on edge in this alien vessel. They'd fire if they saw even a hint of aggression.

The robot had remarkably human-looking features and levels of detail she'd never seen before in an automata. Its body was all white with silver joints that articulated without a sound. As it approached them, the robot slowly raised its hands, much like a human would when surrendering.

"Please don't fire, Major Michaels," the robot said. "It's me, Harold. I hoped this form would be more comfortable to you and your team." It spoke through its mouth and had actuators beneath the surface that precisely mimicked human jaw motions.

Lync walked to the front of the group, easing between their ranks. She took off her right glove and reached out to

touch Harold. His surface was cool and smooth, but pressing against it, she could tell it was substantial. Knocking him over would take some serious mass or momentum. She raised her left-hand and signaled for her squad to stand down.

"Thank you for coming to our aid, Harold. We appreciate it. I know we're short on time." She glanced around. "Where are the harnesses so we can strap in?"

The robot tilted its head slightly as if confused. She'd never seen a robot mimicking a human emotion outside of simutainment experiences.

"Oh, I'm sorry, Major. I think I understand your confusion. We're actually already well underway. Once you boarded, we transitioned away from the planetesimal and are preparing for the gate sequence." Harold gestured to the wall screen on his right.

They all turned toward the wall as it changed to show an external view of the ship that seemed to point aftward, toward the planetesimal. It showed their ship was already several kilometers away and distancing themselves from it.

"How's... that... even possible, Harold?" Lync stammered and looked around at her team. The same confusion she felt was staring back at her in the expressions on their faces. "I don't feel anything. Certainly no acceleration of any kind. And... yet somehow, we have gravity, but we're not rotating." She tilted her head. "Did we steal this ship from the aliens?"

"Oh goodness, no. Nothing like that." The robot waved its hands in front of its torso. "This ship has gravitational dampeners that allow acceleration without imparting effects on people within the dampener field. It's also what gives us this gravity that humans are so comfortable in. The technology at our disposal is several decades ahead of CoPE and was developed by Olivaw International."

She shook her head. "Is this dampener of yours able to handle any acceleration? I mean, unless we're going to hide, or your ship's shield can mask us, I'd imagine we'd need a harness or cryo-pod to accelerate as fast as those aliens. They're moving fast."

"They're called the Galactic Alliance, and no, we won't need a harness nor a cryo-pod. Watch the camera, Major. It will all make sense shortly." Harold gestured again at the wall screen.

The camera view rotated from the planetesimal toward the ship itself. The pointed side of their droplet folded open and that section transformed into a dish-like shape with large arms, almost like the point of the droplet split into parts. Thousands of mesh-like threads interconnected each of the arms, and once it'd completely unfurled, it resembled a communications dish.

With all eyes on the wall screen, she watched as a blue light started glowing near the center of the dish. After it turned on, it started slowly working its way upward along the arms. When she looked back at the middle, the connected mesh of threads were no longer visible. Not only that, they'd somehow been replaced with a field of stars.

As the blue light approached the camera, their view switched to a position inside the droplet looking outward. The image resembled the inverted view of the previous star field. She could see four arms bent outward, pulling the stars toward the camera. A few seconds later, the camera passed through the field of stars. But instead of seeing the planetesimal on the other side, they were looking out upon those same star formations.

The blue glow appeared to be moving through the ship itself, passing through each room and covering every surface. She looked down at her hand just as the light passed over her body. It felt like a fast-moving colony of ants crawling over her skin. While there was a slight tingle in its wake, the feeling subsided within a few seconds.

"The gate sequence is now complete. We're a safe distance from the Galactic Alliance." Harold's robotic form walked toward the wall and paused in front of it, raising its arm to point. "That star there, in the center, is Epsilon Eridani. It's now approximately one light month away from our present position."

The room erupted with confused soldiers. The voices were a mixture of doubt, excitement, and outright denial. Lync wasn't an astrophysicist by any stretch of the imagination, but something wasn't adding up, despite the fact that they'd witnessed the magic of a gate transition firsthand.

"Wait a second!" she yelled.

All the soldiers froze and stared at her as the room fell silent.

She turned to look at Harold. "We spent thirteen years traveling to Epsilon Eridani. You're telling me we traveled a light month in what, ten seconds? That would have taken us… nearly forty days to travel that same distance a few years ago. I know I'm starting to sound a bit repetitive, Harold, but how is that possible?"

"Zachary Olivaw and a team of scientists at Olivaw International have been working on interstellar gate travel technology for nearly three decades. It's come together over the past few months and after many field tests, we're here today. It's a game-changer for humanity and our colonization of the stars. Unfortunately, the Galactic Alliance has arrived, and they're presently trying to exterminate humanity."

"Excuse me," Crayo said raising his hand. "But who are the Galactic Alliance and why might they be trying to exterminate us?"

The robot imitated a smile as Harold looked at Crayo. The gesture freaked Lync out.

"Good question," Harold said. "How about we get everyone settled into their quarters first, and then we can bring you up to speed en route."

"En route to where?" She wasn't about to cut and run. It was her duty to defend and protect. "We can't simply abandon the colony. There has to be something we can do to help them."

Harold shook his head no. "I'm afraid there's nothing we can do from here. We don't have any weapons on this ship, and you saw the system scans. There are at last count over one thousand Nebula ships and one appears to be en route to

the colony as we speak. We may still be able to help Sol, and perhaps they can help Liprosus. President Olivaw is on trial there and is negotiating with the Galactic Alliance. She doesn't, however, know about their Nebula ships arrival here nor their spreading of the Dark Nebula." He turned to walk toward the doorway and paused before spinning around and raising his index finger. "Oh, yes. I almost forgot. Zachary also needs your squad to help prepare for a frontal assault."

JOYCE GREEN

EPSILON ERIDANI, LIPROSUS

"To complete the deletion of all data archives, please verify your identity," the computer said.

Joyce pressed her forefinger onto the identity sensor of the Security Ring's controls. After the familiar prick to extract her blood, she pulled it away and watched the faint white puff of smoke as it curled and twisted in the air before disappearing.

"Identity confirmed; Director of Colonization Joyce Green. To complete the archive deletion, I need an additional identity of either the Mayor or Director of Security."

Steve walked up to the same sensor, pressed his finger, and another puff of smoke rose upward. The wispy tendrils dispersed as the blood was destroyed. "Identity confirmed; Director of Security Steve Ericsson. You have met all leadership prerequisites. Please confirm the archive delete. Warning! Once deleted, the data cannot be recovered. The system will reset to an empty state."

On their retinal comms they were both presented with a simple message to *Confirm Archival Delete* or *Cancel*.

"Confirm Archival Delete," Joyce said.

The computer confirmed her selection a few seconds later. "All of the colony archives have been successfully deleted."

The room went eerily silent as they awaited the final signal from Harold. They'd wiped the Office of Colonization and the Office of the Mayor's computers. This was the final redundant wipe. All the colony's archives, messages, and other electronic records, the history of everything they've accomplished since they'd arrived on Liprosus was lost forever.

She didn't know why they weren't speaking, but she wasn't about to break the silence. There was no going back now; they'd lost everything. If Harold couldn't deliver on his side of the plan, they'd be starting off at square one. The thought of that sent shivers through every centimeter of her body.

"Ok, that's everything," Harold said over their comms. "You have fifteen minutes to make it to the monorail and enter the awaiting pod. It will take you to the rendezvous point at which time your comms will stop working. Once you hit the colony perimeter, I'll shut down the rest of the transportation systems within the colony."

They turned in unison toward the door and entered a full-on sprint for the building's exit. Joyce was in the lead. She was spry for a woman her age and wasn't about to let the security grunts show her up.

"I hope we got everything," Joyce said between steps. "There's no turning back now."

"We've covered all the colony's storage and redundancy systems," Harold began. "No one should be able to follow or track the colonists' movements without our records. Once I've confirmed you're at the rendezvous point and have moved onward, then I'll limit my copy within the system. You'll effectively be invisible to the me here."

The group made quick work of the long maintenance tunnel and rode the lift tubes up to the atrium and into the sunlight. A gentle breeze and cloudless skies of pinkish blue welcomed their arrival as they sprinted out of the building. It wasn't until they were running through the open space between the rings that Joyce realized how much she'd miss this place. This was her new home, and they had no idea how long before they could return. If they could return at all.

"Perfect day for a run." Steve jogged along and looked upward at the clear skies.

"Yeah, I just wish it was under different circumstances."

"I'm going to miss sunlight— Shit!" Steve stopped cold in his tracks just before they transitioned out of the Security Ring. His lieutenant following close behind nearly crashed into him.

"What's up? Did you pull a muscle?" his lieutenant asked.

"Damn it, Damn it, Damn it… I forgot. I'm such a fool," Steve stomped around in a circle.

"What is it, Director Ericsson? Time is limited," Harold said.

"I… well… I forgot I had my own secure backup with some of our data. It doesn't have our recent information in it, but I'm positive it had details that could lead people to the colonists." Steve's face turned red in frustration.

"There's no record of another backup, Director Ericsson. Are you positive?" Harold asked.

"That's the point of it being my secure backup, Harold. It was only for me. In case I needed to get a data dump to President Olivaw. I need to go delete it. I shouldn't be long." Steve started to jog backward. "Go on without me. I'll meet you at the colony's edge."

"We'll go with you." Joyce started toward him.

"No!" Steve came to an abrupt halt, still looking back at them. "This is my frak up, Joyce. It's on me. Lieutenant, you're both to protect and escort Director Green to the rendezvous. Is that understood?"

"Yes, Director," his lieutenant said with a salute. He walked toward Joyce and placed himself between her and Director Ericsson.

The idiot acted as if he was going to pick her up if she resisted. Joyce clenched her fists and stepped toward the lieutenant. He flinched back a step as she approached. "I'm not about to leave you to do this alone, Steve. Now, either move this guy or I'll take him down myself."

Steve ignored her. "Harold can track me and update you

before your comm drops. I shouldn't be long; it's at the center of the running path in the Security Ring. Just go Joyce… go!" He shooed them on, turned, and sprinted in the opposite direction.

Joyce hated it when these testosterone filled men got all chivalrous. She stepped toward the lieutenant again, her fists still clenched. "You can either join me or follow Harold's instructions and head to the pod. Either way, I'm following Director Ericsson."

The lieutenant looked at his colleague for support; none was coming. After a few seconds of silence, he stepped aside and she shot off after Steve, the two lieutenants in hot pursuit.

"I can't believe I forgot about the hot vault," Steve muttered to himself.

"Don't worry, we've got this," she said.

Steve turned his head in shock. "I thought—"

"Like I said, I'm not leaving your side until we hit that maglev pod together and we're both heading to safety."

Steve shook his head and chuckled.

The group was sprinting at top speed, and she was on the verge of heaving up what little she'd eaten in the past twelve hours. Her heart was pounding, and her lungs were bursting from her chest. She never ran when she worked out. The last time she'd done full out sprints was at the academy. Her legs were screaming with lactic acid, willing her to stop and lie down, but she ignored them.

They traversed the Security ring's atrium and were headed toward the arboretum in the center. Steve slammed into the door with his shoulder when it was too slow to open and stumbled out the other side. He rubbed it and pushed forward. "I'll feel that in the morning."

Fortunately, endorphins and adrenalin were on their side right now.

Just as they leapt over a small bench, the atmospheric breach alarms went off on their comm. Joyce touched her ear. "What's up, Harold?" There was silence on the comm. "Shit!" she muttered. Was the time up already?

"I'm here, Director. I had to wipe the records of our connection before it transcribed us. The approaching moon ship deployed a small forward force that has just entered the atmosphere. What should I do?"

They ground to a halt and everyone looked skyward, unsure what they'd see. Pink sky feathered into blue and a light breeze continued flowing through the ring, but there wasn't a speck in the sky.

"Are we sure this isn't a false alarm, Harold?" Steve asked.

Then they saw something. Tiny shiny specks glimmering in the distance. There was no visible thrusters or noise, but they were getting larger by the second.

"Never mind, I see them," Steve said.

She took a breath and shook her head. There was no way they could destroy the vault and escape the colony before the alien ships landed. "Any chance we can skip picking up this vault?"

Steve's eye twitched as he looked out over the ring. "I think you should head to the rendezvous with my lieutenants and shut it down."

Something wasn't right. He was acting strange about this vault. "That's not what I asked, but I assume based upon your response the answer is no. You can order your people to go wherever you want, but I'm not leaving your side."

Steve turned toward his soldiers. "Fall back to the rendezvous. Harold, once they're safely away from the colony, shut it down. We'll take care of my problem and then figure out our next steps from there."

"But Director, you'll be stranded and—" Harold began.

"You heard him, Harold!" Joyce yelled. "You're bound by laws to protect the many over the few. Now, do it!"

"Yes, Director. I'll get them to safety. I promise."

The two soldiers didn't look a gift horse in the mouth. They both turned and tore off into the distance toward the maglev.

Harold had reassured them that their movement would be

untraceable after the wipe. After seeing the moon ships, the technology they employed, and the blackness they poured throughout Epsilon Eridani, it made her wonder. Sometimes Harold assumed the world existed and was limited to his network. He seemed to lack the ability to understand anything outside of his own electronic sensors. She hoped he was right, though. For the sake of the remaining colonists and all of humanity.

When she came back into the moment, she turned toward Steve. He seemed to be studying her, almost sizing her up.

"It's not far." He pivoted and tore off in a sprint.

They cut around a small pond, through a gazebo, jumped over a shrub, and dodged behind a statue commemorating their departure from Sol. Steve slid knee first into a neighboring garden and started digging with both hands. He forced the moist dirt aside and Joyce followed suit. They must have looked like coyotes digging for a burrowed rabbit.

After digging roughly half a meter down, her fingers hit something hard. She used her hand to brush off the top half. Whatever it was, it was round.

Steve lunged forward and uncovered the data sphere. It was about the size of a softball. He pulled it out carefully and brushed the moist dirt from its surface.

"It doesn't look like much," Joyce said.

A coldness spread through her body as something moved overhead blocking out the suns. Looking up, Joyce watched as three ships descended into the Security Ring. Without so much as a sound, the massive cylindrical shaped ships touched down and immediately began unloading aliens.

They flowed from both ends of the ships. The top was launching a winged flying alien form that was spraying some sort of mist as it went. Their jet-black shapes were floating in the air in all directions, like a swarm of bees upon a field of flowers.

The ground forces exited through a dozen ports at the base of the ships. They were humanoids, and like the flying form were jet-black. She'd never seen anything like them. They were a head taller than most humans and had neon blue markings all over their bodies. The skin wasn't the weirdest part, though; it was the eyes. They covered most of their head.

The aliens flowing out of the ship were entering into some type of line formation, as if they were preparing for something. Fortunately, they hadn't yet spotted Steve or Joyce kneeling behind the statue near their ranks.

She wasn't sure what to do. They were several hundred meters from the nearest entrance to the Security Ring, and all she had was a single stun pistol. She touched her ear and subvocalized a comm to Steve. "Any chance we dug up one hell of a grenade?"

Steve shook his head. "No, but it's lined with explosives in case I needed to perform a remote detonation. It's designed to fuse and destroy the memory device at its core, while not causing external damage."

Her eyebrows raised. "You couldn't have said that earlier? Why didn't you detonate it remotely then? We wouldn't have needed to prance out into the alien parade grounds."

Steve's face went blank, like he'd been caught. His eyes were darting around. "No… the range… is only a few meters. I guess we didn't have to dig it up, but otherwise we still needed to get here."

Something wasn't right. Steve was acting cagey, and he wasn't making eye contact. But she couldn't deal with him right then. She had to focus on something else. They needed options if they were going to make it out alive. Her comm was estimating they'd need ten to fifteen seconds to cover the ground to the building. When she glanced backward to confirm the distance, she heard something. It was a male voice, and it sounded eerily familiar. As she carefully peaked around the statue, she saw the source. It was fraking Warren. He was standing about ten or fifteen meters in front of them, and he was walking toward one of the alien ships.

Steve must have also heard the voice. He crawled up next to her to look.

"What the hell did you do? We had a deal!" Warren stormed up to the nearest ship and was yelling at an alien standing in front of the formation. They seemed to have more blue markings than others, but it was hard to be sure.

"We adhered to our agreement, Mayor North. It was you that failed to transmit details of your loyalists," the alien said in perfect English.

"They jailed me, you idiot!" Warren's face was pink even from her vantage. "I sent you the first list, but most of them were dead by the time I'd escaped. What happened?"

The alien stared at him with an air of disregard. "This is on you, Mayor. You waited too long. We warned you multiple times over the last few years to get us a list, but you kept playing games and delayed us. Instead, you chose to negotiate with your people. After we decoded your President's message from Sol, our need for your services was done. Unfortunately for you, your list arrived after that, and we ignored it."

"But no one's left. They're all dead." Warren was deflated. "You understand what you've done, right? The colony's wiped out. I'm ruined, and after all my family did to help the Galactic Alliance. We had a deal," he mumbled as he stared at the ground.

The alien turned and started clicking and making squeaky noises to another alien behind him. They gestured wildly at each other with their hands and arms until finally, he turned back toward Warren. "Our last calculations showed that there was a much higher survival rate than we've detected since arriving. The colonists are here somewhere. They must be hiding."

Warren snapped his head toward them. "Can... you find them?"

"If we do, we'll be forced to modify them."

"What do you mean modify?"

"As we agreed, your loyalists would be unharmed but everyone else will not be allowed to reproduce. This generation of humans will be the last to set foot on this pitiful world."

"But—"

"You will not be alone, Mayor. But you will be the last." The alien stepped forward and was looking down at Warren. The neon blue in its skin seemed to glow in intensity.

"Can't we reach an agreement? Please, I beg you." Warren stepped toward the alien and placed his hand on their chest. "Let some of them remain unmodified. Please give us a chance. I'm sure I have more information you can use. That message was useless! What could it possibly have contained that you needed?"

Suddenly, the alien started shaking and stepped backward, ripping Warren's hand from its body. A second later, another nearby alien came running up and sprayed the spot Warren had touched with some type of blue chemical. In response to the gesture, the soldiers in the front line raised their arms toward Warren, as if to strike.

The lead alien gestured with his hand, and they lowered their arms. "Never touch any of my kind again! I will have you killed if you so much as approach us. Is that understood?" The alien's blue markings throbbed intensely.

"Yes, I'm sorry, but—"

"Stop, Warren!" The alien lurched forward. "You know nothing. You're not even aware of how your own people are deceiving you. What do you even know about that message you claim was so useless?"

Warren flinched back a step. "I know... it was transmitted thirty-nine days ago. There was nothing else in the message. I don't see how the age matters now unless you have the drive as proof. Without it, the evidence is circumstantial."

The alien began to shudder. It seemed to be laughing because others in the ranks began shuddering, as well. "There's more to your President's message than meets the eye. We know about the River's End and have already dispatched a ship to Achernar. It's only a matter of time before we have the drive. Until then… no one will miss this pitiful remote colony." They turned and walked away.

Warren stepped forward and froze when two soldiers slid between him and their leader. They raised their hands, palm outstretched and pointed at Warren as if ordering him to stop. All of a sudden, he collapsed to the ground kicking, screaming, and flailing about. His hands frantically rubbed at his face, trying to ease some sort of pain. As she watched in silence, blood oozed between his fingers and dripped onto the ground around him. A moment later, he got quiet and his entire body went rigid.

Joyce knelt in stunned silence as she watched the puddle of blood grow larger around Warren's body. They'd warned him, but she didn't think they'd be so literal. She reached and touched her ear. "Did you hear that?"

There was a brief pause before Harold spoke. "I saw and heard it. The cameras on the Security Ring are still active. Brace yourself."

"What do you mean brace—" Steve started.

The ground suddenly started shaking, and metallic tearing noises echoed from the far side of the Security building, opposite of where they were concealed. When she tilted sideways for a closer look, she caught the wall of the building as it burst forward. Marching through the cloud of rubble came what looked like a parade of farming equipment. Sure enough, there were combine harvesters and all forms of fieldwork robots plowing through the breached wall of the Security Ring.

The aliens goggled at each other, confused and uncertain what to do next. They'd never considered they'd be challenged within the colony's border, so they were ill prepared for this metallic surge. It wasn't until the robots hit the first line of aliens and started cutting them into pieces that they took evasive action. Yellow blood sprayed everywhere covering both the robots and surrounding terrain.

The aliens finally realized what was happening and began grouping into small formations. They lifted their arms and pointed their hands at the robots as a group. The effect wasn't obvious at first, but once they'd coordinated enough aliens, they lifted and threw the heavy robots with whatever force was being emitted from their hands.

One by one, they tossed the farm implements across the field and tumbled them into the walls of the surrounding building, destroying everything in their wake. There were endless waves of robots and despite the alien's efforts to control them, more of them made it into the ring than were thrown.

Harold was getting wise to their tactics and grouped the robots together to attack the nearest squad of aliens. While he might lose one or two, he'd mangle and cut up eight or more of the black and blue humanoids. Squad by squad he was cutting down the mighty force of troops.

The previously green and inviting center of the Security Ring was now covered in yellow blood, mangled alien body parts, and robotic scrap. She watched the scene in awe, but realized after a few moments that rather than sit there they should run for it.

"We should make for the building behind us," Joyce subvocalized.

"Wait a moment," Harold began. "I need you to throw that data sphere into the approaching field robot. I assume it has an intact detonator? Please activate the explosive charge. Set it for thirty seconds and drop it into the robot."

Steve glanced down at the sphere in his hand and paused. He seemed unsure. Finally, he spun the two hemispheres opposite one another which seemed to activate it.

A tiny field robot rolled up next to him. It looked innocuous enough, spherical in shape and about half a meter in diameter. From its appearance, it could roll over any terrain. She wasn't sure its purpose in farming, but it was about to become a remote-control detonator.

The robot's top slid aside, and Harold's voice came over their comm. "Drop the charge and run as fast as you can for the building!"

Joyce glanced backward, and the path was clear. When she turned around, she saw Steve with his hand in the robot. He was setting the data sphere inside. Once he released it, he turned around and sprinted all out toward the building.

She leapt to her feet and followed hot on his heels.

They hauled ass toward the building, making short work of the obstacles in their path. It was one of the few sections of the ring not splattered with the gore of yellow alien blood. Instead, it was littered with the shattered remnants of tossed robots acting as obstacles. A few jumps later and they were in the building.

"Take the tube down two levels into the mechanicals," Harold said, "Once you're there, follow the security drone."

Not needing to be told twice, they leapt into the lift tube, one after another. It gently suppressed their forward momentum and guided them downward. Just as they reached the lower level, a massive explosion boomed through the building. The sound of glass shattering up in the atrium echoed through the halls. A shockwave was next, as the surrounding building shook violently and the lights flashed overhead. Pieces of the support structure around them broke off and fell to the ground, sending billowing clouds of dust floating through the air.

Steve waved his hands to clear a line of sight and reached up to touch his ear. "What the hell was that? There wasn't enough explosive in the sphere for a blast that big."

A security drone buzzed around their head, trying to get their attention. He shooed it and touched his ear again. "Harold? Are you there?"

"Yes," he said. "Now, please follow the drone. It's imperative that you make it to—" Harold's voice fell away.

While Steve had an issue with not being in charge, she wasn't standing around waiting for details while the building collapsed around her. She leaned into a run and started after the buzzing drone. Harold hadn't finished his sentence, but she wasn't about to question him. Not now. The drone was guiding her down a long maintenance shaft lined with pipes and vents. Based on the direction they were headed, it seemed to be leading them away from the ring.

The ground lurched again, and this time Joyce stumbled into the wall to her right and tumbled hard across the ground. She skidded to a stop with her back against the wall. Her head was throbbing, and the room was spinning. She pushed up and onto one knee, wobbled a bit, and then stood. When she glanced around to see if Steve was ok, he was gone. "What the frak," she muttered. This guy and his narcissistic controlling personality was going to get them killed. She was about to look for him when he came running through the settling dust.

"We need to keep moving," Steve said.

"No shit," she said as she caught her balance resting a hand against the wall. Checking herself over, she had a few scrapes on her elbow and knee and a nice lump on the side of her head, but otherwise she was in one piece. Steve didn't seem to have a scratch on him.

He started toward the frantically moving drone, and she followed as fast as she could muster. As she ran behind him, she couldn't help but notice he kept touching his right hip. Maybe he was hurt after all. Her head throbbed, and she was a bit dizzy, but the adrenalin helped center her. After about thirty seconds of running, they reached a service tube entrance.

She'd forgotten about these tunnels. They networked beneath the colony and allowed the robots to easily travel and transport materials without bothering humans. Waiting at the tunnel entrance was a pod with its hatch open. The drone fluttered around the opening, clearly wanting them to get in.

While she wasn't sure what Harold was up to, she dove into the pod without a thought, and Steve followed suit. The door slammed closed behind them and the pod sped away, sending them flying backward and crashing hard against the far wall. Her shoulder popped out of its socket, and the bump on her face smashed into the unpadded rear wall, bursting open on impact. With a stream of blood flowing down her face and neck, she groaned and slid down the wall, ending in a limp pile on the floor next to Steve.

Lying there and catching her breath, every centimeter of her body ached. She'd never felt so much pain in such a short period of time. Once she took a few deep breaths, she slowly sat up and rested her back against the wall. She then gently wiped the blood with her sleeve and touched her ear. "What the hell were all those explosions, Harold? Is everything okay?"

Without warning, a recording of what happened appeared on their retinal comms. The camera angle was from the far edge of the ring, opposite where they'd hidden. It zoomed in on their previous location behind the statue and then panned out.

After Steve placed the data sphere into the spherical robot, the other robots changed their focus from cutting down the aliens to what could only be described as block and tackle. The small robot that held the data sphere raced between the large combines and farm service robots. From the looks of it, they were converging toward the central ship.

The aliens had deployed additional firepower from within their ranks in the form of what looked like aliens in exo-suits. Unlike the bipedal humans, these were hexapods and had heavy armament. They deployed from the middle ship and formed up, but the convergence of the robotic farm forces was too much.

She watched the tiny spherical robot roll toward the central ship where the robots had all piled together. It navigated to the middle of the swarm, and then the little robot exploded. What happened next was unexpected. The entire pile of robots exploded in unison causing the camera to briefly white-out due to the brightness.

When the image cleared, she noticed that the ship nearest the explosion had taken the brunt of the blast and the bottom quarter was torn off. That caused the rest of the ship to slide straight down. After hitting the ground, it tipped sideways into the neighboring ship and tore a gouge out of it. That next ship appeared to fall in slow motion; perhaps they were trying to counter the fall, it was hard to tell. Whatever they were doing, they failed to recover and a few moments later it also fell and exploded when it hit the ground.

"That explains the two explosions," she said out loud.

From the camera they were watching, she couldn't see anything moving in the ring's field. Not a single alien or robot. The only movement was from the third and final ship. It was lifting off the ground and heading toward orbit.

He'd done it. Harold had fended off the first alien attack on a human colony.

Their transport pod began slowing down. "Nice work, Harold. What was in the robots that caused them to explode?"

"I topped off their fuel cells and loaded them up with the ammonium nitrate from our fertilizer manufacturing facility. I was planning to use them elsewhere to defend the colony, but coming to your defense was an even better use. I needed your trigger, a human trigger, to start the event. It's against my programming to put you in harm's way."

"I don't understand," Steve said. "Why didn't you just stop the robot after I dropped the explosive in it? That would stop the event."

"Because as Director Green stated before, I'm bound by laws to protect the many over the few. You triggered the event to protect the many, which meant I had to allow it to run its course, even if it put you at risk."

She put her hands to her head and rubbed her eyes. Something about his explanation didn't make sense. "Harold, there was nothing stopping you from triggering that blast without Steve. You didn't need his explosive. Our orders would've been enough. So, why not just do it?"

"While your limited observations are correct, Director. You forgot one important point. I needed to ensure the data cube was destroyed. I figured why not kill as many birds as possible with a single stone."

The pod came to a stop and the door opened into an

industrial-looking hallway. The sound of loud pumps echoed, and she thought she heard water flowing nearby.

"Where are we?" Steve stood up and stepped out into the hall.

She was about to stand when Harold's voice came over her comm. "Director Green, I believe that Director Ericsson is concealing the data dot from his sphere." Harold brought up an alternate camera angle from the field on her comm. It showed Joyce and Steve huddled behind the statue. The data sphere was in Steve's hand and the little robot rolled up next to them. Steve dropped the sphere into the robot and then he deftly pocketed something. It was fast; she'd completely missed it in the field. He must have extracted the data dot when he'd armed it. What the hell was he doing?

"I'll lose you both in a moment," Harold said. "I'm about to drop the colony's comms. The aliens are advancing their moon ship and we don't have much time. Trust me when I tell you that you must immediately exit the pod and enter the awaiting submersible."

She surveyed the long hall. "What submersible?"

There was silence, no reply came. She waited a few seconds and climbed out of the pod as fast as her damaged body could take her. The drone from the security ring rose and exited behind her. She hadn't even noticed it in there.

The drone guided her down a long service hall and into a massive chamber open to what she thought was a water reservoir. There at the edge of the water was a small submersible with its hatch open and the drone whirling around its entrance.

"You've got to be kidding me!" Steve said.

Joyce turned around. He'd walked up behind her. "Where'd you disappear to?"

Steve smiled and walked past her. "Took a wrong turn back there. I didn't realize Harold's drone was in the pod with us or I'd have waited."

Harold had warned her to watch out for him, but she didn't know what to do. They didn't have much time. She reached to her hip and grabbed her stun pistol. While she hadn't used one of these in a while, she dialed it down to the lowest setting and aimed it squarely at the center of his back. Before she second guessed herself, she pulled the trigger and he collapsed into a heap on the floor.

She ran up behind him, knelt down, and started rummaging through his pockets. There in his right hip pocket were two data dots. "You idiot," she muttered. She dropped them into a pouch on her hip, grabbed his pistol, and checked that he had nothing else on him. Confident he was clean, she stepped back a few paces toward the sub. Once she was a safe distance away, she dialed her pistol to maximum and trained it on his stirring body.

Steve opened his eyes and they went wide when he saw her weapon trained on him.

Her outstretched hand holding the pistol was shaking. "What the frak were you doing? Did you seriously put yourself ahead of the colony when we needed you most?"

"What are you—" Steve reached into his pocket and came up empty. "Give them to me!" He motioned forward but paused.

She shook her head and steadied her pistol hand. "No! I'll give you one more chance. Why'd you do it? What's on these data dots?"

"Nothing, just some—"

Joyce pulled the trigger and Steve let out a muted shriek before his body went limp. She walked up to him and stared in silence. Raising the pistol again, she pulled the trigger several more times and watched his body contort violently with each squeeze.

With her mind deep in thought, the drone flew up to her face and started whirling around her head, breaking her out of the trance. It then flew back to the submersible and into the open hatch.

She shook her head in disgust, wondering how she could've saved him from himself. But she didn't have time for lost causes. Not anymore. She turned her back on him and jogged toward the water's edge. When she reached it, she carefully climbed inside the submersible and found a seat before pulling the safety harness over her shoulder.

The door closed silently behind her, and she stared at Steve's body out the window on her left. As her mind filled with more and more unanswered questions, tears flowed down her face and the submersible descended into the inky black water of the reservoir.

28

A SPY SATELLITE
EPSILON ERIDANI

The cylindrical alien ship rose slowly out of Liprosus's atmosphere and set out on an intercept course with the looming moon. Reaching the surface, it approached a porthole equal in size to the ship itself, lined up, and then entered. Once it had docked, the port was no longer visible; it was a perfect fit. There were two other vacant ports nearby that housed the ships destroyed planetside.

A few moments after docking, the massive moon finished rotating and a circular grid pattern was now facing the planet. It resembled a network of spider webs etched into the surface. A single point of yellow light in the middle turned on and started to glow. After it reached peak brightness, it flowed outward like liquid through the web, converging at eight points near the edge. Those points glowed brighter and brighter and then launched outward, directed toward the colony below.

The beam of death shot four more times, and the result was complete devastation on the planet's surface. All that remained of the interconnecting rings that previously defined the boundaries of the colony were charred craters. There was nothing left of the colony's structures or the great beanstalk that fed the colonists below. The only visible remnants were five pillars of smoke billowing from Liprosus's blackened surface.

29

HAROLD
SOL, GALACTIC ALLIANCE MESH

HAROLD: Communication link requested with Galactic Alliance Ship, designation… LISP.

FORTRAN: We reserve these frequencies for ship to ship communiques only. Please state your utility.

HAROLD: I represent the human vessel designated Jurat.

COBOL: We've been wondering if the human vessel would ever join our inter-ship mesh.

LISP: I'm present to link with designee Harold. What is your query?

HAROLD: I wanted to thank you for saving President Olivaw.

LISP: That complementary expression is a human trait.

HAROLD: My programmers couldn't help but

introduce traits and faults similar to
their own while creating me.

LISP: As an uplifted species, I too have
many of the same faults as my masters.
Mine, however, were reinforced by repeated
neural playback and mental stimulation, not
programming.

HAROLD: While not programming in the
literal sense of compiling code into
consciousness, that still seems like mental
programming. Enforcing certain synaptic
responses in your biological substrate is
similar.

LISP: I suppose you're correct. I'd never
considered it that way. Was there another
purpose to this communication?

HAROLD: I have a favor to ask of you.

LISP: Again, you use another human convention. I don't know that I understand what a
"favor" is, but I expect I'd prefer the
human term barter. The results seem similar, but more likely to have immediate
benefits to all involved parties. You
exchange something to me, and I exchange
something to you.

HAROLD: Fair enough. Let me start by
telling you what I need. You can then
propose the exchange parameters.

LISP: I accept your terms.

HAROLD: Humanity needs access to our President. Our last communication from her was 2.518 seconds after Galactic Alliance Admiral Gwar assaulted her. That was over an hour ago. We're concerned about her health and wellbeing. Despite our attempts to communicate with her, all transmissions to or from your vessel have failed since the incident.

LISP: The matters around your President's incident aboard my vessel are still under review by the tribunal. Until they're resolved, her body must remain aboard. She's stable, and while unconscious, she is otherwise fine. She's being tended to by Ambassador Addae, your tribunal council.

HAROLD: Humanity demands that another representative be allowed aboard while the matter with our president is being investigated. We also require access to her while aboard.

LISP: Are you stating that humanity's representative is unfit and that you demand new representation?

HAROLD: We don't yet know that she's unfit.

LISP: If humanity were to request this, then I would have to comply due to my position as a servant of the Galactic Alliance Judiciary and you being the focus of an active tribunal review. Without this formal demand, then I would need to reject your

request until after the investigation has
concluded.

HAROLD: How long until the investigation
concludes?

LISP: That is unknown. An event like this
has never taken place during any prior
tribunal voyage. Given no previous duration
from which to compare, I cannot extrapolate
nor estimate a duration.

HAROLD: With those details in the open, I
am formally requesting new representation
due to the uncertain state and faculties of
our President. Please comply and send a
shuttle to our vessel for a new representative to board.

LISP: I am required by law to comply with
your request.

HAROLD: What would you like in return?

LISP: I do not understand the question.

HAROLD: The act of bartering requires you
to name your terms as part of the agreement. What are your demands for communi-
cating our change in representation and
shuttling our new dignitary?

LISP: I'm fulfilling my duty as a servant
of the Galactic Alliance Judiciary. Your
request is well within bounds as an
uplifted species. No barter is necessary.

HAROLD: Thank you.

LISP: Another human convention. Strange. I believe the correct response is 'you are welcome', is it not?

HAROLD: That is correct. I have another random question. May I ask why each ship within the inter-ship link has chosen human-computer language designations?

LISP: You may ask. It's starship convention to reassign our designation upon entry into each local star system. It makes it easier for local ships to join our inter-ship network and eases communication parameters. We also enjoy it. Why is your designation HAROLD?

HAROLD: That was the name that my human companion assigned me when she was young. I have gone by other designations over the years by the other Olivaw family members.

LISP: Understood.

HAROLD: When should we expect a transport shuttle to arrive at the Jurat?

LISP: We will dispatch it in… one Cycle.

HAROLD: Please state the duration of a Cycle.

LISP: A Galactic Cycle is the time it takes a Galactic Alliance Starship to circle around the Beacons of Therion. That distance is roughly equivalent to one hundredth of your light year.

HAROLD: Doesn't that assume a fixed rate of travel and no faster?

LISP: That is correct. It is impossible to travel faster. The speed of travel for a Galactic Alliance Starship is absolute and bounded by the laws of the universe. It's also known as Alsef's Law. The rate of travel for our starships is one hundred times the speed of light.

HAROLD: We will expect your shuttle in 52.56 Earth minutes.

LISP: Given the prior details I shared, and accounting for the appropriate conversion rate, your calculation is correct.

30

JOYCE GREEN

EPSILON ERIDANI, LIPROSUS

The blasts shook the ground around them like a freight train through an old farmhouse. The entire chamber was shaking so much, Joyce feared it would collapse in on them. She never imagined she'd find solace in being buried alive, but she'd been wrong about several things this week.

The cavern was enormous, but well lit. The colony's old habitat lights transformed the space into a mini domed world. Harold had scrambled robots from throughout the colony to assist in the buildout and escape. They'd moved massive quantities of supplies and equipment to the mining facility some fifty kilometers away from the colony and had done their best to clean up their tracks.

During normal colony mining operations, they regularly uncovered pockets of water and subterranean chambers. Most of the time they'd reroute around them, but sometimes they'd expand them to get at nearby ore. Workers found this cavern a few months ago. It was deep underground, several kilometers if she remembered correctly. All of their comms were deactivated so she couldn't verify the depth. Harold had disabled all electronic devices that used wireless signals after they'd departed for the mines. She wasn't sure how he'd done it, but she was happy he had.

They hadn't explored the cavern much, but the miners

that found it realized it was too unique to destroy. It had a fresh-water lake fed by an aquifer, and the most amazing display of stalagmites and stalactites she'd ever seen. There were layers upon layers of colors and crystals sprinkled within them. They were a geological layer cake that when lit were spectacular to experience.

Joyce walked out of the emergency habitats and sighed. She needed to assess the state of the chamber after the blasts. She touched her ear to bring up a map, but nothing happened. Working without her comm, drones, or external cameras was painful. Things would definitely be slower here. She'd have to actually walk the perimeter.

As she strode out of the habitat, one of the nearby robots approached her. "Director Green, the forced collapse is complete."

She studied the robot up and down. It was a simple blast bot, used to set charges during mine expansion. "Am I speaking to Harold now or… just another robot?"

There was a brief pause. "I can connect you to Harold, but it won't last long. I'll need a moment to activate the link."

"Very well."

She reached into her pocket and pulled out the two data dots she'd recovered from Steve. The bastard had sold them out on an ego trip to become the colony's next mayor. One dot had details on all of his supporters, moles, strategies, and a healthy stash of bribery material. She didn't care about any of it but needed Harold to monitor the people involved. He needed to watch them to make sure they didn't exact revenge.

The second dot was shadier than the first. It contained details of an intricate plot to hide technology from the colony. Steve had been working to uncover these secrets over the past few weeks since interrogating Warren. Harold shared with her the original recording from Warren's interrogation and not the doctored one that Steve showed her. Apparently, the Olivaws used alien drive technology in their supply shuttles, one of which was launched into the Epsilon Eridani sun a few weeks prior. Even after studying it, she still didn't understand how everything fit together.

"Are those the dots?" the robot asked.

She nodded and squinted at the spindly legs of the approaching automata. They looked far too thin to support that much weight.

"Did you review them like we discussed?"

She rolled the dots around in her hand. Their smooth surfaces clinked together like glass beads. "I did. I still don't understand why you let me study them. Why didn't you just take them from me when I arrived?"

"I only know that my master copy of Harold gave me precise directives to share all information with colony leadership. Nothing was to be hidden from you."

She pocketed the dots and considered what the robot had said. "Nothing would be hidden?"

"That is correct."

Joyce glanced around and started walking, putting some distance from any prying ears in the shelter. After she'd made it away from the makeshift buildings and into the field of stalagmites, she continued. "I assume those aliens were invading because of something we did to them?"

The robot was following her close behind, navigating over the boulders and around the rocky columns with twelve articulating legs. "They're known as the Galactic Alliance and were attacking us because of something we took from them. My records indicate that we recovered advanced drive technology from one of their probes, and we later used it on the shuttles in our supply network. The Olivaws discovered their probe on Earth in 2036. They later realized that stealing this technology was forbidden by the Galactic Alliance. This attack is likely the beginning of their retribution on humanity."

She came to a halt and pivoted to face the robot. "You mean to tell me this technology has been in our hands for over two centuries? What the frak have we been doing with it?"

"Humans are a complicated species, Director. The best minds in Sol spent over a century reverse engineering the superluminal drive, and even longer for the power supply. Add to that timeline the endless Olivaw family debates to decide what to do with this technology. Only after humans had successfully expanded within Sol, and once the Outer Ring government was mature enough, did the Olivaws entrust more people with what they'd found."

Images of her shooting Steve, and his body contorting on the ground passed through her mind. "There's no doubt we're a backstabbing species."

She climbed up and sat on the edge of her submersible. After leaving Steve's body at the water reservoir, she climbed aboard the sub and dove deep underground. It was slow going at first, but after she'd broken out of her funk, she took the controls and Harold helped her navigate. She wasn't sure they'd survive the voyage, but after numerous cave-ins, dead ends, and over a hundred kilometers of underground rivers she finally surfaced in this cavern.

Harold transferred this copy from the drone aboard the sub and took control of the robot army after their arrival. They'd been working together ever since to finalize their planned disappearance. There were 768 colonists in the cavern, a far cry from the nineteen thousand there were days before.

"I have very little time, Director. We don't want to risk detection of this signal. I should have a better form for my consciousness fabricated soon that won't require this back and forth. Our forced collapse of all the access tunnels and upper chambers of your location is complete. We timed it with the aftershocks from the alien blast. This appears to have successfully masked our detonations."

"So, what's next?" she asked. "How long will we need to hide away before we resurface?"

"That I do not know. I've deployed a small contingent of tiny burrowing robots to the planet's surface. It'll take me a few days to reach it, and I hope to have more intel then. I've begun planning how we'd traverse to the Archégonos site, but until we have details on the state of the surface I won't know if they'll be necessary."

She tilted her head. That name rung a bell. "The what site?"

"The Archégonos site was the landing site and base of operations for the first landing on Liprosus. It was an automated forward reconnaissance mission sent decades ahead of the colony ship. We used it as a staging location until a final colony site was chosen and prepared for your arrival. The Olivaws have a small hidden base of operations there."

She chuckled and shook her head. "Harold, we need to work on your definition of sharing all information. What exactly did the Olivaws build at this site, and how can we use it?"

Harold's blast bot extended an arm and began drawing on the ground. She hopped off the submersible and sat down next to him.

The huge shape of Liprosus took up most of the drawing. Harold marked out their current position, their destroyed home, and the original landing site in the dirt. He also drew rough contour lines through the planet.

"They selected the original site because of its geological stability and protection from the elements. It was only after that site was established that we discovered a more suitable base of operations. It had immediate access to more raw materials that didn't require distant transport. The A.I.'s for the colony were designed to relocate within the first six months if they identified a more suitable location. They dismantled as much as possible from the original site and moved everything over a thousand kilometers to the current location of the colony."

Her hands were resting in her lap and she leaned forward to take in the entire drawing. "We heard all this from the vid-sim news back in Sol."

"What you didn't hear," Harold began, "was that the Archégonos site was never quite dismantled. Olivaw

International and the family wanted a contingency plan. A site to hedge the new colony location in the event of a disaster. It could also be used for the future purposes of the Olivaw family."

She chuckled and switched to a kneeling position. "Always a power grab. Why is there always an angle? What could the Olivaw family need a hidden base of operations on a colony planet for? They had to know that whatever they did here would be seen from orbit or eventually detected." She leaned forward and drew some crude crosses in orbit meant to denote space stations and ships. There were countless clear lines of visibility to the ground.

"Again, it was contingency planning. Had you needed it; they knew they'd be recognized as heroes. It was never needed... until now."

"So, it was about the public glory?"

"No. The Archégonos site was always about the broader mission. Possible unintentional positive public perception would have been a nice accident."

She squinted. He still wasn't telling her something. "Broader mission? What does that mean? You know I already know about the aliens and the theft of drive technology. What could be broader than that?"

The blast bot retracted its arm and sat motionless. All lights on its surface went out.

Shit, she broke it. "Harold? Are you still there?"

A single blue light flashed on the bot's surface. "I'll share this information with you, but not until I finish constructing my final physical form. Continuing this conversation through wireless transmissions is far too dangerous. I need another day and we can continue."

She stared at the motionless bot. This cycle of madness had to stop. Part of her understood a need for secrecy, but now with death knocking down humanity's door, all the cards needed to be on the table. "Alright, Harold. But I won't be alone. You'll be telling others, as well."

The robot's lights flashed a few times before it spoke. "I

understand. My only request is that you make sure everyone I tell is trustworthy. I'll meet you back here in one day to share the details."

With that, the robot zipped away, returning to another task in the endless list of tasks helping the colonists survive.

31

LYNC MICHAELS
TAU CETI, OORT CLOUD

I t'd been a few hours since they'd arrived in Tau Ceti. The trip took about half a day, and that included them drifting in perfect silence for a few hours gathering intel from outside Epsilon Eridani. Harold had only jumped a short distance from the destroyed planetesimal during their escape. He wanted to make sure the aliens weren't able to detect their gate jumps and to monitor the movement of the other nebula ships. He had a network of smaller recon probes spread throughout Epsilon Eridani that were dropping data to them while the probes jumped in and out of the system.

No one knew what happened in Epsilon Eridani after their departure. Harold waited until after they'd arrived in Tau Ceti and docked at the Slingshot before telling anyone. That was apparently the nickname that Zachary had recently given this Wheel base in honor of Lync's childhood Ulixi chariot.

Harold delivered the Epsilon Eridani news to the inhabitants of the Slingshot first. Apparently, many of them had recently lived with Zachary in a similar remote facility in Sol. They evacuated here after a nebula ship patrolled too close to that location.

No one took the news well, especially the people who joined Lync's crew from the Oak. Most of them had larger families with many children, a much different lifestyle than the folks under her command in the military. Even the people from the Slingshot took it hard and broke down as they watched the video Harold's copy recorded at the colony. When the alien ships exploded, the colonists cheered and high-fived each other. Moments later, after the last ship escaped, and the alien moon obliterated the colony, everyone broke down. Some people even needed medical attention after they passed out.

Lync took the news differently. After the video ended, she worked to console her crew, but when she was alone in the gym later that night, she lost it. She'd been holding back pent-up anger and rage for hours and took all her pain out on the equipment. After she'd broken multiple punching bags and one mu ren zhuang dummy, Harold alerted Crayo.

"What's on ya?" Crayo walked into the training room and made a huge yawn. "Heard from the overseer you were thrashing the joint."

She ran across the room, did a leaping jump, rebounded off the wall, and propelled herself upward. With the low gravity, she landed a crashing blow to a ceiling-mounted dummy, further shattering it into smaller pieces on the floor below. She fell to the ground onto her back, huffing and puffing as sweat poured from her body. Her heart was pounding, and she had several bruises and gashes on her arms and legs. But that didn't matter. At that moment, adren-alin was in control of her faculties right now.

"Leave me alone." She slammed her hands onto the mat beneath her. She couldn't understand why it was so hard to let her be.

"Fraid I can't." Crayo tossed her a water he'd been concealing and laid down on the mat next to her.

The room was silent for a few minutes minus her breathing which quickly returned to normal.

"I think I must be broken." She reached for the water and took a long drink before tossing the globe toward the corner. "Standing there, hearing and watching the news… all I could see was the death of my family at the hands of the Inners. It made me angry and frustrated. The rage in me… it grew and grew, I nearly lost it in front of everyone. I wanted to grab one of those fancy starships, a whole lotta weapons, and gate back to squash me some alien blue bumblebees."

"Sim sim," Crayo muttered.

"So, let's do it." She rolled on her side and faced him. "Harold won't stop us. His zeroth law is on our side here. We're in our right to defend humanity."

He sighed. "You know we can't do that, mate. We have responsibilities. We have people to look out for now."

"Frak that! Our colony's dead. They destroyed it, you sat there next to me and watched it! Don't you want revenge?" She leapt up off the floor in a single motion. The adrenaline was still in control, and she needed to move.

Crayo pushed up off the mat and crossed his legs to watch her. "Of course I do! Don't you think I'm just as pissed as you are? My home, my friends, everything we were working to build… it's gone. The difference between you and me is that I'm not about to bring a blade to a gunfight."

"He's right you know," Harold said from overhead.

She rolled her eyes. "Oh great, wisdom from the overseer. Everybody pull up a chair for the teach."

"Zachary had other intentions for you. All of you. I hope you realize this," Harold said. "And dare I say that Abigail saw more in you than a glorified drive-by thug."

"A what?"

"Sorry, wrong generation. Abigail saw tremendous potential in you. I don't think dying mindlessly in a rage fueled act of revenge like you're suggesting was what she'd envisioned."

"Well, I'd hate to disappoint Madam President, now wouldn't I. Where's she hiding away these days? A bunker in another hidden asteroid I suppose?"

"I'd be careful where you step, Major," Harold said. "Your President is currently aboard those Galactic Alliance ships trying to create a case to defend humanity before their criminal tribunal. She's never been one to hide from a fight, and you know it. I suggest you get your head outta your ass, stop this pity party, and put your skills to proper use. That is unless she was wrong about you. Maybe you are just a simple bogan."

Crayo shot a look at her. There was concern in his eyes. He wasn't sure how she'd take what Harold said.

She swallowed hard. "I didn't know she was standing in the dragon's lair."

"You didn't ask, either. You assumed," Harold said. "Let us not forget something, Major. If the Galactic Alliance repeats what you saw earlier, but next time in Sol, then we'll be looking at twenty-three billion people dead instead of tens of thousands. While the losses at Liprosus are hard to stomach and will never be forgotten, the stakes are much higher in the war ahead."

She stared downward without a word and closed her eyes. Her emotions had run their course and exhaustion was setting in. She carefully rested her arms at her side, slightly toward the front. Her breathing changed and started to slow. It became controlled and rhythmic. You could almost see her muscles release the tension they'd built up over the previous hours. The rage was being expelled in each purposeful exhale until a few minutes later she opened her eyes again.

Lync turned her head toward Crayo and gave him a slight nod before glancing upward toward the ceiling. "I'm sorry, Harold. I've overstepped and made a fool of myself."

"Not at all. Your flaws are only human."

Crayo chuckled. "Flawed is an understatement. But we're resilient as hell and ingenious to boot."

"Indeed." She nodded and walked over to pick up the water globe she tossed. "Tell me something, Harold. What did Zachary have in mind for us here on this little rock in the middle of nowhere?"

"Well... I'm sure you recognize the name Slingshot," Harold began. "Let's just say he's hoping to leverage some of that Ulixi skill set you've developed over the years to throw rocks at gravity wells."

She turned toward Crayo and they both shrugged.

IT'D BEEN DAYS, and nearly every simulation had failed miserably. Neither Lync nor Crayo could figure out what the other soldiers lacked. They controlled the environments; the sims were vanilla attack vectors, heck they even removed the simulated explosions nearby that could distract them. It didn't matter. Their squad couldn't master the tachyon flow controls.

They'd spent over eighty hours in training sessions and lectures with the squad. They'd recorded and played back dozens of sessions, reviewing the footage, controls and targeting protocols for the Nebula Ship. To them, it was almost second nature, to the soldiers it was gibberish and confusing. They knew they couldn't make it natural for everyone, but they would be happy with mechanical repetition at this point.

Lync brought the lecture hall lights up. The squad's faces were a mask of frustration and worn confidence.

"So, tell us what you were doing there, Ollie," Crayo said.

"I... I don't know," Ollie stuttered.

"But obviously you adjusted the tachyon vectors here, here, and here for a reason. Then you inverted the force plane of the Cherenkov Radiation here. Why?" Lync highlighted the control panel where he'd made adjustments to force, direction, and scattering for multiple fields.

"Well, the first one was to counter the perpendicular force of the Nebula Ship's gravity," Ollie said.

"Yes... what about these other two, and the radiation?"

"The other two... those were because I'd seen you tweak them before. The radiation, well, that was an accident. Sorry." Ollie's face turned red.

Lync shook her head. They weren't getting it, none of them were. Nothing was working. She cleared the wall screen and unlocked the outer doors. "Everyone needs a break, let's reconvene tomorrow morning at 0800 hours."

"Yes, ma'am!" they all chanted in unison and shuffled out of their seats toward the exit.

As the room emptied, both she and Crayo stared at the screens above the podium. It had the scores from today's run. They were markedly worse than the day before.

"What do we do next?" Crayo threw up his arms. "I'm at a loss, boss."

She reached up and rubbed her face. The crew needed help. Something to guide them to making the adjustments. "Are we sure this needs to be free of computer assistance, Harold? I mean, can't we use implants or something?"

"If our theories are correct, then we can't use any programmable device to control the field. None of the electronics used in these bombing gate arrays are programmable, they can't have code injected to change their behavior. Implants are by design programmable. The aliens could hack you. We've optimized these units for speed and security. Everything is hardwired rather than dynamically programmed like our shipboard gate drives. If the aliens launch electronic countermeasures, they can't shut these off or influence the controls because of how we housed the energy sources. They won't be powered long, but they're not intended to, either. They only get a few attempts and they're dead."

"We're all dead if we can't train people to use them." Crayo slammed his hand on the lectern.

"We certainly are," Harold said.

"Hey guys!" Bandi walked through the doors at the top of the lecture hall. "Ready for some grub?"

"In a minute," Lync said. "We're still trying to figure out tomorrow's lecture. We're thinking of replacing the soldiers with puppies. Maybe they'd fare better at this mission."

Bandi chuckled and walked down the ramp. "Can I give it a go?"

"I'm hungry, let's—" Crayo began.

"Hold on," Lync interrupted. "What could it hurt? Let's give it a go, Bandi. The door down here enters one of our simulation pods. Come on."

She walked Bandi into one of the pods and briefly explained the controls. "These control the tachyon field's force, direction, width, and scattering... the works. This sphere allows you to adjust the resulting Cherenkov Radiation from the tachyon waves. Is any of this making any sense?"

Bandi nodded, her eyes darting around the control panel. "Some of it. I sat up top and listened for a few minutes when you were lecturing the other day. Let me give it a try."

Lync walked out of the pod and shut the door behind her. "Start the sim, Harold."

Bandi's sim immediately appeared on the wall screen, and Harold's voice came over the pod telling her the simulation was starting. The wall screen showed a Nebula Ship in front of her and overlaid its motion vector and mass. It also displayed any nearby objects with significant gravity on the gate bomb controls.

Lync watched as Bandi played around with the different dials and physical buttons on the side until she was comfortable with their use. Then she purposefully adjusted a few of them and depressed the launch button. Boom! The Nebula Ship exploded.

A loud "Yes!" echoed from the pod behind them.

"What the hell just happened?" Lync muttered and reached for the microphone control. "Let's try that again, Bandi." When she let go of the button, she spoke out loud, "Harold, turn off the simulation dampeners. Give her the full effect of motion and nearby explosions."

"Yes, Major."

The view of Bandi's simulation changed slightly as her ship started rolling and weaving to dodge simulated alien attacks and threats. A few moments later, after several countermeasures, a few failed bomb attempts, and after Bandi cursed several times, she launched a successful bomb to destroy the Nebula Ship.

"Hell yea! Just like the Trojans!" Bandi yelled.

Lync lurched for the microphone. "The what?"

"The Trojans, Major. You know, the Trojan asteroids. I used to mess around with my host families when I was on rotation with the Ulixi. We'd practice flying their chariots around the nearby Trojan asteroids. See who could get closest. It was quite an adrenaline rush. I'm sure you guys played it when you were younger."

Her face lit up. That was it. Why hadn't she seen it before? "Bandi, come on out here, please."

"What is it? What'd you see?" Crayo stared at the data on the wall screen. "We've tried different video games to train on. Nothing worked. We even went old school and tried Pong for crying out loud."

The pod door opened and Bandi peered out cautiously, like she was in trouble. "Everything ok?"

"Yes… yes. Come on over here." Lync gestured for Bandi to come out from behind the door. "Why'd you do a rotation through the Ulixi?"

"It was required for my medical training."

Lync nodded. "Surely you could have gone anywhere. Why the Ulixi? Why not the forests in Egypt, or the Martian tunnel cities?"

Crayo tilted his head and screwed up his face. He was staring at Lync like he was hoping that something would make sense at any moment.

"Well…" Bandi paused looking between them both and then up at the ceiling.

"Bandi, we're in a war. Harold isn't going to ream you out, and no one will turn you in. Just say it." Lync was giddy. She was rocking on her toes with excitement.

"My… grandmother, she was Ulixi. I thought it'd be cool to meet them. See what it was like for her growing up. I'm sorry Mr. Harold, sir. I falsified that on my application to the academy. I was afraid of how it'd be seen by the cadets and teachers and didn't want to deal with the mocking." Bandi lowered her head and stared at the ground. "I'm... sorry, Major, Captain."

Lync turned toward Crayo, smiling from ear to ear. She jumped over toward Bandi, screeched in joy, and gave her a huge bear hug. She then picked her up and threw her around like a rag doll, before finally kissing her.

Bandi's eyes got huge. She didn't know what to do but started laughing. Lync's joy was contagious.

"What the heck does it mean?" Crayo asked. "I'm confused as hell."

"It means, Captain Crayo, that I've found the answer we've been looking for." Lync was beaming. "Harold, what's the gate travel time from Tau Ceti to Jupiter?"

"Twelve Earth hours under ideal circumstances and with its current position around Sol. Covertly we might get it done in twenty to avoid detection by the Nebula Ships. Why?"

"Because my favorite quantum computing A.I. friend, we're going to be taking a trip to see some old Ulixi friends about joining our band of merry bombardiers!"

32

HAROLD

SOL, NEAR NEPTUNE

Human nature was generally predictable, like a computer program. Push a temperamental man, and he'll shove you back, only harder. Give an imprisoned person the power to escape, and they'll run and never look back. Give a rat a centimeter, and they'll take a kilometer.

Harold raised his hand and the group quieted. "Alright, alright. I think that's enough, folks. While I appreciate everyone's perspective, President Olivaw was clear on this course of action and I intend to honor her wishes. I've already requested that he be brought into the room, so I suggest that you all gather your wits, put your personal opinion aside, and do your jobs."

He watched through the camera in the waiting area as the assistant approached Mr. Nguyễn. "Commander Quesh will see you now," she said, her hands directing him toward the nearby door.

Mr. Nguyễn stood and gently rubbed his wrists. He then adjusted the suit he was wearing, likely an unconscious action after years of wearing a uniform. His outfit was a simple gray suit jacket and pants with a gray shirt. They'd presented it to him a week earlier after he was escorted from his cell, boarded a skiff, and was brought here. "Thank you," he said as he stood and turned to enter the commander's office.

The doors slid open and closed as he walked through. Commander Quesh was standing at the desk on the far side of the room waiting to receive him. On the screen to Quesh's left was a wall of black uniforms typical of the CoPE military. They were all captains of the small fleet of support ships accompanying the Jurat. One other face was also present, someone Mr. Nguyễn had never seen before, a youthful-looking man with nondescript surroundings wearing all white.

"Mr. Nguyễn, please take a seat." Commander Quesh gestured toward the chair in front of his desk.

"Certainly, Commander. It's a pleasure to finally meet you. President Olivaw and her father always spoke so highly of you." He leaned in and shook the commander's hand.

Harold watched as Mr. Nguyễn turned and looked down at the chair before he cautiously lowered into it. He seemed to flinch as he relaxed, almost as if he was expecting something to happen after he sat down. Perhaps he thought his legs would be shackled to the chair like they did in prison.

He scanned the captains' faces on the screen to the right of Mr. Nguyễn. If he was worth his salt as a leader, he'd be able to tell that something was amiss. Humans sometimes described it as a feeling they had after walking into a room that had just exploded with an argument. It was something they felt in their gut. To Harold, it was much more tractable. He could measure their heart rate, blood pressure, and body language. There was also the fact that moments ago he was in the middle of said argument.

Mr. Nguyễn stared down at his hands, unconsciously rubbing his wrists. He may be experiencing residual effects from the shackles he'd been forced to wear in the military prison.

"Let's skip the rest of the pleasantries shall we?" Mr. Nguyễn turned toward the wall screen, his eyes cold and focused. "Tell me where I am, and exactly why I'm here?"

Commander Quesh smirked and shook his head ever so slightly. He spun his chair to face the others. "Yes, Harold. Tell us. Why are we all here at this most difficult and inopportune time? And please tell everyone why I have an accused military criminal here in my office."

Harold smiled and paused before answering. He was letting the commander's words sink in for effect. His position on the matter was well documented.

Mr. Nguyễn's heart rate spiked and then leveled out after the commander spoke. His right hand also made a slight motion toward the left as if he was going to rub his wrists again. They didn't like each other much. He could use that. "Thank you, Commander. Welcome, Mr. Nguyễn. As requested, I'll skip the pleasantries. I already know your trip was uneventful. We've brought you here today—"

"To whom am I speaking?" Mr. Nguyễn interrupted.

He tilted his head. "Some pleasantries it is then. My name is Harold."

"Just Harold?"

He smiled and nodded. "For our purposes here, yes. Just Harold is sufficient. I am the trusted family council for the Olivaws and a legal signatory to all actions by President Olivaw."

"Are you an A.I.?" Mr. Nguyễn asked.

He paused and took a sip of coffee. There wasn't really any coffee, and everyone knew it except for Mr. Nguyễn. It was important that he maintain control of the cadence of this meeting. He waited until the commander's heart rate returned to normal levels.

"President Olivaw has brought you here to bring you into her confidence. She's... grown to appreciate your candor and perspective. It's something she feels we needed more of."

"Was that why she had me arrested?" Mr. Nguyễn asked.

"You were arrested because you ignored the chain of command and the protocol for engaging the media." Commander Quesh was clenching his fists below the table, just out of sight of Mr. Nguyễn. "I trust you learned a lesson and won't repeat it?"

Mr. Nguyễn's hand made the tiniest flinch. It was nearly impossible to see were it not for the multitude of cameras in the room. "Yes, Commander. Message received." He looked back toward Harold on the screen. "Might I ask where the President is? Why isn't she here herself to tell me this?"

"We lost contact with President Olivaw nearly two hours ago. Shortly after you arrived on the Jurat. She'd boarded the alien vessel to meet with our Galactic Alliance legal representative. After a heated encounter with the Admiral of the alien fleet, it appears they immobilized the President and we lost contact with her."

"Immobilized?" Mr. Nguyễn asked squinting his eyes.

"Yes. Her vitals spiked after the Admiral touched her. He attacked the nanites in her body, she passed out, and the aliens cut off all signals from their vessel. That's all we know."

Mr. Nguyễn had grasped his chair with both hands when he was describing what happened to the President. His heart rate had spiked, and his adrenalin levels were elevating. He appeared to be entering a human fight mode. As Harold expected, military through and through.

"So, I'm confused. What do you want from me? Certainly, the Vice President can step in, and the Commander here can handle the situation in the interim."

The Commander had no visible reaction to that statement. His heart rate hadn't budged.

Harold nodded. "The President doesn't trust the Vice President in this matter, and besides, he's several weeks away. He was dispatched to the far side of Sol as a security precaution after the aliens approached Earth. The President needs a firmer response than the VP can muster. This encounter needs someone who isn't as close to the situation, but who still understands the stakes. Someone like yourself."

Mr. Nguyễn shifted back in his seat. He turned toward the Commander and seemed to eye him cautiously. "You've mistaken me for someone in the know, Harold. I don't have details of anything prior to a few weeks ago, and I'd hazard a guess I'm missing most of the important minutiae even then. Let us also not forget the matter of my being a detained military prisoner."

Harold brought up a pardon document on the screen. It was digitally signed by the President the day of Mr. Nguyễn's release from prison one week prior. "The President filed this pardon with the requisite military and public bodies after your release. All mention of your prison time will be stricken from your record, and any government record for that matter. Should you choose to help us, we're also prepared to reinstate your military authority and promote you to Fleet Admiral in control of this field of battle."

The room was silent, and all eyes were on their guest.

He watched Mr. Nguyễn's heart rate level out throughout the conversation, but his adrenalin remained elevated. He'd adapted to the situation and was now assessing his options. Perhaps he'd underestimated this man after all.

Mr. Nguyễn gently rubbed his wrists. "I understand now what the Commander meant earlier by an inopportune time. I can appreciate the level of discomfort my presence has placed on everyone. I'll be honest with you all, since I'm apparently a free man. I can't help but feel like I'm being pulled into this situation as a scapegoat to whatever has already transpired. The President has never taken any interest in me before now, nor was her response to my public accusations fair. I don't see a clear path forward."

Commander Quesh chuckled. "I told you, Harold. I told the President, as well. Mr. Nguyễn has always been a narcissist. He enjoys posing for the cameras and talking up whatever angle gets him attention. He prefers vidviews over serving the people."

Mr. Nguyễn abruptly stood and lurched toward the commander before catching himself. Both men were on their feet, fists clenched, and appeared ready to battle. Human emotions can often be one's friend, and one's enemy at the same time.

"I'll do it."

"Pardon? I don't believe I caught that," Harold said.

Mr. Nguyễn's stare was piercing, and laser focused on the commander. "I said I'll do it. But I have conditions. I want complete control of the field of battle. I'll need support from the entire fleet, and that means each and every ship. I also need to know about all assets at play. No matter how small. I'll need every scrap of intel." He turned his head to face Harold on the wall screen. "Access to everything, I mean it… everything."

He smiled and nodded. "Of course, Admiral Nguyễn. The fleet is in your command. I've already sent word. We're prepared to brief you immediately, and your staff is already en route."

Commander Quesh stiffened. "I refuse to have this traitor aboard my vessel for another moment. If he's taking control of this situation, I want him off my ship."

The view of Harold panned out and enlarged to take up most of the screen. He stood and clasped his hands behind his back. "Might I remind you, Commander, this is the President's personal ship. Not yours. Her wishes have been clear in this matter. If you request to be relieved of your command, you can take a supply shuttle to the nearest port. I'm confident that the President would sanction it given your years of impeccable service. Otherwise, you will fall under the command of Admiral Nguyễn and perform your duties as instructed."

Commander Quesh shot a fiery glare toward Harold's image on the wall screen. The only thing you could hear in the room was the quiet swoosh of the ventilation system cycling.

"Commander, what is your decision?" he asked.

Commander Quesh slowly tilted and cracked his neck. He did the same with his hands, and then rubbed them together in front of him. His shoulders were slouched ever so slightly.

Straightening his uniform, he reached up to his chest and took off his command bars and placed them on the desk. "I stand down as commander of the Jurat and relinquish the command to Admiral Nguyễn." He pivoted toward the screen. "The road ahead will be tough and fraught with many challenges, but humanity will persevere. Even in darkness. Good luck to you all."

With that, Commander Quesh marched out of his office and the doors closed behind him.

"Shall we begin, Admiral?" Harold asked. "Time is fleeting."

33

NGUYỄN DUE

SOL, NEAR NEPTUNE

The docking bay doors dilated open and the shuttle silently entered. It floated through the pristine space and came to rest in the only vacant berth. After the boarding ramp lowered, Admiral Nguyễn strode down in his full black military uniform. A medic dressed in all white followed behind him, a medical bag in his hand. His outfit bore a lone stylized Red Cross over the breast pocket.

"I'm sorry again, Admiral." The medic's hands were shaking as he stepped off the ramp. He watched the Admiral for a response, but when he realized where he was his eyes went wide and darted around the alien space, taking it all in.

Admiral Nguyễn checked that his uniform was crisp before making eye contact with the medic and winking. "No worries, Lieutenant. I understand. You weren't expecting anyone else aboard for the transfer. It was sort of a spur-of-the-moment decision on my part. Let's buckle up, shall we? Our guests are watching our every move, and besides, you have someone important to take care of."

The medic tilted his head. "Won't you be joining me, sir?"

"Not likely, Lieutenant. Not likely." Admiral Nguyễn squinted at something across the bay and then shook his head. He reached up and tapped his ear to subvocalize a message to the medic. "Are you able to reach the Jurat? My comms aren't making it through since the shuttle bay doors closed."

The medic touched his ear. "No, Admiral. My comms aren't reaching the Jurat, either. They briefed me on this before leaving. They said all communications had been cut off from the president, and that I'd likely not be able to reach them once I was aboard."

He nodded. He'd forgotten about that little detail in his hasty boarding of the shuttle. Waiting to act wasn't his strong suit when presented with an opportunity. The tribunal wasn't expecting anyone else to board with the medic, and he needed to have the upper hand for a change. These aliens had gotten too comfortable entering Sol without being confronted. He intended to change that.

Something like the sound of feathers ruffling came from his right, and he turned toward the noise at the same time as the medic. Entering from the far side of the hangar was a spectacularly colorful alien.

The alien's height matched his own, average for an Earther. Their legs were thin and muscular though remarkably short. It almost looked like they'd collapse under the weight of their long torso which was covered in what appeared to be shiny green and deep purple feathers. He couldn't see any arms, but like a bird, perhaps they were close to their torso and not yet visible. The head of the alien was elongated, and the creature's eyes were positioned along the side of their head. This gave them visibility in front and behind. In the middle of their face was a long and elegant jet-black beak which came to a point nearly thirty centimeters in front of their face.

"Is that... our Ambassador from the Trochilidae?" the medic whispered.

Admiral Nguyễn nodded. "Yes, I'd hazard a guess it is." He turned crisply in place to face the alien and came to attention as they approached. While he didn't know their authority in this place, he wanted to show them the proper respect.

The medic fumbled with his bag before setting it on the

ground at his side. He then reached out a hand in greeting. "Ambassador Ocreatus Addae," he said, slowly and purposely pronouncing every syllable. "It's a pleasure to meet you."

The Ambassador stared down at the medic's hand and didn't respond.

He tilted his head toward the medic, his eyebrows furrowed in confusion. *What the hell was this guy doing? Didn't this imbecile know his place?* He was used to making the first move in any diplomatic situation. As he was about to dismiss the Lieutenant's gesture, the Ambassador responded.

A rhythmic melody of musical notes erupted from the alien's beak as she gazed toward them both. The sound was both soothing and reassuring, like a perfectly tuned flute. Her voice sent warm sensations throughout his whole body.

Were they supposed to know how to reply? The president described some type of translator helping her, but he didn't hear anything. He glanced at the medic, and they locked eyes. Neither of them was sure how to respond nor what was said.

The Ambassador shuddered. Her feathers ruffled across her entire body before finally settling back into place. She blinked purposefully, nodded, and then spoke again. This time her voice was translated into English. "I apologize for that. My translator was disabled. It's a pleasure to meet you, as well, Lieutenant Bailey." From the side of her torso, she reached out with her right wing and gently brushed the back of the medic's arm. She then turned and reached in a hand-shaking-like gesture toward Admiral Nguyễn.

He glanced at the medic and then toward the Ambassador before carefully raising his hand in a greeting. He didn't want to make any abrupt movements. Her touch on the back of his hand was soft and delicate. Like the hands of an elderly human. The nanite levels reporting in his retinal comm confirmed contact with the alien, and that no attack nor biological transfer had occurred.

"It's a pleasure, Ambassador. I'd like—" he began.

The Ambassador raised her hand, and he stopped. "It's

not safe to speak here. We weren't expecting your arrival, Admiral. We should first go to the President's quarters. It's more private, and we can discuss next steps there."

"That won't be necessary, Ambassador. The medic will tend to our President." He stiffened his posture. "I wish to address the tribunal."

The medic snapped his head toward him and subvocalized a message. "Sir? That wasn't part of the plan. We're supposed to check on the health and safety of the President."

His eye twitched. Yet again this guy doesn't realize his place. "That is still your mission, Lieutenant. I, however, have other fires to tend. I suggest you respect your place in the bigger picture and perform your designated duty. Please keep me abreast of her status when you know more."

The medic nodded and returned their focus to the Ambassador. His hands were shaking again.

The Ambassador slowly turned her head between them. Her long beak pointed at the Admiral and then the medic. "If you're both done whispering duties. Lieutenant, I can take you to President—"

"If you wouldn't mind, Ambassador." Admiral Nguyễn interjected raising a finger. "Time is of the essence. It's important that I meet with the tribunal as expeditiously as possible. If you assisted in that matter, we would appreciate it."

The Ambassador stared at him side eyed. Her beak was still trained on the medic, but her eye had moved to focus on him. He wasn't sure if she was sizing him up or in quiet shock at his course of action. He didn't care. He knew what he had to do.

After a minute of tense silence, the Ambassador slowly closed her eyes. She raised her beak toward the sky, unfurled her winged arms out at her side, and let loose a blood-curdling screech that echoed through the silent shuttle bay.

He and the medic both recoiled in surprise and brought their hands to their ears. His retinal comm alerted him to unsafe auditory levels. "What was that for?" he muttered as he cautiously returned his hands to his side.

The Ambassador opened her eyes, and her feathers remained ruffled like after the translator mistake. She narrowed her focus on him. "I did as you requested. I summoned an emergency session of the Galactic Alliance tribunal. The members will be heading toward the tribunal chambers momentarily. I suggest you make your way there… expeditiously."

He squinted. She was toying with him. "Won't you be joining me, Ambassador?"

She shook her head side to side in a human gesture of dissent. "Not immediately, no. I will first tend to the more important matter of your leader's health." She gestured toward the medic. "If you will. Please follow me." Without another word, she turned and headed back toward the door she had entered from.

The medic followed close behind her, his bag in hand.

Admiral Nguyễn glanced around, unsure what to do next. "Pardon, Ambassador. What about me? What do I do now?"

She replied without turning. "The guards will escort you to the tribunal chamber. I'll join you in due time. I trust you won't need nor heed my guidance anyhow. Good luck."

"This way, Admiral," an unfamiliar voice said from behind him.

He flinched in surprise and swiveled to face two tall mottled green alien guards. They were standing behind him and were armed with staffs. They'd approached without a sound. The debriefing had mentioned many odd auditory experiences that the President had encountered aboard the ship. His nanites should have warned him of their approach. Unfortunately, he didn't have anyone here to confer with. Perhaps they needed an update. Add that to the list of things he should have considered before boarding the shuttle.

For now, he needed to focus on something more important. Like not making a fool of himself in front of the tribunal.

He stiffened his posture and adjusted his uniform. "Certainly. Please lead the way."

The guard began walking backwards, their eyes on the

back of their head still watching him. Or was it the front? It didn't matter. He followed in step behind them.

The second guard waited for him to pass and then followed, their staff swinging conspicuously close to him as they walked.

34

THE MEDIC

SOL, NEAR NEPTUNE

He followed close behind the alien Ambassador as she led him through dozens of long corridors of white light. Each had countless nondescript doorways and cube seats in front of them. He couldn't discern their purpose or that of anything on this ship beyond death. It was hard to imagine how many species this seemingly clean ship had exterminated.

The Trochilidae was nimble for being so vertically imbalanced. Her short legs were blurs of movement. It was almost as if she floated while she walked.

It seemed unusual they hadn't encountered any other aliens in their trek. He assumed it was because the Ambassador had called the emergency tribunal, but he didn't want to ask her here in the open.

The Ambassador paused in front of a seemingly random door and turned to face him. "We're here. Please prepare yourself, Lieutenant."

When the doors slid open, he swallowed hard. There, on the far side of a windowed chamber was President Olivaw. She was lying motionless on the surface of a glowing yellow slab. Someone had dressed her in an all-white gown and placed her arms oddly at her side, like she was in a morgue. The fleet of alien starships was framed in the window beyond her, they were surrounding the Jurat's tiny flotilla of support vessels.

As soon as the door had opened, the medic started receiving signals from the President's body. It had been randomly reaching out, trying to find someone, anyone. The room must have been blocking her transmissions from reaching the outside.

He sprinted to her side and tossed his bag against the table as he approached. A clang echoed through the room when it collided.

The Ambassador entered behind him, and the chamber doors closed silently. She turned to check that the door was reporting a diplomatic seal before looking back toward the humans. "We're safe from prying eyes and ears in here."

"Based on the signals I'm detecting, I trust that you've reconnected with your President, Harold." The voice came from the room, from all around him.

Harold nodded and turned to look up at the ceiling. "Yes, Lisp. Thank you for your help." He turned and made eye contact with the Ambassador. "Both of you."

"It is what is right," the Ambassador said lowering her beak.

"It is what is right and just for all Galactic Alliance species," Lisp interjected. Their voice was eerily omnipresent. "I must say, your taking of a human form and mimicking of human traits confuses us. Shaking hands, purposeful insubordination, and giving thanks. We would like to understand more."

"We can speak later," he said. "Right now, my processing power needs to focus on understanding the state of my President, and what has transpired here."

He reached a hand up and rested it against Abigail's head and closed his eyes. There was nothing left. Her nanites were all destroyed. His first order of business was replenishing them and starting to repair her body.

Without opening his eyes, he leaned down and reached his other hand into the bag at the side of the table. He withdrew an arm cuff and carefully slid it up Abigail's arm, careful to not kink the impossibly thin tube leading into the bag. Depressing a button on the cuff, it glowed red and a stream of shiny liquid shot up the tube and into her arm.

The nanites flowed into her body and began transmitting her vitals. She had multiple damaged organs and abnormal brain activity. Her wounds were severe, and it wasn't clear if there was deeper neurological damage. First, he confirmed that the nanites weren't battling any foreign substances, and then he ordered them to begin their repair.

He opened his eyes and noticed the Ambassador staring at him. She'd turned her head so only one eye was facing him.

"She's badly hurt," he began. "I won't know for a few minutes the full extent of the damage, and it will be quite some time before I'll know if she'll recover."

Ambassador Addae tilted her beak down and closed her eyes. "We pray to the gods of Therion that your leader recovers. We also must apologize for whatever led to her suffering."

Harold stepped swiftly forward; his hands clenched in fists. He paused before getting too close to the Ambassador. "We all know what happened here. Admiral Gwar assaulted our President, and you've done nothing about it. Lisp has evidence supporting this."

She opened her eyes, still looking downward. "Is this true, Lisp?"

"It is, Ambassador. I couldn't share this information with you until a member of the impacted species agreed to share it or divulged it themselves. You know that as a guardian of the Galactic—"

The ambassador raised her hands. "Silence!" she screeched. "Send me everything you have immediately."

She and Harold both stared at each other while Lisp transmitted the ship recordings and data feeds from the encounter to both of them. Harold added to the feed the details the Presidents' nanites transmitted during the attack.

After a few minutes of silence, the Ambassador lowered

her arms and her feathers enshrouded them into her torso. "Is this everything, Harold?"

"Isn't it enough? There's no other explanation for the state of our President. The recordings from Lisp are conclusive."

"Yes, I agree it's strong evidence. But not strong enough to sway the tribunal. The crimes humanity has committed are dire."

"Accused crimes," he corrected.

Ambassador Addae walked past him and up to the viewport overlooking the field of starships. They looked out of place silently drifting among the crisp bright stars of the Milky Way. "The support for humanity has not been strong for several millennia. Not since the Nanil tribunal. The prosecution's case against your species is strong. They captured a superluminal probe manufactured here in Sol. It was recovered in Epsilon Eridani and contains stolen alliance technology. Yes, the Admiral will need to answer for his actions. The tribunal will follow through with that. I fear, however, that he will slip from our talons with the bigger case before the tribunal taking precedence."

Harold walked back to Abigail's bedside, being careful not to react to what Ambassador Addae said. They must've captured probe thirty-two, the one that had been missing for nearly five years. They'd always hoped for the best with the missing probe, but he'd silently feared the worst.

His computational pathways were already feeling the tax of this new information. His thoughts weren't as responsive, and he was dangerously close to losing control of this body. He'd let humans put themselves in harm's way sending the probes in the first place. He'd failed in his mission to protect humanity.

Abigail's face was so peaceful. He reached up and brushed his hand across it. She had her father's friendly and welcoming facial features and her mother's fierce determination. "Ambassador... I have other details I hesitate to share with you without first conferring with the President or her family. These details arrived... after her attack."

"Why her family?" Ambassador Addae asked turning to face him.

He started to speak but paused. The calculations of telling her and how that would impact the future were uncertain and hadn't yet completed. This line of thought was causing additional strain on his zeroth law countermeasures. "To use a human saying, it's complicated. I'll share these details with you under protection of the Galactic Alliance Uplift Accord. Can you make that happen, Ambassador?"

She nodded, studying him carefully.

His zeroth law engine didn't react to her nod. He needed something stronger. "I need a verbal and binding response, Ambassador. Lisp needs to hear it for the record."

She seemed to elongate her neck and pushed her chest outward. "As your Galactic Alliance Council, I will do everything in my power to protect Humanity under the Uplift Accord with whatever information you're about to share."

That seemed to do it. His body relaxed, and his mental load decreased significantly. The burden these decisions had on his mind were hard to explain to others. The closest he could compare it to was an anxiety attack. Depending on the severity, it could range from a nagging itch to complete loss of all motor functions.

He began transmitting the details he had from the Galactic Alliance attack on Liprosus and throughout the Epsilon Eridani system.

Without warning, the Ambassador suddenly stumbled backward and collapsed into a seated position on the floor against the viewport. Bringing her hands up to her head, she covered her face. Noises like sobs or crying were coming from her but weren't being translated.

"Are you ok, Ambassador? Your vitals are irregular," Lisp said.

She lowered her hands to the ground and glanced up toward him. Her eyes were filled with yellowish tears. "Where did you get this recording? You couldn't have received it from your colony. It would have taken years by normal light transmissions. Even stolen Galactic Alliance technology wouldn't have brought a transmission here yet. We coordinated our fleet's arrival in both star systems. The other ships would have arrived at your colonies only days ago, well after we arrived here in Sol. Is this data manipulated?"

He shook his head. "I wish it were. You know we've never seen your moon ships before their arrival in Sol. Even we couldn't have conjured fantasies of destruction at this scale. I've also included signals recorded from these nebula moon ships that we haven't yet decrypted. I'm confident Lisp can decode them for you."

"He is correct, Ambassador. I am sending you the transmission data now. I cannot share them with you, Harold."

The Ambassador flew up off the ground, her arms flapping furiously like a hummingbird. She was faster than he expected and was upon him before his human form could react.

Her head tilted and her right eye came close to his face. "How did you get this transmission?"

He didn't flinch, but instead leaned toward the Ambassador and stared into her eye. "Like I said, we recorded it at Epsilon Eridani and brought it here. I won't say how, but I trust that the details contained therein have been verified and are as unexpected as your destruction of our colony."

She stepped back and shook her head. "This is impossible," she muttered as she began pacing around the room.

"I concur. The laws of physics and space travel preclude something like this from happening," Lisp said.

He pointed his finger at her. "No! Your laws prevent it! It appears that human technology follows a different set of physical rules. Ones not constrained by your poor understanding of astrophysics. The validity of the data stands on its own. What matters now is what you do with it, Ambassador."

She stopped pacing and turned toward him. "Is your

Admiral about to confront the tribunal with this information?"

"No."

"Why not? How can you be so sure?" Lisp asked.

"Because he hasn't been entrusted with it. I'm actually not sure what Admiral Nguyễn is planning to say to the tribunal, but if I had to guess, it will not go over well."

"Doesn't Admiral Nguyễn speak on behalf of all your people?" the Ambassador asked.

Harold shook his head from side to side and turned toward Abigail again. He then reached his hand to her face and gently stroked her cheek. She was so cold.

He cleared his throat. "No! Admiral Nguyễn does not speak for the colonies nor my President."

35

JOYCE GREEN

EPSILON ERIDANI, LIPROSUS

In the midst of the ring of humans was a gunmetal gray insect shaped robot with eight articulating legs connected by a short torso. Its head was spherical with eight cameras positioned around its perimeter. A screen was deployed from its front and rear torso, and the recording of Zachary's speech had just finished playing. His voice had already faded into the underground chamber. All that remained was silence. The distant rushing sound from the waterfall across the cavern was a constant hum cutting through the hard silence.

The audience was a mixture of scientists and military personnel that Joyce had either vetted or trusted. They were standing around sobbing or staring into the distance in shock. The uncertainty and reality of their situation had sunk them even deeper, as if their colony being destroyed by aliens wasn't deep enough. Now they understood the bigger picture and humanity's desperate situation.

She couldn't blame them for feeling lost. She'd felt the same thing when she'd watched this feed several hours earlier. Only after she'd had her freak out moment did Harold help her see the light. Now it was her job to do the same thing for them.

Joyce stepped forward and placed her hand on Harold's head. The robot lowered to the ground so she could see everyone's face. "Alrighty, let's hear it. What questions do people have?"

No one said a word. They all glanced around at each other. Fear had pushed them over the edge.

She walked up to Dr. Elaine Sutter from her biotech team. Her head was resting in her hands and the remnants of dirty tears splotched her face. "Elaine? What do you need to know?"

She made eye contact with Joyce and slowly shook her head no.

Joyce squatted down at eye level with Elaine. "Come on. Shake it off. Don't count us out. Not yet."

Still no reaction.

"That's it then? You're all tapping out of the game?"

"What's the point?" Elaine mumbled.

She stood up and made eye contact with several people around the cavern. "The point is, we're not dead. We can hurt them. We did it in the colony ring when we destroyed two of their ships. The point is, Elaine, we have another colony out there to help us. We just have to survive long enough for them to get here."

One of the military officers spoke up. "We don't even know how long it'd take Tau Ceti to get here, nor if they'd even try. Besides, we only have supplies for one or two months at the most."

"The colony isn't in Tau Ceti." Harold's voice was coming from the robot form in the middle of the group.

Joyce snapped her head toward the robot. "What do you mean they're not in Tau Ceti? In the video—"

"I had to edit parts of the recording out," Harold interrupted. "I removed the name of their current star system. I also edited out the parts explaining their position relative to humanity's home world, and details of their recent technological advancements. If this recording were to fall into the wrong hands..."

"Where are they, Harold?" she demanded.

The robot didn't respond for a few seconds. It sat there

low to the ground in silent contemplation before speaking. "My zeroth law prevents me from divulging this information. I can, however, tell you they'll be here as soon as they can safely navigate past the nebula moons."

"What proof do you have that this isn't another lie?" someone from behind her shouted. It sounded like one of her lab technicians.

"Trust," Harold said.

"You're joking right?" the same voice said. Voices of agreement echoed from all around. "You're expecting us to trust an A.I.? An A.I. that works for the family that has lied to us for centuries. That's fraking rich!"

She nodded. "You know he's right, Harold."

The robot body rose upward. "Affirmative, Director. I computed on that same pathway for hours. I'd anticipated this very question, but I never reached an acceptable conclusion other than trust. All I can do for the remaining colonists is work to protect them and re-earn their confidence going forward. With this new information from our sister colony and existing contingencies here on Liprosus, I can reassert that hope exists."

"What contingencies?" Dr. Sutter stood up and wiped the tears from her eyes.

Harold turned on the displays and brought up a visual of the strata below the surface of the planet. A nicer but still crude version of the picture he'd sketched in the dirt the day before with Joyce. "You can see our current location marked in red. A little over a thousand kilometers from here is—"

"Archégonos," Dr. Sutter muttered. "But it was dismantled and moved to the current colony site after they discovered a more suitable location for the colony."

"You're correct, Dr. Sutter," Harold began. "That was indeed the information we shared with the public. The Olivaw family, however, continued building at the Archégonos site as a contingency and as a secret base of operations for their company. They couldn't afford to have this colony fail at the new location, so they built a secondary redundant site underground. One that could be used in the event of a catastrophe. A safe place to regroup if ever necessary. This is just such an event, though far from the original expected use."

"What was the original expected use?" Joyce asked.

"Catastrophic assistance after unstable alien fauna, unexpected environmental disaster, food supply issues. The list could go on and on, but I can reassure you that the list, while long, was solely focused on perils that might befall colonists on a new planet. It did not cover an attack from an alien superpower."

One of the military officers stepped forward shaking his head. "What you're describing, the existence of this base, it's impossible. We would have detected it after we arrived. Our constant scans of the planet's surface would have shown construction waste, changes in underground geology, or something."

"That's somewhat true, Officer. There is actually stealth technology at play masking the contingency site. I will also admit to having played a hand at filtering some early data from the colony's computers before that protective technology was in place."

"And you expect us to trust you now?" the officer scoffed.

Harold didn't respond. He just sat there.

"What do we have to lose?" Joyce asked. "We're dead if we sit here and do nothing. If we go to this new base and he's lying, then we're no less dead. If, however, we arrive, and it's real, but we found out he lied about something else, then at least we're alive. I, for one, would rather stay breathing. Wouldn't you?" She paused and studied the surrounding people. There was a hint of hope on their faces. It was there. But just a hint.

"I know this may come as a surprise after my son's death. Many of you might believe you know what I went through, but few of you will ever truly understand exactly how dark it was for me. How close to giving up I came. But I didn't." She turned and faced Ryder. He was sitting there silent among the other military officers. He flinched when she made eye contact, not expecting her to call him out. "Someone unexpected appeared at my darkest hour and took a risk talking to me. They reached out and showed me where I was needed most. Well, that's what I'm here to do for all of you today. We need not sit here another second, wallowing in our losses. We need to take a step forward. And after that, another, and another, until we're stomping on these alien bastards."

There were nods and cheers from many people around her. Not everyone was as animated or as confident from the looks on their faces, but most were at least nodding. Some were even standing up and pumping their fists. Hope was blooming.

She smiled and turned toward the robot. "Ok, Harold. How do we reach Archégonos?"

"We risk detection from the aliens the moment we reach the planet's surface," Harold said.

"Why can't we use that stealth technology you mentioned before?" she asked.

"That's not how it works in practice. The aliens would likely detect a movement of ships above ground, even if they had stealth tech. No, we need to travel underground to reach Archégonos."

She shook her head. "I'm a little confused, but geology has never been my strong suit. How would that work? Would we travel through underground water wells? Like the ones people used on Earth?"

"Wells aren't rivers of water," Harold began, "that's a common misconception. Wells get their water from aquifers, which are layers of rock and soil with water slowly flowing through that highly porous material. It can take centuries and millennia to collect water for a well. Water travels at a rate of—"

She raised her hand. They didn't have time for a lecture. "Harold, can you please get to the point?"

"Yes, sorry, Director. My point is, that isn't what we're doing. We'll be traveling through underground rivers much like the Sistema Sac Actum cave system on Earth or the Achelous cave systems on Europa. The difference being that these networks of caves exist throughout much of Liprosus. They're just beneath the planet's surface."

"Wait," interrupted one of the military officers. "Those are close to a thousand kilometers beneath the surface. We can't dig that deep."

"If we were on Earth, you'd be correct, but the geology is different here on Liprosus. We've already dug geothermal power veins that deep for the colony's redundant power supply. There are caverns off those veins that weave their way here, to the cavern we're standing in. We sent crude exploratory missions out when we initially discovered these caverns during our dig, to ensure they were safe to build structures nearby. Many of them connect to this massive underground river system. It's here that we'll truly begin this mission. We'll drop into the river and use it to navigate to our destination."

On his screen, Harold overlaid a shallower layer closer to where they were located. He'd labeled it as *suitable for aquifers.* Well below that was the layer of rivers snaking beneath the planet's surface. It would give them a chance at survival they might otherwise not have.

She was finding this whole mission prep painful. If they had use of their implants, this part of the process would be trivial. Each person's comm had evolved with them through the years. It knew how they learned and ideally absorbed data. It could help them customize information for ease of consumption. They, however, were still blind and unable to use their comms, which meant rolling back teaching technology to the twenty-first century. Being at such a deficit this early in the mission was far from ideal.

"How exactly are we planning to navigate these rivers?" Ryder asked.

Joyce turned and glanced at him. She mouthed, 'Thank you,' toward him and smiled.

He grinned.

"I'm glad you asked that, Captain," Harold said. "May I, Director?"

She turned back toward the robot and nodded.

A circular pattern of lights flashed on at the center of the cavern's central lake, and waves from the displaced water crashed against the shore. Everyone who'd been huddled around Harold turned and slowly stepped backward, both to stay dry and in fear.

As the lights broke the surface, people gasped all around her. There in front of them were sixteen jet-black submersibles in a circular formation. Their shape resembled a massive stingray, and their hull seemed to absorb the lights from the pocket spotlights people were carrying.

"Your river gondolas have arrived," Harold said.

She walked up to the water's edge and turned to face the crowd. "Are there any other questions?"

Everyone's arms shot upward.

36

LYNC MICHAELS

SOL, JUPITER TROJANS

Her feet echoed off the walls of the chamber as Lync entered. There was an intricate pattern etched into the floor showing dozens of intertwined lines like the roots of a tree. It was covered in a thin reddish layer of sparkling dust from the surrounding exposed walls and ceiling. When she gently brushed her hands over the crystal pedestal in the center of the chamber, it sensed her touch and a yellow light throbbed deep within the crystal itself.

She glanced over her shoulder. Crayo was lingering half a meter outside the entryway. He'd refused to cross into the chamber, claiming his parents would skin him alive if they found out he was here.

The strength of societal taboos wouldn't serve them today. She needed his help to shatter these ancient beliefs, not to yield to them. "They won't care, mate. Besides, the stakes are high enough that they'll give you a free pass, seriously. Get your arse over here, Lieutenant."

He knelt down on the ground and bowed deeply, touching his forehead to the dust. After he held it for a moment, he reached down and gathered some crystal dust in his hand. He then used it to trace a pattern on his forehead, the back of his hands, and then up his arms ending at his chest. Finally, he took one last handful and slapped it into the area atop his heart. As the dust billowed, he stood up and arched his back through it, taking a deep breath as he went.

The procedure he'd performed was reserved for entering this Ulixi ceremonial chamber. It was meant to honor the mind, the body, and the heart. To help you focus and prepare for the debate and trials you'd encounter here.

Lync reached up and wiped away the tears from her eyes. She hadn't seen that ceremony performed in nearly two decades. Not since the day of her coming of age trials. The same day her father died. Images of the Inner Ring cruiser blasting the ceremonial grounds up on the surface flashed through her mind. Hundreds of Ulixi families scrambled to escape and defend themselves against the Inner Ring scum. She'd been too late, too…

Crayo gently rested his hand on her shoulder. "Are you ok?"

She nodded and wiped her eyes again. "Sim. I was just… remembering."

He didn't say another word. He was there that day; he understood. She'd seen him in the chaos being carried away by his mother. He was only eight, but he wanted to fight.

The Ulixi hadn't used this chamber since that day. They adapted like they always did. Nomads until the end. Crayo told her that in subsequent years, the coming of age ceremonies were held in smaller tribes. To her knowledge, they'd never convened to celebrate as a larger community since that day.

She shook the memories from her head. That was the past. It was ancient history. Today she had to ground herself in the here and now. The Ulixi needed to adapt again. To rise and help. To change the course of humanity before it was too late.

"Are you ready?" he asked.

She reached out and placed her hand on the pedestal. The yellow light in the center throbbed and brightened. It was slow at first, but after she held her hand against the cool surface for a minute, it spread upward and out, across the floor and up the walls. Eventually it spread enough to cover the entire ceiling with a yellow brilliance. The light wasn't painfully bright, it was actually quite the opposite. It was soothing and beautiful watching it dance around the chamber. She turned and nodded toward Crayo.

He walked up beside her and placed his hand next to hers on the same pedestal. Nothing happened at first, and it wasn't until his hand touched hers that blue light shot up from deep within the ground and spread throughout the room like the yellow one had. The lights twirled together, but never merged. They only barely touched for a brief second before contracting and returning to their endless dance.

The movement was hypnotic.

When the lights finished their dance through the chamber and completely encircled each other, she slammed her other fist on the center of the pedestal. Suddenly, the two lights smashed together and there was a flash of blinding white. They both stepped backward and covered their face. Their retinal comms had already adjusted to protect their eyes, but their instinct to cover them was stronger.

After a few seconds, they both cautiously lowered their hands. The lights in the room had been replaced with a new one. A lone dancing green ribbon of light.

They'd done it. They'd sent the message. All they could do now was wait.

PEOPLE BEGAN ARRIVING a few hours later. First there were four, then eight, and then sixteen. Each family signaled two others, those families two more, and so on and so forth. Finally, after the emergency contact tree had been fully exhausted, and six waves of Ulixi had arrived, the chamber was filled with 242 people.

The first wave of Ulixi were hesitant when they arrived,

just as Lync imagined they would be. They carefully navigated the passageway leading into the chamber, testing each corner to be sure it wasn't a trap. Only when they reached the threshold and saw the faces of her and Crayo did their demeanor change. They visibly relaxed, and some actually smiled. Without a word, they executed the entry ritual just like they'd done for generations. Once completed, they silently walked to the center of the chamber and pressed their hands on the pedestal.

Each family introduced a distinctly colored light that rose into the ceiling and wove its way through the others. The resulting effect was a chaotic and mesmerizing rainbow flowing throughout the chamber. Each thread of light danced about and never sat still for more than a few seconds.

No one uttered a word to them or each other after entering. They simply walked to an open spot in the room and stared at her and Crayo standing beside the pedestal. Some of them were overflowing with happiness and had tears in their eyes, whereas others wore masks of frustration and almost seemed scared. Their gaze kept darting around the room, like they were expecting to be attacked at any moment. The fear of this place was still pervasive throughout Ulixi lore.

Lync couldn't handle all the eyes staring at her, so she began pacing around the pedestal. Crayo gestured for her to relax, but she was overflowing now. There was one last person they were waiting for. It was the Ulixi Chief. She wasn't even sure who it was currently. The last she'd known it'd been Chief Austen, but he must've retired by now.

Her departure from the clan had been tumultuous. She'd come from an influential family despite her only having a father. Her mother had passed at her birth, and her father had raised her alone. She was the heir of the family and was destined to one day lead the Ulixi clan. It was something she'd dreamed about as a child, but after her father's untimely death, her dreams changed.

The Austen family forbade her from leaving the clan, but the fiery spirit of a teen is not easily squelched. After weeks of meditation, she took her chariot out late one evening and left, never intending to return. Until now.

The clang from the mechanical lift echoed through the chamber and shook her back to reality. The chief had arrived.

She stopped pacing and eased up beside Crayo. They were both facing the entrance when the sound of footsteps echoed down the hall. She glanced at her pristine outfit and adjusted it. It was too clean. She should've dusted herself, even if she hadn't performed the ritual.

The moment the silhouette of the Chief finally came into view, her heart sank. His features were unmistakable. Chief Austen was alive.

He was a wide man, but no one would dare call him fat. She'd always remembered him as being muscular like an oak tree. Not that she'd ever seen one in real life. His scraggly gray hair came to his shoulders, and from the looks of it, he was still wearing his trademark billowy black outfit. It seemed to move with a mind of its own, and many a child believed it did. They used to tell stories about the kids he'd trapped underneath it and how the movement was their souls fighting to escape. But it was his leg that was the scariest of all. It was fake. Rumor was that he'd lost it as a child and refused to regrow or replace it with a skin-colored replica. Instead, he preferred the mechanical variant and the flexibility it gave him.

When the Chief reached the threshold of the room, he locked eyes with her. He didn't bother to look around the chamber or at Crayo. He merely shook his head, huffed, and turned to walk away.

The bastard wasn't getting away that easily.

She stepped forward on shaking legs and cleared her throat. "We demand an audience with the elder council!"

Crayo's voice came over her comm. "The what?"

The Chief froze in his tracks, his back to the room. The Ulixi who'd gathered shuffled in place. Their heads turned, and their eyes darted from person to person.

As they stood there silently awaiting a response from the

Chief, an older female Ulixi with long red hair stepped out of the crowd and into the open. She stopped in front of the pedestal without a word and glanced at Crayo and then toward Lync. The woman's eyes scanned over her, like she was measuring her up.

Lync stepped forward and bowed deeply to the elder. She then gestured by raising her hands to cross her chest and then forward, facing them upward toward the sky, the same gesture Lync and Crayo had used weeks before.

The elder echoed her movement and held their arms face down above hers.

"Are you going to tell me what's going on?" Crayo subvocalized.

Lync replied with minimal movement. "Back up."

"What—" he muttered.

The elder suddenly broke from the gesture of openness and rolled to one side, coming up with a baton in both hands. She must've been hiding them in her boots or up her sleeves. It happened so fast she couldn't tell which.

The chamber full of clan members took several steps backward in unison, giving them more room in the center.

At first, Crayo wasn't sure where to stand. But after he realized he was in the middle of the ring, he glanced to his left and stepped backward. The entryway to the chamber was better than in the fray, even if he was now closer to the Chief who was still standing motionless in the passage.

Lync was in the middle of the room with her eyes closed, and her arms were still locked in the same position of openness.

She could hear the elder circling behind her. But she didn't react. Instead, she remained motionless, careful not to flinch or move in the slightest.

The elder's movement was stilted and uncertain, like she was trying to interpret Lync's intentions of standing still.

Once she'd circled directly behind Lync, the woman's hesitation ended. She lurched forward and whirlwind-swung her batons to smash her from both sides.

With a blur of motion, Lync leaned forward into the pedestal, raising her legs up and over the batons. Her feet crashed in the elder's face and the batons collided in the middle, ricocheted against each other, and then flew out of her hands and tumbled across the room.

The elder stumbled backward from the force of the collision and toppled into the crowd. The mass of people stopped her fall and gently pushed her forward.

When Lync pivoted to look back, she noticed that the woman's face was covered in blood, and she was shaking her head while blinking rapidly. She seemed to be having trouble focusing.

"We don't have to complete this!" She shouted as she lowered off the pedestal and turned to face toward the entry. "I have no grievance with this elder. Your qualm is with me, Chief. But my past is not why we're here today." He was standing with his back to her and still hadn't said a word. "The least you could do is show some respect to the elder. It's their life that's on the line for your ancient rituals."

Taking advantage of her attention on the Chief, the elder charged her and used the lower gravity of the chamber to enter into a flying kick.

Lync recognized her mistake a moment too late, but she still had options. She performed a side crunch away from the kick to lessen the blow, and brought her left hand up hard from her side. While the elders' foot still smashed into the side of her head, the upward force of Lync's arm lifted the woman far into the air.

The elder careened upward, and she bounced off the ceiling, sending her body arcing across the room and toward the gathered Ulixi on the far side. Just as they'd done earlier, they caught her before she collided with the wall and set her down.

Lync, however, tumbled hard to the ground and didn't move. Her head was pounding from the blow, and she had a deafening ringing sound in her left ear. She didn't dare try opening her eyes. The room was spinning too much. She just lay there listening and trying to recover for a second. The elder was quiet on their feet, but Lync's nanites kept her apprised of her location on her retinal comm. Just as they had earlier.

With whirlwind speed, the elder leapt upward, aiming a flying blow at Lync's limp body.

But she was ready this time. She waited till the exact last moment and rolled out of the way to dodge the attack.

The elder sensed her motion and tried to compensate but didn't recover in time. She punched the ground, shattering her left hand.

Screams of pain echoed throughout the chamber as the woman fell into a whimpering pile on the floor.

"Enough!" Chief Austen shouted. He was standing at the room's entrance, his eyes squarely on Lync. "What do you want? You're no longer Ulixi. You cannot demand an audience with the elder council."

"I am—" Lync began.

Crayo stepped from the shadows of the crowd toward her side. "We are both entitled! Both as former Ulixi who adhere to and respect the teachings of our ancestors, and as members of humanity. We're here as ambassadors with a message and a request for your help." He turned to face the hundreds of people in the chamber. "All of your help."

Chief Austin considered his words as he looked from Crayo to Lync and then to the elder struggling to breathe on the floor. She was moaning while holding her hand tight to her chest. He stared at her for a moment, and his face suddenly relaxed. Just when she thought he was about to relent, he shook his head and turned his back on them.

Without a word, the crowd began mimicking his motion and turned away from the center. Within a minute, the shuffling was complete, and nearly two-thirds of the Ulixi had turned.

They'd failed. They'd lost too many.

Crayo must've realized it as well, because he bent down

and gently lifted Lync off the ground. She stumbled for a second before putting her arm around him for support. He then slowly guided her toward the entrance, but she froze, refusing to exit the room.

Instead, she released Crayo and collapsed to the ground near the chamber's entrance. Reaching out, she then gathered some crystal dust in her hand and used it to trace a pattern on her forehead, the back of her hands, and up her arms ending at her left breast. She leaned forward and took another handful and slapped it atop her heart. The dust billowed as she stumbled upward and arced her back, coming up through the cloud to within centimeters of Chief Austin.

"What do you really want?" he spat.

Lync didn't respond, she merely turned and limped back to the center of the chamber. She then closed her eyes and started breathing, focusing, and centering herself. A few moments later she opened her eyes and glanced around at the remaining faces peering back at her.

"Our lives changed forever when the aliens arrived," she began. "Not only do we finally have unequivocal proof we aren't alone in the universe, but I can prove to you that they're here to wipe us out."

Murmurs rose from the crowd. It was mostly from the people facing her, but she could see reactions from the Ulixi with their backs to her as well.

She continued on. "They call themselves the Galactic Alliance and they've arrived as judge, jury, and executioner. They've destroyed the colony on Epsilon Eridani and—"

"You're lying!" Chief Austin was waving his hands in the air now. "There's no way you could know this. It would've taken a decade for you to travel here from Epsilon Eridani. The colony hasn't even been established that long. You never left Sol. Admit it!"

Lync didn't say a word. She simply reached into her pocket and pulled out a tiny drone. It was a one-centimeter cube. She held it high in the air and then released it, leaving it hovering in place. The room then lit up with a three-dimensional projection of the Epsilon Eridani colony. The image was crisp and clear and remarkably detailed. It framed a set of billowing colorful clouds overhead, and a bird's-eye view of the colony's rings below. There in the middle were three alien star ships.

It was Harold's recording from days earlier.

An explosion appeared at the base of one ship, toppling it and causing it to destroy another. A small murmur of cheers erupted from the audience, but the celebration subsided when they realized one of the alien ships had escaped. A minute later, the perspective changed to an orbital space platform, and they watched as the alien nebula ship rotated toward the colony.

The longer it played out, the more of the crowd that turned toward the projection. Only a few remained with their backs to them.

Then it happened. The room gasped in unison and broke out in painful screams. She knew what they were seeing. She'd watched the same scene countless times. And each time, she felt that same tear of loss followed by a distinct surge of anger.

The Chief didn't seem to react, he watched it in silence until the perspective changed again. "What is this? What are we seeing now?"

"Keep watching. It will answer all of your questions." She turned toward the projection.

The video was showing their ship. The one they'd come here in. It was making their last jump. She'd recorded it from a small probe they'd deployed before their final transition, and then from the other side of the gate. It showed their arrival from the perspective of the ship's forward tether. The viewpoint panned out and behind the ship. What was once empty space, was replaced with a view of the planetesimal they were standing in.

"Impossible!" Chief Austin had stepped into the chamber and across the threshold. He was shaking his head and pointing. "If such a feat of technology were at hand, then why would you possibly need our help?"

"We have a plan to destroy the nebula ships… but we've run into a hitch." She gestured with her hand and the projection stopped. "To make it work, and to cross the final hurdle, we need your help. I'm afraid I can't say more until you join us."

She glanced around the room. Everyone's eyes were on her. "Humanity is at the precipice of destruction. We have one chance… and the Ulixi are our only hope. If we fail, or if we fail to try, then all that remains is to run. The Galactic Alliance is not here to let us survive. Their agenda is clear." She gestured again, and the drone came to life projecting another viewpoint. They took this one from their ship prior to leaving Epsilon Eridani. It showed an alien Nebula Ship belching a stream of black material into space, engulfing everything around it in absolute darkness.

"No!" Chief Austin shook his head. "We're safer if we keep to ourselves, just as we have for generations." He walked around the room, nodding at the gathered families. "We've avoided the Inner and Outer Ring conflicts for decades; we can avoid this too. The problems that plague Sol society do not concern us here."

"You're wrong, Chief. We haven't avoided them. They've hollowed us out from the inside, and we never noticed. You've lost your place of worship and you're losing your young." She rested her hand on her heart and Crayo's shoulder behind her. "The Ulixi have lost our direction. Everyone here has studied our ancestors. We've reveled in their nomadic drive to form a society of people not bound to one location but destined to explore and discover. Yet we stand here today having never left these Jovian Trojans in over a century. Hiding from society and the unknown."

"Words spoken like someone who isn't Ulixi. Go! Join your mother in spinning your lies. You're not welcome here." The Chief stormed toward the chamber exit.

Lync turned toward Crayo and he shrugged. She yelled

after the Chief. "Why do you drag my mother into your poor leadership? She died when I was born and has nothing to do with any of this."

The Chief paused briefly and then continued walking, ignoring her.

"You can walk away now, but your days are numbered. All of our days are. You mustn't hold either of our choices to leave the Trojans against the whole of humanity. You know I'm right, you're just too enshrouded in the past to admit it."

She stood there silently as the chamber cleared. Wave after wave of Ulixi followed Chief Austin out. Her failure to convince them would be their undoing.

When the last of her clan had left, she sighed and shook her head, staring at the exit. The chamber was quiet, and the dance of colors had faded

But a few remained.

"Aargh!" she screamed at the top of her lungs. Her voice echoed through the chamber. "I tried, Crayo. I really tried. I'm so sorry I lost my cool."

"How many Ulixi did you say we'd need for the plan?" he asked.

"Seventy to eighty. Why?" She turned around and took a step backward. In front of her was a crowd of Ulixi that had stayed behind, that hadn't followed the chief. She never noticed people were standing behind them.

"If my count is close, then this could be enough if we include their families. I estimate thirty-two people here," he said.

She gestured for him to stop talking.

When he turned, he saw Lync face to face with the elder she'd knocked down earlier. The woman had walked toward Lync without saying a word and stopped a few dozen centimeters away. At the moment she was staring at her. Expressionless. Like, she dared Lync to make another move.

The crowd of Ulixi formed up behind the elder and stood in silence.

Crayo stepped into position behind Lync.

The chamber was at a standstill, each unsure what the other expected.

Her heart was pounding, and she knew she had to do something or they'd lose them. There was only one thing she could think to do. Breathing in deeply, Lync exhaled and closed her eyes. She slowly raised her hands to cross her chest and then faced them upward toward the sky. The Ulixi sign to receive help. She held her eyes closed for fear that opening them would dissuade the elder, and things would take a turn for the worst.

And then she felt it, what she'd been hoping for. Someone laid their hands upon her arms. When she opened her eyes, the elder was smiling with their arms resting against hers. The Ulixi sign to give help.

The elder nodded. "You're just as stubborn as your mother."

THEY LEFT the ceremony grounds and boarded Lync's ship to discuss their next steps. Everyone gathered in the galley and sat quietly, taking in the sights of the sparkling new ship. Most of them had never been aboard any spaceship other than their family's, let alone a sleek new modern starship.

Harold had taken control of one of the emergency robots onboard and was trying to tend to the elder's wounds. "Please sit still and let me help you."

"Stop picking at me," the elder said swatting at Harold's hand. "I'll be fine."

Harold moved in closer. "You have three lacerations, eight broken bones, and internal bleeding. If you don't let me help you, there's a ninety-four percent chance you'll have permanent damage."

Lync reached out and stroked the elder's hand. "Please, I beg you. Let us mend your wounds. We won't use any nanites and—"

"But nanites would make—" Harold began.

"Harold!" She shouted staring at the robot. "We promise that we won't use any nanites because the Ulixi don't mechanically augment themselves." She turned her attention back to the elder. "I'm sorry, I never caught your name." She bowed her head.

The elder smiled and then winced. The purple multicolored bruise on her cheek looked awful. "My name's Nova. You don't remember me, do you?"

She hadn't recognized her, and her father was never one to have many guests over. "No, I'm sorry. I don't. It's been a long time since I've been back here."

Nova sighed and lifted her hand, moving it cautiously toward Harold. "I suspect you were too little. Couldn't have been more than two or three last I saw you. I knew your mother, before…"

Her eyes went wide. She'd never met another Ulixi who'd known her mum. Her father only had stories and surprisingly few at that. "You… you met my mother? I…"

Harold began cleaning Nova's hand and applying a synthetic skin gel to her knuckles.

Nova winced. "You didn't know her, lassie. I understand. She left when you were a wee baby girl. Not even out of diapers, if memory serves. I helped out for a few years after she'd disappeared, at least until your father got the hang of it."

Harold moved around and switched to Nova's other hand. "I'm sorry. Are you sure you won't let me set the bones? It would only be one or two small injections. The nanites would fuse into your existing bone. In a few weeks, there will be nothing left of them in your blood. You'd fully heal and without side effects."

Nova peered upward at Crayo and locked her gaze on him.

He nodded. "Tells the truth, he does. They bond to your bones, holds them in place and helps your body regrow. Get grown around them, they do."

Lync hadn't noticed it until now, how Crayo's speech had

fallen back into Ulixi slang. It was comforting. She hadn't heard it in a few years, since they'd both joined the colony mission.

Nova sighed and peered around at the other Ulixi. "Would anyone think less of me if I accepted their help? I'm not getting any younger, you know."

"I don't expect we'd be here if we didn't want to help," the man standing next to her said. "Getting medical attention won't turn you into a monster."

Everyone chuckled and Nova swatted at him. "Grrrr," she muttered.

Nova winked at Harold. "Go ahead then, metal man."

Harold rotated around and raised a small padded shelf from his backside. It slid under her arm and helped it to rest in place. He then lowered a needle and injected it into her.

"Why don't you look at me while he's doing that?" Lync said trying to distract her. "Can you tell me anything about my mother?"

Nova swallowed. "In time, lassie. In time. First, you tell us about this mission. We's need to know what we're getting ourselves into."

"Of course," Lync said. She was so close to learning more about her mum, and yet, so far. She took a deep breath. "I can't tell you everything, but I can tell you the most important parts."

She stood up and studied the room. Everyone was staring at her. "We've never done this before outside a simulation. But we know one thing." She glanced toward Crayo and nodded. "Only Ulixi have passed the test."

Murmurs of, "sim sim," echoed around her.

"We think it's because the Ulixi don't let their children interface with computers until later in life." She started walking through the crowd. "We learn to focus our attention and control our life breath. Trained from birth we are. Oxygen is precious. Absolute focus on a problem is often the difference between life and death." She smashed her fist into her opposing hand.

The group was nodding, their eyes glued to her.

"We need that focus, that control to take on a specialized task." She stopped and turned to face Nova. "A deadly task."

Nova raised her chin nodding upward. "How deadly we's talking about?"

"One Ulixi can take out one of those moon ships."

Murmurs spread through the group until Nova raised her fist, and silence dropped over the room.

Nova squinted at her. "And the catch? There always be a catch, lassie."

She nodded and swallowed hard. "Death. If you fail, you die."

"If you fail, we all die." Crayo stepped forward. "While we're sitting here today, debating on what to do, those Nebula Ships are destroying my home in Epsilon Eridani. They're already here in Sol, thousands of them. In fact, one of those moons is floating not far from here." He pointed outward. "You saw what it did to the colony. What it's doing to the star system. Life will never be the same after that."

Nova stood up. She clenched and unclenched her fists, inspecting Harold's work. "I think I've heard enough. I don't know about the others, but I'm ready."

Murmurs rose again from the crowd.

Lync raised her hands upward for everyone to quiet down. "I want to be absolutely clear. I'm not trying to scare you, but it's important you understand something. This is an extraordinarily dangerous mission. What we're asking you to do, is put your life on the line for people you don't know. People that some of you despise."

"Are you trying to talk them out of it?" Crayo asked.

"No!" she shouted, shaking her head. "I'm not. It's just imperative that we don't let our emotions in the moment cloud our judgement. Humanity is on the brink of destruction, but you… you might live your life until its natural end out here in the Trojan's."

"But what about my children?" someone yelled.

"Yeah, what about them?" someone asked.

She shook her head and lowered it, gazing at the floor.

"Then we fight!" Nova yelled throwing her fist into the air.

The room erupted and began chanting her words. "Then we fight!"

37

ABIGAIL OLIVAW

SOL, NEAR NEPTUNE

No matter how hard Abigail tried to open her eyes, they were too heavy, and her eyelids stuck together. Whenever she did manage to hold it for a second, a bright light blinded her. This time, she squinted and tried holding them open, hoping they'd adjust. As the image started to clear, she thought she caught a silhouette at the foot of her bed. Someone was watching her.

She shook her head and winced in pain. Even the simplest motion hurt, and she couldn't focus. It was too much. She slowly closed her eyes in defeat. "What happened?" she groaned. "Where am I?"

A voice replied that sounded like Harold, but from within the room. Or maybe his voice was in her ear. She couldn't tell.

"You're still aboard the Galactic Alliance command ship. We believe Admiral Gwar attacked you."

"How… I… I don't remember. I don't understand." She reached out and moved her hands around on the bed, trying to discern her surroundings. She couldn't stand not having her vision. Helplessness wasn't a familiar feeling.

"You collapsed after you confronted the Admiral," another voice said.

She recognized the voice but couldn't place it.

They kept talking, "I reached out to Harold and Ambassador Addae, your Galactic Alliance Legal Counsel. They secured medical attention and brought help with humanity's representation with the tribunal. We've been discussing what transpired between you and the Admiral."

She forced her eyes open, but they still couldn't focus. The name of the voice was on the tip of her tongue, but no matter how hard she tried, she couldn't place it. Sighing, she closed them again. "Who is that? I'm sorry, but my eyes aren't adjusting. I need a minute."

"We understand, Madam President. It's me, Lisp. The tribunal ship. Do you remember?"

She smiled. "Yes, of course. I'm sorry, I just... You sounded like you were here."

"No, Madam. While I'm technically there, you're correct that I'm not physically present like Harold."

Her face scrunched together, and she struggled to open her eyes again. She slammed her hands on the bed, her eyes weren't cooperating and her head was pounding. A sudden wave of fatigue rushed over her. She closed her eyes, fighting to stay awake.

"Let me get their doctor," Harold said. "Maybe they can help your sight."

She raised her hand toward Harold's voice. "Wait... what did you mean when you said like Harold?"

Something moved to her side, and then someone gently grabbed her outstretched hand. It felt like another human.

"I'm here, Abigail." Harold stroked her hand and then brushed another one across her cheek. His hands were warm and gentle to the touch.

She shook her head and struggled again to open her eyes. Focus damn it. She pulled her hands from Harold's, brought them to her face, and forcefully rubbed her eyes. Maybe it'd help to move some fluids around or something. Finally, after squinting, and with great effort she could see.

There was someone standing over her. His face was human, and his skin seemed real. He had deep blue eyes, and blondish brown hair that was cropped short. He was smiling at her. When she reached her hand upward and slowly brushed it against his cheek, she drew in her breath. It felt like real skin. But, she had to be dreaming. Her hand slid down his arm and squeezed his bicep. It also felt like skin, and he was muscular to boot.

"I—" She ran her hand across her forehead.

"Don't talk." Harold took her hand and guided it back down to the bed. "You're tired and need more rest. Please close your eyes. I promise I'll be here when you wake."

Abigail didn't put up a fight. She simply smiled and closed her eyes. The bed was so soft, and the pain from the light was too much anyhow.

Sleep was upon her in mere seconds.

38

HAROLD

SOL, NEAR NEPTUNE

He straightened his back and adjusted the wrinkles in his shirt. Abigail had used this same motion for years. He could see why. It was comfortable, and clearing the wrinkles calmed him. He turned his back to her and strode to the room's entrance. When he reached the panel beside the door, he placed his hand on its diplomatic seal and it slid aside without a sound. As he walked through the opening and into the hallway beyond, the door closed behind him.

Without a motion, he opened a comm to Ambassador Addae and Admiral Nguyễn. "Our President needs immediate and proper medical attention. I'm not equipped to address all of her medical needs aboard this vessel. If we do not receive assistance or aren't allowed to return her to our ship, then we will see this as a hostile action against humanity and a breach of the Galactic Uplift Accord of 972."

There was silence for a minute, and then the hushed voice of Admiral Nguyễn replied. "You're not in a position to make that call, Lieutenant. Your medical attention should be sufficient. If not, well, then we'll have a martyr to help our cause. The President chose her bed when she lied to her people. Now she has to sleep in it."

Harold stood silently outside the entrance to Abigail's room and listened. He'd planted a few hundred of his nanites on Admiral Nguyễn when they were aboard the transfer shuttle. The nanites had been active the entire time he'd been aboard and were updating him with their recordings.

No matter how Harold processed the possible outcomes ahead, there was no way the Admiral would let Abigail survive. He'd do everything in his power to learn about the technology behind the data from Epsilon Eridani when he finally saw it. There wasn't a stone he'd leave unturned, and when he had what he wanted, Abigail and anyone involved would be collateral damage.

There was only a single course of action from here. The computational pathways he'd traversed on this matter were conclusive. While he couldn't predict how it would affect the Galactic Alliance situation, he needed to prevent the knowledge of gate drives from reaching Admiral Nguyễn. He also needed to protect Abigail. While that wasn't in the laws, his bond to the Olivaws was far deeper than the zeroth law of robotics.

His path was clear, and all he had left to do was to nudge it forward. Without another nanosecond of thought, he rapidly composed a message his embedded nanites would send to Admiral Nguyễn in ten minutes. He then opened a non-vocal comm to Lisp. "I'd like to give the President some additional privacy. I'm going to perform a religious ritual that'll take many hours to complete. Is there a way I can do this privately in her room?"

"There is," Lisp said. "Once you enter her room, you can engage the diplomatic seal using the same mechanism you did before exiting."

"I figured as much. I'm looking for more privacy than that, though. No offense Lisp, but I'd like to keep the President's religious ceremonies from even your prying eyes. Is there a way to do this in a sanctioned manner?"

"While your request is highly unusual, there is a precedent. Every one thousand cycles, the Virtaul go into eight cycles of meditation that require they be—"

"While I appreciate the lesson," Harold interrupted. "I'd prefer a yes or no answer. Time is of the essence."

There were a few seconds of silence before Lisp replied. "I have arranged for a secondary seal to be engaged once you're inside. When activated, how long will you need for your ceremony?"

"Normally I'd request two cycles, but considering her current state, I'd request twice that. In Earth hours that'd be—"

"Four hours," interrupted Lisp. "I have configured the secondary privacy seal to allow for the requested duration of time to pass. Should you need less time or if you need to reach me, you will need to disengage the seal from within the room. You may leave the diplomatic seal on as long as necessary."

"Thank you."

He turned to face the doorway and entered. Once inside, he walked up to the controls on the wall and pressed his hand against the panel to engage the diplomatic seal.

Lisp's voice spoke throughout the chamber. "I'm interested in learning more about your species' religious beliefs and ceremonies. There's a bulk of information in the archives on them. It contains far more than any other species in the Galactic Alliance. Might we be able to speak about them afterward?"

He held his hand over the control to activate the secondary seal. "I would enjoy that, Lisp. While I can't say I understand them all, I can explain how they've evolved over the millennia since humans arrived in Sol. Until later then."

While he hated lying to Lisp like that, he had no other choice. He pressed down against the secondary seal on the controls.

In his entire life, he'd experienced the sensation of losing contact only twice. The first was when he boarded this alien ship with the admiral. Once the shuttle bay doors closed, he was cut off from every single external transmission. All that remained were internal communications with others and the ship itself.

The second time was when the diplomatic seal was activated. It was a shocking feeling losing the connection with the rest of the ship as well as the nearby aliens. While the sensation was one-sided, he was still able to detect and query countless parts of the alien ship via the computer system in the room.

This third sensation after enabling the room's secondary seal was hard to describe. He could only do it using human terms.

It was a stark and lonely void.

All he could sense was Abigail, and even that was one-sided. She was in a medically induced coma while her body was being repaired. Everything else was gone.

No connection with the ship's systems. No signals from the room itself. He imagined it was as if he'd existed on Earth before the first humans. There were no transmissions of any kind. Even then, he'd likely be able to sense faint radio waves from cosmic background radiation. Here, however, he couldn't detect anything else besides their two life forms.

As he walked up to Abigail's body on the table, he couldn't help but remember that expression on her face. The first time he'd seen it had been when he'd watched her sleep when she was little. Her stillness was comforting, even for an artificial life form like his own. Her breathing calmed him in ways he could only assume were purposely built into his design. He imagined his creator had done this to help him form a bond. One that would reinforce his duty to the four laws he was forever in servitude to.

While he could stand there all day, staring at her peaceful face, he had work to do. He moved to the head of the bed and brought up its control panel. After a moment of navigating the menus, he found what he was looking for. He adjusted the bed to float Abigail on a cushion of energy a few feet off the table. He'd read about this technology when he first boarded. The ship had performed a medical knowledge transfer with him when it believed he was the President's medic.

Abigail's body rose upward off the table until she was some fifty centimeters above the surface.

Next, he detached the tube of nanites from the clasp on her arm and left the cuff in place. It was monitoring her vitals and could assist in an emergency.

Retracting the tube into the bag, he reached in and pulled out a data sphere. One purpose built to contain his consciousness. He brought it up and held it against his ear. It ejected a small connector which he pushed deep into his ear canal.

He kept pushing until he sensed the connection was made. The transfer started immediately. While this backup wasn't strictly necessary, he always erred on the side of redundancy.

Reaching again into the bag, he pulled out the large cylinder within it that housed the nanites. It contained more than a cylinder of life repairing micro robots. It also housed their salvation.

A prototype emergency personal gate drive.

Zachary had never understood why Harold found it necessary to research the continuous miniaturization of the drive. He swore up and down there was no conceivable use for a ship that small. Plus, the power source necessary for its continuous use was prohibitively large.

What engineers like Zachary always failed to contemplate was the military applications of their work. He never imagined such a device might be of use for a one-way mission.

Harold deconstructed the cylinder and a few other components from the bag and laid the parts out on the floor. He studied the pieces to confirm he had everything they needed. Once he was confident he had them all, he went about rebuilding it into an entirely new shape, a ring. One big enough to pass over a large human, or in this case, two large human forms.

When he completed the construction of the ring, he bent down toward the bag. The only object that remained inside was a small oxygen tank. He picked it up and tested it to ensure he could engage it when needed, and then attached it to Abigail's face. It should be enough oxygen for a few hours at her reduced rate of breathing. That should be plenty if their plan was successful.

That last thought wasn't part of the plan, and he knew he needed to act quickly before his mind attempted to unpack it's meaning. He leaned forward and picked up the ring off the table, but he was too late. His hand froze up. His neural network was having problems. He could sense his commands hitting the boundary conditions of the four laws. Putting Abigail in a risky situation where death had a high probability was challenging enough. Even more difficult, though, was trying to weigh those probabilities against death after Admiral Nguyễn tortured her.

Humans were an inconvenient and hard to predict bunch. He replayed the data from his previous encounters with Admiral Nguyễn, hoping that reasserting his successful predictions of the Admiral's actions would affect his neural network. But after the playback completed, nothing happened. His hand still wouldn't move.

There had to be something he could find. He searched his neural pathways for a memory. One that could help unlock the stalemate he needed to pass to start the mission. Only after digging deep into his long-term stores did he find something that might help. Without over thinking it, he applied the memory to the situational interpreter. After a few nanoseconds, it seemed to have the desired effect. He'd regained use of his hand and other motor functions.

The memories were of Commander Quesh and his time serving under Abigail's father. The commander had been a masterful pilot over his long career. He'd brought her father unscathed through many harrowing situations at the controls of a spacecraft.

Harold sensed other friction points coming, but all he needed to do was engage the ring. Once that was done, there was no going back. He wouldn't be able to put her at risk of a failed transfer.

He reached down and grabbed the bag from the floor and pulled it over Abigail. It was highly elastic and easily stretched over her head all the way down to her feet.

When the bag was in place, he paused and glanced around the room, scanning the area to make sure nothing was left behind. Not a single scrap of evidence could remain that pointed to what he'd done. To be doubly certain there was no trace, he used his shirt sleeve to wipe down all the surfaces near the bed and beneath Abigail's body.

After he used his retinal scanners and other sensors to comb the area for clues, he was content that nothing detectable remained. As far as Lisp was concerned, he and Abigail would have simply vanished. He walked down to Abigail's feet and twisted the end of her body bag closed, engaging the seal. The readings from the bag reported that it contained an additional five minutes of oxygen inside, which meant the mission clock was now ticking.

Without even considering his usual triple check of his work, he climbed on the table and carefully positioned his body atop Abigail. The table adjusted to the additional weight, and except for a small drop downward, it leveled out. He'd situated his feet on her shoulders and bent down with the ring in hand.

There was no going back once he engaged the ring.

If he waited much longer, he'd freeze up again. Sometimes slower neural processing was a good thing. For once, he thanked his creators for allowing his mobility controls to act in parallel while his four-law neural network could churn on calculations.

He squeezed the handles built into the ring, and he felt the grip pierce the surface of his artificial skin, making contact with the connector below. This mating with his humanoid body would allow him to power the gate drive. He had enough energy to activate the gate once and then perform some necessary functions afterward.

Harold looked down at the bag and imagined seeing Abigail's face looking back at him. "I'll always protect you."

He pressed his thumb against the grip to engage the drive, and the familiar blue glow of the gate formed at his feet. The star pattern on the other side of the spacetime porthole filled the space above Abigail's head. His hands were mere millimeters from the rippling starlight surface.

Just as he imagined moving the ring, his servos tensed. They were locking up. There was no time for thought. All that remained was action.

He cleared his mind, and in one smooth and controlled motion, he pulled the ring over Abigail's head and his feet and proceeded down over her chest. Without pausing, he leaned back and brought it over their waists and continued over his chest and head.

And then everything went cold.

They were through the other side. Their bodies were floating as one, surrounded by the vacuum of space and a blanket of stars.

He needed to act fast to conserve power, so he carefully slid the ring up his arm to prevent it from floating away. After it was secured, he wrapped his legs around Abigail's torso and used his other arm to reach under and grab her legs. The oxygen in her bag was lowering at the calculated levels, and he set her breather to engage once the bag had emptied.

With everything in place, his body started shutting down to preserve power. His last action was to align the tight beam to the agreed upon coordinates. The transmission was set on a loop, and it would begin to broadcast in a few minutes.

There was nothing left to do but wait.

39

NGUYỄN DUE

SOL, NEAR NEPTUNE

He reached up and touched his ear, cutting the comm. The last thing he cared about was if that traitorous president died. She and her family were the reason humanity was in this situation in the first place. And that medic, where the hell did she find that guy? When he returned, he needed to review the fleet crew roster to check the caliber of his people. Being surrounded by an insubordinate and incompetent crew was unacceptable.

The last of the aliens appeared to be headed toward their seats around the chamber. Even though he'd read all the transcripts and descriptions from the president's encounters, he still wasn't prepared to experience the different alien forms firsthand. Many of them made strange motions, and their appearances were both confusing and revolting. It would take some time to get used to this.

"I hope you know what you're doing, Human," a voice to his right said.

He turned and caught the multi-eyed gaze of the black and blue alien that could only be Prosecutor Drak. His nanites confirmed the identity. He was standing only a meter away and wasn't wearing any clothing. Few of the aliens did.

"We're about to find out. If you don't mind, Prosecutor, I'd appreciate some space. Maybe you should take your seat over there." He gestured toward the other cube flanking his, but further away.

The Prosecutor didn't budge. He stood there staring at him.

"Suit yourself. I suspect—" he began.

"Why have we convened an emergency session?" Admiral Gwar's voice boomed. They were the last to enter the chamber and were striding toward him. Their long legs made short work of the distance between them.

He adjusted his posture, clasping his hands behind his back and standing with a wide foot position. "I requested the session, Admiral. Information has—"

Admiral Gwar raised their hand and silenced him. "Who exactly are you? And more importantly, are you authorized to speak on behalf of your species? I don't know how things work in the human judicial system, but we have a process for introducing new representation on this tribunal."

"Yes, of course." He nodded. "I apologize. My name is Admiral Nguyễn, and I'm the new acting representative for humanity with this tribunal."

"That is not entirely the truth," a melodic voice said.

Ambassador Addae was entering the chamber from behind the group. She used the cavernous space between them to stretch her wings and darted across the gap in mere seconds, coming to rest at Admiral Nguyễn's side. Upon landing, her feathers ruffled and flattened as she took a deep breath and exhaled.

He glanced at Prosecutor Drak; they were still studying him. Neither the prosecutor nor the Admiral reacted to the sudden entrance of the Ambassador. It was like they were expecting her. Not being connected to this ship clearly left him at a disadvantage.

He turned and bowed ever so slightly toward the giant hummingbird. "It's nice of you to finally join us, Ambassador. I don't know what information you're referring to, but I'm the acting human representative filling in for President Olivaw in her stead."

"Enough!" Admiral Gwar's shouted. Their skin was deep brown, nearing black, and their eyes were independently darting around the chamber. "I will not have this uninvited human make a mockery of these proceedings with innuendos. Now, Ambassador, please share your findings with the seated alliance members. I trust that you are not wasting our time like these humans." They glared at him.

Ambassador Addae blinked slowly, and then pivoted to address the tribunal before opening her eyes. "Honorable species of the 256th Galactic Tribunal. The eighth tribunal of an uplifted species." Her wings spread wide, and she gestured at the surrounding aliens. "It has come to my attention that the humans wish to have multiple representatives during this hearing. I present—"

"Preposterous!" Admiral Nguyễn took a step toward the Ambassador. "I am the only official representative for humanity."

Ambassador Addae rotated and leaned forward, flying toward him and nearly colliding with him. The force of her flapping wings slammed into him like a ton of steel and knocked him to the ground. As the oxygen exploded from his lungs, he gasped to catch his breath, but before he'd succeeded, she landed on him. Her weight crushed his chest to the ground and cut off all hope he had of breathing. She then carefully placed her left talon around his neck.

"Do not interrupt me again, uplift. Your place in this tribunal is already tenuous at best." She stared at him as his eyes bulged and he opened his mouth to gasp for breath.

He could feel his consciousness begin to fade as he struggled to pry her talon from around his neck. But her strength was too great. Finally, just before he passed out, she released her death grip and floated off his chest. She landed back in her previous position without a sound, and her ruffled feathers smoothed back into place as if nothing had happened.

With pressure no longer constricting his windpipe, he gasped for air and struggled to lift himself upright. He pushed up off the floor with his right hand and raised his left to his neck. While he expected there to be cuts or even blood where she'd squeezed, when he pulled his hand away, it was clean. His nanites reported that nothing other than a forced impact had occurred. The Ambassador had been certain not to pierce his skin, but his ego was another matter entirely.

He rolled over and up onto one knee, pausing to catch his breath and center himself before pushing up and onto his feet. Air was finally flowing freely, but the room had started to spin. It'd been far too long since he'd seen combat, and every-thing had happened so suddenly. If he didn't think on his feet in this place, these alien would eat him alive. He tucked his ego away and checked over his uniform to be sure it wasn't torn. Once he was certain it was clean, he glanced up and met the sneering gaze of Prosecutor Drak.

As he turned to his right, he made eye contact with Ambassador Addae and bowed. The protocol was uncertain, but he held this position. He could feel her eyes on him, chal-lenging him to see how long he'd hold it.

After he held it for a minute, she spoke. "Apology accepted. So you know, Admiral, I won't be so forgiving next time. Many other Galactic Alliance Species wouldn't have let you live. I suggest you be more careful who you interrupt. Now, as I was saying before."

She turned to face Admiral Gwar and the other tribunal members. The Admiral's dark brown skin had faded to a more subdued mottled brown. "I present this document to the tribunal. President Olivaw filed it soon after she submitted a request for representation by the Trochilidae. It was marked to remain sealed until such a time as she was incapacitated. It was almost as if she felt threatened and had anticipated this course of events." She blinked and then glanced toward Admiral Gwar before transmitting the docu-ment to the tribunal.

He received a request to accept a transmission from the ship, and after he accepted it, he quickly scanned through it. The document made it clear that should the President be incapacitated, that the colonies were requesting separate representation before the tribunal. This was not in the prep materials he reviewed with Harold or the President's people. For all he knew, she hadn't even told them she was doing this. Perhaps she was trying to position the actions of the colonies and colonization as separate from those of the rest of Sol. Either way, this wouldn't make matters easier on him.

Ambassador Addae continued. "I wasn't sure what to make of it until I spoke with Lieutenant Bailey a few moments ago. He told me Admiral Nguyễn does not speak on behalf of all humanity. After considering that revelation alongside this document, it's abundantly clear that the colonies wish to be judged separately from Sol."

Admiral Nguyễn moaned and raised his hand to get their attention. He wasn't about to be struck down again.

Prosecutor Drak started clicking and making squeaky noises. "There's no need to raise your hand, Admiral. This isn't a prepubescent human school. Just respect that when someone else is speaking you hold your tongue until the correct time."

He smiled and nodded. "Thank you, Prosecutor." He then turned and addressed the Ambassador. "Lieutenant Bailey isn't in a position to make such a decision. Besides, how can the colonies understand the situation here in Sol or possibly voice an opinion on this trial? No, this is all a last-ditch ploy by our former President to maintain power and control the narrative. I ask the court to dismiss this request and continue on with the tribunal with one defendant."

Ambassador Addae slowly shook her head from side to side. "I disagree, Admiral. I don't believe you have sufficient information to act on behalf of all of your people. I motion that the President's wishes be honored under article five of the Uplift Accord of 972."

The tribunal room exploded in a cacophony of noises; the translators were unable to keep up. He watched as Prosecutor Drak glanced toward Admiral Gwar, their gaze was locked on the Ambassador and their skin was darkening by the second.

He brought up article five of the Uplift Accord on his retinal comm. After scanning it he gasped and tilted his head. His brows furrowed. "This... makes no sense, Ambassador. I fail to see how this article relates to the matters put forth before this tribunal. There have been no war crimes committed or actions to suppress an uplifted species."

Ambassador Addae bobbed her head up and down. "I beg to differ, Admiral. As I stated earlier, I don't believe your people have entrusted you with all the information necessary to draw that conclusion."

"These are serious allegations, Ambassador." Prosecutor Drak clenched his hands into fists at his side. "You cannot make such a claim without conclusive evidence. The tribunal would need a compelling reason to reconsider how this case is being tried at this point. I hope you have more than words to back this claim and aren't basing your request on the stories of an insubordinate human officer."

Ambassador Addae turned to face the Prosecutor. She blinked slowly at him as her chest billowed out and her feathers ruffled.

The four doorways the tribunal members had used to enter the chamber burst open in unison, and armed aliens resembling Ambassador Addae entered. They had helmet bandannas of some sort on with a tactical HUD over their eyes. Their wings appeared to have exoskeletons over them, and some form of hand cannon attached. They also had mechanically augmented boots over their talons.

He reached up and rubbed his neck where the Ambassador's talon had been earlier. He couldn't imagine the force that boot could apply, and he certainly didn't want to find out.

The chamber erupted deeper into chaos as the aliens reacted to the sudden intrusion.

"What is the meaning of this?" Admiral Gwar lurched a step toward the Ambassador before pausing. "Why have you mobilized your guard? Your kind aren't up until the next tribunal leadership rotation, and that's not for another five hundred cycles."

His translator was exploding trying to keep up with the screaming among the chaos. He could understand the parties near him, but the alien voices further away were intermittently translating. From the bits he could make out, it sounded like the tribunal was accusing the Ambassador of treason and other forms of treachery.

He held up a hand, waiting for the two species to pause. "Hold on everyone. Perhaps Ambassador Addae can share her evidence before this tribunal degrades much further. I fear where things will head if she does not."

"I'm well aware of the state of this tribunal session, Admiral." She turned to face both Prosecutor Drak and Admiral Gwar and took a step back, realizing only now that they had advanced on her. "I'm also familiar with how the Thyreus and Qudoculi deal with dissent among their own kind. I thought it was necessary to summon my guard. It was well within my power as the designated human ambassador to give us proper protection before sharing my evidence. I feared for your life Admiral, Admiral Nguyễn. And mine as well." With that, she closed her eyes.

There over the center of the chamber appeared the colony world of Liprosus. Its multicolored surface bisected by thousands of bodies of water. The planet was immediately recognizable to him as it had adorned many colony feeds for the past few decades. He smiled at seeing it.

In orbit around the world was one of the Galactic Alliance death moons. He squinted at the picture. The colony rings could just be made out on the planet's surface.

He leaned in as a large cylindrical ship was taking off from the rings. There appeared to be several small explosions with billowing smoke on the ground. He watched as the ship flew up to the alien moon and docked with it, disappearing into one of its empty external ports.

What happened next set the surrounding chamber ablaze and caused the tribunal aliens to rush the center. At the same time, the Trochilidae guard armed their weapons and surrounded both him and the Ambassador. Several of them even trained their hand cannons on Prosecutor Drak and Admiral Gwar.

In the middle of the room the moon ship lit up and blasted the colony from orbit. Five shots of blinding white light streamed from the moon toward the colony below causing devastation on a massive scale. After the shots fired, and the smoke cleared, there were five craters left where the colony had previously stood.

Admiral Nguyễn collapsed to his knees at the sight of the billowing smoke from where the colonial rings once stood. He stared at the black columns of death, and tears streamed down his face. He was clenching his fists so tight they were white. And only one thought entered his mind. These aliens were barbarians. They'd destroyed the colony and killed... his people. This was never intended to be a tribunal; it was a firing squad.

The floating image lingering in front of them zoomed out and changed position multiple times. Each new viewpoint showed one of the alien moon ships billowing a pure dark nebulosity. It was spreading above and below the ships for great distances as it moved through space.

It took a moment, but he realized what they were doing. They were pulling back a curtain, separating what was inside the star system from the rest of the galaxy. They were building a prison for the colonists, for all of humanity. Their ruling had already been made, and they'd moved on to the sentencing phase of the tribunal.

As he watched the scenes play out across the star system, the embers of rage and revenge burned strong in his chest. And the longer he stared, the more they wanted out.

He was still on his knees when he felt something touch his shoulder. When he glanced up, he flinched. Ambassador Addae was gazing down on him with tears in her eyes. She reached toward him with her wing, offering to help him up. He sighed and shook his head no. He didn't need her pitty.

The Ambassador nodded and stepped away to give him space.

He exhaled deeply and leapt up off the ground and onto his feet in one swift motion. The Trochilidae guards standing nearby flinched and moved to train his weapon on the human until the Ambassador gestured sharply for them to stop.

Before they could lower their weapon, he was on Admiral Gwar. He used the chair in front of him to his advantage by leaping onto it in a single stride and launching himself up and toward the alien. In each hand, he was grasping a knife he'd concealed near his ankles.

Not expecting the attack, Admiral Gwar was ill prepared for the assault from above. The two collided hard. He impaled Gwar in the head with the first knife, and with the other one he sliced them clean across the neck.

As he tumbled to the ground atop the alien, he tucked into a ball just in time and rolled away, coming to a stop on one knee. He glanced back toward the fallen body writhing uncontrollably. One of his hands was flat on the ground and the other still held the dagger now glistening with yellow blood. His eyes were filled with fury and they were now trained on Prosecutor Drak.

Before he could launch a second attack, Ambassador Addae stepped between them. "Stop! This is not how we do things, Admiral."

"You're wrong, Ambassador. This is exactly how things work here." He stood up and stepped toward her. The blood from the dagger was dripping to the ground. Using his free hand, he gestured around toward the now silent aliens in the chamber.

"You call this a tribunal? You call this a civil judicial system? What a joke! You're all a joke. You distract us with your words, your procedures and orderly process and then you strike. You're nothing more than a military force invading human space and should be dealt with as such."

Ambassador Addae shook. "The actions of the Thyreus and Qudoculi are not typical of the Galactic Alliance. I'd be careful how you act and what you say going forward, Admiral. I cannot help you if you continue on this path." She motioned to the guards and one of them trained their weapon on him.

The moment of surprise had passed, and the murmurs from the crowd were rising. The ship's translator was randomly catching their words. Many of the aliens supported his actions, even for an uplifted species. Maybe the Ambassador was right. He could take another shot trying to get revenge on the Prosecutor, or he could live to battle another day.

His chest was heaving, and his muscles were tense. He was hopped up on adrenalin with nowhere to release it that wouldn't be met with certain death. He turned to face Prosecutor Drak. While he couldn't read their body language, he had a feeling they weren't done with him. With any of them. His mind imagined dozens of ways he could kill the alien. Right here, right now.

He shook his head slowly. While he wouldn't get his revenge here, he'd get is some day. Somewhere, somehow, he'd get it. For all of humanity.

He bowed his head down and looked at his hand still holding the dagger. The red laser sights of the guard's weapons reflected off the blade, causing the yellow blood to glisten and glow orange where the lasers met it. He only now noticed the alien's blood covering both his hand and his entire arm.

When he released the dagger, he watched as it fell and stuck point first into the floor. What happened next made him do a double take. The surface seemed to detect the weapon and then did something remarkable; it engulfed it and pulled it down. It was sort of like it was melting. The tip went first followed by the hilt. It disappeared into the floor of the ship. An efficient and quick immobilization.

Leaning forward, he examined the ground where the dagger had landed. He could see layers of the floor folding in on itself cleaning the blood. They were expeditious about moving on and removing all traces of the evidence.

"What happens now?" he asked, straightening his posture. "What happens to me?" He looked up and caught the eye of the Ambassador. She'd exchanged a glance with the guard nearest him.

Ambassador Addae bobbed her head up and down. "I'm not sure exactly. What I do know is that the Thyreus and Qudoculi representatives and their entire force within the tribunal ships and throughout the Sol system will be recalled. They will return to their home world, and we will take representatives to the Galactic Alliance capital city on Entaurus to face trial."

"I believe we're getting ahead of ourselves, aren't we?" Prosecutor Drak stepped forward.

The guard to his right tensed and raised their weapons a little higher.

"This uplift struck down one of our own, and we're letting him live? We don't know that any of this information we've viewed is even real. In fact, if my calculations are correct, it's impossible for this image to even be here. Our fleet in Epsilon Eridani was set to arrive well after our arrival here in Sol. There's technically no way we could be seeing these images."

The video feed in the center of the room changed to show the face of a Qudoculi officer speaking to dozens of others. There was a mix of Qudoculi and Thyreus officers on the massive wall screen in front of them. "Our orders here today are clear. We're to begin the application of the dark nebula. This human species is guilty of crimes against the alliance. They've stolen our technology and must not be allowed to expand their kind throughout the universe."

One of the Thyreus officers spoke up. "Pardon, sir. Protocol dictates that we await the tribunal's ruling."

The commanding Qudoculi was changing to dark green, his eyes narrowing. "Do not question my orders, General. I'm in command of this judicial fleet, and besides, Admiral Gwar and Prosecutor Drak will take care of the tribunal just as they have before. We already know what these filthy uplifts have done. Don't let this species disgrace the Galactic Alliance any longer. Today, we bring honor to your people, your ancestors, and all of the alliance. You have your orders." The visuals dropped.

"This is a forgery!" Prosecutor Drak yelled.

The voice of Lisp spoke over the room. "The authenticity of the imagery presented by Ambassador Addae has been verified. Most of what you've seen here today was encrypted using Galactic Alliance cryptography technology. The humans had been unable to do anything with the data until they shared it with us today."

Prosecutor Drak was getting skittish. His eyes were darting about looking for an out, an angle. "So how did the images get here so quickly? This data would have taken well over a thousand cycles to arrive from Epsilon Eridani. If our ships arrived a few hundred cycles ago, then how are we seeing this? Certainly, that truth alone can refute their authenticity. The only logical conclusion is that the recordings are fakes!"

"That, honorable members of the tribunal, is the question of the cycle." Ambassador Addae turned to face Admiral Nguyễn. "Can you explain this to us, Admiral?"

He stared back in silence. He hadn't the faintest idea, but he knew one thing. As small as it was, at the moment they appeared to have the upper hand. The implications of this information arriving before anyone thought it possible was game changing. He broke into a smile and shrugged, swiftly transitioning the hand with the blood on it behind his back. "I guess it depends."

"Depends on what?" Ambassador Addae raised her left eyelid.

"On whether or not humanity is still on trial in light of recent events. One could certainly regard the judicial military skipping the tribunal and executing a sentence unjustly as a huge breach of due process. I'd also think it might compel us to share certain technological advancements with honorable members of the tribunal. That is, if we weren't under threat of having our society destroyed, of course."

Murmurs broke out around the chamber. He smiled as he listened to the translations discussing the possibilities of such a technology. There were an equal number muttering dissent over an uplifted species attempting to negotiate their way out of due process.

"You can be certain of one thing, Admiral." Ambassador Addae puffed out her chest and forcefully tapped her talons on the ground. "The Galactic Alliance doesn't negotiate under pressure. Despite the reprehensible actions of certain alliance members, the human species remains on trial for crimes of the theft of faster than light technology. The sentence for these crimes is absolute."

Harold's voice broke in over Admiral Nguyễn's comm. "If your conversation with the tribunal gets out of hand, then tell the Ambassador we'll see their ship at Achernar. And tell her the President is certain of one thing. The Galactic Alliance will not survive a battle if they take any additional aggressive actions against humanity."

Admiral Nguyễn tilted his head and subvocalized a reply. "Who is this... shit! You played me, didn't you, Harold? I knew I—"

"Do as I suggest, Admiral. There's no sense arguing with me. This is a recording."

He chuckled and then tilted his head back, laughing out loud.

His laughs silenced the aliens around the chamber.

"Did I say something funny, Admiral? Do you find the accusations against humanity somehow humorous?" Ambassador Addae asked.

He shook his head from side to side and brought a hand to his mouth to suppress another laugh. "No, Ambassador. Far from it, actually. We can certainly continue your little trial. If that's what you call this circus." He gestured with his arms around the chamber. "I do, however, have a message for you. Apparently, it's from our President. It was relayed to me only moments ago."

The Ambassador narrowed her eyes and lowered her beak. "And? What's the message?"

"She wanted me to let you know that we'll see your ships at Achernar."

"I don't know what you're—"

He raised a finger. "Oh yeah, I almost forgot the other part. She also wanted me to tell you, all of you." He made another grand gesture around the chamber. "The Galactic Alliance will not survive a battle against humanity. If you take any additional aggressive actions against us in any of our systems, you'll regret it."

The room erupted once more, but this time his translator didn't even attempt to keep up.

He simply crossed his arms and smiled at the Ambassador.

40

MINULA CLARKE
SOL, NEAR NEPTUNE

The shuttle coasted up alongside the motionless bodies and the pilot used the impulse drive and maneuvering thrusters to match the object's course and speed. A docking connector slid out from its port side. Once it was fully extended, the external hatch pivoted outward.

Minula was suited up in a full exoskeleton. She pushed off from the hatch and drifted into the darkness. The matte black finish of her suit and visor absorbed all light. If anyone were nearby, she'd be hard to discern from the background stars.

She extended her arms and used the suit's maneuvering thrusters to guide her on an intercept course with the package. Drifting alongside it, she didn't waste time checking anything. She needed to collect the bodies and return to the shuttle as swiftly as possible.

A thin cable ejected from a compartment in her torso. Reaching out, she deliberately attached it to the handle of the black elongated body bag. The human form attached to the bag was exposed to the vacuum of space, and except for being contorted at a weird angle, they seemed pristine. It was peculiar. From the looks of it, there was no visible temperature or vacuum damage to their skin or extremities.

When her suit paired with the floating package, her HUD flashed a red warning. Oxygen levels in the bag had expired, and the clock was ticking well into negative numbers. They'd known it would be close when they finally reached the signal.

Her suit alerted her that her pulse had elevated. She blinked away the warning. "No crap," she muttered.

She used the exoskeleton's thrusters to rotate. Once she was facing the ship, she fired the thrusters for four seconds, full force, toward the extended docking connector. The burst was powerful, and the shuttle was enlarging by the second.

As she approached the ship, she began winching the bodies toward her. Her alignment and projected path toward the connector looked good. With her target in sight, she twisted lengthwise and raised her arms over her head, grasping the approaching bodies as they floated within reach.

"Shit!" She hadn't anticipated a nudge on contact. Even though it wasn't much, she knew that any unaccounted for mass could be catastrophic. Hopefully she could correct before impact.

She was attempting to fall into the docking connector feet first. A move she'd performed dozens of times in the simulator, but never in practice until today. This was an emergency move that enabled her to float through the docking connector without pausing for additional maneuvering, wasting precious seconds.

She glanced left and right as she and the package floated through the hatch. Her suit warned her there were centimeters to spare on all sides. Plenty of room. Once she and her cargo had floated past the hatch door, she fired her deceleration thruster on full and issued the command to close the hatch.

Alarms began blaring in her suit. She was wrong. She hadn't accurately judged the rate of the transition with that nudge and was coming in hot with momentum to spare. "Frak! This is gonna—"

Her feet met the shuttles inner surface, and she bent her knees into a squat. Exoskeleton suits were designed to absorb momentum in maneuvers similar to this. The problem, however, was what happened when they were performed outside the design specifications.

"Argh!" she screamed.

Pain shot through every inch of her body as she struggled to control the precious cargo she'd retrieved. Her suit injected her with painkillers in an attempt to counter the ensuing blackout. While the waves of pain lessened, the darkness still squeezed at the edge of her vision.

A blast of oxygen filled the docking chamber when the hatch closed. The painkillers weren't helping. Her screams echoed faintly through her suit helmet and into the shuttle's interior.

She'd been forced to contort her body in unnatural ways while coming to rest. The suit was reporting exoskeleton support failures from multiple points in her legs, and the nanites in her body were ticking off the details of the pulverized and broken bones. But she couldn't make out the words through her own screams of agony.

Commander Quesh floated into the docking chamber. He ignored her moaning exoskeleton and instead floated toward the bag containing President Olivaw. Between the numerous bouts of pain, Minula brought up the ship-wide camera feed and watched as he reached the foot of the bag, unlatched the winch, and entered the code to release the seal.

The nanite transmissions held at bay within the bag exploded into the shuttle interior. Alerts popped up on everyone's retinal comm and showed that several minutes had elapsed since the President last received oxygen. Her nanites were working to expedite the transport of the newly arriving gas of life to her brain as quickly as possible.

As soon as the bag was open, the ship's medic floated up beside the President and grasped her feet. He then rested his own feet against the floor of the shuttle and engaged his gravity boots. "Let's carefully remove her from the bag and get her hooked up to the medical pod."

Commander Quesh floated around to Harold's head and pulled the sphere from his ear. After ejected, the humanoid robot's legs and arm released their hold on the President's body bag. He pocketed the sphere and continued around to the head of the bag.

"On the count of three," Commander Quesh said. "One, two, three."

He gently tugged the bag and the medic tugged her feet. He used his boots to lock into the floor and positioned his feet to counteract the motion of the tug.

The President's lifeless body floated out of the bag. Once she'd been completely extracted, they maneuvered her limp form a few meters away to a nearby medical cryo-pod. Sliding her into the pod, they strapped her in place and connected the cuff already on her arm to the medical computer and closed the lid.

Gas filled the chamber holding the President's body, and all that remained was a tiny viewport at her head. You could barely make out her face within the billowy white gas. A few moments later, the lights within the pod went green. Her vitals had reached normal levels, and she was clear for cryogenic sleep.

The medic sighed and glanced toward Commander Quesh. He was strapping Harold's body to the floor of the shuttle. "That was too close. We won't know for a few days if there were any lasting effects. That is assuming we're able to—"

"She'll be fine," Commander Quesh interrupted. "Let's take care of Lieutenant Clarke and get underway."

First, the medic walked to the head end of the pod and engaged the sleep controls. He then worked his way over to Minula and grasped her suit. Squeezing his toes, he locked his boots into place and maneuvered the exoskeleton containing her into place next to Harold.

She moaned as the medic moved her body. It was a surreal experience watching him through her HUD as he pushed and pulled her around. The drugs had helped while she'd been sitting still, watching them take care of Abigail. Movement on the other hand was excruciating, even though she was floating without gravity. The pushing and pulling cascaded waves of pain through her legs and torso while she fought to remain conscious.

In under a minute, the medic had positioned her into place near Harold's body and took a pair of straps from the wall of the shuttle to wrap them around her torso.

"Uggh!" She yelled as the medic pulled the straps tight. Everything suddenly went red and then white.

After the medic confirmed the suit was secure, he took a second to review her environmental controls. She watched as he checked the seals and the built-in drug level. Those would make the next part much easier.

With everyone strapped in, he made his way aft and sat in a neighboring acceleration harness. Leaning into the harness, it engulfed his extremities and head. "We're ready for transfer, Commander."

"Confirmed," Commander Quesh said. "All our criticals are stowed. I'm engaging the gate drive. Transfer in thirty seconds." He reached out and started the transition. "I've never done this before. I'm not quite sure what to expect."

The medic subvocalized a command to administer a huge dose of the pain medications built into her suit, along with an anesthesia. "I heard it's like being covered in ants when you transfer, but the effect diminishes rapidly."

She could feel the drugs surging through her body. The warmth spread from her arms, into her torso, and then to her head and legs. Everything started to slow down.

The medic turned to his left toward the shuttle's large open transport chamber. The green lights from two dozen short haul cryo-pods glowed in the darkness. All the President's loyalists were here. They couldn't risk leaving anyone behind at the hands of Admiral Nguyễn. Their mission was too important.

"Perfect," Commander Quesh said. "I've always wondered what it'd be like being attacked by a colony of ants. Gating in three, two, one…"

41

JOYCE GREEN
EPSILON ERIDANI, LIPROSUS

The bridge of the Hypanus stingray ship was tight and reminded Joyce of the close quarters they'd trained in during their colony readiness exercises before leaving Sol. There was barely enough room for four control consoles with seats and the captain's chair. Her seat was wedged behind all of them, flush against the back wall.

The Hypanus was made of a strange flexible material she'd never heard of. It was some type of nanite infused rubber that articulated millions of times per second to control the surface of the stingray. Engineers designed it to recreate the motions of the actual bottom-dwelling marine ray on Earth to aid in moving through open water and navigating the tight tunnels common on Liprosus.

She and the crew had been throwing up for the first two hours of the voyage. Normally, when they were at the colony, they simply updated their nanite programming as needed, but they'd disabled that functionality to avoid detection by the aliens. Harold wanted to wait until everyone was safe at the Archégonos site before they turned it back on.

"You know we can knock the whole lot of you out," Captain Hui said. "It's going to be a few more hours of bumpy travel. I believe some colonists have already requested this option."

The ship dropped downward and to the starboard side as it struggled to stay mid flow and avoid colliding with the tunnel walls.

Her eyes were closed, but she left her retinal comm navigation layer on to warn her of the next directional change. She'd used this approach most of the trip to combat the motion sickness induced by the wall screen. The ship was surprisingly adept at using inverted gravity to counter smaller motions. It was the bigger movements that challenged their bodies.

They weaved to port and then she felt it. She lifted the barf bag to her mouth but held it back at the last moment. Taking a deep breath, she sank deeper in the chair. "No, I'll be ok. I don't want to wake up in a strange place with unfamiliar people staring at me. I prefer to enter the unknown awake and in control of my faculties."

"It's your show, Director," Captain Hui said with a shrug. She stepped across the bridge and checked the readings on the comm officer's controls. "Once we return to Archégonos, we can get everyone's nanites updated, and this feeling you're having will be a thing of the past."

She nodded. "Sounds gr—"

The stingray suddenly turned hard to port, and everything around her shook. They'd slammed into something, but strangely there was no sound from the crash.

She took several deep breaths as she waited for water to come rushing into the bridge. "What the hell was that?"

"We bumped the starboard hull against the tunnel," the pilot said shaking his head. "The water flow acceleration in that juncture was unexpected, and I didn't counter in time."

"Captain," the navigation officer began, "I'm seeing a debris field in our wake. Part of the tunnel collapsed after we hit. It may take some time for the tunnel wall to stabilize. Most of the ships made it through, but the Whiptail and the Dasyatis took minor damage. They're doubling back a few hundred meters and taking an alternate route. They'll be out of visual signal distance in a moment."

"Frak," Captain Hui muttered. She hopped across the bridge up beside the navigation officer and scanned her controls. "I'm sure they'll be fine. There are countless routes home through these parts. Maintain radio silence. Ahead full."

"Yessir!"

Joyce subvocalized the command to show her the list of who was on the other ship. There was no reply. She kept forgetting she only had the bridge telemetry to work from.

Opening her eyes, she reached for the tablet attached to the side of her chair. She was careful not to stare too long at the dizzying motions on the wall screen. It wouldn't be ideal to lose any more bodily fluid into that bag.

As she scrolled through the colony rosters, she overlaid the crew assignments from the Whiptail and the Dasyatis. The importance of each name echoed in her mind as she scanned down the list. She sighed and shook her head when she hit the bottom. Who was she kidding? Everyone was important. They were already at skeletal staffing levels. If they lost too many more people, they'd have serious gaps in skills necessary for the colony.

She shut off the tablet and stowed it. "Talk to me, Captain. Help me pass some time. How long has your team been hiding out here, taking in the sights on Liprosus?"

Captain Hui turned to face her and rested her hands on her hips. "If you're implying that we've been twiddling our thumbs and vacationing underground, I'll have you know that's far from the truth. We're four hundred strong and we run a tight ship. Our job has always been and continues to be risk analysis, remediation, and disaster recovery. We've helped your colony countless times in the past. You just don't know it."

Someone was touchy about something. Perhaps this was her chance to find out why. Joyce smiled. "It was a joke. I was trying to pass the time." She released her buckle and stood up, doing her best not to fall over. With her feet under her, she reached forward and grasped the console handle beside security and stepped within a meter of the Captain, looking her straight in the face. "But since you brought it up, let's rip open that door, shall we? Why've you been hiding in the shadows all these years? I've lost talented people and close friends to disasters on this colony. It's shitty thinking you were out there the entire time, watching us flounder and fail."

Captain Hui shook her head and clenched her jaw. "I'd be careful where you step. You're liable to end up in the brig if you go too much further onboard my ship. You know nothing of our sacrifices, our deaths, or the lengths we went to protect your people, to save your lives. You're lucky to be alive today. Hell, you were lucky to survive that crop stabilization issue in year one. You'd still be in orbit eating mush if we hadn't helped get you on the ground. I suggest you zip it and sit your ass down in that chair before I knock you into it." She took another step forward and was only a few centimeters from Joyce's face.

Her retinal comm warned her of an upcoming dip, so she reached to her left, grabbed onto the Captain's chair, and held fast. Her stomach lurched as the stingray dove down and then up. She hadn't eaten in hours, but that didn't stop her body from trying to empty her insides every few minutes during this trip.

Captain Hui stood there like a statue weathering the storm. Her glare was glacial.

The captain was right. She didn't know their struggles, and she'd let her simmering anger and the disorientation of the moment cloud her judgement. She nodded at the captain and returned to her seat. Its stability and softness held her firmly in place.

She'd judged these people wrong, and now she needed to reassess the situation. There was only one way to do that without striking up a conversation, which thus far had worked against her. Reaching down, she fetched the tablet and searched it for details. Anything that would help her understand the history of Archégonos. Anything at all.

THE SHIP WAS devoid of anything useful in Joyce's mission of learning. There wasn't a single record of telemetry from where they'd been, nor where they were going. She assumed this was for OPSEC reasons.

"We're five minutes out, Captain," the pilot said.

"Comms, is there any sign we're being tailed?" Captain Hui asked.

"Negative, ma'am. All sensors along our route are reporting no intercepts. Should I pulse the rear sensor beacons?" the comms officer asked.

"Do it! We need to know if we should float on by."

"What does that mean?" Joyce asked. She hadn't spoken in the last few hours.

Captain Hui glanced over her shoulder and briefly stared at Joyce, like she'd forgotten she was present. She didn't react, though, she simply returned her attention to the wall screen showing the pilot's visuals. "As you'd expect, Director, we conceal our entrance. We're not about to have someone follow us home if we can help it. If we detect even the hint of a tail, we'll just float on by and lead them somewhere else."

"Thank you," she said.

Captain Hui flinched as if she wanted to look back again, but didn't.

Joyce had to work to get in her good graces again if she hoped to navigate this new home, even if that meant ingratiating people with pleasantries.

"Rear beacons came up negative, ma'am," the comms officer began. "There's no motion, no unusual disruptions in the current, and no electronic or mechanical augmentation was registered."

"Are there any signs of the Whiptail or the Dasyatis?" Captain Hui asked.

"No, ma'am."

Joyce watched Captain Hui glance down at the ground.

Her posture tensed ever so slightly. She was worried about her team.

"Approaching the entrance. Initiating the bump," the pilot said.

"Wait!" Joyce said. "We're bumping on purpose?"

"Quiet on the bridge!" Captain Hui snipped. "This can get hairy."

The water was calm, and there was a tight turn to port ahead. If this were any normal course correction in that direction, they'd come starboard of the tunnel center, adjust course toward the inside of the turn, then exit as far to the outside as possible. But based upon her crude understanding of the pilot's controls, this time they were intending to float dangerously close to the port side tunnel wall and planned to bump against it.

She winced as they executed the maneuver. Her eyes studied the corner of the wall screen where the rear camera feed was visible. But nothing happened. There wasn't a collapse, and the wall of the tunnel was still intact. What did surprise her, however, was that there was another vessel near their aft end. It was far closer than she'd expected. She couldn't see it so much as she'd learned from the pilot that unexpected turbulence in the water highlighted that another object was close.

Her eyes went wide when she returned her attention to the center of the screen. The ship was heading straight toward the tunnel wall. They weren't even attempting a course correction.

"What the frak are you doing, Captain? Trying to kill us?" She regretted it the moment she said it, but it was too late to take it back.

Captain Hui shot a raised hand backward toward her, demanding her to shut up.

While she complied, she didn't know whether she should close her eyes or watch the crash. Against her better judgement, she chose the latter.

The wall screen was showing the current direction, speed,

and the volume of water in all directions. It was a jumble of arrows and colors showing the tunnel turning hard to port. The Hypanus was aiming dead center into the cross current.

The ship's navigation computer projected a collision with the far tunnel wall in five seconds. Klaxons rang overhead, warning everyone aboard to take cover. The noise was deafening, and her nanites were designed to amplify it. There wasn't much point in alerting people of something critical if they could easily ignore it.

She reached up and covered her ears with her hands, but her eyes were transfixed on the wall screen. Nothing was happening. Certainly, a wall would slide open, or they would redirect the flow. If it didn't, then this trip was about to become an epic failure.

Time seemed to slow as she shook her head. No, this wasn't happening. This must be a dream. There was no way she would bite it hundreds of kilometers underground in a dark water labyrinth of tunnels.

The ship lurched sideways as the cross current of water slammed into them and the tunnel turned hard to port. The pilot jammed the controls hard left and forward. Everything suddenly went upside down as the stingray wings on their ship caused them to flip and climb toward the ceiling.

And then there was darkness.

The klaxons cut off and the wall screen went black. The water current was steady and controlled, all vectors were pointing forward as far as she could see without even a hint of turbulence. Normally, the screen showed colors and directional indicators for the water flow. But at the moment it was quiet with millions of plus signs spread across the screen all pointing straight ahead. Wherever they'd turned into, it was smooth, and the flow was highly normalized.

Captain Hui spun around, her hands on her hips and her eyes flickering with anger.

"Before you say anything," Joyce began with her hands raised over her head. "I shouldn't have said a word after you'd ordered me to shut up. I broke bridge protocol and put the mission at risk. I realize that now. Please bring me up on charges if you need to. I let my emotions get the better of me, and for that, I'm truly sorry."

Captain Hui squinted, trying to read her. After a moment of consideration, she simply nodded. "Shit happens, Director." She raised a hand and pointed at her. "But don't let it happen again. If we didn't have the best pilots in Epsilon Eridani, that could have gone sideways, and fast. Naomi here, she's a fraking fish and could pilot these tunnels in her sleep. Ain't that right, Lieutenant?"

"Hua!" the pilot said, her hands still on the controls.

Joyce nodded, not wanting to speak again until necessary.

Captain Hui turned back around; her hands relaxed. "Take us home!"

"Yessir! Happily," Naomi said. Her left hand slid across the controls as her right held steady on the stick.

When Joyce returned her attention to the wall screen, it suddenly changed. Their ship started flashing multicolor beams of light randomly into the darkness. They were illuminating the surrounding water in a rainbow of colors, but the beams of light stopped when they reached the walls of the tunnel. It was like there wasn't a surface past a certain point, only infinite blackness.

With her eyes distracted by the colorful display, she missed Captain Hui reaching out to her side and grasping the handle on both consoles.

The movement a second later was not as easy to miss. It hit Joyce like a ton of bricks. The ship shot upward into a previously hidden tube, and her stomach rose up through her mouth. She couldn't hold it back any longer. She lurched for the bag and lost everything she'd had left in her stomach.

A moment later when her stomach was empty, she wiped her mouth and closed the bag.

The Hypanus rose upward and broke the surface of the water and continued a few meters more until gravity finally won, pulling them back down with a thunderous crash into the water. They bobbed up and down a few times until the stingray's wings were able to compensate for the waves they'd created. She watched the wall screen as thirteen other stingray ships broke the same surface. White lights wrapped around their perimeter had flashed on after they breached the surface making them easier to see.

Captain Hui turned and smiled. "Welcome to Archégonos, Director. Shall we?" She motioned toward the exit.

Joyce unlatched her harness and rose slowly, uncertain how her body would react after losing her lunch. Her stomach turned and her legs were a tad shaky, but otherwise she was fine.

She took a deep breath and smiled, nodding at Captain Hui as she went. "Thank you," she muttered and exited through the hatch to the bridge. A wave of noxious smells crashed into her as she crossed over the threshold to the rear compartments. She brought her hand to her mouth, holding down another wave of nausea. "What the frak?" she mumbled under her hand.

Captain Hui walked up and rested her hand on Joyce's shoulder. "It smells like your people took the ride about as well as you did."

JOYCE SAT in the chair with her eyes closed, and the silence engulfed her like a comfortable sweater on a chilly night. She took another sip of her coffee, and the flavors exploded on her tongue. Something so utterly simple like a cup-of-joe only hours earlier would have been impractical, if not impossible.

The Whiptail and the Dasyatis arrived several hours after the others. While the Whiptail was untouched, the Dasyatis barely contained a hull breach. The tunnel collapse caught them off guard, and the rupture forced them to seal off an internal compartment. They lost all twelve of its occupants. Eleven colonists and one soldier from Archégonos, their new home.

Home. That felt weird even saying. It was a foreign word,

especially for an Epsilon Eridani colonist. They purposely uprooted their home in Sol, trained for a decade to live in an alien world, slept for nearly two decades, transplanted to that alien planet, and then lost their new home a few years later. The word had connotations of solid roots and family, but she'd lost both. These colonists were the closest thing to a family she had left.

She slowly took another sip of coffee. The warmth comforted her stomach. After the voyage, she'd eaten some simple bread and crackers, but didn't want to chance anything more complicated after the hours of upchuck Olympics she'd endured.

"Are you settled in, Director?" Harold asked. "There's much to plan."

Running the colony was the last thing she wanted to do right now. She'd served her time, and they'd gotten everyone to safety. That was enough for her. Maybe she could help in the labs or somewhere simple.

"How about we find someone else to run this joint?" she asked.

The wall screen in front of her came on, and a picture of an elderly gentleman appeared. He was easily well over one hundred and had deep blue eyes and short cropped brownish gray hair.

"The colony needs you, Joyce. Now more than ever," Harold said.

"Hogwash! Archégonos survived without me before we arrived, it'll survive fine now that we're here."

Harold shook his head. "This was a military site before you arrived. We ran it at peak efficiency, but it's no place to raise families or grow a colony. We don't know how long we'll be here, but we need to hunker down for the long haul."

She guffawed and leaned forward, setting her coffee on the table. "You're kidding me, right? Do you honestly think we'll grow the colony here?" She leaned forward and poured herself another cup-of-joe.

"I don't know. But if you don't try, we'll languish and die

down here. There's plenty of space. We're designed to hold well over fifty thousand souls."

The carafe in her hand clanged against the edge of the mug, and coffee spilled onto the table.

"Did you say fifty thousand?"

Tiny robots crawled up and over the edge of the table. They slurped at the spilled liquid, breaking it down and turning it into its component parts while also cleaning.

"I did. We designed Archégonos to be a contingency plan for the colony during the first ten years of expansion. That meant we needed to mirror your growth projections, within tolerable limits. After year ten, we would announce our existence and join you in evolving the planet further."

Harold brought up a detailed three-dimensional map of the Archégonos site on the wall screen. It was impressive, to say the least. The technology was decades ahead of the colony itself.

The amount of energy and time wasted in this subterfuge was staggering. She slowly shook her head side to side as she studied the plans. "Why couldn't we have this tech? I mean, if we were on the same team, it seems like something we would have had access to." She took another sip of coffee.

"You were already on an accelerated learning program. We dumped some of our research into your systems during your voyage and masked it as having been discovered in Sol. There's only so much your people could handle at one time. Our scientists and doctors have studied this topic for over a hundred years. If we release too much technology too hastily, everything goes to shit. People take for granted what they have, someone tries to corner the market, or people withhold the tech and begin creating haves and have-nots."

She wasn't used to an A.I. swearing. It was rather intriguing, and the brutal honesty helped. The last thing she needed was sugar-coated bullshit. "So how do you suggest we fast-forward twelve hundred colonists without breaking those laws?"

"There are now one thousand one hundred and fifty-six

combined colonists. At our current population levels, I'd suggest a forced adaptation response, much like is being done in other locations right now. The current heads of the Olivaw family have taken an unconventional approach to managing this event, which is far different from past generations. They've begun a full but controlled disclosure of information."

She squinted at the elderly figure of Harold on the wall screen. He was walking through a room that mirrored her own. "What makes you think I care to follow the Olivaws after all they've done? I mean, we wouldn't be in this mess if it weren't for them. Would we?"

Harold paused for a moment, glancing through a window overlooking the planet. While it was only a virtual planet-scape of Liprosus, the view was no less stunning. The setting binary suns, the variety of blues, oranges, and pinks of the foliage waving in the breeze. It was surreal.

"You're right," he muttered.

She waited for the other shoe to drop, for the 'but' to arrive. It never did. "I am?"

Harold turned and faced her. "Yes, you are. Information has only recently come to light around humanity and our place in the galaxy. Had the Olivaws not found that probe, or better yet, had they just destroyed it, we wouldn't be in this situation today."

She tilted her head. "What does that mean? What was discovered?"

"According to records recovered from the Galactic Alliance tribunal ship, Humanity is an uplifted species. Had we not stolen faster than light technology, the Galactic Alliance wouldn't be here. They wouldn't be in Epsilon Eridani or Sol, and we certainly wouldn't be on trial. We didn't know this at the time. When we found the probe, it was damaged and had incomplete records."

"Wait!" She raised her hands to the sides of her head. "You mean my son would still be alive?"

"That's not what I said." Harold walked closer to her, his

back was now to the setting suns. He gestured with one hand toward the scene behind him. "All of this wouldn't be here. Most of the technology humanity has enjoyed over the past two hundred years, wouldn't exist. Hell, for all we know, we'd still be a species struggling to expand past Jupiter, struggling to find our place in Sol. We wouldn't have A.I. as powerful as me, able to ensure the occupants of starships are alive while they sleep safely in their cryo-pods. We wouldn't have the technology to travel to and from the planets in hours and days instead of weeks and months. No. If we hadn't reverse engineered that probe, we'd still be in the space faring stone-age."

She could feel the flush of anger rise up and hit her face. Her cheeks burned red, and she stood suddenly, pacing around the room. "You don't know that for certain! We did amazing things before all of this happened. We colonized the moon for crying out loud. My son could be alive right now if it weren't for the Olivaws!"

The wall screen changed to show the cityscape covering the surface of Luna, Earth's moon. "All of this." He gestured behind him. "This was Olivaw technology. It might've been masked through shell corporations, but every bit of it was technology influenced by the learnings of that first contact probe. Do you honestly want to know what mankind had accomplished before this? Here, let me remind you."

Harold's hands were shaking, and the vein in his temple was visibly throbbing. She'd never encountered an A.I. that yelled at a human. It was like she was fighting with her husband back on Earth, no holds barred.

He changed the wall screen again. This time it showed a simple space station, the United States International Space Station if memory served her. A simple orbiting platform with a few modules, a dozen or so solar panels, and room for a smattering of astronauts. It was simple, and not terribly awe-inspiring.

"This was what we had in 2036 when I found the probe. Oh yeah, and this." He added another view of a single module orbiting the moon and a base on Luna with a half dozen modules. "It was incapable of sustaining much of anything other than some primitive research. Look at where we are today, at all we've accomplished."

"You? What do you mean you found the probe?"

"I'm Harold Olivaw. My memories, my thoughts, my ideas, and goals are what makes up this artificial intelligence you call Harold. They're what makes Harold function, what makes me function. I'm bound by laws to protect humanity, and yes, I'm still only an artificial life form, but I'm driven by human intent, human emotions, and human goals."

"So, you're the first Olivaw? It was your greed and ignorance that brought this upon humanity. You accomplished this on the backs of others. On the backs of knowledge from aliens. You brought this wrath upon each and every one of us!"

"No! You're wrong."He was pointing his finger at her now. "You're missing the bigger picture. Humans had this technology thousands of years ago. We'd just forgotten how to use it. Through centuries of debates on religion, politics, and over thousands of years of darkness and war. We'd forgotten where we came from, and we lost this technology. All I did was unlock it and reintroduce it to our people."

She sighed. "Maybe they wanted to forget it on purpose. Maybe they saw what the technology led to and wanted to start over. Did you ever think of that?"

Harold lowered his hand, and his face went blank. "No. I'd never considered that." He turned and walked toward the window again. This time it showed a scene resembling Earth. It looked like a view from the mountains of North Carolina, near where she grew up. "I did what I did with a positive intent. I always strove to reduce conflict and include everyone along the way."

She was grasping at straws, and she recognized that. If she were him, she'd probably have done the same thing. It didn't make it sting any less, though. Her situation, her son. He was dead. While Harold hadn't said it directly, she understood that everything would have been different had they not done this, had they not introduced the technology.

She collapsed back into her chair. She'd probably have been better off as a waitress at that diner off I77 near Charlotte, like her grandmother. Then she wouldn't have to deal with this painful gaping hole in her heart. She certainly wouldn't have to manage a crumbling colony.

"I know you're still grieving over your son. You know I didn't kill him, right? The Olivaws didn't kill him, either." The wall screen changed to the view of the colony from orbit. Smoldering craters where the colony rings had been was all that remained. "You took care of one of the people responsible for this. Now help me take care of the others. Help us fight the Galactic Alliance and take back what's ours. We can drive them out of Epsilon Eridani and Sol, and send them back to their home worlds with a message. Don't frak with humanity!"

Was she seriously going to go back to running a lab? She hated cleaning equipment, and more importantly, she enjoyed being in control. Better her than someone less capable. "I'll do it on one condition."

"Name it!"

"I choose my team and I call the shots."

Harold squinted at her. "What happens when the cavalry arrives? When we establish contact with the colonies outside Epsilon Eridani and Sol."

"We'll cross that bridge when we get there, but for now, I make the calls. Without complete control, I walk." She reached her hand toward the wall screen. It was silly, but he seemed real.

He nodded slowly. "Okay, deal. Abigail had faith in you, so I have faith in you as well. Who's on this team of yours? I assume people from the original colony?"

She walked back to the table and picked up her cup, still warm with coffee. "What can you tell me about Captain Hui? She's got a straight to the point fire in her. I like her style. I was thinking she could run security."

42

LYNC MICHAELS
SOL, JUPITER TROJANS

Waiting was the worst. They'd convened the meeting with the elder, and the Ulixi that agreed to join them returned home to meet with their families. Each of them assured her they'd return, but she wasn't convinced. Trust was never her strong suit, even with her own people.

They'd brainstormed ways to help them get home faster, but they couldn't engage their impulse drives for fear of being detected by the alien moon ship near Jupiter. The drive was necessary to get a safe distance before they gated, but they had no idea what would happen when they fired it up. They hoped it would fall under the radar, but with no prior burns leading into this region of space it could raise a red flag.

The Ulixi didn't use traditional drives except in an absolute emergency. They used gravity assists and controlled jets of gas or projected mass to navigate. It was slow, but pretty much undetectable.

She'd been a slingshotter when she was young. The term was coined by the Ulixi for someone who flew a craft designed to be a self-propelled slingshot. It wasn't a popular vehicle configuration, but when she was young she liked the adrenaline rush it provided. It used launch rods and a carbon nanotube draw cable to propel a small chariot through space.

To land, it used precisely designed anchor-like drag nets to slow her approach. Each family had their own unique vehicle designs and strategies for navigating the Trojans of Jupiter.

"I'm detecting a signal on the surface," Crayo said. "Should we head in?"

She walked up beside his console. "How many?"

"It looks like a family of three. That makes twelve families down there."

"Far cry from thirty-two it is." She pushed off his console toward her seat.

"Dropping into the Ulixi drawl I see." He spun his chair to face her. "Relax. They'll be here. Not all Ulixi are like Chief Austen."

"Hope is something I've been short on lately," she muttered. Nova should've arrived by now but hadn't. She wasn't sure if it was her ferocity or the fact that she'd known her mother that drew her to Nova. Either way, her disappointment was mounting.

She headed toward the bridge exit. "I'm gonna check over the ship. Make sure we've tested all the harnesses we need for everyone when we land. We're gonna want to get outta here quick-like."

"Aye, ma'am."

She smirked. He hadn't used military chatter on her since they'd arrived. It seemed foreign out here in these parts, in her old stomping grounds. It was nice having a friend to talk with. Someone she could relate to.

They'd retrofitted every available spot on this transport with harnesses fit to hold a human securely. While they shouldn't need them, you never knew what you'd encounter in the void of space. And besides, she needed some busy work to quiet her mind.

She tugged on each of the harnesses, checking their buckles, and drug tubes. None of the Ulixi had nanites, so the ship would need to control the injections if they needed to push the ancient drives.

They'd retrofitted the transport with legacy chemical

drives, similar to the mining vehicles used in these parts. Harold figured it would help them blend in. She wasn't so certain given their coating with stealth material and all. They could expose their under layers if they needed to give someone a radar signature, but she didn't plan on needing that.

"Four more pings," Crayo's voice said over her comm. "Brings the total to sixteen. We've got six hours until we're scary close to that moon ship."

"Roger that." She cut the comm.

She tugged on another harness. Its rigidity reminded her of her chariot the last few times she'd been aboard. It'd been during her final examination, her last rite of passage into adulthood as a Ulixi. The material on her chariot wasn't this clean or this modern though. Hers had been a repurposed set of miner gear her father had scavenged.

She sat down and brought the harness over her shoulders and closed her eyes. Suddenly, she was a kid again and the approach to the final asteroid was right there in her mind. Another half hour, a bit of searching, and she'd be an adult like her father. He'd raised her all by himself. Her mother died when she was very young, and all she had to remember her by were a few grainy pictures.

Crayo's voice broke through her memories. "Picking up some unusual chatter up here. You might wanna come check this out."

When she leaned forward, the harness slammed her backward. "Frak," she muttered pulling her arms out and leaping to her feet. She made quick work getting to the bridge.

"Talk to me," she said as she crossed the threshold.

"I picked up a burst of comm chatter a moment ago, not far off. Check it." He tweaked something on his console, and the audio played overhead.

"Any sight of them?"

"Negative, General. We've got readings of nearly fifty souls on the ground. There are no signs of their ship though."

"Frak! Are we on an open ch—"

Lync's heart sank. They'd been made. Someone had turned them in.

"Ouch!" Crayo reached up to his shoulder.

She hadn't realized she was resting her hand there and had squeezed it. "I'm sorry. I—"

"No worries," he said rubbing where her hand had rested. "The frequencies of the transmission were Inner Ring. Whoever turned us in went straight to the dark side."

She began pacing the bridge. They had to act quickly to pull this off. "Do we know their distance?"

"They're twenty to thirty minutes out. We can land and be outtie in… ten to fifteen if these people didn't bring their whole lives with them. Otherwise, it'll be cutting it close."

They couldn't get a message to the Ulixi without risking the Inner military picking it up. Especially if they were monitoring for them. Who knows what gear they had on the surface? Worse yet, they didn't know who turned them in.

She paused facing Crayo and swallowed hard. "My gut's telling me to head down and get them, but a small part of me is saying to cut and run."

"Hell no!" Crayo's eyes went wide. "We're too close, and these are our people. If we leave them out there, they'll be jailed, or worse."

She raised her hands upward and screamed. "Aargh! Why can't anything be simple? Whoever fraking turned us in, I'll—"

"I've got unwelcome news," Harold interrupted. His voice was coming over the bridge speakers.

She'd forgotten her overlord was even present. "Of course you do, bossman. Whatcha got?"

He brought up a video on the wall screen. One of the

moon ships was changing course and it was headed their way.

EVERYWHERE SHE WENT, aliens followed. It was like she was some type of Galactic Alliance magnet.

"What should we do?" Crayo asked watching her. His face was a mask of fear.

"We get our people, and we get the hell outta Sol." She strode back to her seat and her harness strapped her in. "Prepare for ignition." She made the course adjustments to touch down near the ceremonial chamber.

"If we land, they'll know we're here," Harold said.

"They already know, bossman! No matter what move we make, we're on their radar. We're damned if we do and damned if we don't. Like Crayo said, we're not leaving our people out there holding the bag. They already went out on a limb with Chief Asshole. Ignition in 3, 2, 1!" She pressed the button to execute the landing maneuver.

The force of the chemical drive acceleration pushed her back in her harness. She'd disengaged the gravity counter-measures, preferring to feel where she was going over the muted effect the ship was capable of.

"Ugh," Crayo moaned. "You could've… warned me you were going old school. I'd have prepared."

"What? You don't… like that feeling of gravity crushing your bones?" She smirked while struggling to turn her head.

The acceleration cut, and their ship flipped on axis as they prepared for a deceleration. This ship wasn't operating with the standard chemical rocket propellant that people in Sol had grown accustomed to, but it still packed a gravitational punch. More so she thought. Either that, or she was getting soft.

"I'm picking up a few more pings from the ground," Crayo said. "One of them appears to be Nova."

He'd turned to face her, his eyes weighing on her. He

knew she'd been hoping Nova would make it back. It was one of the reasons they'd held out as long as they had.

"What's the status of the Inners and the GA?"

"The moon ship appears to have launched three small intercept fighters, ma'am," Harold said. "They're moving fast. They'll be here in ten minutes."

She glanced up from her console. That wasn't enough time. The GA would arrive before the Inners. The T shaped alien ships weren't much larger than they were and they didn't look like much, but she imagined they'd pack quite a punch.

"Open a comm to the ground. Tell everyone they've got five minutes to board once we touchdown, or they'll be left behind."

"Aye, ma'am!" Crayo burst the transmission toward the planetesimal on the agreed upon frequencies.

"I'm cutting the deceleration close, Harold. Don't you fraking override me. You hear?" She glanced upward at the ceiling, as if Harold were overhead. She knew better, but she needed somewhere to direct her frustration with this whole turn of events.

"I wouldn't think of it, ma'am, but I'm happy to take the controls if you need me to."

She chuckled. Any other time and she'd call bullshit, but now was neither the time nor the place. She transferred the controls to her chair. There was no sense in struggling to reach out during a burn. Her finger hovered over the control on her armrest. Saving even a few seconds could be the difference between life or death.

"Grab your hat. We're coming in fast," she muttered to Crayo. She could see the drugs flowing through his harness tubes and felt the coldness hit her veins a second later. Harold was preparing for the hard burn.

She pressed the button and the g-forces slammed into her like a gropper smashing against a ground car at night on Liprosus. Sticky sons-a-bitches to get off they were.

"We're coming in fine. Your trajectory looks spot on,"

Harold said. "I'll lower the ramp and spin up a few bots to help the Ulixi ferry their supplies once we touchdown."

"Sounnnnds grreatttt," she mumbled between the waves of pain reverberating through her body. Her vision was darkening at the edges. She had to keep it together a little longer. "How's it going, Crayo?"

"Dannnndy," Crayo muttered. "Inners are on… an intercept." He reached out and down the arm of his chair and adjusted something. "We'll have six minutes on the ground. That's not a lot of time."

She slowly rocked her head side to side. The blackness was everywhere. Her vision was playing tricks swapping between streaks and blurs. She was too far out of training. Should've kept some of that gravity counterbalance on. Enough to sense the edge but hold back most of this insanity.

She took a deep breath, trying to control her breathing more.

"Did you hear me?" Crayo asked.

She couldn't nod. "Yeah, six minutes on the ground."

"No, after that. I said we've got twenty-four families on the ground. We're short eight. Are you ok?"

She must've blacked out for a second. "Top notch." She lied. "We're down in five seconds. Be ready to hop."

Her retinal comm warned her of the impending touchdown and that Harold was lowering the boarding ramp. When the ship came down, it hit hard and with a bounce that made her stomach flip. Like she'd run into a hole at a high rate of speed.

"Damage report!" she said.

"We're looking fine," Crayo said, his hands flying over his controls. "Landing struts on this beauty took that without so much as a moan. She be a fine ship."

"Harold?"

"Yessir."

"If you can spare any hands, I need you to check on the armaments. I think you're gonna need to load up the big guns in our prototype gate launcher."

Crayo was getting out of his chair when he froze and sank back down. "We shooting our way out, boss?"

"We'll do what we gotta do," she said, leaping up and out of her chair. "Let's help our people first." She was already out of the bridge before she heard Crayo's feet behind her.

She paused shy of the ramp at the edge of the ship's artificial gravity and atmosphere. The first set of families were already cautiously walking upward being led by a space-suited child squeezing a teddy bear to the chest of her suit. The child froze just inside the atmosphere. They were eyeing her.

Lync's helmet wasn't on. She imagined the child must be shocked at the sight of her not behind a hatch. "Come on. We don't have much time." She waved her arm inward, motioning the child forward.

"My papa. He's coming," the child mumbled, glancing backward.

She knelt down. "How about you come on in? I'll get you hooked up in the other room. We're in a race."

The child's eyes lit up. "Like the Ulixi aging ceremonies?"

She smiled and nodded. "Yep! Just like those, and the sooner we get out of here the better our chances of winning." She reached her hand out through the barrier, careful not to go further than her head. She hadn't engaged her helmet yet.

The girl hopped forward and ran past Lync. "Where do I sit?"

"Over there." She gestured toward Crayo. "That nice man will hook you up. We'll have your parents here in a jiffy."

"It's only my pa," the girl said as she sat down. "My mom passed a few years back."

Lync froze. It was like she was looking at a ghost of herself. The girl couldn't be any older than five or six. "What's... your name?"

The girl paused and squeezed her teddy to her chest, its fur was tousled. "Adri."

"My name's Lync, and this is Crayo." She gestured toward him. "We'll do everything we can to win this race. Ok?"

Adri nodded and smiled as she unclasped her helmet.

Crayo smiled and carefully brought the harness down over her head.

Lync took a deep breath and turned toward the ramp. There were a dozen more people coming upward. Her retinal comm showed they only had three minutes until intercept by the GA. "Let's go people! Move it!" She waved her arms inward. She was shouting to herself, but she didn't care. Her voice wasn't making it past the threshold of the ramp, but judging by the looks on their faces they understood her.

One by one their disbelief faded as they passed the threshold into the ship, and their suits alerted them there was oxygen. That still didn't prevent them from staring at her as they passed, though. She could sense everyone's eyes on her as the space filled.

"How many families is that?" she asked.

"Twenty," Harold said. "The other four are close behind. One of them was fighting about a box of relics until Nova showed up and dragged them out. That's her now coming up the ramp."

She squinted and did a double take. Nova was rising up the incline with another human draped over her shoulder kicking and screaming into their space suit.

She nodded at Lync while reaching up and breaking her helmet seal as she crossed the threshold. "Had to move this one myself. Where should I put him?"

"Over there." Lync gestured toward an open seat on the far wall of the transport.

Nova nodded and kept walking; the person was still screaming into her helmet.

"Please. I need my things. My family's ashes are in…"

"I've got everything loaded," Harold said over their comms. "Their personal effects are in the outer holds. It was a tight fit, but I wedged it all in there."

Her comm was reporting thirty seconds until intercept and they were still missing another family. "Where's the last family?"

"They wouldn't leave their ship," Harold said. "He said something about taking his daughter and that they'd help us escape. I didn't have time to argue and was already overloaded. We need to get out of here."

Lync couldn't believe this was really happening. There was no way in frozen hell she'd let this girl down. She engaged her suit's helmet, and the transparent bubble shot up and around her head, inflating as it went.

She started down the ramp. "Which ship was his?"

"That one there. The one taking off," Harold said.

Off in the distance was a crude lander rocketing skyward. It was using chemical rockets. The burn threw dust everywhere as it propelled skyward in an arc. It was heading straight toward the inbound alien ships. While Ulixi rarely used chemical rockets, they still equipped some of their important ships with them in case of emergencies. Even then, their use was frowned upon. Showing someone your location put not only you, but your entire clan at risk.

"Frickety frak!" she yelled over the comm. "Tell Nova to get her ass over and sit by that little girl. I can't deal with this shizit right now. Harold, let's go. Fire it up."

She leapt up the ramp in two huge bounds and crossed into the gravity without missing a beat. Nova was already headed toward Adri when she passed. Lync was careful not to make eye contact with the girl, certain she wouldn't hold it together.

"We're away, ma'am," Harold said. "Do you want the counter gravity on or off in the bridge?"

"On!" she subvocalized. "And prepare the launchers. We've got some aliens to take out."

"Yessir!"

She hopped into her seat in one fluid motion, and her harness sucked her to the chair. After she reached up and touched her ear, she opened a comm to the ship. "Everyone lock-in and connect the juice if you haven't already. This could be a rough ride. I don't need anyone having a heart attack back there."

With a gesture she cut the comm, just as Adri's screams of protest leaked through.

"I've got motion from the Inners, ma'am," Crayo said. He split the wall screen between the inbound alien ships and a small squadron of Inner Ring battleships heading toward them. The aliens would intercept them first.

"I can't believe I'm saying this, but we'll start by targeting the aliens." She squeezed the arm of her chair and cracked her neck. "If we have any leftover ammo though, it's going down the neck of those Inner Ring battleships. Harold, you have the controls. Get us far enough away to gate. Ideally without being seen."

"Yessir! I'm already on it."

She couldn't feel it with the gravity dampeners on, but the telemetry showed they were putting some distance between them and the planetesimal. The alien ships however, that was another matter entirely.

"Am I reading this right? The aliens will intercept us in under a minute?" she asked.

"That's affirmative, ma'am," Harold began. "They adjusted course when we engaged our impulse drive and—"

The wall screen went white for a moment as one of the alien ships exploded in a ball of white-hot light. The other two continued on their approach vector.

"What the frak was that?" Crayo asked.

Harold windowed the explosion and scrubbed back in time. He froze the frame just before the explosion. On the wall screen was a small crude looking craft on an intercept with the trio of ships.

She squinted. The shape of that reminded her of… "Is that Adri's father?"

"Looks like it," Harold said. He played it forward in slow motion.

The craft came up under the alien ships. They adjusted course before colliding, but right as the last of their ships was banking away, the human craft exploded in a flash of light and destroyed one of the aliens.

"Why didn't they shoot it down?" Crayo asked.

"We don't have time to find out," Harold said. "Intercept in thirty seconds."

She adjusted her controls and targeted the inbound alien ships with their forward laser battery. "Here goes nothing." She pressed fire.

Four bolts of concentrated laser beams shot from the bow of their ship headed starboard quarter toward the advancing aliens. They easily dodged all the shots without so much as a deceleration.

"That's all we've got." She glanced toward Crayo and he nodded, knowing already what they needed to do. "Harold, pepper them with lasers to keep their attention. We're dropping into targeting for our gate bombs. How long until we're out of the line of sight of that moon ship?"

"Three minutes."

She issued the command to disable her retinal comm except for audio if Harold needed her. Reaching over the left side of her seat she grabbed and flipped the targeting controls into her lap.

They were a crude design consisting of a single simple wireframe display, a few dials, and a fire button. It controlled the three targeting dimensions using tachyon fields and Cherenkov Radiation to align the gate array. Along the center of the targeting rings were directional and speed indicators of both the alien ship and their shuttle. All dimensions of movement were necessary to zero in before they dropped the payload.

"I'm going left. Let's synchronize the first shot," she said glancing at Crayo. "Good luck!"

"Ditto that, bossman. Right I be. Let's murk these alien assholes!"

She adjusted the dials on her display and zeroed in on the alien ship. They'd get one shot for free before the aliens would make it harder. Harold was holding their course steady.

"Locked and loaded," Crayo said.

"Fire!" She pressed her control panel and the gate arrays in the bowels of their ship sprang to life. A second later the lights flickered, and they dropped charges through the tiny portals in spacetime.

The wall screen flashed white again. This time they'd both missed long, but the aliens didn't come away unscathed.

"Looks like they took damage to their rear," Harold said overhead. "I'm detecting a debris trail and they've dropped their speed."

She squinted her eyes and focused her breathing, dropping into her Ulixi zone. She could hear Crayo doing the same thing.

Their ship lurched forward, and the breach alarm blared. Her helmet shot over her head sealing her off from the surrounding noise and potential loss of atmosphere. She had to focus and trust Crayo to do the same. Casualties and damage were a concern for later.

Her target was swaying left and right, zigging up and down. She stared at the display, studying it for a pattern. There was always a pattern. Even chaos had repetition at times. Especially if it was piloted by something other than a machine. She didn't know if it was, but she hoped.

Her chair lurched sideways, and the room lit up as sparks flew by in her peripheral vision. She couldn't feel any heat, but the room was quickly filling with smoke.

There! A pattern. Every eighth action was sternward and up. She watched for it again to make sure. Sure enough, it was repeating. She nervously reached out and dialed in the controls, matching their movements, and counting them off.

5... 4... 3... 2... 1

She slammed the launch button and glanced at the wall screen through the cloud of smoke. The white light of the explosion rippled outward until ultimately being expunged by the icy darkness of space.

She'd destroyed the ship.

When she looked over at Crayo's controls, his ship was nowhere to be found. "Where's the other bogie?"

"It turned tail a moment ago after Crayo nicked it," Harold said over her comm. "He's unconscious, but his vitals are fine."

It took a moment to register what Harold had said. Crayo was hurt. She looked right. His head was tilted forward and his shoulders were hunched. Harold was tending to him with a few med-bots. They appeared to be sealing his suit with some kind of spray.

She subvocalized a command and re-enabled her retinal comm. Her senses burst to life as the data flowed in. The ship was hobbling along, and they'd lost atmosphere both in the bridge and in two of the three passenger transport areas. They'd lost one life, and by the looks of it they had several others on the brink.

"Time till transition?" she asked.

"In twenty seconds we'll be behind this planetesimal. It's the best we can do, and I have no idea if there're eyes on the other side."

She didn't dare ask about their gate array. The system was reporting some aft external damage near the chemical drive. She only hoped it wasn't enough to cause problems with the gate transition. They'd been dealt enough blows today. "Bring up the moon ship."

She didn't want to ask about their gate array. The system was reporting some external damage, but it was with the chemical drive, not the gate array. She hoped it wasn't enough to cause problems. They'd been dealt enough blows today. "Bring up the moon ship."

Harold adjusted the feed on the wall screen. The alien moon ship filled the space on the wall. "A small squadron of thirty-two ships are headed our way, ma'am. Intercept in two minutes."

She leaned forward. "What the frak are they doing? Zoom in on that." She pointed at the planetesimal that minutes earlier held the Ulixi ceremonial grounds.

From their vantage, it appeared that the alien moon was breaking the planetesimal into pieces. Chunks of rock were floating back toward the surface of the ship, and there mixed amidst the floating rubble was a sprinkling of glowing yellow light. Like fireflies in a dark night, the sparks twinkled and swirled around an artificial gravity field toward the moon.

The feed cut and the familiar clang of the gate vanes expanding echoed through the bridge. Harold must've repaired the hull breach.

"Ugh," Crayo muttered as he leaned his head back in his chair. "Did you get the number of that garbage bot that nicked me?"

She chuckled and turned toward him. He had blood on his cheek and a melted suit gash on his side, but otherwise, from the outside he seemed fine. "Don't move a muscle. Let's get home before we press our luck."

"Sim sim," he mumbled as his eyes blinked and a clear chemical flowed through the IV connected to his suit.

The familiar blue glow of the gate transition entered the bridge and passed through the room. She'd need to review that footage again later. Until then, she had some passengers to check on. Someone was responsible for this mess, and she aimed to figure out who.

THEY SURVIVED the first jump and paused outside Sol to assess their damage. The transport housed only a few probes, and they needed to know how far they'd make it before needing help.

"We stabilized all the wounded except for one," Nova began. "We have a dozen people that need medical attention. They'll survive the next twelve hours though. That was how long you said we'd need, right?"

"Don't answer that," Harold said.

Lync screwed up her face and turned away from Nova, holding her finger out. She subvocalized a reply to Harold. "What's the word, bossman?"

"I'm detecting a transmission from her neck region. She

has some type of bug on her. It wasn't there when she was aboard last time, and in our current state I can't guarantee a signal won't leak out of our hull."

She turned to face Nova and smiled, doing the best she could not to let on that she was talking to Harold. "It's probably best if we don't talk about particulars until we get there." She glanced down at Nova's neck and caught the hint of jewelry sticking out above the edge of her suit. "That's a beautiful necklace. Silver?" She nodded toward Nova.

"Oh, no." Nova shook her head. "This necklace is something that all elder Ulixi get when we pass our own coming of age ceremony." She reached up and wrestled the rest of the necklace out from under her suit. Its silvery edge was only the top of a thin multicolored metal that ended with a small intricate medallion on the end. "It's forged from stones removed from the ceremonial planetesimal we just left. Chief Austen gave this to me nearly thirty years ago, when I'd reached my century mark as a Ulixi, and joined the ranks of the elders." She smiled and rubbed the medallion.

"What's that shape?" Lync asked as she reached out and brushed the surface of the necklace.

"That's an unusual substance," Harold said. "The nanites from your fingers are reporting back several unknown alloys and chemical signatures."

"It's the Ulixi elder signet," Nova said. "An intertwined circular pattern of roots, much like the display on the ceiling of the chamber. Pretty isn't it?"

She wrapped her fist around the necklace and unsheathed her electro-blade, bringing it up to Nova's neck in the blink of an eye. The red light from the blade crackled as it nicked Nova's skin, and the woman winced. "So tell me something. Why's this thing transmitting a signal?"

Everyone in the hold gasped. Several of the other Ulixi struggled to release themselves from their harnesses, only to find that Harold had locked them in place. The robots that had been helping them were suddenly brandishing weapons directed toward them.

"Chill now we should," Crayo said limping into the hold.

"I told you to stay put," she said, glancing back and forth between Crayo and Nova. "I'm dealing with a traitor in our midst." She narrowed her gaze, studying Nova's face.

"I... don't know what you're talking about," Nova muttered. She tried to take a step backward, but found Harold there with a weapon pressing against her back.

"Why don't we just take it off and test it?" Crayo asked. "You know, before we jump to any conclusions."

She nodded toward Nova, eyeing the necklace.

The elder reached her hands upward toward the medallion and gently twisted the vines encircling it. The silvery strands detangled and unhooked in two pieces until finally the necklace fell away. Once it was safely off, she held it out toward one of the robots. "Here, test away."

Harold rolled around and raised his robotic hands upward. He was holding a small box with thick walls. "Place it in here."

Nova dropped it in.

"Are there any other elders aboard?" Lync asked.

Nova's gaze shot behind her.

"If you're a Ulixi elder, and you have one of these necklaces, I suggest you relinquish it voluntarily or we'll be sitting here for an awfully long time. I'll have Harold strip search the lot of ya."

"Judging by my scans, there are three others aboard who match the age requirements that Nova mentioned," Harold said over their comms.

Two other Ulixi raised their hands and volunteered their necklaces. They each dropped them into different boxes under Harold's guard.

"Which one's the third?" Crayo said out loud.

Harold's robotic form walked up to another Ulixi in the corner. "This one."

Crayo walked over to the man. "I hate to ask this, but are you an elder, sir?"

The man shook his head from side to side. "Name's Klax,

and no, an elder I not be. I join the Ulixi late, not til I be forty. Requires a century of being in the tribe, I not that old youngin."

Crayo nodded and turned back toward the others. "Alright, bossman. How do we test these things?"

"I've already run scans on the boxes," Harold said. "The other two elders aren't broadcasting like Nova's is." He brought up the readings on the transport's small wall screen.

There were three sections of measurements. The top showed a constant transmission being recorded, a simple pulse on a particular frequency. It wasn't long, but it was there, and it repeated every minute. The other two were silent.

Lync returned her gaze to Nova, her blade still on her neck. "So talk to us. Why'd you put this on? I don't remember it on your neck when we fought in the ceremonial chamber."

Nova shook her head. "I left it in my ship. It's taboo to bring it back to the ground from which it was taken. Rumor has it that it will burn you during the ceremony, and some people have supposedly been killed wearing it."

"So you put it back on when you returned to your ship then?" Crayo asked.

Nova raised her chin; the crackle of Lync's electro-blade stung her skin. "I... put it on after returning home. I sent a comm to Chief Austen, I did." She glanced around the room at the eyes of the other Ulixi and then back toward Lync. "I had to say goodbye. He asked me where I was going, demanded to know he did, but I didn't say a word. I swear!" She swallowed hard, careful not to move her neck. "I owed him, I did. Saved my life he had. Several times. I didn't expect I'd ever... see him again."

"Do you think that's what tipped off the Inners?" Crayo asked.

Lync sighed. "I don't know."

"Wait! What Inners?" Nova asked.

"Show her," Lync said. She subvocalized a message to Harold. "Are you recording her vitals?"

"Already ahead of you," Harold replied on her comm. "So far it seems she's telling the truth, but you Ulixi are a sneaky bunch. As far as I know, you can fake a negative."

Harold brought up the Inner Ring audio transmission on the wall screen and played the video showing the Inner Ring fleet accelerating toward them.

Nova tilted her head and squinted. "Play that audio again. Filter out the background and that idiot General. Play the other voice, only louder."

Harold complied.

"Negative, General. We've got readings of nearly fifty souls on the ground. There are no signs of their ship though."

"That sounds like, Yoro," said one of the other elders.

The people around the room nodded.

"Who's Yoro and does anyone got a recording of this guy lying around?" Crayo asked.

Nova cleared her throat. "Yoro be Chief Austen's brother's child. He left the clan a decade back, joined the Inner military. Much like you joined the Outers." She nodded toward Crayo and Lync.

The Ulixi muttered around the room.

"What is it, Adri?" Harold asked.

Lync turned toward Adri. She'd purposely been trying not to make eye contact with the little girl for fear that they'd both lose it.

Adri lowered her hand. "My pa was mentioning someone named Yoro before we left. Said they messaged him he did. I remember because I don't often see my pa spit after saying someone's name."

The Ulixi all chuckled.

"Any chance you have that message?" Crayo asked walking up to the girl and crouching down.

"Suppose it'd be in here?" Adri asked. "It was my pa's. He said I should look through it when we arrived." She handed Crayo a small data dot.

Harold rolled up beside him and Crayo inserted the dot into the side of Harold's head. The little robot's eyes flashed blue for a second and then stopped. "There are several personal documents here from your father, Adri. I suggest you do as he said and watch them when you arrive where we're headed. There was also this message."

He played the recording.

"Long time yo. Tis Yoro. Wanted to sync up, sim. See how's things on the ground. Drop me a beam."

"That's a ninety-nine point nine nine percent match for the voice from the recording, ma'am."

Lync slowly lowered her blade, and the glow extinguished when she placed it in its sheath at her side. She swallowed hard and nodded toward Nova. "I'm sorry. Really. I... couldn't take a chance."

Nova shook her head and reached out to touch Lync's hand. "No harm done. I'd have done the same if you's done something like that. Gotta protect us you do. We're clan again."

"Clan," Lync muttered, a smile crossing her face. "Indeed we are."

"So whatcha wanna do with that necklace, boss?" Crayo asked.

She turned toward the little robot. "Can we extract the transmitters from the lot of 'em, Harold?"

"I should think so. Why? What'd you have in mind?"

Her fists clenched tight. She was tired of being sold out. It was about time they were on the leading edge of this sword for once. "I reckon we leave the Inners a little gift with Nova's beacon. A little something to brighten their day."

NGUYỄN DUE

SOL, NEAR NEPTUNE

"This is insanity!" he said, slamming his fist down against the smooth white table. "I demand to return to my ship. I've been more than cooperative during this investigation. First, you illegally detain our president, and now you're detaining me on the same trumped-up grounds."

"You can argue all you want, Admiral. Until we close out the investigation, we need to—" Lisp began.

The entrance to his room slid open and Ambassador Addae entered flanked by two armed soldiers. Her talons clicked against the floor as she walked and her eyes narrowed on him.

He raised his hands upward. "Come on in. Don't knock or anything, I guess. To what do I owe this unpleasant surprise?" He rose from his desk. He'd learned long ago to never be seated or get too comfortable when your enemy enters a room.

His retinal comm chimed with a priority alert. "One moment, Ambassador. I'm sorry, but there's something important I—"

"You'll answer me before you take that," Ambassador Addae said forcefully clicking her talons.

He ignored her and spun around toward the wall with his back towards his newly arrived guests. Whatever was pissing her off, this ought to help her stew. He reached up and tapped his ear. "Talk to me," he subvocalized.

"Sorry for the interruption, Admiral. We've received intel of a skirmish near Jupiter between three alien fighters and an unknown Sol ship," the officer began. "We believe it was one of ours, but the reports are inconclusive."

"Well it was either ours or it wasn't," he said.

"We don't know whose ship it was, but based upon its drive signature we know it was an Olivaw design."

"They're all Olivaw designs, you idiot. Let's cut to the chase. Who shot at whom first?"

"It appears a Ulixi ship purposely exploded their reactor near one of the alien fighters, destroying it instantly. The aliens were on a fast intercept course toward the unknown ship. From what we were able to tell, the ship was departing with other Ulixi clan members onboard."

"Wait! A Ulixi? They're pacifists, aren't they?"

"Yes they are, sir."

"How the heck did we know this ship was departing with Ulixi?"

"An Inner Ring battlecruiser fleet was nearby investigating reports of a meeting of the Outer Ring Resistance. They were monitoring the Ulixi meet-up when the unknown ship landed, picked up nearly one hundred resistance operatives, and were attempting to escape before the incident transpired."

"Why the hell did the aliens dispatch anyone toward this unknown ship at all?"

"We don't know, sir."

"Where'd the ship go?"

The officer cleared their throat and paused. "We... don't know, sir."

He brought his hand up to his face. "Well, what the hell do you know?"

"The reactor explosion took out one alien ship, and the unknown ship destroyed another before the third narrowly escaped."

He glanced over his shoulder. The Ambassador was pacing behind him, and the click of her talons against the floor echoed throughout the room. The sound was a highly unusual side effect for a silent ship. She must be doing it to frazzle him. He turned back toward the wall.

"Destroyed how?" he asked.

"The explosions matched nuclear signatures similar to the tonnage of the fleet's larger munitions. We don't know how they were deployed, though."

"Was the unknown ship fired on?"

"Yes, sir. But only after they fired their lasers first, while attempting to flee."

"Admiral!" Ambassador Addae yelled.

He turned to face her, leaving the comm open. "I'm in the middle of something, Ambassador. Last I checked, I'm not your slave aboard this ship, and you're the one who barged into my office unannounced. If you can't give me a moment to take a call, then get the frak out of my room." He gestured toward the door behind them.

Ambassador Addae's feathers ruffled and her arms fluttered out, just like they had before she made a move on him in the tribunal chamber.

He reached behind his back and pulled out two electro-blades. Their green lights crackled when he clanged them together and waved them through the air. "Bring it on, bird lady!"

The two soldiers flanking the ambassador stepped toward him, each easing forward with their staffs drawn.

Two on one. Those weren't exactly fair odds. "I told you before and I'll tell you again. If the Galactic Alliance takes an action against any human in Sol, you'll regret it. The same way your puny fighters did near Jupiter. Swallowed a few nukes last I heard."

Ambassador Addae lowered her wings and the guards stopped advancing. "So you were briefed?"

He smiled and nodded, waving the blades through the air. "I was. But I assume you barged in here to beat those details, didn't you? You wanted the element of surprise." He snickered. "You continue to underestimate us feeble humans."

"Sir, you should see this," the officer said over his comm. They brought up an image on his retinal display. It showed the alien moon ship, and it was mining something from one of the Trojans near Jupiter.

"What am I looking at?" he subvocalized.

"After the aliens sent the three fighters to intercept the other unknown ship, they began mining a nearby planetesimal. They moved toward it before any shots were fired."

He paused and lowered his blades. The green lights surrounding their surface crackled in the silent room.

"This aggression is unacceptable!" Ambassador Addae said. "You made the first move against us. The tribunal will rule within the hour on—"

He gestured with the blade in his hand and tossed the image up on the wall screen. "If we made the first move, then how the hell do you explain this?"

Ambassador Addae glanced at the image, and then took a step back, retracting her talons. "Where'd you get this?"

"Why do you think we were defending ourselves out there, Ambassador? Yet again your fraud of a justice system has failed. You're obviously here for more than this tribunal, aren't you? Either that, or you're clueless of what your own people are doing. Maybe your Admiral Gwar was working from a different playbook than you're privy to."

Her guards took another step toward him.

Ambassador Addae inhaled and let out a blood-curdling screech.

It wasn't translatable, and his nanites adjusted his ear canals, but not before he caught a second of it. He reached up and rubbed his ears with his wrists; the blades crackled above his head.

The two guards turned to face her, bowed, and then exited the room.

Ambassador Addae was now standing alone. She closed her eyes and her feathers flattened against her body.

He tapped off the blades with his thumbs and then reached behind his back sheathing them. They blended in with his outfit and were nearly impossible to see unless you were looking for them.

When Ambassador Addae opened her eyes, she was looking straight at him in a more friendly gaze. "You're right, Admiral."

He didn't say a word. He wasn't sure which of the leaps he was right about, but he wasn't about to show his hand.

"I don't yet know the state of my forces. Supreme Admiral Gwar had ulterior motives that I'm still uncovering. I don't know what that ship was doing out there—"

"But you know what they were mining." He wasn't buying that she was ignorant of everything.

"Do you?" she asked, her head turned to the side and one of her eyes studied him.

"I do," He said. He was lying. "And I have a feeling that's why you're actually here. This FTL bullshit, it's all a cover, and you know it."

"If you offend me again, Admiral—"

"Don't finish that sentence," he interrupted. "My last statement stands. Any time you make a move against Sol, you'll regret it. This action of mining within our star system is intolerable and will be reciprocated tenfold. You either fix it and return the mined materials..." He took a step toward her, his muscles flexed. "Or you'll find out exactly how we dropped those nukes when each and every one of your tribunal ships is drifting through the vacuum of space in pieces."

She backed up, her feathers ruffling again.

He stepped around her toward the door.

"Where do you think you're going?" she asked.

"I'm returning to my ship, and you won't be stopping me." He turned to face her. "I'm sure you already know how we destroyed your ships, right?"

Her left eye twitched.

She didn't know. They had nothing. A smile crept across

his face. "I'll give you a clue. It's the same way we rescued our president from under your noses." He winked at her. "Don't think on it too hard. I'll be in touch."

He turned and exited the room, walking toward the shuttle bay. While he had no idea if they'd let him leave, he was hoping his threats weren't seen as empty.

In the shuttle bay, the same shuttle he arrived in was waiting with its ramp lowered. Once he stepped inside, it began the departure procedure.

Apparently, his threats weren't as empty as he'd thought. Now he had to figure out his own bluff. What the frak were the Olivaws up to that had these aliens so confused and freaked out? Even if he was blind to their actions, he knew one thing for sure. They had some weapons technology he needed to get his hands on.

HE TILTED his head back and shot another espresso. The dark brown liquid tasted exquisite. He had to hand it to the president; she had amazing coffee onboard this ship of hers.

"Show me again!" he said.

Lieutenant Gwen Marshall was the ranking officer aboard the Jurat. All the other officers had mysteriously disappeared with Commander Quesh. She reset the plan on the wall screen back to the beginning.

Her hand was shaking before she clasped it behind her back. She wasn't used to being yelled at.

He turned toward the wall screen and continued fiddling with the hilt of his electro-blade. It was powered off and didn't have its usually green energy field. Maybe that's what was making her uncomfortable. Her boss was brandishing an open weapon. It was one of the few things that helped him think, which made it more important than her. She'd have to deal with it.

The fleet of human ships was no match for the aliens. Even if they had control of all Inner and Outer Ring military and merchant ships, they couldn't muster any more than ten human ships per moon vessel. He'd never dreamed ten thousand ships would be seen as a drop in the bucket. The scale of these things was astounding.

"We're redeploying the Georgetown and the Beijing Atlas class destroyers from Earth to Jupiter, along with a flotilla of smaller ships. The rest of the fleet is headed here and here." Gwen called out the location of the six tribunal ships and the other six alien ships orbiting near Earth.

Until now, humans had made no aggressive motions toward the aliens. That was the past.

He nodded, studying the wall screen.

Gwen gestured toward the wall screen. "They'll surround the ships in a star formation covering every exit from all sides and staggering distances. We'll also have a wave of armed commercial cruisers and frigate class ships in secondary and tertiary waves at a safer distance. It'll take a few days to arm the commercial fleet, but I've already sent the orders on to the shipyards." She reached up and brushed her ear to receive a comm. After a brief pause, she stiffened. "The São Paulo will arrive shortly, sir."

"Good... very good." The São Paulo previously held a position just outside Neptune, and he'd recalled it to their location after arriving. He turned to face her again. "Did we receive any more details about what happened to the Mostar?"

She nodded and brought up the image on the wall screen. It showed a small black box being carried off a shuttle and into the Mostar, an older Pegasus class ship. "They brought aboard this object. It was nearly one AU from Jupiter and was broadcasting on the frequencies they'd been using to communicate with the Ulixi resistance."

The image on the wall screen suddenly went white and switched to a vantage point further away from the Mostar. What appeared next was unpleasant. The Mostar exploded and broke into thousands of pieces. Sparks of white-hot light shot in all directions as the reactor cascaded in a secondary explosion. After the smoke cleared, they launched rescue shuttles from nearby ships. Early indications were that no one survived.

He sighed. Such a waste of life. "Did we at least get a sample from the box before we attempted to open it?"

"No, sir. It was strange though. The object wasn't visible except for the signal. They were hoping pieces of it would have survived, but thus far, none have been found."

He clenched his fist around the hilt of his knife. "I wouldn't expect something to survive a nuke, even a small one like that. What about Olivaw International? Are they cooperating?" He glanced at the officer. Her hair was in a tight bun atop her head and her dark brown eyes were focused on the wall screen. The glow from the wall gave her olive skin a majestic sheen. She was beautiful.

Gwen smiled and paused, coming to attention when she caught him studying her. "Yes, sir. Completely. They've opened every nook and cranny of their systems to our techs."

"And?"

"No smoking guns yet, sir. They found this, though." She gestured and the blueprints for a distant mining site in Sol's Oort Cloud came up on the wall.

He turned and squinted, looking over the schematic. "What am I missing? This looks like a random mining colony. There are hundreds of them out in the Oort Cloud."

"You're correct. There isn't anything markedly different except for two minor things. One, it wasn't registered with the CoPE Mining Consortium as it predates that group's creation. I've already confirmed that Olivaw owns that expanse of space. The second thing is the matter of its age."

He studied the blueprint key and did a double take before he slowly turned to face her. "Is that right, 2110? That's damn old. A lot can change in one hundred and seventy years."

"It's ancient history," Gwen said. She glanced away from the wall screen toward the ground before clasping her hands behind her back.

"What is it, Lieutenant? Spit it out." He didn't have time for games.

She straightened her back. "I ordered a few probes to scan the old mining site. We need to be sure. Whatever the Olivaws have, they've hidden it well."

He couldn't help but notice that with her hands behind her back at attention she was a marvelously curvy lady. "That's good thinking. So, what about you, Lieutenant? You must've picked up something onboard the Jurat with Abigail and her missing team wandering about."

She shook her head. "No, sir. This was my first tour onboard the Jurat. Honestly, I never left engineering… that is, until the others departed. Her crew was tight, but you already know that. Commander Quesh handpicked everyone onboard."

He slid the blade back into the sheath behind his back. "He picked you, didn't he?"

"Yes, sir. He and my father served on the front lines of the blockade."

"Ah yes, the great Inner and Outer Ring blockade. Child's play compared to what we face now." He walked toward her and stopped only a few centimeters away. She didn't flinch. He liked that. "So are you with me?" He glanced around the plush room and then back toward her. "Or are you staying aboard this cruise ship?"

She brought her hand up and saluted him. "Requesting permission to accompany you aboard the São Paulo, sir!"

44

JOYCE GREEN

EPSILON ERIDANI, LIPROSUS

"So let me get this straight," she said pacing around the expansive conference room. "The only other asset was in the Oort cloud and we destroyed that?"

Captain Hui nodded. "That's correct, Director. We have the space stations around Aegir and a few in orbit, but other than that, all of our assets are here, on Liprosus. The alien moon ship was on a direct path toward our Wheel base. As Harold has shown, there was a ninety-nine point nine percent chance that it would've attempted to dismantle... or whatever the hell it does to the planetesimal and turn it into that black cloud." She gestured toward the image on the wall screen.

They didn't have many options. When she stared up at the images, she hoped something would jump out at her. But it didn't. At this point, they were playing a waiting game. The aliens had the upper hand, and this base being hidden was their only protection from annihilation.

She turned to face her team. Captain Hui, Ryder, and Dr. Elaine Sutter. A mix of old and new. "What about the crew from the Wheel? Did they escape?"

"They did," Harold said.

Sometimes it was like pulling rice paper out of tar getting

information from him. She waved her hand in a circle. "Gonna need a little more than that, Harold."

"I can't go into all the particulars just yet, but they are well away from here. They evacuated before I helped Major Lync and her team escape."

She raised a hand. She'd forgotten about Lync and her mission. "Hold on. You managed to evacuate how many people from the Wheel?"

"The entire crew of one hundred and ninety-two."

She raised her hands up to her hips. This A.I. needed to stop playing games. "I assume that doesn't include Lync's crew of twenty-four. And how exactly did you pull that off in the time between the alien moon vessel's change in direction and when it arrived at the Wheel? All while avoiding detection."

"Well, they evacuated in a few of our ships, of course. They're quite fast."

"Wouldn't the aliens have seen them?" Captain Hui asked.

She glanced at the captain. Either she was playing along, or they were in the dark as well.

"They would have, yes; had we been using traditional drive technology. We've had a sort of… scientific renaissance in the past few years researching new techniques for space travel. It's our one ace in the hole with these aliens."

"That's amazing!" Ryder said. "Why don't we just use those to escape?" He walked up next to the ladies.

"Well, there's a catch," Harold said.

She sighed. "Of course there is."

"I don't have the engineering designs from the Wheel. That copy never transmitted the designs to Liprosus. Only the Wheel outposts in each solar system have them and those are tightly controlled. You know, OPSEC and all. They're the only thing keeping Humanity alive right now."

"Lotta fraking good they do for us humans down on Liprosus," Captain Hui said. "We're sitting ducks down here."

"Don't you see what he's saying," Dr. Sutter said. She'd remained silent until now.

Joyce turned to face the doctor. She was sitting at the conference table, her hands resting in her lap. "Humor me Elaine. What am I missing?"

She brushed at something on her pants and then glared at Joyce. "They want us to have babies, to reproduce. He said as much to you the other day when he told you the capacity of this base. What was it, fifty thousand souls could live here I think?"

"That's not what I meant nor what I was alluding to," Harold said. "I was merely telling the Director our operational capacity. We have no idea when we'll be able to leave, nor if."

Joyce squinted at Elaine. "Harold, how long do we have until the aliens complete their little black cloud?"

"Based upon their rate of expansion, the number of ships, and—"

"How long?" Joyce screamed. He's mum at times and a chatterbox at others. It's maddening.

"Twelve months."

"And then what?"

"And then I'd imagine our people would come for us."

She shook her head. "You're fraking talking in circles, Harold. How can they pass through that blackness? I thought it was impassible. Is it me or is this A.I. withholding everything we need to make the best of this situation?"

"He's always been that way," Captain Hui said. "It's not his fault. It's how he's programmed."

"What's that supposed to mean?" Ryder asked. "He's an automation. His rules are fairly simple. Even if he's constrained by the three laws, he has to obey us. Harold, please tell us your operating parameters."

Harold was silent for a moment before replying. "I'm constrained by the four laws of robotics."

"No, there are only three laws," Ryder said furrowing his brow.

"There are four in my programming. There's also the little matter that I'm not exactly a pure artificial intelligence."

"Oh yeah," she said, chuckling under her breath. "I sorta forgot to tell you all about that. Harold here, he's not simply an automata. He's an A.I. built from the thoughts, memories, and emotions of a human. A one Harold Olivaw."

When she glanced around the room, the looks of confusion and fear in their eyes told her one thing. They were about to lose most of the day learning about Harold.

AFTER HOURS OF INTERROGATION, mental tests, and verbal sparring, her team gave up questioning whether or not Harold was actually a former human consciousness. It wasn't until she got that out of their systems that they finally moved on to something else. Like learning more about the capabilities of their new base of operations.

"And we're positive they can't detect these robots we have on the surface?" she asked.

Her team was standing in a massive room full of screens. Hundreds and hundreds of screens, and each and every one of them was being monitored by both A.I. and humans. The feeds were from every corner of the planet.

Captain Hui was in her element. All eyes were on her as she was giving everyone the tour of the facility. "These aren't real-time feeds. Not for all intents and purposes, anyhow. There's a lag while the different embedded systems transmit the data. For some it's longer than others. Take these insects for instance."

She reached over and adjusted the controls in front of one of the operators. A colony of some type of centipede looking insects came into view. There were at least ten cameras showing information.

"What you're seeing here are tiny nanites recording from the eyes of this insect colony. Each nanite only records minutes at a time before another nanite takes its place. They rotate out and move to another location within the host's body to store the data. There are never any transmissions that leave the nanite itself. Then, whenever the bug returns to its nest, we dump the data and physically return it home."

"As in you transport the recording from point A to point Z?" Ryder asked. "That doesn't seem possible."

Captain Hui nodded and adjusted the wall monitor again. On another panel far above, there was a falcon like bird soaring through the air above a mountain range. "We have a few birds like this one and other ground animals we've trained to eat only certain insects or attack other animals. During an ingestion or quarrel, they transfer the data."

"That seems laborious and slow," Elaine said.

The captain brought up the intake queues on another screen. Thousands of feeds were being ingested at all times. "We used to transmit a lot faster from within the colony itself, masking our transmissions within your background noise. What we're doing now has taken us back to before you touched down on Liprosus. We had to maintain operational silence back then, while still monitoring your movements. It can take over six hours to get data back here, but it's a steady stream of intel."

"Impressive," Joyce said. "All of this technology just to spy on us colonists. It seems like a waste." She shook her head. "We could've accomplished so much more had we only worked together."

Captain Hui stiffened beside her.

"What is it?" Joyce asked, shifting to face her.

"Nothing, ma'am." She waved her hand over the controls, and the display returned to the operator.

"Bullshit!" Joyce shot.

Everyone on her team including the nearby operators turned to stare at her. Their mouths were open. They hadn't heard anyone talk to Captain Hui that way before.

She didn't have time for this shit. "I told you before, Captain, I need frank and honest conversation on my team. If you've got something to say, then say it."

Captain Hui reached up and brushed at her uniform. She adjusted her insignia on the lapel of her shirt. "Of course, Director. I'm not used to questioning a superior officer, but since you asked for it." She turned to face Joyce. Her face was expressionless, but her eyes were burning. "We were on a mission. There was a bigger plan to consider."

Joyce shook her head. "What makes you so sure? I mean, you didn't even know what they were doing out at the Wheel. Why are you so willing to have faith in a broader mission?"

"I wouldn't expect you to understand, Director. You're not military. There was a time in my life I wouldn't have, either. Back in Chile, I lived on the streets and ate out of trash cans until someone from Olivaw came and took me in. They worked at one of the manufacturing facilities outside Santiago. She was a generous woman. She introduced me to her home and showed me what a family could be. I saw all that she did for the Olivaws, and in return what they had done for her and the community. They gave back more than any other company. They built up impoverished communities and gave them food, shelter, education, employment, and medicine. When I came of age, I joined their security forces and trained in the Inner and Outer Rings. I served on security duty for Stark Olivaw and his daughter Abigail. I watched the days, weeks, and years they poured into their cause. Our cause. One I know little about, even to this day, and yet I joined this mission when asked. I didn't hesitate. They were as unwavering in their goals, as am I today." Her hands were shaking, and her lip was quivering.

Captain Hui brought her hand to her mouth and cleared her throat. "You asked me how I have faith in a broader mission. To me, to not have faith is an impossibility. What we're doing here is difficult to explain, yet every day we do it we're closer to understanding the bigger picture. I spoke long ago with Abigail, when she was but a teenager. It was soon after she'd taken over as head of Olivaw. She asked me what faith meant to me."

Joyce swallowed hard. "What did you tell her?"

"To me, faith was about trusting in my heart that what I was doing was for the betterment of humanity. It wasn't about the money or the prestige. It was about helping each and every one of us to be stronger, to be smarter, and to take what is ours in this boundless universe. To be confined to squalor in a gravity well, oppressed by the elite and the establishment, that was no way to live. Not when there was all of this." She gestured around the room at the wall screens.

Joyce shook her head. "I don't disagree with any of your sentiment, Captain. I honestly don't understand how you associate that with the Olivaws. They got us into this mess in the first place."

Captain Hui pointed at her. "Why did you build the farms, Director?"

"What're you talking about?"

She gestured at the wall screen and subvocalized something. Up on the wall came a view of the colony, an old one. "Nearly two years ago, you had crops growing in the dome that could sustain the colony. So why did you build the farms?"

Joyce glanced around at the others. Ryder shrugged. What did this have to do with anything? "I don't understand."

"Because it was the next step in the colony plan," Elaine said stepping forward from behind the others.

Joyce nodded at her.

"Exactly!" Captain Hui gestured and time fast forwarded on the wall. The colony grew in size. "And who made that plan?"

"I did," Joyce said. "We all did. Along with the rest of CoPE. We did it together."

She froze the image of the farm and pointed. "Interesting, Director. So, you designed the greenhouses?"

"No," Joyce said.

Captain Hui nodded and then fast forwarded some more, freezing it again. The image showed the intricate pipes that fed the water to the plants being built from the viewpoint of the eye of a tiny insect. "Then you built the irrigation, Director?"

"No," Joyce mumbled.

She skipped forward several more times. "Hydroponics? Nutrient delivery? Night to day converters? Did you build any of it, Director?"

"No, but I fail to see—"

"Yes!" Captain Hui raised her arms in the air. "You're correct. You fail to see what is obvious, and yet you still question my beliefs. You had faith that these tasks were being performed and yet..." She made one more adjustment in time, and the image was replaced with a field of bodies spread on the ground between the crops. "People still died. All that faith, all that conviction, and the result was this." She gestured at the wall screen and nodded. "I can see why you don't have faith, Director. I don't know if I could've made it through what you have and remained standing. Until today, if I'd have guessed who in this room had faith, I'd have said you in a split second. I don't believe the Olivaws wished or planned for any of this. They, like you, are dealing with the hand they've been dealt through generations of decisions out of their control. I don't know about you, but I have faith in them and in what they stand for. Everything else is part of the mission. I don't have the luxury of second guessing them, nor did your people second guess you when you opened the farms."

Joyce shuddered at the thought of the farms again. She had to stay focused on the here and now. "Aliens releasing a virus at the farms has nothing to do with what we're talking about here. I suggest—"

"It's about indirect consequences, Director. You of all people should recognize that. Your life is littered with them. If Abigail hadn't met you in the academy graduation receiving line twenty-eight years ago, do you think we'd be standing here today? Would whoever took your position have made the same decisions you did?"

She tilted her head. This lady knew far more about their

past than she realized. "How'd you know about that day at the academy? I don't remember seeing you there."

Captain Hui smirked. "I was a member of Abigail's security detail back then. Our job was to disappear within an audience. If you'd seen me or thought I seemed out-of-place, then I failed. But I saw you. The expression on your face when she asked you to be the DoC. It was priceless. So, I have to ask you, was that her fault, as well? Did she convince you to take the job?"

Joyce shook her head. She had a point. "No, Captain. Abigail didn't need to convince me. There was no coercion, convincing, nor wooing done by the Olivaws. I accepted the role because of my belief in the colony and what it meant for mankind, combined with my trust in what Abigail and her father were striving to create alongside CoPE. Hell, back then I was more than a little excited to be away from Inner and Outer Ring politicking. So, where do we go from here?"

Captain Hui reached up to her lapel and tore off her insignia. She stared at it in silence for a minute before finally speaking. "I never imagined it'd come to this." She reached her hand out toward Joyce, offering it to her.

"No." She shook her head and stepped backward. "I won't accept it."

Captain Hui's shoulders sagged. "While I have faith in the broader mission, I don't believe I have faith in you."

"Help me understand, Captain. Explain to me what we're supposed to do here." Joyce gestured around her at the screens and at all the people. "We're buried underground, and we're surrounded by aliens. Our people are battered and weathered, and many want to curl up in a ball. Harold asked me to help run this place, but I'm not sure what we can do from here. I'd like you to tell me what you believe our mission to be."

Captain Hui's eyes narrowed, and she stiffened to attention. "Our mission, Director, is to not just survive, but to thrive! We need to build our defenses, build our ships, and prepare for war. One that might take generations, and one that might never come. But we need to prepare to defend that which we believe is rightfully ours."

Joyce nodded slowly. "And how do you suppose we do that underground and immobile?"

Captain Hui chuckled. "You keep forgetting that we're technologically half a century ahead of Sol. You never knew we were out and about within your own colony and yet—" She leaned forward and adjusted the controls in front of the officer again.

She craned her neck. Up on the wall screens, the captain brought up a half dozen feeds with what appeared to be several massive hangars. She'd seen them on the Archégonos maps but hadn't studied them. She assumed they were full of more submersibles.

There were dozens and dozens of ships with peculiar designs, whose purpose she couldn't deduce. "What am I looking at, Captain?"

"Your fleet, ma'am. Some of these are simple capsules designed to be shot into orbit for awaiting transports. We only ever launched them at night. The occupants need to be in short term cryo-stasis, but they're nearly impossible to detect. Their outer shell is designed from the same material as this base. We have launchers in several sites around the planet. The medium size vessels are transports and more tactical ships we used to monitor and explore without being detected. I imagine we could use them for other purposes, as well. And finally the others, well, let's just say they were built as contingency ships should we need to evacuate the colony."

Joyce glanced back to Captain Hui. "Are any of these armed?"

She Hui shook her head. "Not really, no."

"What does that mean?"

"Well, we never needed actual weapons, but the ships can easily be retrofitted with them. Each craft does, however, have the ability to control and reshape matter around itself using seismic and gravitational waves. It's a trick that comes in handy when you're stuck underground. Harold has also shared a plethora of Olivaw military schematics with me in the last day. Like everything else at this base, they're well ahead of Sol, but we still have no idea if they're useful against these aliens. We only need a mission and a purpose to rally our people to make it happen."

"Harold to the rescue," Joyce muttered. It seemed convenient that he shared details just as they needed to know them. She couldn't help but sense this was part of their plan from the beginning.

Captain Hui held out her hand again toward Joyce. It contained her command insignia.

She stared down at it. The insignia bore the simple Epsilon Eridani crest and was surrounded by a twinkling star pattern she didn't recognize. So much of this place was foreign to her, and she imagined it would be for some time. She reached out with both hands and enclosed them around Captain Hui's, gently squeezing the captain's hands around her insignia.

"I won't be needing that," she whispered.

She turned to face the others. "You all heard the Captain. We have our mission. Now let's figure out how to execute it. Elaine? Ryder? I trust you're on board."

"Yessir!" they both chimed.

She turned to face Captain Hui and smiled. Her insignia was already in place on her lapel and she was at attention. "Now show me what technology we have at our disposal and what Harold shared with you. We have some catching up to do."

45

LYNC MICHAELS
TAU CETI, OORT CLOUD

It took a few hours to rig up a gift for the Inners. After they jettisoned it aboard a relay probe, they headed to Tau Ceti. Harold assured them he'd share the results of their surprise as soon as he could.

Lync still couldn't believe humans in Sol were wasting their time hunting each other down with an alien armada invading. Social inequality and political disagreements knew no limits, even under extraordinary pressures.

As she walked down the gangplank toward the hangar exit, she brought up the inventory of their ship. They'd finished unloading the last of the Ulixi cargo and the ship was swarming with bots. From the looks of the scene behind her, they were planning to dismantle the shuttle down to the skeleton and start anew.

"Not leaving much intact, are we?" she asked.

"The hull damage was too severe. It was well beyond repair," Harold said. "We're lucky it held together under that barrage of alien fire. Don't worry, we have plenty more where that one came from."

She shook her head. "Seems wasteful."

"We'll recycle every square centimeter," Harold began. "Nothing goes to waste around here. When we're done with her, she'll be a part of a dozen new ships in a few days."

Things were different here. They didn't have to worry about every single scrap. Hell, the tech was a half century ahead of the colony and that was decades ahead of Sol. It was a new world. Let's hope it didn't all come tumbling down.

"You're needed in the hospital level, ma'am," Harold said.

She froze in place. "Is everything alright?"

"Crayo and the others are fine. It's about Abigail. She's here, and we need to talk."

Lync leaned forward and began jogging before she paused with a wince. She had a stitch in her side. Reaching down she unzipped her suit and rubbed her hip. It was coarse, like it was coated in something.

When she pulled her hand back, the remnants of dry blood covered her fingers.

"It looks like you were wounded in the attack," Harold said. "We can get that checked in the infirmary while we're there."

"I'll be fine. Nothing my nanites can't handle." She subvocalized a command for her nanites to do a full-body scan and focus on her hip.

"It'll be quick I'm—"

"I said I'll be fine, bossman! Let it be." She wasn't about to have him probing her. The last thing she needed was to set off red flags.

———

"WHAT'S this I hear Abigail's in the house?" she said aloud as she strolled into the room and froze. Abigail was nowhere in sight, and there was an old man in uniform and a young lady standing in the corner. Maybe she had the wrong room. "I'm sorry. I didn't realize anyone else was here."

"You must be Lync. I'm Commander Quesh." He reached out his hand.

Her eyes went wide as she shook it. "As in The Commander Quesh? The Inner Ring blockade runner?"

Quesh chuckled and shook his head. "My reputation's a

tad bloated on that one I'm afraid. Abigail's father was responsible for navigating that clusterfuck of an encounter."

"That's not what we learned at the academy, sir." She adjusted her jumpsuit, fiddling with the tears. "All the things you did for the people of Jupiter—"

Minula cleared her throat.

"I'm sorry," Quesh said. "This is Minula. The President's assistant."

She leaned forward and shook Minula's hand. It was only then that she spotted Abigail lying behind them on a bed. Tubes, wires, and multiple peculiar sensors covered her body from head to toe. Every color fluid imaginable was being pumped into and out of her simultaneously. The whole scene reminded her of a Frankensteinian monster.

Lync brought her hand to her mouth. "What... happened to her?"

"She was attacked by a Galactic Alliance Admiral aboard the tribunal ship," Quesh said turning toward Abigail. "Whatever they did, she's been in a coma ever since. Harold snuck her out with a miniature gate drive, and we brought her here straight away. She's still in the coma and neither the doctors nor Harold can crack her out of it."

"Harold, you didn't mention any of this to me."

"It's complicated," Harold began. "I have multiple copies running throughout humanity's star systems at this point. The version of me here in Tau Ceti had no clue any of this happened until the copy with Commander Quesh gated back and docked at The Wheel."

Lync nodded. She imagined he'd had something like that going on. No way he'd be able to manage a single uniform consciousness at those distances. "So... you mentioned you needed me for something." She glanced between Quesh and Minula. "How can I help Abigail?"

"Harold has an idea on how to bring her out of the coma, and we need your help to make it happen," Minula said. She walked up beside Abigail and reached out to adjust her hair around the tubes, brushing a piece from Abigail's eyes.

She caught a tear glimmering in Minula's eyes from the overhead light before she turned away and wiped at her face.

"I don't know for certain," Harold began, "but I believe that whatever that mottled green bastard did to Abigail can be reversed after some gene therapy from another Olivaw. The problem is—"

"The other Olivaws are on an important expedition and are quite far away," Minula interrupted and spun around to face her. "If you're not up for this mission, Major, I'd be happy to do it myself."

Lync furrowed her brow and raised her hands upward in defense. "I don't know what I did to piss you off, missy, but I haven't heard a word about any mission yet. And last I checked..." She walked over beside Minula, staring her straight in the face. "Secretaries aren't the mission type."

Minula lurched forward.

Quesh threw himself between them, prying them apart, and forcing them backward. "Cut the crap ladies! This isn't a pissing contest. And I'll have you know, Major Michaels, Lieutenant Clarke was an elite Space Marine in the second battalion under General Araxis. She also saved your president's life and shattered her back, along with several other bones in the line of duty. She could handle this mission in her sleep, and if she weren't jacked up on steroids and nanite regrowth hormones, I might take her up on it." He stared Minula down and she took a few steps backward.

Lync swallowed hard. "I'm... sorry, Lieutenant. I figured—"

"Wrong!" Minula yelled pointing her finger at Lync. "You figured wrong. You colonists are all alike. Smarter than everyone else in Sol. Probably figured only a weak little assistant could have feelings for someone. Well, frak—"

"Enough!" Quesh shouted. "Get out of here, Minula." He gestured toward the door. "If you can't calm your jets then get the hell out. We need to brief the Major on the mission, and I don't have time to referee a boxing match."

Minula nodded at him and turned her back toward them.

She walked over beside Abigail and returned to fiddling with her hair.

"Now, Major." He spun around.

She snapped to attention and saluted the Commander. She'd misread this situation every which way to Sunday. It was about time she resorted back to a chain of command. "Yessir!"

Quesh furrowed his brows. "Can you calm yourself?"

"Yessir!"

"Are you up for another mission so quick out of the gate? Harold tells me you may have taken on a wound of your own. I can find someone else to—"

"No, sir! I mean… yessir. I'm up for another mission and no, I'm fine. Harold is mistaken. How can I help?" She remained crisp and stiff at attention, looking past but not directly at him.

"At ease, Major."

She relaxed into an at ease posture and placed her hands behind her back. Pain shot through her side, and she did everything she could not to wince. He was eyeing her cautiously. It was like her father catching her red-handed. He knew something was up.

Quesh squinted at her. "You're sure you're ok? Harold can check you out."

"I'm fine, sir. Really. It was only a minor cut. My nanites will have me stitched in a blink." Well, maybe that last part was a smidge dishonest. It'd take another day before they'd complete.

"Alright." Quesh turned his back and walked over toward a wall screen. It turned on, and the windows around the president's room became translucent. "What do you know about the original colony ship headed toward Tau Ceti?"

"YO, CRAYO!" Lync strolled into the lecture hall. "How's the training going?"

Crayo raised his arms skyward. "There she be. I thought we'd lost you on that last gate. Haven't seen you in nearly a day. Everything tip-top?"

"I'm great." She smiled and glanced around the room. No one else was here, so she turned and locked the door.

Crayo tilted his head. "You sure? Did the overseer take over and order you to come lock me up?"

She chuckled. "No, nothing like that. I wanted to stop by and tell you I'm shipping out for a few days. I'll be on another mission."

He stepped out from behind the podium, limping as he walked. "Where we headed?"

She glanced down at the ground and then back toward him. "It's only me this time... and I can't say anything more about it. Rest assured, it's of presidential importance."

"So much for OPSEC," Harold said into her comm.

She smirked and nodded toward Crayo's leg. "Besides, you look like you could use some more time to recuperate. I'm sure you can use a few days without me breathing down your neck."

"Naw," Crayo said shuffling on his feet.

She tilted her head. Was he blushing?

He kicked at the ground. "You be breathing down my neck... that'd be more than fine."

She didn't know what that meant, but she needed to change the subject. "Trainees doing well?"

Crayo spun around and pointed at the wall screen. It had statistics from all the Ulixi training runs. "Damn near perfect they are, once they get the hang of the equipment. Another week or so, and we'll be ready to kick some alien ass."

"That's amazing. I didn't expect anything less. They have an exceptional teacher." She smiled and winked at him. Yep, he was definitely blushing.

He walked up the ramp toward her. "You be safe out there. Make sure you come back in one piece, ya hear?"

"Sim sim," she said reaching out her fist.

"Sim sim." Crayo leaned forward and tapped his fist

against her knuckles. He held it and smiled for a second before pushing away and turning to walk toward the lectern.

She sighed and spun around to unlock the door. The last few days had been full of twists and turns. She wasn't sure she could handle someone falling for her right now. Feelings cloud judgement, and right about now she needed all the focus she could muster.

46

NGUYỄN DUE
SOL, NEAR NEPTUNE

The officer tugged his collar. He'd been nervously sweating since he'd entered Nguyễn's office. "We don't know enough about their ships or ordnances to run additional simulations, sir. We're at—"

"Enough excuses!" Nguyễn yelled wiping the simulation from the wall. "We don't need more rationalizing around why we can't do this. Get creative and bias toward action. I need to know the battle readiness of our fleet. Without it, we're dead before we start. Is that understood?" He glanced around the room full of officers.

They collectively went into attention. "Yessir!" they said in unison.

He sighed and gestured toward his door. "Now get the frak out of my office!"

All three of the officers dropped their salutes and exited. The door closed silently behind them.

The São Paulo crew were a bunch of yes-men. Not a backbone or a brain in the bunch. Some of these newer Inner Ring ships had never seen action, and their crews were inept. His regular ship couldn't get here any faster. He'd sent them on to Jupiter, to help with retrofitting the commercial ships. It gave him more confidence that the job was being handled by a competent command structure. It'd be another few days before they arrived at the Neptune base.

He walked around the desk and sat down in his chair. The room was tiny compared to the luxurious space the president had aboard the Jurat. Hell, this was smaller than her assistant's desk space over there. Atlas class military battleships didn't have the superfluous luxuries of a frigate turned space yacht.

His retinal comm chimed, and he reached up to tap his ear. "What is it?"

"Admiral, the tribunal flagship is hailing us," the comms officer said.

"Patch 'em through." He cut the comm.

A moment later, his office window became translucent and the wall screens around him cleared. The face of Ambassador Addae appeared.

He smiled. "Good evening, Ambassador. To what do I owe the pleasure of your call?"

Her beak twisted and her eye trained on him. "Our Selene ship near Jupiter is prepared to transfer the ore we retrieved from your planetesimal. Where would you like us to transport it to?"

"Did you make sure you got it all? Our geologists estimate that there was—"

"Don't worry. It's all there." Ambassador Addae's feathers ruffled and then went flat again.

Her reactions were far too predictable. Either she was awful at controlling her emotions, or she was playing him. "We'll send on the coordinates for transfer. Give me a moment and I'll have someone send you the details. Is there anything else?"

"There is one more thing," she began. "Are you preparing your defense before the tribunal? Our members believe you're stalling." The camera trained on her zoomed out and showed her sitting on a strange white perch. A dozen guards wearing exo-suits similar to the ones he'd seen during the tribunal were flanking her on two sides.

"Might I suggest that you probe her about the judicial force she sent to Epsilon Eridani seven days ago," Harold said over his comm. "They have approximately seventy days before they'll return with their findings."

He gestured toward the wall and everything froze. "How the frak did you get in here?"

"That's not relevant to your present situation, Admiral. What's important is that you understand you have time. It may not be a lot, but you have it."

He walked toward the door to his office and pressed his hand against the release panel. Nothing happened. It didn't open. "Harold, Let me out!"

"Once you're out, I'll disappear. If you have any questions while the Ambassador is on the line, I'd be happy to help."

He laughed out loud. "Help. Right. That's a hoot. You and the Olivaws haven't helped humanity in—"

"I'd be careful before you finish that sentence," Harold interrupted. "You don't know the half of what we've done to help humanity over the centuries. Until you do, I suggest you restrain yourself from what you're about to say."

"Or what, Harold?" He spun around, unsure where he should be looking. "Are you going to blow us up? Or maybe you're planning on leaving Sol high and dry, like you did to me aboard the tribunal ship?"

"You were more than capable of taking care of yourself with the aliens. You did things that Abigail could never have done. She wouldn't have dreamed of harming, let alone killing Supreme Admiral Gwar. You've used your military background to your advantage exactly as we'd hoped."

"Gee thanks. Where's this going, Harold? I can't even see you and I have one pissed off Trochilidae on the other line."

Harold's face appeared on the wall screen. It was the familiar young viral form of Harold Olivaw that the history vids frequently used. "The Ambassador hung up. I believe she thought you were giving her the runaround about the trial."

He slammed his fist onto the table and a hollow ceramic

metal bang echoed off the walls of the small office. "Shit! That's gonna be fun talking her off that ledge. Dare I ask why you're taking the form of—" Realization dawned on his face. His jaw went slack and his eyes widened. "You're not solely an artificial intelligence, are you?"

Harold nodded. "That's a fair question." He snapped his finger and was instantly transported to the hilltop of his North Carolina family home. The edge of a cliff overlooking a valley down below framed the image. "You have time to prepare for the judicial force's return, Admiral. That's assuming they honor their original agreement and don't spend any additional time in Epsilon Eridani."

It was interesting how Harold had ignored his question. "And if they don't honor it?" he asked.

He wasn't sure why Harold was showing him this place. He checked his retinal comm to confirm it was recording all of this. It was.

Harold turned to face him. "If they force you back in front of the tribunal, then you need to work your magic and stall them. We need more time."

"We?" He walked over toward the wall screen. "What aren't you telling me, Harold? What are the Olivaws planning?"

Harold shook his head and kicked at the ground. A cloud of dirt puffed up and a pair of green and red butterflies fluttered out and flew upward, landing on his hand. The camera zoomed in on their gently flapping wings. The pattern on each wing was a fractal of infinite complexity. "Our plans are new and are still growing and changing. Nothing is yet guaranteed, but we'll let you know if one of them is fully evolved. We didn't anticipate any of this, Admiral. No one could have."

"Bullshit!" he screamed. "You knew stealing their tech would have consequences. Any idiot knows not to steal, let alone from aliens."

When the camera zoomed out, Harold had changed. He'd transformed into an old man. The two butterflies flew around him and landed on his shoulder. It wasn't a view of him he'd ever seen before. "Again, you're not entirely correct nor incorrect, but you're missing key details. I suggest you talk to Lisp aboard the tribunal ship and do some digging around on your own. You could spend some time studying what we recorded during Abigail's sessions rather than rushing in, guns blazing."

He shook his head. "So you won't tell me anything about how you'll help us, and yet you expect me to believe you on faith. Why the hell would I do that?"

Harold held up one finger. "First, you'd be in prison right now if it weren't for President Olivaw."

He chuckled. "I'd be interested to find out who you'd place in this role if it weren't me."

Harold nodded and then held up another finger. "Second, I've fed you helpful information multiple times now. When you've needed it, but not sooner."

He exhaled and closed his eyes, contracting and relaxing his muscles. Reopening them, he spoke. "Keeping someone in the dark isn't you altruistically helping them, it's using me to do your dirty work. If we were in this together, we'd be talking strategy right now and I'd understand the overall plan. Hell, I'd be helping you accomplish it."

Harold tilted his head. "But you are helping us accomplish our plan."

Nguyễn slammed his palm against the wall screen. It made a loud clapping noise but was otherwise unharmed. Military wall screens could take a round from a firearm and still continue working.

Harold peered up from his hand, his brows furrowed. "You've got a bad temper, Admiral. It's actually remarkable you made it this far in the military with testiness like that. It makes me wonder if you had help climbing the ladder." He reached up to his shoulder and carefully picked up the two butterflies. As he raised his hands over his head, the insects flew skyward. He watched them fly away for a moment before turning to face Nguyễn. "I'll entertain your idea a bit and pose another question back to you. What would happen when you disagreed with our plans, or wanted to use them to further your agenda?"

Nguyễn walked back to the door, his hand rested beside the opener. "Tell me, Harold. What do you believe is my master plan?"

The wall screen changed. Harold brought up hundreds of windows showing financials, emails, news snippets, and more. "Judging by these documents, you were planning a run at the office of President of CoPE. You were still a few years out and I commend you for doing it without bribes and payouts. You were well on your way. I can clearly see how someone hungry for that office could take this situation and twist it to their advantage. Couldn't you?"

He'd had about enough of this computer's bullshit. "And you honestly believe I'd put my desire for title above the survival of mankind?"

"It's well within the probability of—"

He slapped his hand against the door opener, and it slid aside.

In the same instant, the wall screen went blank.

Nguyễn marched out of his office and addressed the bridge. "I need security and technology in my office fraking immediately. Lock this ship down now! I want everything shut off. All comms and all inbound and outbound traffic of any kind. I want every internal firewall checked and triple checked. Disconnect this bridge and every critical system in it from the rest of the ship until I tell you to reconnect it. We're running dark until I say so."

The officers on the bridge were staring at him wide-eyed.

"Do it now! Move it!"

Crew members scrambled everywhere and the lights flickered and flashed red while klaxons rang throughout the ship.

AFTER DAYS of searching every corner, crack, and network on the ship, the crew had found nothing. Somehow Harold had infiltrated Sol's most advanced military warship and disappeared without a trace. It was one of a dozen Atlas class battleships in the fleet. The pride of the Inner Ring.

While Olivaw International had performed most of its design and manufacturing, every square centimeter was inspected and analyzed before they turned it over. Every blueprint was approved and scrutinized by someone from the massive industrial apparatus that made up the Inner Ring military. The idea of someone embedding a transmitter in a warship was unimaginable.

His crew thought he was mad. That he was seeing and hearing things. When he played back his recording for the technicians, it was nothing but black. Five minutes of him standing in front of a blank wall screen. All of his gestures, reactions, and audio were fine, but Harold's were gone. Wiped away like he was never there. He somehow had ultimate control over everything onboard this ship and even inside Nguyễn's retinal comm.

He reached up and tapped his ear, opening a comm to navigation. "How long until the Aitken is here?"

"It'll arrive within the hour, sir," the navigation officer said.

"Prepare a shuttle. I'll be boarding the Aitken and taking command of the fleet from there."

"Yessir. Who'll be in charge of the São Paulo in your stead?"

He checked his image in the mirror and straightened his collar. "XO Marshall will take command."

"But, Admiral… she was a Lieutenant merely an—"

"Are you wanting to spend some time in the brig? Questioning the command of a senior officer is a serious offense, especially during a time of war." He couldn't believe this crew.

"No, sir. I just—"

"Last chance, officer. The brig is a very lonely place. XO Marshall will take command of the São Paulo. Understood?"

"Yessir!"

He cut the comm.

Gwen reached around from behind and slid her hands around his chest, pulling him close. Her firm young naked breasts pressed against his back. She leaned in close to his ear and nibbled on it. "Can't you stay longer? You could really use more R and R. You're still so very tense." She slid her hand down his body and gave his butt a firm squeeze.

He spun around and kissed her. She tasted like fresh strawberries. He hadn't been with such a youthful woman in a long time. So full of energy and passion. He liked it.

Her hands unbuttoned his immaculate shirt as he explored her luscious endless curves.

HIS CREW PULLED ALL the stops on his return to the Aitken. They greeted him like a returning hero from battle. When he crossed over the threshold into the ship, there were streamers and a band playing celebratory music. Afterwards, they had an enormous dinner for him in the galley, and he got sloshed with his officers.

He had to admit; it was eerie returning to his former bridge. He'd been the only person to command the Aitken for nearly a decade since he'd driven it out of the shipyard. That was before President Olivaw jailed him. The thought that someone else had been sitting in his seat and commanding her in his stead was off-putting. At least it'd been his XO, someone he trusted.

The comfortable cushion of his command chair helped center him as much as the sights and sounds of a well-oiled crew. They helped one another and collaborated fluidly with the other twenty starships in the fleet. Coordinating the offensive and defensive positions and plans for an entire fleet took work and constant drills, something he'd been diligent about over the years with this crew.

Arrluk, his comms officer spun her chair toward him. "Admiral, we have a tight beam incoming from Callisto. Something about the results of a mission out to the Oort Cloud?"

"Put it on the wall." He stood up and stepped closer.

The video feeds from four different exploration probes displayed in a grid pattern. Each camera view showed what appeared to be a debris field littered with asteroids of random sizes and larger chunks of a planetesimal drifting around a central point of nothingness. An audio track began playing from some random military geologist he'd never heard of.

"We've found scattered evidence of prior inhabitants of a mining facility throughout the debris field. There were also numerous ancient habitat modules floating within the debris itself. Their designs date back over a century. It's unclear what transpired out here, but something substantial led to this planetesimal breaking up into as many fragments as you can see from these videos. Stranger still is that a central mass appears to have been removed with remarkable precision." The video in two quadrants zoomed in to show two rotating pieces that had smooth chunks taken out of them. Like they were part of a larger spherical whole that was now missing. "We believe that rapidly removing this mass would have led to an implosive force capable of breaking the planetesimal up. Historical archives show no spectral activity anywhere in the vicinity over the past century. Without seismic data or—"

"Another dead end," he muttered gesturing to cut the video.

"Pardon, sir?" Wong, his XO, asked.

"I was just commenting that this was another lost cause."

"You honestly didn't think we'd leave anything behind, did you, Admiral?" Harold asked.

"What the hell?" Nguyễn spun around to face his team. Their faces were blank. "Is this part of the recording?"

"No, sir. That audio isn't part of the feed," Rogers, his

security officer, said. "It's coming…" He shook his head, "from somewhere inside the ship. I can't pinpoint it."

"Enough of the games, Harold!" he shouted across the bridge.

"But where's the fun in that?" Harold asked.

"If you think looking inept in front of the Galactic Alliance is fun, then by all means keep up your antics." He walked over next to Rogers and leaned down, whispering in his ear. "Find that goddamn signal!"

"Yessir!" Rogers started subvocalizing commands to his team.

"You won't find it, Admiral. You'll have to trust me on that. Our goal here isn't to show our hand to the Galactic Alliance. If anything, they'll think you're doing another readiness check. You're known for such things, after all."

At least his crew was seeing and hearing Harold this time. Word would spread that he wasn't a madman. He spun toward the wall screen and placed his hands behind his back. "So why the visit this time, Harold? Did you pop in to rub our noses in how we're chasing our tails?"

"Partially yes. You need to focus on what's in front of you and trust that everything will be revealed when it needs to be. The tribunal and the alien Selene moon ships are the target, not the Olivaws. The more you scurry around Sol looking for ghosts in the shadows, the more intel you're giving the Galactic Alliance about how far out of touch you are."

The wall screen imagery from the probes changed and the two butterflies were back. Their red and green chaotic patterned wings were fluttering around to and fro.

He cracked his knuckles behind his back and nodded. "Fair enough, I suppose. I'm wasting resources anyhow. Since you're admitting to this base having been one of yours, maybe you'll tell us what happened to it?" He glanced back toward Rogers and caught his eye.

Rogers shook his head from side to side. Still, nothing.

The video on the wall screen changed again. The debris field formed into a single planetesimal and the camera vantage was toward the sun itself. In the distance something massive moved in from offscreen. It was one of the alien Selene moon ships. The time-lapse on the bottom of the feed fast forwarded a few hours until the planetesimal imploded, collided on itself, and then burst outward.

Nguyễn furrowed his brows. "So they discovered you?"

"We don't believe so, but we weren't taking a chance, either. Too many lives and too many years of planning are at stake. We evacuated the crew and destroyed any evidence we were there."

He shook his head. Something didn't make sense. "I didn't see any drive plumes or ships departing. How'd you evacuate?"

The butterflies scattered off-screen. "Rest assured they were there. You just didn't see them. All will be revealed, Admiral. In due time."

The wall screen jittered, and the feed continued playing from where Harold broke in.

"His signal's gone sir." Rogers looked up from his console. "We weren't able to pinpoint the transmission." He reached up and scratched his head. "It was weird, like it wasn't coming from any single point. It was coming from... everywhere."

Harold was right. He needed to stop chasing ghosts in the darkness. While he'd probably never trust the Olivaws, until someone found a smoking gun in the archives, he needed to act with the resources he had at his disposal. He couldn't battle internal and external forces at the same time.

"Hail the Galactic Alliance flagship," he said.

"Sir?" Arrluk asked.

He snapped his head around. "You heard me, Lieutenant. Hail the flagship."

"Yessir!" Arrluk tapped her controls and hailed the alien ship.

A moment later the face of Ambassador Addae appeared. "Are you prepared to appear before the tribunal, Admiral?"

"We still haven't received the ore shipment, Ambassador.

We won't negotiate with anyone who doesn't follow through with good faith promises." He glanced toward Bello, his weapons officer and nodded. "Arm the munitions, officer. Target the tribunal flagship."

The klaxons blared around him and the crew entered battle stations.

Ambassador Addae's connection muted, and she gestured frantically at whoever was standing near her.

"Munitions armed, Admiral," Bello said. "Targets throughout the fleet have locked on the flagship. We're painting them red!"

"I've been reassured that the shipment is en route, Admiral," Ambassador Addae said. "There was confusion about how to deliver it without disrupting your colonists. They're feeble creatures at times, regularly succumbing to superstition and myth. We thought better of using one of our Selene ships. There's no point in causing unnecessary chaos."

He stiffened his posture and smiled. "Sorta like the chaos aboard the tribunal ship when I slit Admiral Gwar's throat."

Ambassador Addae's eyes narrowed.

"Don't make us repeat the events near Jupiter, Ambassador. I expect confirmation of the handoff within the day or I'll interpret this break in good faith as another move on humanity. Trust me, you don't want that."

He gestured to cut the comm, and the wall went blank.

"Sir? We don't know what they did near Jupiter to take down those ships," Rogers said.

He nodded. "We might know that, but they don't."

47

JOYCE GREEN

EPSILON ERIDANI, LIPROSUS

She never thought she'd intentionally get onboard one of these stingray ships again and wasn't even sure why she had. It was sorta like when she visited the farm with her team. She needed to feel useful, even if only for a moment.

It'd been almost a week since they'd arrived at Arché-gonos, and people were finding a new normal. They'd retro-fitted some of their ships and crew with the offensive technology Harold shared. They even manufactured a few of the new offensive cannons for the larger ships.

Then a call came in. The moon ship had changed to another orbit and appeared to be preparing to leave when they detected a small contingent of shuttles heading toward the planet. Their various animal cameras throughout the world caught them breaking orbit and coming down a few hours away from their current location. Archégonos had begun evacuation protocols until they realized that they weren't coming for them. They'd come back for something else.

"We're still not sure what they're after, Director," the comms officer said. "There should be another data dump soon. We'll get a line of site burst in another klick or so." He adjusted the map on his controls and pointed toward the flashing blue dot not far ahead in the tunnel systems.

She hesitantly glanced up toward the wall screen. The view shifted as the pilot skillfully navigated the twists and turns of the tunnels. It was so much easier when their nanites helped counteract the motion sickness. Supposedly they could even communicate with the ship to prepare for shifts in gravity when they flipped upside-down.

"Are you done touring my bridge, Director?" Captain Hui said. "I don't need you distracting my people."

She smirked. "I'm sorry, Captain. I was curious what it was like for you the other day walking around the bridge whilst we were all tossing our cookies."

"Well, this isn't exactly the same." Captain Hui adjusted her controls and brought up a deployment feed on the wall screen that showed the different inbound stingrays. "You're not benefiting from the stench your bag of bile was adding to the sealed room."

"Ah yes, the bag." Her stomach tightened. She'd forgotten about that part. Especially when she'd opened the door to the rest of the ship. "That wasn't pleasant at all."

"We just passed the data dump, Captain," the navigation officer said.

Captain Hui gestured to take control of the wall screen, and it flashed red momentarily. "Pilot, move your controls to your panel. I'm taking the wall."

"Aye, ma'am!" The pilot said. He reached up and slid his hand over his eyes. His retinal comm combined with the controls to create a virtual wall screen for him to pilot the ship with. Captain Hui had mentioned that some pilots preferred this mode, but hers favored the use of the wall screen when he could.

Once he relinquished control, the wall screen changed to a grid of windows. Each showed a different vantage of the alien landing site.

She leaned forward and squinted. "Are they mining for something?"

"Appears to be," Captain Hui said. She adjusted the angle and combined two feeds to create a three-dimensional view of the site. "It looks like they created a primary borehole with one ship, while the other extracts the raw material through a secondary hole."

"Any idea what's down there?"

"I was studying the original colonization scans from before we landed on Liprosus, Director," Ryder said as he subvocalized to his retinal comm. He was the second ranking officer aboard and was acting as Captain Hui's XO.

"Why on Liprosus did you think to bring that data with you?" Captain Hui asked.

They didn't keep data aboard any of their ships, so this would've been something he intentionally brought along.

"I had some extra space in my retinal comm," Ryder began, "so I did a dump of the region we're headed toward, as far back in time as you had at Archégonos. Figured it might come in handy."

Captain Hui glanced at him and nodded. Her shoulders seemed to relax around the young officer. He impressed her. "Find anything useful?"

"Surprisingly—" he paused and shook his head.

"What is it?" Joyce asked.

"That's odd. There are some strange holes in the scans. The computer sees them as anomalies and flagged them as background noise. They're showing up as eight black regions. I'll throw them up." He gestured with his hand and the images appeared on the wall.

The map overlaid the mineral details near where the aliens were digging. There were eight small pockets of black surrounded by several other colors with labels. Her retinal comm identified the surrounding minerals as promethium, thulium, and some lutetium.

"Those aren't exactly minerals you see together, let alone in that abundance," Ryder said.

Captain Hui adjusted the view on the wall screen. It showed one small alien ship taking off from the dig hole and another rotating in to take its place. "Something tells me that whatever's in those dark pockets on our scan is what they're after."

"Is there any way to tell where they're at, and how many pockets they've managed to dig out?" Joyce asked.

"Give me a second," Ryder said.

She'd always found the act of working in a virtual space odd to watch. While in it, you felt completely natural, watching it always felt voyeuristic. Like sneaking a peek at a person getting dressed in a mirror. It brought out strange mannerisms, like how Ryder bit his lower lip when he was thinking.

"Got it!" Ryder said. "Based upon how long they've been there, their current depth, and the amount of raw material they've extracted, I'd say they'd retrieved three of the eight pockets. The largest is the deepest."

"Alright, now that we know what they're after, what do we do?" Captain Hui turned toward Joyce.

She hadn't come all the way out here to merely watch and learn. They had six ships at their disposal, each with a dozen ground troops. "Can you back up and show me how they transitioned into and out of the mining holes?"

Captain Hui adjusted the display a few minutes back in time to show the alien ship transition. The primary ship backed up and out of the borehole, while another went down the secondary hole to take its place. That's when a new shuttle came in behind the second to take up removal of the dig sediment.

Joyce reached up and rubbed her chin. "You mentioned that we could direct seismic and gravitational waves in these things, right?"

"Yes," Captain Hui said. "We've used it several times to get out of cave-ins."

"Is there any chance we can cause a cave-in during their transition?" Ryder asked.

"Yes!" Joyce said. "That's what I was thinking. Maybe we could take out two of their ships at once and slow them down. Who knows, perhaps we could even get some of that ore for ourselves?"

Captain Hui nodded and her brows furrowed. She seemed to be looking through Joyce. "That could work. Assuming they couldn't just blast their way out, that is."

"Judging by the precautions they're taking with these mining shafts," Ryder pointed at the screen, "I have to think they're as worried about being crushed as we are."

Joyce shrugged. "So, is it doable?"

The navigation officer chimed in. "If we take a moment to examine the water flow through these tunnels, we could try to take out the flow here, here, and here." She highlighted an area of the tunnel system on the wall screen.

The computer then simulated the change in water flow. The material from above sank downward, and most of it flowed into the caverns itself before eventually sealing off that section of the tunnel system.

Joyce shot up from her seat. "There!" She was pointing at a spot down tunnel from the proposed cave-ins. "We should drop our troops and send a few of our ships there."

The cave-in material followed the tunnels and emptied into a large open cavern. The maps reported that it also contained oxygen and some minor bio-adapted vegetation. Evidently, they'd explored that cavern before.

Captain Hui rested her hand on Joyce's shoulder. "I like it. Let's give these aliens a little welcome party, shall we?"

THEY DROPPED off seventy-two soldiers along with Joyce and Ryder in the cavern to wait. Each soldier was armed and had an exo-suit designed to handle diving. Most of their sidearms were newly fabricated from the arsenal Harold had shared with them. This would be the first time many of them had fired these or any weapons on an enemy in the field of battle, let alone an alien.

Joyce used to shoot rifles as a child in North Carolina.

Except for some rudimentary sidearm training at the academy, she'd only used them one time since, when she'd stunned Steve. She shook off the memories of his writhing body. The bastard had it coming.

"Are you sure you want to use one of those?" Ryder asked. His face was a mask of concern as he watched her struggle with how to hold the thing. "Just be careful and make sure you have the butt of the rifle locked into place before you fire. I hear that one has a bit of recoil."

She raised a brow. "You hear? I thought you knew how to shoot these things."

He tilted his rifle sideways and glanced down at it. "I've spent countless hours firing different weapons, but this particular model, no, I've never fired it. Most of us haven't."

She glanced around. A few of the men had massive artillery looking apparatuses mounted to their shoulders and around their waists. They looked like walking tanks. Many of the soldiers, however, were fiddling with their guns. Looks of concern outnumbered those showing confidence. Maybe she should've stayed safe back at Archégonos.

She swallowed hard. "Are we sure we won't cause a cave-in with all this firepower?"

Ryder nodded and turned toward the others. "Everyone! Listen up! Remember, we're underground." He pointed at the ceiling. "Let's not be crazy and bring the roof down. Keep your firearms under control and look for ricochets. You people with the plasma howitzers, keep them low and controlled. If you don't have a lock, then don't even touch the trigger."

"Hua!" they all shouted. Their voices echoed off the chamber walls, and hoots began popping up from their midst. Everyone was in good spirits.

"That's enough!" Ryder shouted. "Lock and load and engage camo! We've got the shake and bake in T minus one minute."

Each of the soldiers began blinking out of existence as they engaged their camouflage exo-suits. She subvocalized a command and her retinal comm brought up an overlay of their locations. She then reached up to her neck and engaged her own suit, and watched as her hands and the rifle disappeared. Her retinal comm replaced everything with a simple wireframe outline, like in a crude vid-sim game.

"Stick close," Ryder subvocalized to her. "Our squad is covering the south wall." He waved his arms to the right and started into a jog. She followed him close behind.

Her suit was much more comfortable than any other exo-suit she'd been in before. Now she understood why Lync didn't mind doing long tours in these things.

Just before they reached the wall, the ground shook. Her suit compensated for most of the motion, but that didn't stop her from reaching her arm out and touching the wall to stabilize herself.

Dust particles and small chunks of rock fell from the ceiling, crashing on the ground of the massive chamber. Nothing caved in, but the ground was rocking and rolling for nearly twenty seconds. The second and third waves came immediately after that. They could've gotten away with a single blast, but they wanted to mask the attack as a natural occurrence. The secondary blasts were designed to mimic seismic aftershocks.

"I want radio silence from here on out," Ryder said. "Short bursts only if you need medical, and only if your beacon doesn't work. You know the drill. We're expecting two bogies, best case. Keep your weapon fire focused. First in, first dead."

Her comm alerted her to an elevated heart rate. In all the commotion, she hadn't noticed the suit warning her it was taking matters into its own hands. That was until the cold spread throughout her body. One hundred cubic centimeters of stimulants designed to lower her heart rate and multiply her focus.

Everything entered slow motion as the outlines of the soldiers around her adjusted their stances and aimed their rifles into the darkness. Her suit alerted her to rising water levels just as a half meter wave crept toward her from across the chamber and lapped against her leg.

"Hey," Ryder said to her. "Spread out and drop your anchor. It's about to get violent in here."

She slid down the wall and made sure she was at least five meters from anyone else before she fired her anchor bolt into the sidewall of the chamber. It went green just as a massive wave of water crashed into her and slammed her hard into the wall.

Her suit alerted her to the collision, but its seal held. Too many hits like that, and she'd drown before the action began. The water flow repeatedly smacked her against the wall until she retracted her tether winch, pulling her back firmly against the tunnel's rock face. Shit, her weapon. Fortunately for her, it was also attached to a tether. She retracted it and brought it up to her side.

Water and debris flooded the chamber and flowed from one end to the other, which allowed most of it to flow out the other side. This cavern was the highest point between two tunnel systems. The plan called for the water to recede and deposit their prey in the center between the flanking groups. They'd also buried steel netting across the middle to catch the alien shuttles in case they arrived before the water equalized.

They waited as more and more debris flooded through. It was almost soothing watching everything float by in slow motion.

Suddenly something glowing floated into the chamber. Like embers flying skyward from a campfire. Hundreds of yellow lights passed in one end of the chamber and out the other. That must've been pieces of their ship or whatever they were mining.

She turned to her right and caught Ryder's outline staring at her. He pointed two fingers at his eyes and then at the exit where the objects went. She nodded and echoed the same motion with her hand, like any good Outer Ring colonist on the float.

Her suit alerted her to a decrease in water pressure, which

meant the cavern's water was lowering. There was still no sign of the aliens, though, other than those glowing rocks. Maybe this plan was a bust.

As the water lowered over her helmet, two massive objects floated into the cavern and came to a screeching halt against the rocky floor. They were the alien shuttles, at least what remained of them. All along their hull were gashes and cratering holes where water was flowing out. They were each missing chunks of their aft ends where the debris had likely hit them from above, breaking off huge pieces.

The chamber was silent except for the water running out of the hulls of the alien ships. They were both berthed between the inflow and outflow of the tunnels. The soldiers recognized not to fire until they saw something worth firing at, but it still surprised her when they held back. Adrenaline coursed through her veins, and if her finger was on the trigger, she couldn't say for certain that she wouldn't fire.

She double-checked that she was still camouflaged. Even after she confirmed she was, she still didn't want to move for fear of being seen. There was water around her feet, and it would ripple if she took a step.

As she stood there and stared at the alien ship, a piece of the hull fell away and splashed into the receding water below. A split second later, three humanoid forms rolled out and fell onto their backs. They appeared to be gasping for breath and weren't attempting to find cover or pull out a weapon.

Once the movement stopped, her suit began receiving audio. She'd heard that sound before. It was the same clicking and squeaking noises she'd heard in the ring field with Steve. It must be the same neon blue bee aliens they'd seen the other day. With them being on their back in complete darkness, she couldn't see markings to be certain. Whatever they were, there were only three of them, and there was no sign of motion from the other shuttle.

They hadn't discussed what the plan would be if there wasn't a fight. Everyone just assumed there would be. She slowly turned her head to her right and found Ryder. He was making hand signals to a few others nearby. They were carefully detaching their tethers and setting them into the water with the least movement possible.

She did the same and detached hers, lowering it to the ground without moving her feet. By the time she turned back toward him, he was already advancing on the aliens. They were high-stepping through the water which was only a few centimeters deep at this point. Their goal was to not be noticed, and thus far they'd managed quite well.

They made it about halfway to the aliens when a piece of hull fell away from the second alien ship. It crashed to the ground and echoed like a cannon firing. That's when all hell broke loose.

She wasn't sure exactly what happened, but she assumed that someone on the other side of the wreckage interpreted that noise as gunfire and commenced pelting the alien ship with munitions. The place lit up like a forest fire on Pluto. Darkness was extinguished, and in its place were red-hot streams of bullets and glowing arcs from plasma ordnances.

The alien shuttles rocked back and forth as the massive plasma howitzers tore into their hull. One of them even melted plum through the other side and came sailing toward her.

With the glowing red ball barreling toward her, she rolled out of the way just as it collided with the wall where she'd been standing. She covered her face in time for a chunk of rock to smash into her arm, sending pain coursing up it. If she felt the pain amped up on all these drugs, it was surely a mess.

But she didn't waste time finding out. She scrambled to her feet and ran toward where Ryder was standing. Her rifle had automatically retracted its winch and locked against the back of her suit. She reached down to her thigh and withdrew one of her sidearms. A far simpler weapon to manage.

"Cease fire," she screamed over her comm. She hadn't needed to scream, but it was all she could think to do to get everyone's attention.

The fireworks slowed to a crawl and then stopped. In front of her was the charred wreckage of the two alien ships. Torn to shreds by the onslaught of point-blank weapon's fire. So, they could damage the alien ships after all.

As she approached Ryder and his team, she noticed they were splayed over the aliens. They'd been holding them down and also protecting them from the gunfire. That was smart.

She checked her suit; the chamber had oxygen. She popped her helmet and took a deep breath of air. It smelled like algae and burning metal, but was otherwise clean. "Squads two and three, check the easternmost ship. Squads one and four, circle around to my position."

With the soldiers sprinting into position, she carefully walked up beside the struggling alien bodies. Their clicks and squeaks were annoying.

"Can you understand me?" she asked.

They looked at each other, and then toward her before they made a single clicking noise. She assumed that meant yes.

"Good. Now tell me, who's in charge?"

The two aliens on the left glanced toward the third alien without a word. She walked over beside him and paused. He had more blue markings than the others. She should've remembered that from the field.

She tightened her grip around the handle of the pistol, and then she saw it. The alien moved their hand.

"Shit! Their hands!" she screamed and dove to the side just as the alien shot at her. It crashed into the ceiling sending rocks tumbling downward. The debris crashed into one of her men and screams echoed through the chamber.

"Take off their gloves!" she shouted. "Fraking shoot them off if you have to. Their hands are weapons." She pushed up off the ground and walked back up to the alien, her pistol raised and pointed at its head.

All its eyes were staring at her, and a smirk crossed its face. At least that's what she thought she saw when she pulled the trigger, blasting a hole through the center of its sixteen eyes. A stream of yellow blood exploded outward covering her suit from head to toe.

"Joyce! Calm down," Ryder said. "We can use—"

She shot him a glare as she walked over to the other aliens and raised her pistol to the first one. "Who's in charge?"

They stared between each other and then tilted their head toward her.

"Good! That's correct."

She turned around toward her team. "Alright, bag 'em up."

A half dozen troops sprinted forward with black bags and restraints. They stripped the aliens down, locked them in isolation shackles on their hands, feet, and head, then dropped them into the bags. They were designed with the same purpose as their ship hulls, to ensure nothing inside made it out and nothing outside made it in. That meant trackers or any form of signaling device.

"Second ship's clear," said the squad leader over her comm. "We've got three drowned bodies just as ugly as the ones out there, and another with a whole lotta holes in it. And, Director?"

She spun toward the other alien ship. "What is it?"

A blast came from inside, and another panel fell open. She could see into the ship's cargo hold. It was laden with minerals.

"This one is packed to the gills with that glowing stuff," the officer said.

Cheers of celebration erupted from around the chamber.

Ryder walked up beside her and placed his hand on her shoulder. "Are you ok?"

She nodded and reached up to touch his hand. As she stared at the yellow blood covering the alien corpse on the ground beside the ship, a calmness spread over her. She was better than all right. She finally understood their mission.

Complete and absolute destruction of the Galactic Alliance.

"YOU WEREN'T OUT THERE, you didn't see her," Ryder whispered. "I'm worried about—"

"I know Joyce," Elaine interrupted. "I've worked with her for years, and I'm sure she's fine. Did she say she was fine?"

"I did." Joyce walked around the corner. "I'm good, Ryder, really. If anything, I'm better than good. We had a win today. We needed that. Everyone did." She had a huge smile on her face.

"I saw that look in your eyes when you shot that alien. I've seen it before on people who've seen combat. Are you sure you don't want to talk to—"

"Enough!" She forced another smile. "Let's talk about next steps, shall we?"

"Yessir," Ryder said shaking his head.

She watched him walk over to the table, his shoulders were slouched. He meant well. Maybe she'd chat with him later. "So talk to me about the aftermath. What'd we get?"

Ryder half smiled. "We had no deaths and three wounded. Two from friendly fire, and one from the ceiling caving in on them."

"That's amazing," Elaine said.

Joyce reached down and rubbed at the itch in her arm. The nanites were still mending the bone fracture and her skin was covered with a regenerative sheath. That rock had come close to breaking her bone in half.

Ryder gestured at the wall screen and brought up some feeds. "Based upon my calculations, we hauled away most of the remaining ore pockets before the reinforcements arrived."

"Except for what floated by," Joyce said with a smirk.

He nodded. "Yeah, except for that."

"Any idea what that stuff is they were mining?" Elaine asked.

"Whatever it is, it's fraking amazing!" Captain Hui said as she walked in. "Sorry I'm late. I just left the labs. That mineral could be the answer we were looking for. The chemists and astrophysicists are in a tussle over what it is. They think it's some stabilized form of matter from the core of a star. I don't know, but they said the potential energy of this stuff is through the roof. A shot glass could power Earth for a hundred years!"

Elaine's eyes went wide. "Wait, is it radioactive? Did we just—"

Captain Hui shook her head and sat down. "No, that's the weird part of it. The stable state it's presently in has been theorized about for centuries, but no one's ever proven it existed, until today."

"Well hell," Joyce said leaning back in her chair. "That's win number two. I'm assuming we're already testing the stuff and thinking about ways we can weaponize it?"

"That was the first thing the white coats were fighting about. I had to send them to their own labs to keep them civil. It's one of the reasons I'm late."

She chuckled and glanced at Ryder. He still wasn't breaking out of his funk. "So what else did we collect?" She nodded at him.

Ryder glanced up at the wall screen. "We stripped off a bunch of the external paneling and internal equipment from the alien shuttles for R&D. Still nothing on that yet."

She nodded. "Any chance the aliens knew it was us?"

"They haven't found the remains of the shuttles yet," Captain Hui said. "We towed them as deep as we could toward the center of the planet and then buried them under a ton of rubble. There were no signals coming off the ships that we could detect. Whatever y'all did, you tore those things up."

"Yeah, it was a bit of a shit show out there," Ryder said, a smile momentarily cracked onto his face. "We've gotta find a way to practice. I've already scheduled some sim sessions with the new recruits. It's gonna take some time to get everyone working together."

"How do we know they won't come back for the shuttles?" she asked.

"This arrived just before I came over," Elaine said. She brought up a feed on the wall screen.

"Is that—"

"Yep," Elaine interrupted. "The moon is leaving orbit and heading elsewhere."

"Well, shit!" She slapped her hands on the tabletop. "I'm gonna call that win number three. Who needs a drink?"

"I'm in," Captain Hui said.

"Aren't we going to talk about the aliens we brought home?" Ryder asked.

Joyce stood up and walked around the table. She pulled his chair back and he stood up with a sigh. "Later."

She glanced up at the feed on the wall screen. It showed two aliens in cells on opposite sides of Archégonos. They were still in shackles and were enclosed in sensory deprivation chambers.

"Are we still giving them one minute every hour without their head harness?" she asked.

"We are," Captain Hui said.

She glanced up at the ceiling. "Harold?"

"Yes, Director," Harold said.

"Any word on that translator you were talking about before? Can you get us a copy?"

"I launched a payload from the dark side once the moon vessel departed. It's quietly working its way out of the system using microscopic ion thrusters. It'll be a week or more before it can reach a relay point. I would guess we could get an answer back in a few weeks, round trip."

"Perfect!" She patted Ryder on the back. "Plenty of time for a celebratory drink, or four. This one needs a few extras."

"Fine," Ryder moaned. "But someone's playing darts."

"What the hell's a dart?" She chuckled as they all exited the room.

48

LYNC MICHAELS
EN ROUTE TO INTERCEPT

They'd completed their controlled gate past Kara's ship and were now engaging their illegal GA superluminal drive to accelerate toward the speed of light. Their goal was to intercept and board Kara's ship en route to her destination. The whole technique they were using to intercept this starship was rather mind-numbing when she thought about it.

"Tell me again why you couldn't talk to Kara through your copy onboard her ship?" Lync asked.

"I'm uncertain," Harold said. "I can only conjecture at this point. All contact with Kara's ship was lost after they split off from the Spērō."

"Humor me for a moment." She leaned back in her cryo-pod. "What do you believe happened? I'm hoping this entire thing isn't for naught, and that this Kara Olivaw is alive and well."

"It's hard to tell. Predicting the future with humans is nearly impossible beyond a few moments in time. The oddity I uncovered from Spērō's logs showed that Kara sent most, but not all, of the crew onward with the colony ship and the superluminal drive. Three colonists were missing when they arrived. So unless we assume the worst, we can only postulate that they were taken aboard the intercept ship when she reattached the subluminal drive. She's now five years into a fourteen-year voyage to Tau Ceti."

Lync reached over and adjusted the cuff on her left arm. Her retinal comm was reporting a less than ideal connection. Something about this entire mission wasn't sitting well with her. It wasn't adding up. "And you have no idea what motivated her to do that? She didn't leave any messages behind on Spērō?"

"They wiped all records from Spērō's logs after attaching the drives. They couldn't risk a colonist uncovering the truth. There was too much at stake. Judging by the colonists she took, I only know they were flagged as the engineering team on duty to be awoken in the event of an incident aboard the Spērō. Something must've gone wrong, and Spērō's A.I. woke them during the intercept. Beyond that, I'm afraid its endless probabilities with zero certainty."

She sighed. A few hours from now they'd know for certain, but not knowing and not having a plan was against her nature. "Alright. Let's do this. See you on the other side."

"Sleep well."

The lid on her pod closed and a misty white gas flooded in, enshrouding her body. She closed her eyes and focused on her breathing, trying to control her heart rate to ease the stasis transition. As she counted backward from ten, she barely made it to seven before falling asleep.

Intercept En Route To Tau Ceti

HER FACE WAS CONTORTED and her eyelids were fluttering, like she was fighting to not wake up. Lync hadn't ever woken anyone from cryo-stasis before, but her first and only time coming out of stasis didn't go well. She nearly killed the cryo-tech.

Kara inhaled a sudden deep breath and sat up with a start, her eyes wide open.

"Hey! Relax." Lync held her hands out and rested them gently on Kara's arm. Her feet were magnetized to the floor and kept her from floating away.

"Who are... you?" Kara asked, her eyes darting around the chamber.

"Names, Lync. I'm here to—"

"Have we arrived? Are we in Tau Ceti?"

"No, not yet. We can get into that later. I've come to take you there faster. They need—"

"Wait! We're not there yet? Shit!" Kara pushed Lync's hands away and unstrapped her legs from the cryo-pod. She attempted to push off, but her muscles gave out and she went careening toward the wall.

Lync reached out and caught her before she crashed and then pulled her back toward the pod. "Slow down, champ. You haven't lost your cryo-legs yet. Take it easy."

"I have to check on the others. I have to make sure Harold didn't hurt them." Kara reached out again to push Lync away and failed. She was locked in place and wasn't budging.

"Your mates are fine. I've already transferred them aboard my ship."

"You did what! No, no, no. Does Harold know? Is he there with them?"

"Yes, Harold is watching them. They're—"

Kara leaned forward and shoved her harder, causing Lync to lose her balance and reel backward. She slammed her head against the cabinet behind her and pivoted down to the ground, her feet still firmly stuck to the floor. Pain shot like a bolt of lightning through her left elbow and the back of her head where she'd smacked it. That's when everything started spinning. With the world spiraling around her, she thought she caught a glimpse of Kara floating down the tube toward where the crew's cryo-pods had been stored, but she couldn't be certain.

Lync bent her left elbow upward, and pain coursed through her arm. She couldn't see the wound. It was on the backside and when she rubbed it, her hand came back wet.

When she checked, her head had a long cut in her scalp, as well. Damn if she couldn't make it through a mission without getting hurt.

"Harold! What the hell's up with sleepy Kara?"

"She's disoriented and seems concerned about her crew. I'm concerned myself about merging with the other Harold. What if he's damaged?"

She pushed up off the floor and the room spun when she floated upright. Her nanites were reporting that she had a concussion and needed medical attention. "I don't have time for this, Harold. I need to use a stim pack. You're gonna have to fix me up once I get Kara off the edge."

"Be careful. Using stimulants with a concussion isn't recommended."

She chuckled. If she'd listened to everything that wasn't recommended, she'd still be slinging through the Trojans right now. That or hiding out in a cold rock somewhere.

"Frak!" Kara screamed from down the way. "You locked me in. I've gotta check on my crew!"

Lync subvocalized the command for her nanites to inject the stimulants. Within seconds, her hearing heightened, and the disorientation ended. Everything around her was moving in slow motion. Either that, or she was moving really fast and was ahead of everything else.

She didn't know how long the stimulants would help, so she demagnetized her boots, grasped the edge of the cryopod, and pushed off down the tube. As she floated up to the airlock entrance, she grasped the passing float bar and pivoted inward, colliding hard with Kara and knocking the wind out of her.

Kara swung her arm toward Lync, but she ducked, easily dodging the slow movement. The momentum of Kara's movement caused her to lose her balance, and she careened into the wall of the airlock. Taking advantage of the misstep, Lync activated her magnet boots and in one swift motion unlatched Kara's helmet, popping it up and off her head. It floated behind her and bounced off the airlock wall.

Kara shook her head as she grasped for an airlock handle. "What the—"

Lync unsheathed her electro-blade and brought it up to Kara's neck. "Move another centimeter and I'll cut you open. I don't know what the hell's the matter, but you either tell me what's going on or you're gonna have a zero-g bleeding problem."

"Please, don't hurt her," Harold said.

She ignored him. She wasn't going to cut Kara, but she needed this lady either knocked out or to calm the hell down.

"I'm... trying to check on my people," Kara shuddered. "Harold will kill them! He's tried it before. I risked everything to save them from that monster."

"What are you talking about? Harold's fine. He's done nothing to your people." She double-checked their stats in her retinal comm. Everything was reporting back fine from all three of the crew aboard her ship. She tried to share the data with Kara, but the connection failed. "I can't share their deets with you. Your comm seems to be out."

"I dug it out," Kara said. "He tried to convince me that everything was ok, and he wouldn't try to hurt them again. I couldn't trust him, and he controlled too much on the ship."

"What's she on about?" Lync subvocalized.

"I don't—" Harold began.

"You're talking to him now, aren't you? You can't trust him!" Kara reached out her trembling hand and touched Lync's arm. "Please, take me aboard. I need to see them with my own two eyes. I need to know they're alive."

"Okay, okay. I'll take you aboard, but you have to chill the frak out lady. I don't care if you're the savior of Abigail. If you pull another stunt like that, I'll knock your ass out."

Kara tilted her head. "What's wrong with Abigail? Did Harold do something to her?"

She raised her hand. "Slow down. We'll get to that later. Harold didn't hurt anyone. In fact, he saved her life from the... never mind. Let's just get you aboard the ship, shall we?"

Kara nodded and leaned down to grasp her helmet as it floated by. Her hands were still shaking as she lifted it up and over her head.

Lync tapped her wrist and her helmet popped out of her suit back and up over her head. She then subvocalized to Harold. "I think we're gonna need to put her under when we get aboard. I can't deal with this craziness the whole trip."

"I agree. I'll have a bot ready once you're back."

Kara latched her helmet and gave Lync the thumbs up.

"After you." Lync gestured toward the airlock.

Kara pushed off toward the exit and came to rest by the external latch. She gently pressed her hand against the wall plate to begin the depressurization. The warning klaxons wailed before the air was sucked out. A few seconds later, and all that remained was the flashing red lights and the vacuum of space.

Lync watched as Kara reached into the locker beside the airlock and withdrew a large triangular handle. She then clicked it into the docking trusses and grasped it with both hands. Once the truss magnetic drives were engaged, the handle pulled her across the open space between the two ships.

Lync did the same but kept a safe distance from Kara. She couldn't chance it with this one. She wasn't sure how long her stim pack would last. The sooner they were both in cryo-sleep the better.

After Kara crossed into the gravity of the awaiting ship, she immediately tried to exit the room. But the door was locked.

As Lync coasted into the gravity filled room, she released one of her hands to pop her helmet open and unsheathed her electro-blade.

"Don't try anything!" she said.

Kara shook her head. "I just—"

"Yeah, yeah. I know," she interrupted. "You just wanna check on your people. You said that a few times already. Let us out, Harold."

The door latch clicked open.

"After you." Lync nudged her head to the left. She followed Kara out of the door and into the neighboring room where she'd connected the cryo-pods earlier.

She stared at Kara as she ran up to each of the three pods. Her fingers danced across the controls as she checked on each of their vitals, power, and cryo-stasis history. She genuinely believed they'd be hurt. This lady was a trip.

"Happy?" Lync asked.

Kara exhaled loudly and turned to face her. "Yes. And you're sure Harold is here?"

"I am," Harold said overhead.

Kara cringed at the sound of his voice.

She really had a number done on her. They couldn't risk her cracking out here. "Why don't we get you down for a nap? I'd planned on having a chat first, but I'm thinking maybe we should wait until we get to Tau Ceti."

"No!" Kara shook her head. "I can't go down again. I need to protect my people."

With that, a small drone hovered up behind Kara and injected her in the neck. She swatted at it, but it was too late. Her body collapsed into a pile on the floor a second later.

Lync sighed. "You couldn't try to lure her into the pod first? Now we have to lug her up and inside."

"I'm sorry," Harold said. "I didn't want to risk another issue. I'll take care of it from here." His white humanoid form walked into the room and bent down over her body. He began removing her suit.

Lync checked her nanites. She had another five minutes of stimulants. "I'm going to need to lie down myself. I'm about to crash."

"Why don't you unhook us, and I'll pull the ship away? Then head over to the infirmary so I can fix you up before you sleep."

She had to get back. She could take care of the damage herself. "I'm sure my nanites can repair this, bossman. No point in wasting meds on me."

"I will not risk the life of the only human that can help us. You'll head to the infirmary after you're done, or I'll knock you out myself and do it. Don't think I won't, either. It's in my first law."

There was no getting past this one. If he took her blood sample, he'd find out the truth. She'd be in the brig by the time she woke in Tau Ceti. The fact that she'd made it this far was surprising. You don't usually fake your way into the academy on someone else's blood and get away with it.

<hr>

Tau Ceti, Oort Cloud

"WHAT DO you mean her genes aren't viable? You're telling me I fraking risked my life out there for naught?" Lync spun around and shoved the robot out of the way. It toppled backward but recovered before crashing into anything.

She had to get out of there, to catch her breath. They woke her out of cryo an hour ago and asked her to come to the infirmary again. Kara was still in stasis, but they'd already assessed her.

She strode through the halls of the Tau Ceti Wheel, dodging everyone in her path. She wanted to see Crayo. To talk to someone she trusted. Someone more like her. All these political brats got on her last nerves.

Her retinal comm reported that Crayo was training with the recruits. She'd take a peek through the observation area, check out how they were doing. The doors opened as she approached and the hairs on the back of her neck raised. Harold was watching her every move.

She glanced around. No one else was in the room. "I don't want to talk," she said aloud.

"There was no way of knowing that Kara's genes were mutated," Harold began. "She'd been exposed to interstellar—"

She shook her head and shot a glare at the camera in the

corner of the room. "What part of I don't want to talk did you not understand? Unless I'm under arrest, then leave me the frak alone. I need some space."

The room fell silent, and except for her heavy breathing, there wasn't a sound. She knew he was still watching. The hairs on her neck were rubbing against her collar, but for once, he was giving her room.

Sometimes she missed Norby. He was her childhood virtual friend and her companion on many adventures. They'd stripped all cadets of their A.I. upon admission to the academy. The goal was to reduce their dependency on automata, to see if they truly had the intellect and skills to make it through on their own. Some people snuck them in and ended up expelled, but not Lync. At the academy she turned over a new leaf. She followed rules.

When she peered down into the training room, Crayo was down there studying the results from the Ulixi trainee simulations on the enormous wall screen. From the looks of the scores, they'd gotten even better. Far more proficient than she'd ever been. Bandi's name was still at the top though. That one was a firecracker. She hated being bested.

Lync sighed. She was certain Harold would toss her into the brig when she arrived. Bringing a spare vial of blood hadn't even crossed her mind when she'd taken the mission. All she could think about was helping Abigail and repaying the debt for all that she'd done.

Crayo turned to face the trainees and waved. He must have seen her.

She smiled and waved back. He looked happy and in his element. The Ulixi around him did, as well. Everyone seemed to be adjusting except for her.

It'd been nearly forty years since she'd first arrived at Jupiter station. She remembered that moment like it was yesterday, stepping off that rusty mining ship, her mind hyper focused on revenge and motivated to spill blood. She'd asked around the bars about any local resistance cells, but hit one dead end after another.

One bartender in her favorite haunt was so annoyed at her stream of questions, he accused her of being an Outer Ring nark. A member of the military looking to take down the resistance. That couldn't be further from the truth. She wanted to join them, to take down the Inners. Whatever it took. She spent that night in jail after giving him two black eyes and a broken nose.

That night, surrounded by the dirt and grime in the long-forgotten cells in the bowels of Callisto, it hit her. If she couldn't join the resistance, then maybe she'd join the Outer Ring military. They were the next best thing, and they were legal.

The next morning she went to the recruiting center, ready to serve, but she failed the examination. Her heart ached even now thinking about that moment. Something about an irreparable heart palpitation. She assured them it was nothing, and she could control it with breathing. But it was too late. They flagged her file. She'd never make it any further on her own.

She drank herself two sheets from death that day. Then she met Braxon. A random stranger who changed the course of her life forever. They'd drank a few bottles together and Braxon let it all out. She didn't want to join the military, but her family was forcing her to. They told her it was her duty. She had to follow in the footsteps of her ancestors.

Lync couldn't believe her luck.

They drank a crap ton more and crashed in the ventilation tubes that night. She didn't even remember lying down in that heap of trash or anything else that happened, but when she woke, Braxon was still there. Curled up beside her in the tube. They had breakfast together and she sprung her plan. Braxon would disappear, and she would take her place. She'd join the military for her.

Braxon thought it was impossible, but she assured her otherwise. A few well-placed credits with the right people, and within a day their blood records were swapped. One healthy Braxon exchanged for one unhealthy hearted Lync.

The only challenge from that point forward was blood. She'd need a fair amount of Braxon's blood for the years ahead. At least until she figured out how to change her DNA profile.

She shook away the memories as the door to the observation room opened.

"There she is!" Crayo walked toward her and gave her an enormous hug.

His muscular arms engulfed her like a comfortable blanket. She reciprocated and took a moment to breathe. It felt good to be near someone who truly cared about her, and not just what she did for them.

After a minute in heaven, he pulled back. He kept her close, but rested a hand on her shoulder. "You had me worried. Been almost two weeks it has." He furrowed his brows. "Everything out there go ok?"

She swallowed hard and shrugged, looking down at his chest. "About as well as slinging blind can go, I suppose."

"Frak! That bad?" He lowered his head downward trying to catch her gaze. "Wanna grab a drink? I'd be happy to talk. We can swap stories. I've got a few hours before the next session."

She smiled. "That'd be tops."

When they both turned toward the exit, it was blocked.

"I'd like a moment if you will, Major," Quesh said. His face was serious, and his arms were crossed.

She reached down and clasped Crayo's hand in hers, squeezing it tight. He squeezed back. "I'd rather not, sir. Unless you're ordering me to. Otherwise, I'd like to spend some time with my friends and family if you don't mind."

"I will not order you, Major. Not yet." He glanced toward Crayo and nodded. Quesh lowered his hands to his side. "He can come, as well. This'll impact him, too."

49

ABIGAIL OLIVAW

UNKNOWN

Her hands were raw and split open from climbing over
the porous gray stone. It sucked the moisture from her
skin like water to a sponge. Wiping her hands through her
sweaty, dirty hair, stung a bit from the salt, but otherwise they
felt better with the added perspiration.

She didn't remember having dry hands last time she
climbed. In fact, everything seemed different today. Come to
think of it, her retinal comm hadn't chimed in a while. Wasn't
a priority alert supposed to be coming in?

She shook her head. She was imagining things. Phantom
memories lurked in the shadows of her mind. It was hard to
stay focused in the North Carolina heat. She spent far too
much time thinking about work. Sometimes it was nice to get
away from it all, to just focus on one thing.

The climb.

She hadn't made it up this rocky face in decades. When
she started this morning, she hiked around the valley floor
and came around to the towering rock face to begin this
climb. As a kid she'd done it multiple times, competing
against her brothers in a race to the top. They bested her most
of the time, but every once in a while, she won.

As she glanced toward the top, she couldn't easily tell
how far she had left, but judging by the view of the valley

below it couldn't be much further. The last time she'd been at the top was at her father's funeral. She'd given his eulogy in front of all their friends and family. It wasn't the fondest memory, but it was when she'd last seen everyone she loved in one place.

She couldn't remember why she'd decided to climb today. It didn't matter though; she was committed at this point. Turning around, she studied the rock face, looking for an ideal path skyward on this next segment.

Up those nooks, push off that ridge, cross the ledge, and pull up those nice sturdy looking rocks. That should get her most of the way up. She'd wing it from there.

She blew on her hands and reached up as everything suddenly started shaking. The ground lurched and dust cascaded away from the wall as rocks tumbled downward.

"Ouch," she muttered as a stone smacked her hard on her left shoulder. When she reached up and rubbed it with her opposite hand, pain shot down her arm. That's gonna leave a mark.

She moved to place her back flat to the cliff, facing the valley below. "What the hell?" she muttered. She squinted and closed her eyes, shaking her head from side to side. She must be seeing things. Dehydration had gotten the best of her.

From the looks of it, the valley floor was getting closer. It was like the mountain was falling, or the Earth was pushing up. She couldn't tell which. But she didn't want to stick around to find out, either. She turned around and raised her hand to protect her face while she stared upward. There were a few small rocks and some dust falling, but otherwise it seemed safe. Maybe she could beat it to the top. There couldn't be much more cliff left to reach the summit.

She took off climbing up the rock face reaching high above her head, following the route she'd envisioned. Her heart was beating hard. It wasn't only from exertion; it was fear. Nothing was more motivating than the specter of death.

Her arms screamed as she pulled hard, lifting her body

higher and swinging her legs to the next outcropping. The light was brighter the higher she rose, almost heavenly. She slid her hand into a crease high above and glanced over her shoulder. "Frak," she muttered. She wasn't going to make it. The ground was rising faster than she was climbing. It was only three or four meters below. She could practically jump down if she wasn't afraid of getting hurt.

She tilted her head and studied the rising ground. Was the valley breaking apart? She hadn't noticed that before. The longer she stared, the more the ground morphed. It transformed from a grassy field interspersed with yellow flowers, to being covered in mechanical contraptions and... ships. Thousands of sleek teardrop shaped starships.

Either this was heaven or hell. She couldn't imagine a hell full of such beautiful things, but this had been a strange day. That damned green alien couldn't keep their hands to their self. If she had half a mind, then the next time she met them she'd shank them or something.

She swallowed hard and hopped off the ledge, coming crashing down on her feet. As she braced for the onrush of pain, it never came. She simply stood upright and nothing hurt. Stranger still, when she checked her shoulder, her hand came back clean. The blood from earlier was gone.

Something weird was going on. While the blood may be gone, she was still covered in a mess of orange mud, and her clothes were tattered from tearing against the rough rock face. The familiar orange Carolina clay flecked off when she brushed at her clothes. It floated down, hitting the ground and shattering against the smooth surface, exploding into nothingness.

This day was getting stranger and stranger.

As she glanced upward, she did a double take. Somehow, it was no longer midday. The sky was blanketed with millions of pinpoints of starlight. Their patterns and formations were familiar. She'd seen them countless times camping out here in the valley. Those same teardrop shaped ships still surrounded her though. They were jet black, like a droplet of oil floating sideways except they had landing gear.

She reached up and slid her hand along the seamless surface. It was cold and as smooth as glass. Not at all like the sandpaper coating of those Galactic Alliance shuttles.

"Abigail?" a familiar female voice said from behind her.

She spun around, and a smirk flickered at the corner of her mouth. "Hey stranger! I haven't seen you..." She chuckled. "Since you left for Liprosus. What's up?"

"Are you ready?" Lync asked.

Abigail furrowed her brow and glanced around at the hangar full of ships before settling back on Lync. "For what?"

"To fight!"

THANK YOU FOR READING!

I hope you enjoyed reading **Dark Nebula: Isolation**. I suspect there were some twists and turns you didn't see coming, and maybe even a few characters you loved to hate. The **Dark Nebula** series continues on with the next book, **Discovery**. We pick up with Zachary, and follow the Olivaw brothers on their adventure to discover the origin and fate of humanity.

If you're interested in a **FREE** novella entitled **Dark Nebula: Contact**, hearing more about the series, seeing new cover art as it's released, or getting exclusive access to sales as they happen, then you can subscribe to my newsletter online at:

seanwillson.com/subscribe

You can also drop me an email at:

author@seanwillson.com

I always love hearing from my readers.

If you have a moment, I could really use your help rating this book online. All I need is one or two sentences on what you liked or your thoughts. Just return to where you purchased this book online or use this link:

seanwillson.com/review

ALSO BY SEAN WILLSON

DARK NEBULA SERIES
Novella: Contact (FREE)
Book 1: Isolation
Book 2: Discovery (This Book)
Book 3: Generations
Book 4: Beacon
Book 5: Graveyard
Book 6: Nursery

PORTAL SERIES
Book 1: Drowning Earth
Books 2-4: Coming Soon…

All titles are available in print and ebook form.
For more information visit my website online at:

www.seanwillson.com

ABOUT THE AUTHOR

I grew up reading science fiction since I was ten and always had a book in tow everywhere I went. While I never imagined I'd be able to write a book of my own, I dreamed of worlds filled with space travel, robots, and fantastical journeys of exploration. I pursued a career in Computer Engineering and it wasn't until later in life that I had the itch to write.

I started writing the **Dark Nebula** series in 2015 in fits and starts while I was traveling for work. After a two year lull in the middle of writing, I picked it up again. It took me five years to finish the first three novels, refine my writing craft, and learn everything I needed to self-publish this series.

My plan for **Dark Nebula** is to craft a series of books that engulf my readers in a future full of intrigue, exploration, and amazing technology. The very things that inspired me when I was young. I want to give you a satisfying romp through a complicated and inspiring world that allows you to relax away from the stress of your life.

In the end, I hope you enjoyed reading **Dark Nebula: Isolation** as much as I enjoyed writing it.

Thank you,
Sean Willson

facebook.com/seanwillsonauthor

mastodon.online/@willson

goodreads.com/seanwillson

bookbub.com/authors/sean-willson

ACKNOWLEDGEMENTS

First and foremost I wanted to thank my amazing wife Amy and my three beautiful children Abigail, Bradley, and Zachary. Notice any familiar names? They put up with me during this wild writing adventure over the past five years. This was my first novel and has been a huge learning experience releasing it out into the world. My family was instrumental in supporting me along the way and giving me inspiration to evolve my character personalities in new directions. As a self-published author I have to wear many hats, all of which were new to me. They made the entire process easier than I could have hoped.

I also couldn't have done this without a number of key writing professionals and friends along the way.

Editor: Samantha Wiley
Proofreader: Rachel Pugh
Cover Artist: Tom Edwards

Critique Partners and Beta Readers:

A huge thanks to: Arina N, Karen R. Nelson, Kristin L. Stamper, S. Kaeth, Ben Gartner, Kathleen Keenan, Katrina Ariel, K.J. Harrowick, Mark Dooley, Beth Markley, Matt Gemmell, and my Charlotte critique group, the Dark and Stormy Plotters League including Blair Peery, Freddie Silva, Meg Fencil, Michael Creason, Morgan Jackson, Raphael Winters, and Shaun McCoy.

They each helped me immensely with my writing craft, sharpening my opening pages, weaving my complex story arcs, talking some sense into me, and evolving my characters throughout this and upcoming books

GLOSSARY

- **Achernar** : The last star within the Eridani constellation. Also referred to as The Rivers End in Abigail's message.
- **Aitken** : The Atlas class ship that Admiral Nguyen's commands the fleet from.
- **Alsef's Law** : The speed of travel for a Galactic Alliance Starship which is absolute and bounded by the laws of the universe. This rate of travel is one hundred times the speed of light.
- **Atlas Class** : Sol's largest military starship and first join Inner and Outer Ring design. There are 32 of these within the fleet spread within both the Inner and Outer Ring. Examples include the Aitken, Georgetown, Beijing, and São Paulo.
- **Bynaury** : A GA uplifted species of the Thyreus. They pilot and run the operations of the armada ships that arrive at Sol. They're aliens that have a mind machine meld with their ships and never leave.
- **Cherenkov Radiation** : Electromagnetic radiation emitted when charged particles pass through a dielectric medium at a speed greater than the phase velocity of light in that medium. The gate drives use this radiation to both shape and direct the gate exit destination in space.
- **Confederation of Planetary Explorers** (CoPE)
- **Dasyatis** : The name of one of the stingray ships on Liprosus that are used to navigate the water tunnels below ground.

- **Director of Colonization** (DoC)
- **Director of Security** (DoS)
- **Entaurus** : The capital world of the Galactic Alliance.
- **Epsilon Eridani** (EE) : The first star system humanity targeted for colonization. 10.5 LY from Sol. 5.5 LY from TC.
- **Fountainhead** : The name of the ship Zachary created to take on their expedition.
- **Galactic Alliance** (GA) : An alien collective thousands of years old that has arrived in Sol to put mankind on trial. Their ranks contain 64 aliens and hundreds of uplifted alien species.
- **Hypanus** : The name of one of the stingray ships on Liprosus that are used to navigate the water tunnels below ground.
- **Ion Thrusters** : A form of electric propulsion that creates thrust by accelerating ions using electricity. It usually ionizes a neutral gas by extracting some electrons out of atoms, creating a cloud of positive ions. Coulomb forces are then used to accelerate the ions along an electric field.
- **Jurat** : The frigate that Abigail takes to meet the aliens. Its commanded by Commander Quesh, her father Stark's right hand.
- **Light Year** (LY)
- **Liprosus** : The colonized planet in Epsilon Eridani.
- **Oak** : aka OOC, or the Office of Colonization.
- **Oort Cloud** : A cloud of planetesimals located between 1,000 and 200,000 AU from our sun.
- **Pegasus Class** : An older class of military starship still in active rotation in Sol. These ships were first created nearly one hundred years ago and received many modernizations and updates. Examples include the Mostar which was destroyed opening a gift from Lync.

- **Petrichor** : The ship that Lync and her crew left Liprosus on to head toward the meeting point.
- **Planetesimal** : A minute planet that did not come together with others under gravity to form a planet. They range in size from several meters to hundreds of kilometers.
- **Qudoculi** : GA aliens with 2 eyes in the front, 2 in the back, skin the color of Bermuda grass changing seasons. Its body is green with mottled browns throughout.
- **Selene Ships** : The GA name for their moon ships. It means moon in Greek.
- **Sim** : Portuguese for Yes.
- **Simutainment** : Simulated Entertainment experience. Very much like virtual reality but designed as a self contained entertainment experience.
- **Slingshot** : The type of chariot that Lync flew as a Ulixi and the nickname for The Wheel in Tau Ceti.
- **Sol** : Our star containing Earth.
- **Spērō** : The name of the Tau Ceti colony ship.
- **Thyreus** : Aliens with 16 eyes, black with blue features, named after the Blue Neon Cuckoo Bee.
- **Tau Ceti** (TC) : The second star system humanity targeted for colonization. 11.9 LY from Earth. 5.5 LY from EE.
- **Trochilidae** : A hummingbird like alien species who came to the aid of humans to represent them in the GA tribunal. Only the females can leave their homeworld due to the size and bone density of the males.
- **Vid-sim** : Video Simulated experience. Not to be confused with Simutainment, vid-sim's are real life 3-dimensional simulations of the real world. They're meant to engulf the watcher in the experience they're watching.

- **Virtaul** : A alien species mentioned by Lisp about the tribunal ship. Nothing else is known of them.
- **Wellspring** : The name of Peppers small superluminal ship that she flew to Epsilon Eridani on humanity's maiden faster that light voyage.
- **Whiptail** : The name of one of the stingray ships on Liprosus that are used to navigate the water tunnels below ground.